T0245817

# I AM THE
# DARK

THAT ANSWERS WHEN YOU CALL

PRAISE FOR

# I Feed Her to the Beast and the Beast Is Me

"Almost euphoric in its embrace of the horrific, and Laure's transformation will speak to girls who have had enough of being dominated and knocked down."

—*NPR*

"Shea has executed a perfect series of pirouettes—effortless to the eye, but technically difficult to achieve."

—TOR.COM

"Jamison could have easily taken this story down well-traveled roads and delivered a cautionary tale about power corrupting, but they don't, and it's all the more satisfying . . . A unique take on a classic horror tale, this brutal ballet story is gruesome and satisfying."

—*SCHOOL LIBRARY JOURNAL*

"Shea's raw, tension-filled emotional roller-coaster of a novel delivers frighteningly gory depictions of body horror. While the scares are grisly, Shea skillfully uses them to reveal hard truths surrounding institutions that capitalize on exclusion, and to depict the lengths one teen goes for acceptance and recognition."

—*PUBLISHERS WEEKLY*

"Gory, gripping, and visceral; examines how supernatural and systemic power unleash the monster within all of us."

—*KIRKUS REVIEWS*

"A charged series starter, drenched in gore, that uses horror to interrogate the brutalities of a calcified institution and its impact on real lives. Horror and ballet fans alike will find much to love."

—*BOOKLIST*

"With its monstrous ballerinas, beautiful monsters, and writing that drips with both beauty and gore, *I Feed Her to the Beast and the Beast Is Me* is a glorious debut. I would follow Jamison Shea down any dark path."
—ERICA WATERS, BRAM STOKER AWARD–WINNING
AUTHOR OF *THE RIVER HAS TEETH*

"Cutthroat competition and eldritch horrors—of both the human and monstrous kind—collide headfirst in *I Feed Her to the Beast and the Beast Is Me*. Gloriously haunting and darkly thrilling, Jamison Shea's words will leave you breathless."
—AIDEN THOMAS, *NEW YORK TIMES*–BESTSELLING AUTHOR OF
*CEMETERY BOYS* AND *THE SUNBEARER TRIALS*

"A beautifully wrought horror story that has you rooting for the monster in the face of insidious institutions. Shea's writing is as graceful as the dancers in their book and will leave readers screaming for more blood."
—TRANG THANH TRAN, *NEW YORK TIMES*–BESTSELLING
AUTHOR OF *SHE IS A HAUNTING*

"A hungry novel that smears your teeth with blood and ambition, then asks if you'd be willing to rip them out. Jamison Shea has cemented themselves as a force to be reckoned with—and reminds us that when your enemies go low, you can always bury them there."
—ANDREW JOSEPH WHITE, *NEW YORK TIMES*–BESTSELLING
AUTHOR OF *HELL FOLLOWED WITH US*

"A sinister, delicious dive into a truly captivating villain origin story. In lyrical prose and a cutting pace, Shea explores the ways power corrupts and the way racist, elitist systems push us to hunger for it."
—COURTNEY GOULD, AWARD-WINNING
AUTHOR OF *THE DEAD AND THE DARK*

"Brutal and beautiful, this book will drag you through the bloodied depths of fierce ambition and into a raw, untethered world of chaos, where salvation comes from crossing the line between girl and monster."
—LYNDALL CLIPSTONE, AUTHOR OF THE WORLD AT
THE LAKE'S EDGE DUOLOGY AND *UNHOLY TERRORS*

# I AM THE DARK

# DARK

THAT ANSWERS WHEN YOU CALL

JAMISON SHEA

HENRY HOLT AND COMPANY

NEW YORK

FOR THE DREAMERS,
DEFERRED AND HEADING
FOR A SUPERNOVA—
WE ARE COSMIC,
THE THING OF STARS

Henry Holt and Company, *Publishers since 1866*
Henry Holt® is a registered trademark of Macmillan Publishing Group, LLC
120 Broadway, New York, NY 10271 • fiercereads.com

Copyright © 2024 by Jamison Shea. All rights reserved.

Our books may be purchased in bulk for promotional, educational, or business use. Please
contact your local bookseller or the Macmillan Corporate and Premium Sales Department
at (800) 221-7945 ext. 5442 or by email at MacmillanSpecialMarkets@macmillan.com.

Library of Congress Control Number: 2024937969

First edition, 2024
Book design by Rich Deas and Meg Sayre
Printed in the United States of America

ISBN 978-1-250-90958-9
1  3  5  7  9  10  8  6  4  2

# — AUTHOR'S NOTE —

With *I Am the Dark That Answers When You Call*, Laure's story of blood, godhood, and devotion comes to an end. Are you ready?

Having walked (or technically, been carried, corpse-like) away from Coralie and the prestigious ballet, our heroine must now see who she is without them both. As such, this story explores heavy themes such as grief, death and dying, mourning a loved one, parental abandonment, and surviving abuse. As Laure rebuilds herself, there are some depictions of gore— particularly blood, bones, corpses, and animal carcasses (due to natural causes)—as well as body horror, murder, torture, vomit, gaslighting and manipulation, heavy drinking, canni- balism, and forced confinement (being buried alive). Just girl things, am I right?

Thank you for your support as I tell this story. Along the way, I hope you find a bit of comfort, like a cozy park bench in the middle of spring, within its pages.

I don't want to be at the mercy of my emotions. I want to use them, to enjoy them, and to dominate them.

—Oscar Wilde, *The Picture of Dorian Gray*

# CHAPTER 1

I f I'd died like I was supposed to, l'église de la Madeleine would've been the perfect place to mourn me. The church was grand, standing tall in the heart of Paris like a temple where the king of gods doled out punishments, where other greats like Josephine Baker and Camille Saint-Saëns were honored and celebrated by the masses. Above strong Corinthian colonnades on every side were sculptures of judgment, severe and aimed down at its guests. Big bronze doors, though open, didn't bother at all to feel welcoming. Its statues of saints were poised for war instead of supplication. It would've been perfect.

But all of it now had the effect of making me want to shrink away or get out of Dodge. Like perhaps I was a monster to be put down when all I'd ever done was try to survive.

Because I didn't die like I was supposed to. Coralie did.

People climbed past me while I stood at the bottom of the steps, gazing up at Jesus while his angels glared down at me. It didn't matter that the icy winter wind nipped at my cheeks and fingertips, or that a few older people cast me glances of recognition from within their bundles of wool. It'd already been more than a month since my face first appeared on the news: one of the missing, then one of the survivors, and according to the very superstitious few, the reason the house fell.

I couldn't move because I didn't know if I was allowed to be here. I didn't want to be here, but I needed to say goodbye.

"We don't have to go in if you don't want to," Keturah said as she pulled her long coat tight around her. Her afro was in full bloom today, voluminous and freshly dyed a radiant shade of lilac, and the coils and kinks fluttered in the breeze.

Andor nodded his agreement and stepped closer, hunching his broad shoulders to try to shield me from the cold and the stares and all that was holding me back. As if he could read my unease as effortlessly as I read his.

He'd carefully framed his handsome face with dark curls in an attempt to cover his milky eye and the scar that ran through it, but it was no use against the wind. And in public, every secret glimpse of me was another pointed at him and all Coralie took from him. Us.

If I were a braver, more considerate girl, I would have seized his hand and taken him away. Spared him the spectacle. Only, we weren't *together* together—any potential we could have had seemed to stay behind in Prague, and here we were only distant friends—so instead, I adjusted the lace gloves and turtleneck I used to cover my own scars and pivoted on my heel. "Maybe we just should go—"

"Nope!" Niamh snapped, snatching up my elbow in her small, strong grip. Her hazel eyes glared at me from behind overgrown black bangs. "I don't know what your problem is, but I'm freezing my tits off. We're going in—"

Keturah pried the girl's hand away. "Niamh…"

But I didn't continue my retreat.

It wasn't her fault she didn't know. She wasn't there when the walls collapsed with me and more than a hundred others still inside. She didn't know what I did and what was done to me before and after. All she knew was that I needed to be here for some reason, that I'd invited her along, and now I was being unusually spineless. Not at all the girl she met back in Prague.

Niamh studied us, sharp gaze flicking between Keturah, Andor, and me with interest, searching for the secret we held that she didn't. Then finally she relented, shrugged, and waved goodbye.

"Fine. Do whatever you want, but *I* am going inside to defrost."

And so reluctantly I was forced to march up the stairs after her.

It had been only a couple weeks since we'd met and even less since she became one of us. It was *my* doing that recruited her and brought her into the fold, so I'd be damned to let my only disciple out of my sight so soon, not with Acheron's power so fresh in her untrained veins and so many vulnerable people she'd be tempted to try it on. No, I'd brave the silly memorial and fundraiser, because I still remembered every craving and dark thought that caught me off guard when I first became an acolyte. And I could never forget the urges that followed long after I knew what I was doing.

To my surprise, Acheron lay dormant as I approached the church. Though I expected it to recoil, to hiss and spit and shirk away from the house of another god, the wicked dark gave neither a lazy glance around nor a passing interest in this place and the growing line of mourners at the entrance. In fact, despite my newfound status as its vessel, despite my harboring some unknown breadth of its eldritch existence in my very body, it shared so little—what it all meant, its plans, its thoughts and relationships to anything. Maybe none of this mattered because Acheron was something so much "other" than I'd ever known. Without any indicators one way or another, I was left to only guess.

By the expressions on Andor's and Keturah's faces, I knew their little shards of Acheron weren't giving off warning signs either.

Shifting from foot to foot as we got in line, Niamh asked, "So, did you, like, know someone who died or something?"

Though she sounded casual, I didn't miss the prying sideways glance.

She wore her scheming plain in her eyes, like she wanted to detect some other answer in my set jaw. Like I was a mark she was preparing to swindle.

My hand flitted to my wallet in my coat pocket, just in case, which she also took note of. No one else noticed.

Inside, the nave of the church was filled to the brim. People crowded the pews, adults and children wiping their eyes and hugging each other while more circled the displays. All around the interior were decorated easels with blown-up pictures of the deceased, framed and showered in flowers and cards and stuffed animals, flammable and dangerously close to the candles. I knew Coralie's was somewhere among them, but I didn't want to find it. Near the entrance was a table set up for donations to help the impacted families, and the very sight made the space between my ribs itch.

That day was still crystalline in my dreams, and I remembered all the diamonds and expensive watches twinkling in the light as everyone stood by. The silks and sateen that didn't shift because no one bothered to help me before it all came down—no one bothered to reach for me, ask after me, when Coralie threw my battered body on display. My blood had pooled on the marble floor, and they only inched away to avoid sullying the ends of their couture gowns.

No one ever contacted me about this fundraiser—would I see any of those donations to soothe the nightmares? The death of my career? Or was I not a good enough victim?

Bitterness burned in me as I raised my chin. I wouldn't hide from the gazes of recognition, not when I deserved to be here. This was my tragedy too. Though my body was taken away and repaired, part of me had died in Palais Garnier with the rest.

"It's so sad," Keturah mumbled, her eyes frozen on a well-dressed couple. They clung to each other before a large easel of a girl my age with a round face, dark hair, and porcelain skin. Olivia Robineau, who glued a razor blade in my shoe.

I swallowed and turned away to study a printed itinerary, thinking that maybe this was a bad idea, after all. Unlike the 113 bodies recovered from the collapse, half of them company members I either studied or trained with, I woke up. Not just alive but more powerful, whether I deserved it or not. Then my attention snagged on the itinerary's first line, on the name that could only amplify my dread.

"Rose-Marie, thank you for coming."

Behind us, an event organizer held a tall, model-esque woman with familiar golden hair and rosy cheeks. She wore a long, tailored coat of royal blue, which I knew was her favorite color after platinum and silver—like the brooch pinned to her lapel to catch on the candlelight all around her—and her posture and gentle expression could only be found on a seasoned ballerina. Achieved through years of conditioning, on and off the stage.

Rose-Marie Baumé, Coralie's famous, star-powered mother, stood in the entrance of the church, looking exactly as I remembered her: harsh and regal. Even in grief, she was cold and unmoved, and even in grief, Coralie's father was absent from her side. Looking at her, you wouldn't even know she'd lost someone. That the "natural disaster" the authorities determined had leveled the building was, in fact, her daughter.

Though it occurred to me that she *could* come, I didn't think she would. I didn't realize I'd have to brace myself in case she noticed me.

For six years, I'd lived as Rose-Marie's unofficial ward, her daughter's best friend and living shadow who followed her everywhere. Every insult, every twitch in her mouth when I'd surpassed and danced circles around Coralie, I'd memorized. I'd also watched as Rose-Marie ran for her life, leaving her daughter to self-destruct. With me still in her clutches.

For all my guilt about killing Coralie, even if I had to, Rose-Marie had created the monster she became.

"Just great," I muttered.

Rose-Marie parted from the event organizer and quickly came to a halt when those emerald-colored eyes found mine. It only lasted for a breath, but it felt like we'd held each other's gazes for so long that anyone might have picked up on it. Picked up on how my shoulders climbed to my ears, like some small dog raising its hackles, how she frowned almost imperceptibly before she kept walking.

She marched past, so close I even smelled her freaking Dior perfume. No acknowledgment. No apology. No well wishes. All I was worth to her was a minuscule frown. Years of knowing each other reduced like I was a speck of dirt on her precious coat. A nuisance, and not the girl her daughter had chosen to torment in her final moments.

As always, despite everything, my thoughts went quiet in the wake of Rose-Marie's condescension. It was so easy to lash out and throw someone down the stairs or rupture muscle, but her? The only way to survive in her orbit was to make myself small, and I just did it all over again like a reflex.

"Bitch," Keturah cursed after her, loud enough for her to hear. She placed a protective hand on my shoulder.

But Rose-Marie carried on, the famous church transformed into a catwalk, her expensive stilettos clicking loudly on the old, stone floors.

Power flooded my veins in the flip of a switch. Acheron was awake and paying attention to my panic now, attuned sharply to the rhythm coming from Rose-Marie's direction. From her steady, unflinching heartbeat.

**We could correct this situation, if you want**, it said, curling around my spine, voice rolling through my bones like thunder.

And it was right—I did want.

But I took a slow, centering breath to quell the temptation instead. It was so easy to be a monster now, with so much power at my disposal and so much spite to keep me going. It would take nothing at all to unfurl my darkness and make Rose-Marie small for once in her wretched life.

**You should snip the tendons behind both knees and make her crawl to you like the worm she is.** *We* **could make her beg for mercy and kiss your feet in worship, and then—**

"Shut up," I snapped through gritted teeth, to the thing no one could see or hear but I could feel now slinking away. That only earned me even more glances, the girl talking to her shadow. Just what I needed.

Even Niamh noticed and resumed her appraisal of me. She didn't know that Acheron and I talked, and I wasn't sure how much I wanted to share when I was still trying to understand myself what it meant to have an eldritch god riding around in your skin.

As casually as I could muster, I dropped my shoulders and found a comfortable place to stand in the back of the pews. "Forget it. It's whatever."

The memorial talks would begin soon, and that mattered more than some imaginary war with Rose-Marie. A dark-wood podium had been decorated with flowers at the head of the church, and Rose-Marie rose to it, in rapt discussion with another organizer. She was to lead the introductions, according to the itinerary, and give her heavy endorsement to the event. If there was ever someone the public trusted, it was her. Still, Acheron was right to call her a worm.

"You don't like her?" asked Niamh with a glint in her eyes as she went back to watching Rose-Marie. "I don't get why, if you can do something about her, you don't."

There was no easy way to explain the futility of it, fighting these kinds of people in these ways—Rose-Marie and her ilk would never see me as an equal, even if I held her at eye level by her throat. And besides, she was a vestige from an old life. She didn't *matter* anymore.

"She has every right to hate me," I explained instead as stonily as I could, keeping my gaze ahead and locked onto Rose-Marie as she took the podium. "I'm the reason her daughter's dead."

I didn't want to see Niamh's expression, to catch it change into distrust or, worse, even *more* intrigue. Though I'd survived, though I'd stopped a situation from becoming worse, I couldn't say without a doubt that I'd done something good.

Rose-Marie tapped the microphone, cleared her throat, and smiled. It was the same bland expression on all her Bulgari and Dior ads, a look I'd seen on TV and in person for years. Nausea rolled through me as I thought of how once I'd wanted to be like her, even as I despised her.

"I hope you can hear me well," she started, eliciting chuckles from her enamored crowd. If we couldn't, no one would ever interrupt to say, anyway. "I come to you today, not just as a member of the board at Opéra Garnier, but also as a mother. A grieving mother."

Here, a profound silence descended over the church. Faces of my classmates and colleagues frozen in time surrounded and watched us, while Rose-Marie Baumé stood in the holy rays of light like some walking parable, and they all ate it up. None of them knew that she was a coward. She didn't try to save her daughter before the collapse, and she certainly wasn't screaming her name in the rubble after. I'm not sure they would care either.

Rose-Marie gestured to one of the largest portraits, positioned conveniently right next to the altar, and it was like staring at a younger version of her. The same eyes, the same coloring, the same nose, the same posed and airbrushed face. My Coralie was different: Her hair was wild and frizzy, cheeks freckled, grin defiant, attitude petulant. Nothing like the sweet, poised doll on the poster.

"Her name was Coralie, and she was a dancer in the company. It was to be her debut night, in fact. She'd worked so hard to get there."

I rolled my eyes again.

Coralie had never worked hard at anything in her entire life except trying to please her mother by controlling me. She'd always expected her face and name to grant her everything she'd wanted, and she was only debuting with the company because she put me in the hospital to steal my spot. And I'd quit to let her keep it.

Rose-Marie continued, "Ballet was her whole world. She'd wanted to follow in my footsteps for as long as I could remember, and I thought, as a parent, that I was doing the right thing by encouraging her. I'd believed she was safe."

More lies. This was the burden mothers gifted their daughters: Rose-Marie forced Coralie to dance and berated her anytime she wasn't exceptional.

"Some mornings, I wake up and hope that I have an answer for how it really happened, how this took my Coralie away. Other mornings, I know it won't make a difference because there are many others—you all—who know exactly what I mean."

**You can stop her anytime**, Acheron whispered when I balled my fists. My scalp prickled as if it were stroking my head from the inside of my skull.

It would have been easy: telling her to come here, watching her kneel at my feet and whimper. Tears twinkling down her cheeks as she gouged her own face in penance. The scandalized gasps and horror from the crowd. After all, she *owed* me.

White-hot anger mixed with Acheron's essence and began to transform me: My gums stung, teeth sharpening until they shredded my bottom lip, and nails became claws that pierced skin. Blood welled on my tongue and in my palm, but the pain was grounding. It gave me something else to focus on, to cling to and pull myself out. Turning into a monster, after all, was what got me here.

I looked through the pews, packed with nodding heads soaking up all of Rose-Marie's falsehoods. They didn't hear what Coralie had told her mother before it happened, what made Rose-Marie flee: They didn't understand the lengths a girl would go to just to appease her mother.

But *I* did.

*You want me to be great? This is the cost of greatness!*

I wore that cost, those great lengths, as scars on my wrists and ankles and throat.

Among the crowd, a figure who looked eerily familiar caught my attention. She had skin the color of mahogany, with dark curls pinned back neatly in a bun. From the side, I glimpsed her dimpled chin jutting out as she nodded, scowling deep in concentration. Her eyes, even from the profile, looked a little like mine.

I squinted.

Acheron reared its head from inside me.

"Coralie was innocent," Rose-Marie said pointedly, and when I glanced away from the mysterious woman in the crowd, I found her looking directly at me. "As was everyone else, but it didn't matter in these acts of god."

Fuck this memorial.

I didn't know what I expected, but it wasn't this. It wasn't Coralie's absolution while my whole life and future lay in rubble. She strung me up like a hog and tried to cut Acheron out of my skin, and when she realized it wasn't permanent, she imploded and took a whole building down with her. And even in death, she still had the world scrambling over itself to defend *her*.

The bronze doors clattered behind me as I stormed out into the cold, the others on my trail. Tears stung my eyes.

Nothing had changed.

It wasn't too much to ask to be acknowledged, to not have them commemorate the girl who shoved glass in my heart. Was I so unlike them that my suffering was this forgettable?

Well, I wouldn't think about them again. And I didn't have to be that girl anymore, the one constantly begging to be seen. If we were destined to be worlds apart, if I was destined to be something more, something other, something *worse*, then so be it.

PART ONE

# THE HARBINGER

# CHAPTER 2

## *TWO WEEKS LATER*

Nestled in a corner of the dance floor of En boîte, I lost myself to a bottle of prosecco and some girl's pillowy lips. They were soft, glossy and pink as ballet satin, homing my senses to only the feel of the almost empty bottle in the grip of my left hand, her cheek in the other, and her fingertips roaming up and down my spine.

And that was all I came for, night after night.

It didn't matter that I didn't know her name. That she was the second stranger's kiss of the night. Most important was the spark in her blue eyes as she approached me, as she slowly wrapped her arms around my waist and complimented my lace gloves, and we proceeded to dance. It didn't matter what initially drew me to her, whether I wanted her or wanted to recruit her, how they felt one and the same.

When I leaned in, close enough to smell the beer on her breath, she didn't hesitate in closing the gap.

Colors from the disco ball swirled all around us, and the music was so vibrant that for one beautiful moment, in the hands of one beautiful person, all my thoughts were drowned out. Reduced to nothing. I could just *be* for as long as this lasted.

I'd come here with Vanessa Abbadie of all people, a former classmate from the ballet who turned to partying after her best friend died in the collapse too. We'd collided one night, both tipsy on our feet, and crashed to the floor in a fit of laughter. Those years of hostility and competition faded away because, after all, what was the point now when we were all that was left?

She was somewhere inside, celebrating her birthday. She was always slipping off to the bathroom, to the bar, to have a smoke, into some guy's waiting lap in the VIP lounge I'd compelled for us. Eventually she'd slink back and suggest we go home, expecting me to believe that her red nose and sniffling were from the outside chill alone. Lucky for her, I'd have to stop dancing and flirting and kissing and doing all the things old Laure couldn't to care. Which I wouldn't.

The girl—whose name was Sara, or Sasha, or something with an *S*—pulled out of my grasp and shouted, "I'm gonna go to the bathroom. Then wanna get out of here?" Her pale blond eyebrows wriggled mischievously.

I nodded thickly, head swirling, blood rushing, and she and her silver sequined dress were swallowed by the crowd.

And then all alone, I was spinning, spinning, spinning. If I spun fast enough, I could escape the person in the wall mirror staring back at me. The pitiful one, the one who was so full of melancholy and other *feelings* I wasn't interested in dealing with. Anger was easy, especially when it was righteous—it was the other, uglier things that this new monster of me didn't know what to do with. Like what use was grieving a cruel girl and a crueler ballet? What if all of this had been a mistake? Was I supposed to be this lost?

But because I was a ballerina in my old life, I was damn great at turning away from those thoughts. I didn't even get dizzy.

The bass was thick, and the buttery-smooth treble glided across my skin. Sweat clung to my arms, hair sticking to the back of my neck, heat burning in my thighs, all offerings to the god I once worshipped. The one before the fall.

The throng of people around me was possessed by the same thrum. Their heartbeats brushed against my palms, steady and strong and eager and drunk. In a mess of static, Acheron too watched from my reflection, feeding off the chaos and revelry while I treaded water. Here, it was let out of its cage: steering a pair of drunk girls away before they stepped on my shoes, sending a wild dancer to the other side of the floor before he thrashed into me. The DJ replayed my favorite song for the fifth time tonight with just a glance.

And soon I'd have my hands buried in some girl's hair, feeling the room spin as we crashed onto her mattress right before I offered her the world soaked in blood.

I was aware of the boy before he even approached. He was as scrawny as the strings of his heart, dressed in an ill-fitted silk button-down, with a diamond stud in his ear. Like me, he was on the younger end of the crowd, only the beginnings of facial hair dusting his chin whenever the strobe swept the floor. In his hands were two sweating drinks with too much ice, one of which he held out to me. A tribute.

Acheron beamed from the mirror.

"Hey!"

In every spin, I studied the boy more closely. His mousy-brown hair was moussed in waves the way French boys were prone to now. And the want in his chocolate eyes was plain, even as he'd *just* watched me make out with that girl. When I slowed, he leaned in close. Too close.

"What's up?"

Rather than answer, I kept turning. The boy remained, doggedly waiting for my answer, looking around for the girl's return.

I slowed—because I couldn't stop, otherwise those feelings would creep in again—and said frankly, "Why don't you say what you came to ask me?"

Too eager, he abandoned his drinks on the nearest ledge and stepped even closer. Orbiting around me to hold my gaze. I smelled mint and tobacco on his skin. "This party sucks. You girls want to try somewhere else?"

That wasn't what he wanted to say, not really.

I pressed a finger to the scrawny boy's lips to silence anything else he'd say, shook my head, and picked up my pace. "No."

Not because of the girl, who I'd only met less than an hour ago. And not because of Andor, my distant not-boyfriend and whatever *his* problem was either, but because this boy seemed weak. Afraid. The wicked thing inside me wanted to eat him up and pick his bones clean, slurp the marrow from within. Knew it *could* and then go back to spinning without missing a beat. He didn't know he'd be devoured, that I only looked the part of a girl, but the creature inside was vicious and always hungry.

So I set off, tottering through the crowd to fetch my girl. Now, *she* was worthy.

Thursday night at En boîte meant that everywhere was crowded—the dance floor, the tables, the bar. Even VIP, which I never had a problem talking my way into, not with my gift, was ready to turn me away at the volume. Crossing the floor took a constant effort to remain upright, to draw in breath with bodies sloshing into me.

One moment I was fine, and the next, it felt like a building was coming down all over again. The noise of the room dulled to loud silence. The lights dimmed. The air thinned, and my chest tightened painfully in response.

**You're alive**, Acheron insisted quietly as I stumbled free from the mass. Its voice purred against the back of my neck.

Standing in the middle of the hall with my eyes closed, stiff, I waited for the memories to subside. I wasn't in the tunnels beneath Opéra Garnier. I wasn't surrounded by marble and stone, wood and dirty water. She wasn't coming for me. There wasn't glass in my heart, and I could breathe just fine.

"I'm alive, alive, alive," I whispered to myself.

Sometimes it didn't matter, stillness or not, when the pitiful part of me slipped out. Sometimes it forgot that we weren't *her* anymore, even if I didn't know who we were now.

When my head cleared, my pulse no longer roaring in my ears, I took a step and immediately crashed into a body outside. Acheron lurched to attention under my skin. The prosecco bottle slipped from my hand and shattered at their feet.

"I'm sorry!" I leapt and steadied myself against a pillar.

And when I glanced up, the other person was already walking away. No utterances of *Excuse me* or an acknowledgment that I was here. She'd come from the women's bathroom, the door creaking shut behind her as she stepped over the puddle of fizzing wine and glass.

So I gave chase.

My hand shot out and grabbed her wrist before I understood what I was doing, nails pinching skin. It was a reflex born of too many years treated as everyone's inferior, but I was god-made now, and at the very least she owed me deference.

"Hey!"

"Back off—" the woman started, twisting out of my grip.

She was shorter than me, wearing black leather pants and a thin white tank that exposed her bare, bony, olive-toned arms. Her hair was cut short, a bleached blond pixie cut with bangs falling around sharp eyes a shockingly familiar shade of hazel. And young.

*Too* young to be here.

"*Niamh?*" I shouted before reeling back, but my voice was lost to the music and the chatter of the crowd.

My recruit didn't show any sign of hearing me as she kept walking, rounding the corner without a backward glance and melting into the mob.

It didn't matter that I'd hardly seen the girl in the weeks since the memorial, that she'd dyed her hair. I recognized the sinister gravity of her presence, a magnetism and otherworldliness that pulled at the room and bent light around her narrow shoulders. It was the signature of an acolyte with Acheron in their blood.

But I thought she'd returned to Prague—what was she doing here?

Acheron hummed with excitement nonetheless, high off itself.

Stunned and still watching over my shoulder, I pushed through the door to the bathroom. The sudden quiet inside felt odd against my ears. No stirring, shuffling, sniffling, pissing. There was only the sound of a lone sink fully open, though no one was standing at the row.

"Hello?"

I'd only shut my eyes for just a moment—there was no way I'd lost my sparkling blonde, Sophie or Simone or Stephanie or Sylvie. Not when she was as drunk as me. But the restrooms here were devoid of life. There was no sign of any pulse inside.

Which meant she blew me off. She changed her mind and let me down smoothly.

"Nice," I mumbled under my breath.

With a sigh, I crossed the floor to shut off the water, though not careful enough to avoid my reflection. And the pitiful version of Laure within it.

At some point, deep into that bottle of prosecco, my face had gone numb like it always did. When I was kissing that girl, it felt like the flesh of my cheeks had lost its elasticity and was sagging, hanging free like I'd never again pull it up into a smile, like kissing someone was the closest I'd ever get to feeling good again. Like the person underneath was shrinking. The depths of those red eyes staring back at me were fathomless and empty, while the horrors within me had grown boundless.

In leaning into the monster, I wasn't sure if I really knew *her* anymore—I feared whatever the human me was hiding, what I'd find if I came to a complete stop.

And then, of course, there was Acheron. Looming over her shoulder like a great shadow, all static and chaos drawing over itself. Spiking and spinning in constant, agitated motion.

**You will always have me**, it offered. And it didn't sound even a little sorry.

In fact, it felt like it was grinning. Though the shape had no head, no face, no mouth to speak of, in my gut, it felt like Acheron was sneering at me, like it knew something I didn't. A hyena baring its teeth before a cornered gazelle.

Only I wasn't a gazelle, and Acheron needed me. I was its vessel—it couldn't hurt me.

My brow furrowed. "Well, of course I will—"

In the corner of the mirror, the reflection of a shoe caught my eye. And when I turned around, I clapped a hand over my mouth to kill the shriek rising in my throat. Icy slush filled my veins.

There, sprawling on the stall floor, her back pressed to the toilet bowl, was my girl, the girl I'd just kissed, her silver dress twinkling in the fluorescent light. Her rosy mouth was agape, twisted in a silent scream. Mascara- and blood-mixed tears streaked her soft, round cheeks. As if she were a gruesome portrait that'd been frozen on the spot.

And because of what I was, I felt the absence of her pulse weighing like a brick. She was definitely dead, and unlike me, she wasn't coming back.

So with unnerving calm, I marched into the neighboring stall and hurled all the prosecco that had previously gone down.

# CHAPTER 3

The sky was already beginning to lighten by the time the Uber dropped me off on a small street in the 7th arrondissement. My thoughts teetered between images of the dead girl in the silver dress and Niamh's blond hair, so that I hardly cared about the driver sneaking not-so-subtle glances at me in the rearview mirror. But it wasn't until we arrived at the address, as I shrugged on my coat, that he finally spoke.

"Aren't you the girl from the opera?" he asked quickly, with a high, nervous voice. He took a break from squinting at my throat, the high neckline of my dress trying to cover the scar, and turned to the worn-down cathedral looming over the car, its wall full of pockmarks and cement patches from its war with time.

I could see the new theories he was thinking, the questions people kept asking me. *You live near here or you just really religious?* Both and neither.

"Did you see what happened? Do you really think it was an accident?"

I was too distracted and tired to think of a clever quip. **"Thanks for the ride."**

And I let the door shut behind me without watching for the vacuousness of his expression—the slackness of his mouth, the gloss of his eyes, these things that followed anytime I spoke like this, extending my will over someone else. Getting my way. It was the look of a simple mortal crossing paths with something divine, and though Acheron's favor had been enthralling once, now it was nothing special.

It was almost...boring.

The cathedral walls absorbed the sound of the car driving away as I strolled inside, through the archway and across the shadows of dawn. I could feel my buzz fading fast, as it had been ever since I found that body, called the police from an abandoned phone in VIP, and fled. Every motion—lurching open the hidden iron door, going down the hundreds of steps into the Catacombs—brought more and more clarity. Which I was hoping to avoid.

Only six months since I'd followed ballerina superstar Joséphine Moreau into the depths of the city looking for a miracle, but it felt like a lifetime. I was so desperate then, for a friend, to be found worthy of anything, that I descended several meters underground and pledged myself to Acheron. The network extended far beneath Paris, more than any of us probably understood. The longer I walked these paths, the more I lent credence to urban legends of mole people, of strangers belonging to the underground.

By now I could walk to Elysium drunk and with my eyes closed, following that pull from my sternum to the warmth and humid air. When it all swelled to a crescendo, I knew I was passing Acheron's altar, the alcove carved out in bloodred stalactites. Sometimes I expected to see Joséphine or even Ciro there, waiting, kneeling by the pool of blood and scrying for their futures.

But they were gone. Coralie killed them because of me, and I'd found their bodies just like I found that girl tonight.

"It can't be Coralie," I insisted to Acheron, because it was always listening. "Aside from the fact that she's dead, she used Lethe to take their marks and strangle them, and this girl wasn't strangled. She didn't have a mark."

Before I ran, I'd needed to be sure. There was no bruising, no frost-bite, no burns. No sign of violence at all except for the fear in her eyes and bloody tears down her face. I'd even searched both arms for a tattoo.

"She was normal. Died a normal death, right? It wasn't Lethe?"

If the thing that possessed Coralie had done the killing, I would have felt it like a chill down my spine. Like insects crawling under my skin, I wouldn't have missed it.

Acheron took a beat. **No, it wasn't.**

Just beyond the alcove was another, heavier door, and my skin hummed as I hauled it open. Elysium was a dimension beyond Paris, the place where gods lay, where fields of papery-white asphodels and hot, blood-scented air greeted me as soon as I crossed the threshold. We knew so little of the lush forest before me, but also trying to discover more was hard when Andor and I kept dancing around each other, nei-ther of us knowing the steps. At least now, alone but not alone, it didn't matter that I was clumsy on my feet from so many hours of dancing and drinking in thick platform boots. No one cared that my body was sore or my makeup runny from sweat and then panic.

All that stayed at the door to Elysium, while Acheron called its favorite little monster home.

**Now come rest,** it said finally, gently enough to mollify me. It didn't care about one mortal girl, and her mortal death, and I wasn't supposed to either. Least of all here.

So late into the night, so early into the morning, the forests beyond the meadow and the two rivers slicing through the land felt still. Hardly any creatures around to disturb with my noise. The very sight of the leftmost river of red made my heart pick up speed, and my legs fol-lowed Acheron's immortal song eagerly.

"So when did Niamh get back?" I asked as I marched through the trees.

Acheron shifted under my skin. **The comings and goings of my disciples are of little matter to me.**

I fought the urge to roll my eyes. "Okay. Well, where is she staying?"

As far as I knew, Andor, Keturah, and I were the only people Niamh knew in Paris. She wasn't staying in our little white cottage in Elysium, and Andor would have told me if he'd handed over the keys to Ciro's apartment aboveground. But more importantly, if she wasn't staying with us, then what was she doing here?

I was still so deep in replaying the night, reading into Acheron's nonanswers and silences, how I didn't even learn the girl in silver's name, that I didn't notice the rustle of pages at first. The soft shift of fabric. The tall figure wrapped in a tartan blanket and curled at the base of a tree, overlooking the blood river with a very thick book in his lap. In fact, I was so tired and distracted that normally I would have *felt* him: the low thrum of his heartbeat, the sheer magnitude of Acheron in his marrow. Especially so close.

If anyone had a pull to them, a weight to their presence, it was Andor. With his many deals, he used to have the most of Acheron until I died and took it all.

I hesitated there, toddling between two trees. The loudest part of me wanted to run, embarrassed. Surely I looked a mess, smelled rank, and had death clinging to me like a residue, and it was so late. But a smaller, quieter part wanted to crawl closer. Seek shelter inside whatever remained between us.

Andor wasn't my boyfriend exactly, and he wasn't nothing either. He was my *something*, though I didn't know what. I was too mortified to ask, and he was too soft to ever say. He certainly never asked where I went, what I did, with whom I spent my time. And though I ached to be enveloped in his orbit, I didn't know what to do with it. If he still wanted it. If I even deserved it, being what I was now considering I had to kill the

Laure he knew to get here. The one who danced, who had drive, who felt things was gone.

So the louder part won, and slowly, I took a step back in retreat.

A dry twig snapped underfoot, and like a predator, Andor lifted his head. The massive antlers carved of garnet shifted, and the four eyes filled entirely with black ink trained on me.

"Laure? Am I awake or dreaming?"

The wry smile on his lips pained me. Surprise and confusion covered his face as I neared, drawn to him though I knew better.

He didn't bother to change his shape, to hide his grotesque antlers and bloodred skin that shimmered in the light. Though Andor was capable of looking human, looking *mortal*, he never did around me because we were... something. I wasn't the fragile ballerina he once painted, who confessed her developing feelings in these woods—I came back feral and dangerous. Still, being able to feel how his heart stammered as I approached, that was enough to make me keep going. A direction to get unlost.

"Couldn't sleep?" I asked, trying to appear as calm as possible.

A week after the collapse, on our trip to Prague, I often woke to the sound of him stirring in the other room, the low groans and whimpers of a nightmare. This seemed a nicer way to ask if they were still happening.

Andor shrugged and made room for me to sit. "Early riser. Plus, I'm meeting Ciro's parents for breakfast..."

His voice trailed off, mouth hanging open, as he drank me in, the blush and lipstick and mascara, the hair frizzing at my temples. All four of his dark eyes, including the two sliced down the center by a fine white scar, followed my every feature as I sank to the ground beside him, the ends of my short dress fluttering.

"Have you been..." Andor cleared his throat and glanced away to hide his gawking. His brow furrowed. "Have you been out all night?"

I caught my bottom lip between my teeth, heat rising above my collar, and nodded. "It was Vanessa's birthday."

We sat so close that our shoulders brushed, and it grew harder to stay here in the moment rather than think about how we were in these woods the last time his lips were on mine.

**If you had any sense, you would set your eyes on sights higher**, Acheron grumbled from the base of my spine, as if it wasn't the dark god's fault I found Andor so intoxicating in the first place. **More *suitable* ambitions.**

Good thing I didn't have any sense, and it couldn't make me. Most of my sense died in the collapse, and I crushed whatever remained at that rotten memorial. And besides, Andor wasn't like all the kisses I'd drunkenly exchanged; I didn't want to devour him, even if he'd let me survive and come back for more.

"You've been pretty busy lately. I hardly see you," Andor remarked, gaze turned out toward the gory rapids. "Is everything okay—"

"I'm fine," I chirped.

"But—"

Just like with the scrawny boy at En boîte, I silenced Andor with a finger to his lips. The contact made my skin prickle, pins and needles traveling down the length of my hand, even through the lace of my gloves. He scowled but didn't say more.

"It was just a birthday."

I settled back and breathed in the dewy and floral scent of his skin, savoring his warmth as my knees pressed into his leg. I didn't want to talk about me or if I was "okay," whatever that meant. What I wanted was to keep spinning, keep looking forward instead of looking back, to bury my hands in someone's hair and press closer until I lost my mind completely.

But then I saw *her* standing five feet away, leaning against a tree with her arms crossed casually. When our gazes met, she even wiggled her fingers in greeting.

*Coralie.*

She was dead, and yet here she was, menacing me every time the buzz faded. Every time I returned to Elysium sober. Her hair was no longer a golden halo of waves but instead pale algae, still wet and clinging to her neck. Her big, green eyes were fogged over, round cheeks sunken, body gaunt. Like her body was frozen in what death made it.

The first time she appeared, I'd rubbed my eyes until it hurt to be sure I wasn't hallucinating. Now I could do little more than glare.

"Hope I'm not interrupting anything," she said with a grin.

Acheron's exasperation flared in me and blended with my own. But Andor didn't see or hear her. She was my own personal haunting.

To cover my unease, I batted my lashes and focused back on him. "You worry too much. Maybe next time you should come out dancing with me."

This worked.

Andor chuckled and dropped his attention back on his book. "I don't dance."

Compelling fellow monsters, like acolytes of Acheron, wasn't the same as making a mortal step aside or buy me a drink. Andor, and others like him, could resist my power—Acheron's favor—if he knew to, so I tried softness instead. I was a performer, after all.

"I could teach you."

His throat bobbed, and his pulse fluttered. And when he finally noticed me looking up at him, his eyes widened almost fearfully. The monster in me trained on it.

"*I could teach you.*" Coralie pitched her voice high to mock me before retching. "Do you hear yourself? Are you really that lonely without me?"

Oblivious, Andor braced a burning hand along my jaw, long fingers sliding through the hair at the nape of my neck, thumb brushing my cheek. Tingling spread along my throat, across my face, and reverberated through my scalp. He made the threat of poison in his touch enthralling.

It was heady enough to make my eyelids grow heavy, to keep the dark thoughts at bay—the dead girl in silver; Coralie, who was still watching; Acheron's disappointment. For a moment, I even forgot why Andor and I weren't a *thing* now. It was impossible for us to just be *nothing* to each other.

His gaze swept across my lips.

"Shouldn't you be looking after Niamh?" Coralie continued, her tone taking on an edge. "Wonder what trouble she's getting herself into—"

I swayed in my seat and turned on her. "Would you shut the hell up?"

Coralie glared at me, unsmiling. As if she was telling me something without saying it, or just baiting me to ruin my life from beyond the grave. Considering I still had scars from her last stunt, probably the latter.

Beside me, Andor dropped his hand and sighed to himself. "*Acheron.* How could I forget there's three of us now?"

I stiffened. "No, it's not—"

But it was too late. His resignation was piercing. That moment, like all the others, was over. Fumbled, just like I fumbled my future. Ruin was what I did best.

If I told him the truth, that it wasn't just Acheron butting in, but Coralie too, he'd worry more. Want to talk more about why I was seeing my dead friend while he couldn't. And if I lied and blamed it all on Acheron, well then, I couldn't be helped. I had the feeling that this thing with Acheron was permanent, everlasting, such a small cost for such a great honor. But what boy would want that?

Andor leaned forward and pressed a warm, simple, unfortunately *chaste* kiss to my forehead and then climbed to his feet. "You should really get some sleep, Laure."

The sadness in his voice killed me. Enough to go submerge myself in the blood of Acheron and never come back up. I stayed seated, leaning against the tree and glaring at where Coralie once stood. Of course she was gone now that her trolling had worked.

Tears threatened to spill over.

"I'm *fine*," I reiterated, wiping my eyes and spurning Andor's helping hand to stand on my own. I didn't care how he flinched, if he had anything else to say, because I turned my back on him and set off through the trees without another word.

He didn't call after me, and he didn't follow. He understood that this Laure, the newer model with a worse attitude and something rotten in her core, the one born from mass death and haunted by it, wasn't worth the pursuit.

I bit my lip hard enough to bleed, to fight the stinging in my eyes, the heat in my face, the tightness in my lungs. At least now I knew clearly where we stood. At least now I was sure why being a vessel meant I would always have Acheron: because I couldn't have anything else.

# CHAPTER 4

Coralie was standing over me when I opened my eyes.

I stirred from a few hours of restless sleep on the riverside with a feeling of being watched, a bed of moss fluffing around my head, Acheron flowing calmly at my side, and too much silence. Sunrays shone through the dark leaves of plum trees overhead, and then her visage of gold blocked out the light.

"Sleep well?" my dead best friend asked, unsmiling.

"You know I didn't," I mumbled as I rubbed my face.

Every time I closed my eyes, there was always something—walls falling down around me, tendrils made of light reaching up from the water's depths, choking the air from my lungs. Sometimes I was back onstage, surrounded by strangers who tore the skin and meat from my bones. Sometimes it was me sinking to the bottom of the water while Coralie rose victorious.

I pushed myself up and sighed. The girl before me may have been a product of my imagination, some manifestation of trauma maybe, but I didn't want to sit through whatever she had to say. Acheron wasn't inclined to pay her any attention either, simpering in the ball of my chest as I asked, "What do you want? Why are you torturing me?"

Coralie tried to smile, the corners of her mouth twitching disjointedly. "Shouldn't I be the one who's mad at you? After all, *you* killed *me.*"

"We killed each other."

When she clasped her hands before her and rocked on her heels, she looked so real that I might have reached out and touched her. But I'd felt her pulse sputter to a stop, and I'd left her body at the bottom of the water beneath a pile of rubble. She didn't even cast a shadow.

"Agree to disagree." She cocked her head and reconsidered. "Though, I suppose that's just what friends do in some sense. Kill each other in little ways, over and over again. Just like you and Acheron."

My shoulders tightened. *Acheron?*

The wicked dark in my bones homed in on her.

It was nothing like me and Coralie. We didn't bask in the flames of each other's ruin. She burned me and shoved a shard of glass in my heart as a parting gift, and I bit her and held her underwater, kicking and gasping for breath; nothing about us was the same. Even if, in some way, Coralie and I loved each other. Even if that love was brutal and rotten. Even if we couldn't escape each other in death.

And it seemed that even in death, Coralie still hated what I'd become.

Suddenly I had the urge to drown her all over again.

"No," I insisted, my voice steady even as I pressed the heels of my palms into my sockets. I dug and dug until they hurt, until stars erupted in the dark. "I'm not doing this with you."

A footstep shuffled through the foliage. Coralie's voice grew closer. "You don't have a choice. Who else are you gonna trust? With what time?"

"What the hell does that mean—"

"You shouldn't have come back."

When I tore my hands from my face, Coralie was gone again. There were no traces in the dirt, no footsteps or broken blades of grass, no lingering scent of lemon verbena perfume, muscle cream, and standing cave water. It was just me and the light scattering through the canopy. Me and the gentle trickle of the dark, red river.

*Killing me is killing everything you know about yourself. And who would you be without me?* Coralie had taunted me in our final moments with those words, and every so often, I heard them in my head, that voice with so much surety I couldn't help but question if maybe she was right. Maybe she knew more about me than I did. I wasn't dancing because I'd quit right before the ballet fell to ruins. Soil and sand stained my skin, coat, and dress in a smear that resembled dried blood because this was where I'd fallen asleep. My remaining friends were so far from reach. I was aimless and hallucinating.

I hung my head and groaned. My mouth was dry and cottony, and a headache—from too much booze, too little water, and too little sleep—began to throb at my temples.

**You run yourself ragged entertaining your delusions**, Acheron chided as I got moving. Anywhere, to do anything. **It would be wise to ignore her.**

"Well, if you know how to make her go away, I'm all ears."

And of course it said nothing.

I cut through the trees, back out of the woods, and into the cottage for a quick shower and change of clothes. What little I possessed, I kept in a corner of Keturah's closet, and enough of the morning was underway that there was no chance of running into either her or Andor, with the former already at work at the recording studio and the latter probably sulking around his gardens or whatever he did when he wasn't embarrassing me.

As soon as I smelled like something other than sweat and stale beer, I was on my way through the quiet meadows and back into the Catacombs. It was easy to just pick a direction and run when you didn't have a job.

In another life, I would have been at Palais Garnier by now, two hours into an eight-hour day where I did nothing but eat, drink, and sleep ballet. My muscles would have been warmed up by the conclusion of morning class, turning my heart in yearning toward Madame Demaret in the hopes she noticed me. Coralie, walking into the studio behind Hugo Grandpré with a clipboard in her arms. In this life, we would have made up—Coralie wouldn't resent me for getting in when she didn't, and I wouldn't have Acheron slithering under my skin, whispering in my ear always. Maybe we'd stay up late planning my strategy to beat the other apprentices. Vanessa and I would be enemies still, and I'd get a feature in a show like *Le corsaire* or *Ballet Impérial* for my troubles.

The bright light of day seared my eyes the instant I shoved through the door to the outside. It was getting worse as the days grew longer, the extent of brightness and sun from which I was spending longer apart.

In this other life, I didn't have to shield myself from the mornings—I welcomed them. I didn't grow pale and gaunt from so long down below. I wasn't so comfortable in the dark so as to become it. That other Laure dealt with nightmares about missing her cues, being late for rehearsals, falling onstage. She didn't keep finding dead girls. She wasn't lost.

JULIEN flashed on my phone as I breezed through the cathedral gate and onto the lively streets of the 7th. Cars and students bustled in every direction, and I imagined myself as one of them as I silenced the call.

Sometimes my father grew nervous when I went silent for too long, like he was afraid I'd drop dead again, but he didn't care enough to fight to hold me close. He'd been relieved to know I'd survived the collapse, but that didn't mean we ever talked about what happened. That we ever saw each other. He had been calling a lot more recently, every week or so, and I was avoiding him like I avoided the rest of the world without really trying. I didn't want to perform the happy and well-adjusted and go-getter Laure everyone knew, the one I sacrificed, and I also didn't want to be at the mercy of whatever she might be feeling right now.

No one paid any attention to me as I strolled down the avenues with a baseball cap on and my coat collar up, gazing through storefronts.

There were stationery shops whose windows were filled with delicate wrapping paper and floral notebooks, a specialty toy boutique with puppets and wooden dolls hanging from the ceiling. Comic books cluttered the entrance of another store nestled next to a dark tattoo parlor decorated with a neon sign. None of the others on the street cared that I wasn't sleeping. They didn't care who I used to be or what was talking to me where they couldn't hear.

"Maybe I should get a tattoo," I murmured, as I drifted along.

**You already have the one that matters most**, Acheron chirped brightly.

It was the muffled music from the other side of the narrow street that lured me closer. "Une fantaisie," from *Raymonda*. A variation I once dreamed of dancing. And beyond the wide glass windows was a studio covered in mirrors. It was tiny, probably an independent teacher of many styles, but today there was only one girl inside, rehearsing the variation alone.

Something I would have done, in another life.

Her neat bun, her pale leotard that almost looked translucent on her milky skin, all of it arrested me on the spot. She'd paired sweatpants with pointe shoes to keep the muscles warm, something I sometimes did when no one was watching, when I didn't have to keep up appearances. And she was gliding across the floor, spinning on an arc as if she were weightless.

I felt a pang in my chest. Once I was her.

Even with the uncharacteristically clear blue skies working to obscure the inside from view, I couldn't miss the flush of the girl's cheeks, the way her eyes drifted shut as physics took over. She was strong on her ankles, steady on her toes, a talented dancer and the most perfect machine, even if she'd never make it anywhere else.

And because I was so damn good at spinning to avoid looking at myself, for once, just for this moment, the Parisian skies gifted me with sun overhead to force my reflection in the window. Suddenly I wasn't looking at this girl anymore—I was staring at the sad thing in front of me. Dark hair frizzy, tangled, unstyled, peeking out from beneath the baseball cap. Grey sweatshirt that still had red dirt stains from the last time I wore it. Deep purple bruises under my eyes that were getting harder to cover with makeup, a starving, feral emptiness in my scowl. And the loud static and shadow that pitched an arm around my drooping shoulders as I reared away.

**When will you accept that you are so much more than just a *ballerina*?** Acheron asked, and though it had no mouth, no lungs, it spat the last word like a curse. Like it was such a small, weak, boring thing to be.

Maybe it was right.

Chewing the inside of my lip raw, I snapped a photo of a flyer in the window advertising auditions for some company and hurried away. Even though I was running, the old Laure and her pitiful aches continued to find me. Buried under a monster's mask but still seeping through, inescapable nevertheless. Yet another ghost.

So I'd have to run harder. Toward something.

Once I was safe inside the cocoon of the crowd, letting the flow carry me toward a bigger street, I called Niamh to set up a time to talk, and Acheron nodded its approval.

# CHAPTER 5

Theatre Illusorio was a far cry from the splendor of Opéra Garnier. The exterior looked run-down and poorly maintained for somewhere in the middle of the 5th arrondissement, the signs full of broken and shattered bulbs, the façade so heavily plastered with faded posters it all became illegible. The street before it smelled strongly of piss and vomit, the pavement strangely colored. On the other hand, it *wasn't* Opéra Garnier, which worked in its favor: no stolen gold adorning the entrance and walls, no statues of slave traders or tourists eyeing me like I didn't belong.

That was more than enough.

"Dancers, this way!" A scrawny man with a thin mustache shouted down the hall.

My phone buzzed as I followed among a sea of others in athletic gear, the caller unknown, and I declined it.

I'd forced myself here, to Theatre Illusorio, where they advertised auditions every month to join their vaudeville cast. It didn't matter that I'd never seen any of their shows before—all that mattered was that it was *something*. I was lost now, dwelling on dead girls and soured futures and what-could-have-beens, but eventually I'd find myself somewhere recognizable, right?

In Prague, Keturah had taken me to a variety performance with girls who were classically trained; I could tell by the point of their toes, the turn in their hips. Though I'd done nothing with it, watching them had felt like maybe there was hope for me. That there wasn't only one way to do this, to dance and live in time with the music. To be happy and whole again.

I still wasn't sure I believed it—if monsters like me were even capable of being happy. What did it look like? Where could I find it?

*What would you be without me?*

*You shouldn't have come back.*

The other dancers gathered around the tables—because Theatre Illusorio was more of a club than a *theatre* in the proper sense—and I scurried off to the restrooms. I felt my stomach climbing up into my throat, tasted bile the instant I saw that stage.

I doubled over a sink and splashed water on my face.

**What are you doing?** Acheron asked, the buzzing of its voice making me shudder.

In the mirror, the dark mass seemed a little more person-shaped today, the head and shoulders more defined, though there were still no features. It crackled and blurred like static on an old TV, or something in the periphery of your vision that you couldn't quite make out. And it looked as though all the energy and shadow in the room were trying to coalesce but couldn't stabilize. This was as physical a manifestation of its eldritchness as it could take.

"Auditioning." I looked away to focus on sudsing my hands. "Or is there something else I should be doing?"

The sinks remained blissfully unoccupied, sparing me from judgmental glances from my competition because I was trembling. The realization that I'd never in my life faltered like this before auditions, that I used to revel in forcing my competition to see my level of focus, only worsened my nerves. I was out of it. I wasn't the Laure who could do this.

After a long pause, Acheron replied, **Do you want this?**

"No, but I need it."

This was the closest Acheron and I got to a face-to-face, staring at each other through a mirror, and it was uncanny seeing its mannerisms play out before me. The bend of its neck as it tried to cock its head, the inelegant slope of its shoulders, the long beats of its silence—none of it was human. And it was in me. A part of me. More of me than *me*.

**But you are perfect. You don't *need* anything.** It spoke without affectation, though I detected an arcane lack of understanding. As if this great, old god couldn't fathom why a lifetime of nightmares and isolation was not enough for me. Or anyone.

I dropped my head and pulled a paper towel. "Not if you ask Andor. Or Keturah. Or Coralie. They think I'm broken. And if I can't prove I'm fixed, pretty soon, I'm sure they'll throw me away."

**Broken? You are the anchor to the Daemon King.** In the mirror, it placed its hand—or the buzzing, crackling shape of one—at the cradle of my throat, stroking idly across my carotid. Almost possessively. Because the god had given me all this power, a new life, at such a low cost. **You are *my* vessel. You cannot break.**

"Thanks," I whispered, my hands slowing over the trash bin.

Though I'd definitely revisit *the Daemon King* thing later, somehow, I did actually feel better. I was sure it meant it literally, that my limbs wouldn't shatter, that I could heal from a head-on collision with a truck, but there was something to be said for the comfort of never being doubted. Of belonging to something without question, for once.

Even if I could never forget what sat in my body, I was wanted. Important.

**You have yet to understand the breadth of a Great, Old One's power, my many names, what is in store for us. You could be a god on earth if you wanted—you do not know how far from breaking you are, but you will soon.**

"All right, much more ominous," I muttered under my breath before stepping back out onto the floor.

Dancers gathered onstage while Thin Mustache and an older woman with curly copper hair sat together at one of the round tables. There appeared to be no structure, no one to direct me or tell me what to do. I helped myself to pins and a paper numbered 17 and joined the others.

Everyone did their own thing. Some stood around back and talked, half-heartedly stretching their arms overhead. One folded over in a wide split, another jumped rope, another balanced in an inverted yoga pose. Some dancers wrapped their toes in bandages and tape, something I might have done if I put any forethought into this at all.

And I stood on the edge, flexing and extending my feet, watching.

At the Paris Ballet Company, and even at the academy and before, all warm-ups were a group activity, led by an instructor who formulated a routine to target every muscle you'd ever need to dance that day. It was systematic, starting low and slow, building in heat and intensity until every muscle was awake and on fire. They had no choice when the dancers were cash cows and an injury could ruin a season.

"Ten minutes!" Thin Mustache shouted.

After ankles, I moved on to calves, knees, and thighs, and I pretended not to notice how a few imitated me. Feigning to follow even if they lacked the flexibility. From my position onstage, I could see interest sparking in the eyes of the judges. They didn't miss me now.

I could do this.

So I hung my head and smiled, my pulse slowing some. The others around me wore tee shirts and sweatpants, while I was in my classic ballerina leotard, shorts, and leg warmers. I didn't have much anymore, most of it left behind at my old apartment in the 19th, but I had enough for this at least, so it would serve me well. I wouldn't go back to that apartment I'd shared with Coralie unless hell froze over.

Still, even from dress, it was apparent that we were on opposite ends of the dance spectrum—the street dancers probably with tricks up their sleeves, but with a ballerina, you always knew what to expect. It didn't make sense how we were all vying for the same thing.

I barely made it to the hips when a tall white woman with a messy ponytail leapt down from the stage and clapped her hands. "Are we ready to dance? Let's begin with a ball change."

Even more confusing, the choreography was a simplistic modern number to a lo-fi pop song without any words. We moved our arms and legs in some disconnected attempt at interpretive, and it hardly mattered how new I still was to *this* body, how strong every motion felt. There were no complex turns, nothing that required even the barest hint of flexibility or precision. Rhythm was a suggestion.

And that was probably why no one had ever heard of this place.

Still, I learned quickly and ran through it again and again. That the steps were rudimentary wouldn't stop me, especially considering my background; the directors had to want me, and I'd show them what a real professional looked like.

Yet when the choreographer shouted, "Okay, let's break into three groups," I startled for just a moment.

And because I was trained to never let it show, I kept up my sharpened ballerina smile to mask my discomfort with the disorganization. I could be dancing with thumbtacks in my shoes, and no one would have known.

For once, *I* had the pedigree in the room. *I* was the shoo-in instead of the underdog.

I didn't have to crack some spines, twist some ankles, or crush hearts to pulp. The audition was so easy, in fact, that when it was my turn, ushered into some group at random, my body still went on autopilot. I hardly felt the motions, hardly noticed it was over until we were lined up on the stage at the end. Waiting for the directors to call numbers.

I wasn't even flushed. My heart was steady, wondering how many they'd choose. Thin Mustache didn't say, just "as many as we need." And as the copper-toned director rattled off a list of numbers, my eyes fluttered shut.

"Two, five, six, and seven... Twelve..."

All around me, the dancers' heart rates spiked, a chorus of pitter-patter as they stared at the papers pinned to their chests. Their hopes and hunger were thick enough to taste, rich enough to feed on.

"Twenty-two, twenty-five, and thirty-one. If I didn't call your number, you're dismissed."

Though I didn't hear my number, ballerinas showed no fear. We were the perfect machines, and it made sense that the best part of old Laure—the ballerina—had withstood death and Acheron. She had to.

But the director waved a hand. "Thank you for coming, and you're welcome to try again next month."

Dancers began streaming from the stage, but in the center of them, I went rigid. Not even breathing. A girl about my age sniffled beside me as she too dragged herself away. Then I was back to drowning. My head underwater, unhearing, unseeing, kicking and paddling and hoping to find my way to clarity soon. Someone's hand laced with mine, pulling me down.

How could I be dismissed? It wasn't possible. Of course people failed auditions and got rejected—it was the reality of our world. But *I* didn't fail. Laure was... We were better than this.

My every step off that run-down stage was stilted, a concession of defeat wrenched unwillingly from me. I was a classically trained ballerina. I put in thirteen years of nearly daily practice—rehearsals and classes, practicing at home, in the shower, in the kitchen, while I brushed my teeth and while I sat in waiting rooms for doctor appointments. I danced on bloody toes, pressing and pressing until the nail fell off. At Opéra Garnier, I breathed perfection—

But this wasn't Opéra Garnier.

And I wasn't that girl anymore.

"Moving on," the thin-mustached man barked with a smile, as if he'd promptly forgotten all the discarded people shuffling behind him. Discarded people that bafflingly included me.

Somehow I was already at my table, shoes changed and ready to go. I tightened my grip on my bag and coat, waiting for it to add up. For someone to stop me and ask where I was going, to insist with a smile that I'd misunderstood, laugh out, *Didn't you hear your number?* So stunned, I didn't even think to force my way through.

Instead, a woman with braces and a neon-pink crop top nudged me and said, "Better luck next time, huh?"

*Next time.*

Nausea rolled through me at the thought, and Acheron studied me curiously.

I'd have to do this again. Even if I didn't know which way was up, I had to keep swimming and hope I broke the surface. Even if this was proof that the ghost was right, that I was broken, and maybe I'd made a big mistake.

# CHAPTER 6

By the time I arrived back in Elysium, worn down from the audition, I was already late. I found Niamh waiting for me in our old spot, sitting atop a tree stump with a butterfly knife flipping around her hand.

She didn't stir as I approached, but rather continued twisting the knife, open and closed, wincing whenever the blade nicked her fingers. I watched her work, how she moved deftly to unlatch the handles, spin one in her grip while the other went flying, and then catch it quickly to expose the glint of silver. How confidently she flicked her wrist despite the blood running down her fingertips. Were she mortal, Acheron and I would have been intrigued, but her blood was no different from my own.

"I'm pretty sure that knife is illegal," I teased as I strolled into view.

"You're late," Niamh snapped without breaking her concentration, "and I'm bored." Her hands stilled for just a moment when her hazel eyes flicked to me.

I could feel the impatience of Niamh's heart like an itch on the roof of my mouth. We'd barely managed a day of lessons on Acheron before she quit, complaining she was uninterested in *understanding* the wicked dark—she just wanted to go and use it. She'd knelt at the pool eagerly when we brought her, but apparently after that, I wasn't going her speed.

Repetition, practicing for as long as she could stand it, patience—this was how ballerinas earned our skill. We repeated the same movements and positions over and over and over again, for hours every day for years on end. It gave us strength and flexibility, and I didn't see why it couldn't do the same for Acheron-given power.

But Niamh had never shown up again, and I quickly grew tired of waiting for her and found my distractions in a club and in a bottle.

Some people didn't make it as ballerinas solely because they lacked the drive to do the same thing every day. I had a teacher in junior classes who'd smack our thighs with rulers whenever we whined of being tired or *bored*, sick of sweeping one leg front and then back, our tiny muscles screaming for a reprieve. Niamh was too undisciplined for what eight-year-old me could accomplish.

So undisciplined, in fact, that we never even figured out what Acheron's favor to her looked like. Did she have power at all, or was it a passive favor like Ciro and Joséphine, where doors opened and blessings just fell into her lap? Would she ever have the focus to find out?

"So, when did you get back?" I asked, rather than dignify her complaint.

"Who said I left?"

There was nothing particularly hostile in her tone that I detected but nothing pleasant either. It spurred guilt in the pit of my stomach, that I'd recruited her and left her to fend for herself.

I shoved my hands into my pockets in my best attempt at casual. "We just assumed you did, because you packed some of your stuff and disappeared. Where are you staying, then?"

Niamh tucked fried, white-blond hair behind both ears, stood, and focused her gaze on me intently. "I made some new friends. We have a place outside of Nanterre. I've been meaning to swing by the cabin and pick up the rest of my stuff."

A shiver rolled down my spine.

Again, none of her words were weapons themselves, but everything from her tongue felt sharpened nonetheless. Like she was planning to wound or obscuring a blade. It reminded me that none of us really knew Niamh at all. We didn't even know her last name, only that she didn't hesitate to follow us to make a deal. She seemed to be running like we all were.

Sometimes I wondered if I'd done the right thing, following the impulse, introducing myself and Acheron to her, bringing her to Paris so that she could have some power of her own. Sometimes I felt like I'd given her a loaded gun while Acheron exhibited no regret. But with me as its anchor, its chosen vessel, its hunger was indistinguishable from my own. Its needs enmeshed with mine until we blurred together and I couldn't tell us apart. So when it wanted Niamh, *I* wanted Niamh, and that was that.

I wasn't so naïve as to invite it in and not expect to be changed. Maybe it'd change her too.

"Want to go exploring?" I asked brightly, so that she wouldn't see how unnerved I was.

On the other hand, the mortal world wasn't my problem. I'd tried to belong among them, to be like them, and still I was cast out. If Niamh went rogue, set the world on fire, and watched it burn, as far as I was concerned, the world deserved it, and I'd be fine to stay in Elysium, unaffected by the smoke.

Niamh nodded, and we began trekking through the forest, her shoulders slumped in front of her. I followed at a pace, pretending to enjoy the sounds as six-footed foxes darted through the foliage, birds with sharp teeth nesting overhead.

"I saw you at En boîte the other night."

"Oh yeah?" she said without glancing back. Unbothered, she snatched a long branch from a thicket of bushes and used it to swat at spiderwebs ahead of her.

"Yeah, I called your name. Guess you didn't hear me."

She shrugged. "The music's pretty loud."

*Liar*, I wanted to say, clamping my mouth shut. The more I thought about it—that far from the dance floor, my fingers around her wrist—the more it made sense that she'd just pretended to ignore me. But why?

"True. Did you hear that a girl died that night?"

Niamh stopped walking, turned on her heels, and raised a brow. "What do you think you're doing?"

*Caught.*

I drew to a stop and assessed her. The rigidness of her shoulders, the slight narrowing of her eyes. Niamh and I were not friends, and I did neither of us favors pretending. She was my recruit, and I was Acheron's favorite—she would tell me what I wanted to know.

**"Did you kill her?"**

The muscles in Niamh's neck strained for just a flash before I pulled the answer out of her. "No."

Relief flooded my body as I loosened up. **"Did you know her?"**

"No," she answered. The vacuousness that I expected from mortals would never cross her face. Instead her expression was stony, guarded. Even though there was no way she could lie to me, know how to resist my commands, it still made me uncomfortable.

"Thank you."

We kept walking in silence, weaving through the forest in search of nothing at all while I ignored the suspicious glances Niamh threw at me when she thought I wasn't looking. Though she'd witnessed my peculiar persuasiveness before, I didn't think she knew how it worked. Who it worked on. But wheels were turning behind her eyes as she tried to figure it out.

"So, what do you do with your time?" I prodded, brushing aside more guilt that blossomed in my chest from treating her like a criminal. Finding my suspicions unwarranted. "Since you're not with us?"

Niamh shrugged. "Hanging around. Mapping the Catacombs. Trying to learn all I can about us—"

**You still mistrust her.** The words seeped from my bones and plumed through me like fog. It was inside my skull, in the back of my throat, under my skin. **Even though you are on the same side.**

I couldn't help the scowl that came. "There are no *sides*."

**You think I made a mistake,** the eldritch god continued, and though there wasn't really a tone, because its words were less spoken and more just *expressed*, I still detected reproach. **But I am what you would call a god. I do not make mistakes.**

"Well, of course."

And it settled back down in me, because while I could detect reproach or self-satisfaction, Acheron couldn't detect sarcasm.

Niamh gaped. "You're talking to it, aren't you? Acheron?"

My cheeks flushed. "Sorry—"

"Why does it only talk to you? What makes you so special?"

And again came that look, sizing me up the way a thief catalogs all the bits and pieces to snatch away. The hunger of an animal who's found something that looks and smells like dinner.

We never told her I was a vessel.

I feigned nonchalance. "Don't know. It's probably because I fell in. Maybe I'm, like, radioactive or something."

She looked unconvinced.

As we walked, I scanned the landscape for something new. The white cottage we all called home was the only structure I'd ever come across here, the rest of sprawling Elysium remaining a mystery. So I took a page from Joséphine Moreau's book and documented everything— typing out notes on my phone, snapping photos at new heights, of changing soil and new plants, anything about or surrounding the blood river. None of us ever mentioned its white twin.

All of Joséphine's notes were lost in Coralie's clutches, but she'd done exactly this: balanced on fallen trees to cross ravines, documented the berries and ferns, the locations of fox dens and birds' nests. Tried to comprehend the tangle of primordial beings whose bodies fed this place. Chaos, the originator of everything. Acheron as its blood. Lethe as its bones. And what of the trees? The soil and rock? What was their divine source?

Then my feet came to a halt of their own accord, and I snapped my head to the side. "Do you feel that?"

"Feel what?" Niamh mumbled, gaze darting nervously between me and the trees.

Before I could find the word to articulate the tremor in my bones, I was already drifting toward it. It was less a sound—like birdsong overhead—or a feeling but more a scent: something new and sweet I hadn't found here before. Even the red ink on my arm was reacting to it, itching as I neared.

The trees thinned, and the forest went quiet the farther from Acheron I went.

"Uh, Laure?" The apprehension in Niamh's voice was new, but she didn't understand—this was Elysium. Our domain. *We* were the danger.

I could feel Acheron incline its head as it cautioned, **You should turn around**.

With its favor, its power in my blood, what did I have to fear? Stopping a heart, making someone swallow broken glass, or driving a scooter into a street pole was as easy as breathing.

I waved them both off. "We'll head back in a second. I just want to get this down so I can come back later."

**You won't like what you see**, it hissed.

But so strong was the itching in my arm that I couldn't resist scratching with my nails, then scraping the skin against the zipper of my pocket. Like something inside of me was dying to get out. My teeth ground together. I *had* to keep going.

And the silence grew more pronounced when I entered what appeared to be a clearing, where not a living thing resided. There was only me and Niamh, but no woodland creatures above or below. Nothing at all, really.

"What..."

The sparse trees were gaunt, and instead of the usual rich colors of plum or onyx, they were grey. A sickly, faded grey spotted with white around the roots that thinned as it climbed higher. Above, bark peeled away in strips like rotting flesh. Branches broke off and hung limp and ragged, devoid of leaves.

"...happened here?"

One more step and the ground squelched under my boots. It was soft and wet, not the sponge and bounce of a healthy forest floor full of mycelia and moss, but soggy, more like a swamp's edge. My foot sank and sank, and muddled, grey water seeped out.

Still deep in the trees, Niamh called out, "I don't think we should be here."

I only nodded, staring as the brackish water bleached the leather of my boots before my eyes. From black to brown, then tan, and finally white, all along the soles, up the heel, to the tip of the toe. And so fast, I could only gape in wonder.

It didn't smell like bleach, though—it smelled sweet, like rot. It triggered some faraway memory in my head, an ache it begged me to remember.

"Acheron?" I asked quietly, to prevent waking something up. "What is this?"

Waiting for an answer, I turned in a circle, examining how the tree line gradually thickened and turned to forest again. The remains of dead and fallen trees filled the mush that I waded through. The bloated corpse of a jackalope lay some feet away, the red sky reflected in one wide, red eye. There were others—sickly white frogs, an entire murder of five-eyed ravens whose feathers were sticky and bleached white too.

And through it all, Acheron was noticeably silent. It didn't stir or turn away from me. It almost felt like it was . . . dormant.

"I *said*, what is this?" I demanded as I nudged a raven with the ruined toe of my boot.

The water wasn't fully water either. It was iridescent, a stream of colors and separated in places, like water and oil. Some of it was white and creamy, and the longer I stood there, the more it pulled at me to place that scent, the profound silence.

Chilled to the bone, I turned back and moved quickly. Genuine relief flashed on Niamh's face. Every step squished and shifted, more mud mixed with milky white, until I remembered where I'd encountered it.

Where I'd *tasted* it: when Acheron brought me back from death.

When I first awoke after dying, I'd vomited something just like this—thick, white, oily, tasting sweet and old like rotting bananas. It'd bleached the floorboards too.

And now it was all over.

As I joined Niamh on dry land, scraping the bottom of my boots on a fern, my shadow stirred to life. Agitated, flickering, Acheron gave a curt answer that only begot more questions: **It has begun.**

# CHAPTER 7

The good thing about having Niamh with me when I stumbled into the brackish water was that I knew it was real. She'd eyed where the color bled from my shoes just like I did, which meant this wasn't like Coralie's ghost. It wasn't in my head—the water turned my favorite boots white in weird patches, and it wasn't even the nice white of snow or pearls. It was the stale, dry white of bone.

We said nothing to each other on our slow, stilted way back to the cottage. I stopped every so often to mark down our path, and Niamh shifted her weight from foot to foot like she couldn't wait to get out, long after the itching and unease had subsided.

*What has begun?*

Acheron didn't say any more than that, no matter how many times I asked. There was only the cold seriousness of its words and a stiffness in my spine as I veered west. The cottage was in view through the trees, its chipped white paint calling to me like a beacon. I figured maybe it'd mean something to the others.

"You go on ahead," Niamh said, her voice unsteady. She jutted her thumb toward the meadow. Toward the iron door. "I need to get out of here for a bit."

And before I could say anything, like maybe she should stay and hear what the others had to say, or at least back me up so they knew I wasn't losing it, she was already gone, darting through the woods as fast as she could without running. I felt the flutter in her pulse;

she'd sensed a bigger threat and decided to run. Maybe she was the sensible one.

"Will you tell me now?"

Stubborn as ever, Acheron said nothing other than **I warned you**.

The high grass brushed against my fingertips as I wrung my hands. Smoke drifted from the chimney, and through the wide windows I glimpsed Keturah on the couch, a fire dancing in the hearth behind her. Beautiful and uncomplicated in a way I couldn't be.

She didn't see me standing in the yard, waiting for an answer Acheron wouldn't give. For all its annoying chatter when I wanted some peace, it had nothing useful to share now.

"It's me," I shouted over the creaking door.

Her voice cut out immediately, as if she was waiting for me to worm through the hall and into the living room before she continued. The force of Andor's gaze hit me the moment I cleared the arch.

Four eyes glinting in the firelight brought heat to my face, throat, and chest. The center of my forehead seared like a brand, and I froze, debating if maybe I should have run too. Maybe it would've been better to follow Niamh out instead of embarrassing myself even further. He had to know what I wanted last night—this morning—when I'd leaned in and closed my eyes.

"Everything…okay?" Keturah asked, gaze shifting between Andor and me. She didn't know, but she could sense it.

"Fine!" Though I wanted to sound chipper, it came out a rasp instead. Every thought bled from my mind until it was empty. "I just thought I'd…pay you a visit."

Stiffly, I crossed the room and sank onto a blue velvet settee, wishing it'd swallow me whole. My heart raced, feeling them both watch my every step, but I chewed my tongue bloody to avoid looking up.

"Were you just with Niamh?" Keturah clutched a teacup in her palms despite its steaming surface. The lipstick she'd worn to match her neat, violet plaits left prints along the rim.

I nodded. "Yes, we were just walking through the woods when—"

"Haven't seen her lately. What has she been up to?" She cast a quick glance at Andor, saying something he understood that I didn't. A look that sent my mind reeling.

Did Niamh tell them something? Did they know about the girl in silver? That she was dead? That I'd kissed her?

I swallowed and looked away. "Nothing much. Why?"

"And it's going all right with her? Acheron's favor?" Andor prodded. Much less slyly. "Whatever it is."

My shadow stirred at my feet in suspicion. I asked in a low voice, "What's this about?"

Keturah shifted in her seat. "We're just... concerned about her, okay? We're not sure if she's..." Her hesitation was going to make me jump out of my skin. "If it was a good idea—"

"**You doubt me.**" Acheron's voice just slipped right out. Because challenging me was challenging it.

The air crackled with power I didn't intend to summon, to let slip. And the instant the words left my mouth, Andor and Keturah exchanged more knowing glances I couldn't bear to witness.

They'd been talking about a lot of things lately, it seemed.

"No—" Keturah started to deny.

"You think I made a mistake," I interrupted, fully myself again, though my head was so full of static, of noise, that I could barely hear my thoughts. "I don't make mistakes. I'm a—"

*No.* I stopped myself.

Those were still Acheron's words, not mine.

Yet they were my friends. They were supposed to trust me, to stand by me, to understand. I'd spent years being doubted and dismissed, and they knew that. They were supposed to be different. When all the world thought me dispensable, they were supposed to see the truth. I shouldn't have to fight by myself anymore.

I shouldn't have had Acheron echoing in my head: *You will always have me.*

"It's just concern." The corner of Keturah's mouth twitched as she tried to smile and placate me. She set her teacup down on the table and reached to take both my hands. It should have soothed me, but it didn't. "I just noticed that when she was here, she seemed a little... Intense. And secretive. I was a little scared of her, to be honest. She's got a lot of rage—"

"*I* have a lot of rage," I countered pointedly. "*I'm* intense and secretive. Maybe she's just coping with this shit the best way she knows how."

After the finality of my words descended a quiet so palpable that my palms slicked with sweat. Neither looked as if they were willing to surrender, but rather as if they were preparing their next offense. Even if I didn't trust Niamh completely, it shouldn't have mattered.

From his seat on the couch, Andor asked a little too sharply, both too loud and too soft, "Is that what you're doing, Laure? Coping the best you know how?"

*We aren't talking about me.*

The buzzing in my skull swelled to a scream. I wanted to kill him. I wanted to tear him limb from limb and collapse into his arms so full of sobs that he'd realize how easy it was for him to hurt me. I wanted to break the antlers from his stupid skull and spear myself so he'd see how easily I bled. To make how haunted I was something for them to finally comprehend.

Fighting the lump forming in my throat, I replied as steadily as I could, "I'm. Fine."

It was all I knew how to say.

Rather than defend me, or put him in his place, Keturah just sighed. "Maybe now isn't a good time—"

I balked.

"The constant partying, the late nights." His gaze hardened at the implication, as if he knew exactly what I was doing and who I was wrapped up in. Did it hurt him or was he grateful to be spared? Yet his voice was so tired at what he said next, it could shatter me. "When was the last time you got some sleep? In a real bed, and not outside in the dirt?"

"It's where I sleep the best," I answered automatically, hating how little I sounded. I was a child being scolded instead of the vessel of an old god who'd *survived death*.

I knew exactly how it appeared to them: They thought an unhealthy attachment was forming, even if they didn't know about Coralie's ghost. If I mentioned her, that was all they'd hear, and then they'd really think I'd lost it. Who'd want to stick around after that?

Andor arched his scarred brow, inadvertently drawing attention to his scarred eyes, the silver line threading down the inky black of both. "That sounds normal to you?"

"You're a recluse in a poison garden. I don't think you're one to question me about what's 'normal.'"

He flinched.

But I wanted to be cruel and covered in thorns. I wanted my existence to bruise and break skin. The anger made my skull throb, there was so much of it, and I raked my hands through my hair to give myself pause. To clear my thoughts and handle this like...Like old Laure would. Laure before the fall.

But I wasn't her. I wanted to make it worse, and being worse was so much easier.

"Besides, I'm auditioning for dance companies," I teased. "I'm ready to dance again. How's *art school* going?"

The muscle in Andor's jaw ticked, but he didn't reply. He wouldn't. And the shadow behind his eyes—the dark, primordial thing buried under *his* skin, *his* bit of Acheron though so much less than mine—flickered to show his agitation too. I was there the day he went on leave, and I damn well knew why: He'd lost Ciro and then his eye in the span of a week.

Still, I broke eye contact first and shifted to the fire, hoping the glow obscured the flush of my cheeks. Andor thought I was better than this, but he was wrong. Right now being hated seemed easier too. At least it was familiar.

After a long pause, Keturah cleared her throat and poured herself more tea. "That's good, Laure, you dancing again."

That only made me want to crawl into myself even more.

"Anyway," Keturah continued, trying to soften the air that had grown tense, "I really just wanted to get your thoughts on Niamh. In case something happens. In case she—"

"In case she hurts someone, and it's my fault," I surmised without looking away from the fire. It couldn't be any plainer now: They thought Niamh was unstable, and I was unstable too, so who would stop her if something went wrong?

Andor added softly, "It wouldn't be your fault, Laure."

Only it was too late. He had already made it clear what he thought of me. Twice over.

Nodding, I climbed to my feet, ready to be anywhere but here, around anyone but him. He'd always had a way of seeing too much of me, even the parts that were supposed to stay hidden, and now it had served up my worst. At the very least, I didn't have to see it reflected in his face.

He wanted the other one back. *Old* Laure.

Yeah, well, sometimes, me too.

**I tried to tell you,** Acheron drawled. **They aren't like you. They aren't capable of understanding.**

"Well, I'll keep a closer eye on her, then." I felt my jaw tremble in spite of myself. "Thanks—"

"What happened to your boots?" Keturah asked. She leaned forward in her seat on the couch, squinting at the uneven splotches of white around the heels.

*Right.* From the water. What I originally came here to share, before all of this drained the life from me. What did any of it matter now when the messenger was so untrustworthy?

I could only shrug and head for the door.

# CHAPTER 8

There was already a long line snaking outside of La Tempête when Vanessa and I arrived on foot. It was probably double its usual length with En boîte closed for the investigation, full of scantily dressed bodies shivering in the cold, teeth chattering, while they waited for their chance to slip inside.

I couldn't just stay home. Between the fraught talk that afternoon with Keturah and Andor and my failed audition, I was a live wire. My grip on myself had weakened to where I could hardly summon any emotion unless the remnants of pitiful Laure inside me unleashed them all. I was a volcano verging on cataclysm, but in the City of Light, there was always a distraction.

"Just come and audition at my new company," Vanessa insisted as we marched past the queue. "Maison Lumina is always recruiting."

*So they can reject me too?*

The more I thought about it, the more I couldn't help but wonder if Coralie was right. Maybe I was out of practice, sure, but maybe I just wasn't *meant* to dance anymore. Or do any of this normal stuff. I had my shot, and I quit, and without ballet, the version of me that could do this had died, so now it was over. Maybe I was still dead in a way and just running in the wrong direction when I shouldn't have come back in the first place.

Maybe now I was meant to be an old god's vessel and nothing else, to have people kneeling at my feet and offering me champagne rather than dancing on some small, obscure stage for tourists who wouldn't even throw tips and pining over some boy. Fate had determined that I was only good at being cruel and selfish, so who was I to argue?

At least *Acheron* got me.

We strolled up to the front door ceremoniously. Beside me, her brown waves bouncing with every step, Vanessa squinted at the line and wrinkled her nose. "We don't have to wait, right?"

She didn't know about Acheron exactly. She didn't understand how I got what I wanted, or what it cost to be able to do such a thing. She didn't know about my mark or the others, and since we never talked about *before*, I was spared from having to explain. All that mattered was that I worked miracles, and she always knew of a party I could escape to.

With just my glance to security in thick coats, the doors were already parting for my arrival, Vanessa on my heels. Complaints from the waiting crowd followed us inside, and I couldn't have cared less. For all I had to put up with, this was the least I deserved.

Then Niamh found me. The gravity of her presence, of an acolyte, struck fast like a serpent, slipping under my skin before I could even hand off my coat. It was the unexpectedness that made me freeze and then slowly wind around to trace it.

She was watching me from the hall, arms crossed and leaning against the wood-paneled wall with a smirk on her face. She'd slicked her white-gold hair back tonight and wore a sleeveless white shirt, her Acheron's mark on full display, and others glanced between us as they walked past. Even Vanessa looked at us with interest.

"When you asked where I'd be tonight, I don't remember giving an invitation," I quipped as I approached. And with a haphazard glance to Vanessa, I commanded, **"Go home. I'll talk to you later."**

Niamh eyed Vanessa closely, narrowing in on the emptiness in her eyes as she strutted away without a backward glance. Then she pushed off the wall and shrugged. "We need to talk."

I raised a brow and started toward the main hall. My phone was vibrating again, yet another persistent call from an unknown number that I ignored. "Already? Didn't we *just* talk?"

And it was also only hours ago that Keturah and Andor laid out their complaints of how angry, intense, and secretive Niamh was. Suddenly my lack of warm feelings toward her had transformed to wanting to protect her. From them. Because apparently she was even more like me than they ever were.

"It's time I tell you—there's a bunch of us living just outside of Nanterre." Her tone was matter-of-fact, sharp and to the point. "And they told me some things."

I slowed. "A bunch of what?"

She gave me a sidelong glance rather than answer, willing me to understand. *Us.* She said she'd been learning about us. About acolytes.

My heart skipped a beat.

"H-how much is 'a bunch'?"

There were more of us. Here. *Anywhere.* And somehow Niamh had found a cluster of them on her own while I was off drowning my woes in cute strangers.

Niamh shrugged again. "I don't know. Fifteen, maybe? I don't keep a roster—"

"*Fifteen?*" I seized her arm and dragged her through the crowd, stepping on toes and shoving everybody out of my way.

She was always doing this, being so casual, so lackadaisical no matter the context—Acheron had *fifteen* other acolytes that we knew of in the Paris area, yet she was shrugging. It never said anything to us about others. How many had I crossed without paying attention? There could be hundreds more, maybe thousands, with concealer and foundation powdered all over their arms to hide the marks. Sure, I hadn't felt them, but Paris was a big place. It wasn't impossible, but to hear she'd found more...

"How did you find them? Where?"

I nodded to security blocking the lounge half obscured by thick velvety curtains, climbed the stairs, and slipped inside, all while pulling Niamh behind me.

She frowned at my grip. "Through the Catacombs. There are other doors to Elysium, doors all over the city. They've been there all this time."

Inside the lounge, Niamh looked around, piecing more of it together: how we met, my vague allusions to influence, Vanessa, security. I left her to it, flopped down at a table in the back, the chatter of the club muffled low, and got started on the waiting bottle of chilled prosecco and two glasses. A table of older women eyed us with distaste.

"So spill—"

"You did that, right?" She clambered closer.

I only nodded impatiently and began to pour.

"Can you, like, walk into any room you want? Or how does it work?" Her hazel eyes were aflame; she hardly acknowledged her prosecco at all.

I didn't want to talk about me. I was sick of always talking about me. Acheron never bothered to explain anything unless it served its interests—I wanted to get back to the fifteen other acolytes in the area. But something told me I shouldn't show my hand, appear so eager and ignorant. Not in front of the girl *I* recruited.

Enforcing calm, I held my glass close and took a bracing sip. "Whatever I want someone to do, I just have to ask. I definitely don't need to pay for anything anymore."

And I left it at that, to let her imagination run wild. She nodded slowly, not knowing the rest of it: how blood called to me too, how easy it was to stop a heart from beating, to send a muscle into spasm. Those things, I wouldn't tell anyone if they didn't already know.

"But enough about me, what more have *you* learned?"

Niamh grinned. "You mean besides my true face?"

I arched a brow. I didn't know what the hell a true face was.

Rather than elaborate, she turned her head to the neighboring booth and grinned. "Watch this."

She studied the three older women all dressed in finery, sharing toasts, talking, laughing. The pearls around their necks, the diamonds on their fingers twinkled in the low light. Electricity crackled in the air as Niamh's fingertips drummed on the table. I tasted ozone. Her concentration deepened.

Then one of the women arched her head back, opened her mouth, and released a bloodcurdling scream.

I startled, along with everyone else in the lounge. We all craned to look as the woman screamed and screamed, as if she were being chased, as if she were being *murdered*.

"What—"

When I whirled around, I found Niamh still grinning but watching me. My reaction.

The woman's friends reached for her, and she bounded out of her seat, away from their table. Her hands flailed around, fighting off some invisible specter. She clawed at the air and herself. Tufts of her own straight blond hair fell from her grip as people wrestled to calm her. In the struggle, the string of pearls broke and skittered across the floor like raindrops. Then her screams devolved to low, full-body sobs, her shoulders shaking as she sank to her knees, as security came close, shouting orders to each other.

The rest of us in the lounge just stared, and some whispered. And while we all gaped in horror, Niamh didn't stop smiling.

"Is that what you..." I started to say, crossed between a grimace and confusion. I wasn't entirely sure I understood what I saw. *Is that what your favor can do?*

As quickly as it started, the woman's screaming and crying faded to nothing. Her companions huddled around her with concern, cupping her face and smoothing her hair, but now she only shook her head at security, looking just as confounded as I was. As if she didn't know *why* she screamed so suddenly, but couldn't bring herself to stop in the moment.

"I make people feel things," said Niamh calmly, breaking my concentration. She was frank again, no more grin on her face, but the traces of it were cold enough to chill me to my core. A look unaffected by how she'd made a woman sob just by looking at her. Like that was a totally normal way of the world.

I swallowed and kept my voice steady. "What...did you make her feel?"

The moment the question left my lips, however, I wasn't sure I wanted the answer. Something about it felt wrong and still raw, and in the back of my mind, I couldn't help but remember when I'd looked at a girl and snapped her shin in half. That once I'd nearly stopped Andor's heart.

I didn't want to look at Niamh and see another problem—not when I already had plenty.

"Fear." Niamh shrugged. "But I can pick anything—thirst, joy, despair, excitement. I asked to make people feel how *I* was made to feel. Some people need to be punished."

I couldn't fault her. The world made people like us inevitable. Who was I, or Andor or Keturah, to judge her? How was I any better? Didn't I punish people too? Coralie? Andor?

So I only nodded in understanding and forced the woman's tears and my discomfort down with more prosecco, savoring the bitterness as I capitulated, "Acheron is good at giving exactly what we ask for. I said I was sick of being ignored."

"I think it likes being enigmatic. Like, every one of our relationships with Acheron is unique so we can't compare notes." Niamh tousled her hair and leaned forward conspiratorially in her seat. The hair color was such an odd choice, so bright that it was harsh again, but something about it and her features seemed so much more serpentine the longer I was exposed to it. "Some people don't know what it's like to be chosen by Acheron, but even some of Acheron's chosen don't really even want to *be* chosen."

Right then, despite what she just did, I could have seized her shoulders and shaken her in agreement. This was the thing that Keturah and Andor didn't get—they didn't *want* to be tied to Acheron. They didn't seek that connection to something greater, to something that *made* you greater, no matter what they got out of it, and they doubted us for it. They didn't think us strong enough to handle it. I'd always gotten the feeling that Andor resented Acheron for all that it offered, that it knew what he wanted, but Niamh and I didn't. We'd invited Acheron in, sought out its company.

The fluttering in my chest slowed to a rest, relief flooding me at how clearly Niamh got it. At how I didn't have to justify or explain myself. Somebody that just understood the truth for people like us.

And the wicked dark in me mirrored that relief. The simmering that was normally an undercurrent in my veins at all times had extinguished entirely. It said there was no threat here. That Niamh wasn't dangerous or a problem at all. That now I was finally among my own kind.

I sank back into my seat, feeling the bubbles go right to my head. "They don't get that in this world, only the people with power get to be happy. We went and got the most."

Niamh's grin returned. "And are you?"

"What?"

"Are you happy?"

*No.* Right now, I was miserable, drowning, and haunted. Everything was ruined, all I fought for either lost or slipping away. Like the harder I tried, the further I sank beneath the surface. But wasn't this what I signed up for? Didn't I do this to myself?

I swallowed and reached for the bottle. "I'm still learning what that looks like now. It's not exactly easy being a vessel."

Niamh cocked her head.

*Shit.*

The interest was plain on her face. If I changed the topic now, she'd drag it right back. But there was no way I'd tell her about Palais Garnier, about Coralie and Lethe and dying. I didn't want to explain having to learn how to reinhabit a body I'd vacated, watching her salivate as she took notes to replicate later. Even if Acheron didn't mistrust her.

"Not that Acheron ever explains what that means," I admitted before downing another glass of prosecco in one go. And noticed how her first glass was still conveniently untouched while I'd blown through—how many? Three? Four? "Just that I'm special."

There was new intensity to how Niamh looked up from whatever text she was firing off to regard me, as if I'd somehow become a specimen, as if there was *more* to expose beneath all the muscle and fat, and she was going to explore it all. I pictured her cracking my ribs to get to Acheron underneath. The sharpened edges of her long, coffin-shaped nails seemed to glimmer, ready to cut me open and dig through my insides.

She raised her glass to me in toast, though it almost felt like she was toasting to something *past* me, to something I couldn't see. And finally she took her first, very small sip.

"Anyway, that's what I wanted to talk to you about—we think you should come stay with us. People who think like us. The chosen. Fuck Elysium; we'll make our own paradise."

I frowned into my drink—my fifth? I should've kept count—having suddenly lost my taste for revelry and unclear exactly why. Unclear if this direction I was running in was any better either. If it made me any more alive. "I'll think about it."

# CHAPTER 9

As it turned out, despite Vanessa's cavalier attitude, Maison Lumina didn't *hold* auditions. The only way to snag a place was to snag its founder's eye, but after my talk with Niamh last night, one more try at this seemed like a good idea.

Anything was better than sitting with the hangover beating against the inside of my skull, thinking about the hurt in Andor's eyes, that Coralie was right, the absence of news on a nameless girl in silver, or even contemplating Niamh's invitation. *We'll make our own paradise*—whatever the hell that meant.

Gabriel Trémaux was one of the Paris Ballet's most famous former dancers. He was popular the same way Rose-Marie was popular, only where Rose-Marie rode out the glory of her career as an étoile until a very appropriately timed and tasteful retirement, Gabriel quit. It was news even when I was a first-year at the academy—Gabriel named étoile one month, and then resigning the next. After a year of touring with other ballets, of posing beside models and rock stars, a body covered in salacious tattoos and a rumored temper problem, he returned to Paris to form his own dance company. One that held "a spotlight on the future instead of the past," he'd said in the press release.

The company rented space at what looked like an old storefront near les Champs-Élysée, the avenue full of bright, luxury brands, bustling with people. Tourists eyed me warily as I followed Vanessa through the crowd, both of us in our dance gear, sweatpants over tights, leotards under hoodies. Something in my expression told these outsiders, desperate for spectacle, to get out of the way, and they all readily obliged.

Even standing in the lobby, none of it felt real. Maison Lumina was something we joked about at the academy, because we looked down on Gabriel as much as we envied him. The critics called him the best of his generation, one of the best of all time, one of a kind, just like Rose-Marie Baumé and Joséphine Moreau. He was so great that he alone could survive walking away from the Opéra. And Maison Lumina never put on a bad show. I'd seen the videos, they all were good. By all means, it wasn't a bad company to be at; I'd be lucky if I convinced Gabriel to give me a chance.

It was just . . . not what I planned. Palais Garnier was always supposed to be my future.

The lobby was hip and unexpected with a free-to-use espresso machine and a wall of snacks: protein bars and fruits and a refrigerator full of yogurts and smoothies. Low indie music playing on speakers throughout, cozy chairs with massage attachments and pillows, foam rollers propped in a corner. It was like a start-up, but for dancers.

In a row of mirrors, I caught Vanessa smirking at me while my mouth hung open. "So, how exactly do I just get his attention again?"

She gestured to the back stairwell, and we climbed to the main studio. "Just talk to him. Tell him that you're interested in joining."

"But there's no audition process."

"Not a formal one. It's what I did, and it took some begging from my brother-in-law, the prince, but it worked."

At Theatre Illusorio, I'd been too stunned and confused to even think of compelling anyone. My feet were carrying me outside before it occurred to me that I could have just demanded a place, and by then I was too embarrassed to return. Maison Lumina could very well end the same way.

"Lucky me," I muttered.

We stepped into the spacious room, where massive windows flooded the studio with light. Dancers scattered all around, chatting or sprawling on the floor in groups with food in hand. I tried not to stare, the mix of classic ballerina leotards and just tee shirts and shorts again, some buns neat and others messy, braids and afros dyed vibrant colors. There were more tattoos and dark-skinned dancers than I'd ever seen at the ballet, and a range of body types the academy used to sneer at.

Curious glances turned my way nonetheless, and I raised my chin in challenge. Just in case. It may not have *looked* like the Paris Ballet Company or its academy, but I didn't see why they'd act any differently. A new person was yet another thing between you and the role you wanted, always.

"Don't look so mean," Vanessa said before breaking out in high laughs. "We don't bite."

And a tall person with umber skin and a buzzed head dyed peach pink quipped in passing, "I do."

For a moment, I wondered if they were an acolyte. Another one of Acheron's hidden in plain sight. But the eldritchness in my veins made no acknowledgment, and their presence didn't press against my lungs like Niamh's.

Vanessa dropped her bag near the windows and scanned the room. "So, Gabriel is over there, and I told him you were coming. Just go, introduce yourself, tell him what I told him—you're looking for a new company because your old one literally collapsed. Say you're staying for the lesson."

I nodded and followed her line of sight.

Gabriel Trémaux looked different in person. In videos and photos, he seemed taller, shoulders wider, muscles bigger and more defined. Like Achilles or some great, marble-carved hero instead of just a man who grew up dancing ballet. Now, standing by the mirrors and drinking water, he seemed both more and less mortal: He had the complexion of a fair-skinned person who never stayed out of the sun, the leathery, crispy orange look of a surfer. The circles beneath his eyes were dark, cheeks bony. There was the remains of stubble shaved low. His dark hair was beginning to have lines of silver. And though certainly he was muscular, he wasn't seven feet tall.

His scowl, however, gave me pause.

"He seems angry," I remarked back to Vanessa, who was nonchalantly eating a candy bar and texting. "Maybe I—"

She shook her head without bothering to look up. "No, that's just his face. Like yours! Go ahead."

I took a step and then pivoted back. "Hey, why are you helping me, by the way? With this. Here." We were once each other's competition, rooting for the other's downfall. What if this was a prank to kick me while I was down?

Vanessa raised her gaze to me and shrugged. "It's exhausting being hated all the time. I figure it doesn't have to be like that everywhere. Now, hurry!"

And with that, I slid the bag from my own shoulder and crossed the room. My movements caught his eye in an instant, and in the mirrors, I saw other glances follow me toward him. Like they all knew I was here to beg for a job. The skin of my mark writhed in revolt from the scrutiny, Acheron's reflection flickering behind me.

It wasn't just an audition anymore. Keturah's smile as she watched me get ready, that irritation in Andor's face, the aimlessness that followed me through the days and nights—I needed this so that I'd recognize myself again. So that I'd find one thing that differentiated me from the cold severity and detachment of Niamh.

"Vanessa's friend?" Gabriel asked as I neared.

His voice was grittier than I expected, like grains of sand were scratching against his vocal cords. Up close, I could see the little scars from the street fights and bar brawls that were always in the tabloids.

I nodded quickly and pinched the wriggling skin of my mark through my sleeve. "Laure, yes. I was at Opéra Garnier."

I left it up to him to wonder if I was in the collapse or not and wouldn't mention that technically I'd quit only minutes before.

His face showed no expression, acknowledging neither my name nor my past. "Well, I'm sorry Vanessa brought you all the way here. We're not looking for more dancers right now."

"W-what?" My heart skipped a beat. I might have reared back, my ears ringing as if I'd been struck.

Gabriel shrugged and gave his best attempt at a sorry smile. It only appeared like baring teeth, with no emotion behind it. "The roster's full. We don't have room for another. You might as well take your stuff and head on home."

Static crackled through the air like a whip. A flame came alive in my veins as I balled my fists at my side, as Acheron's buzzing became my own. Of all the things I expected, it wasn't this, being told to go home before I even started.

I shook my head. My voice came out a rasp as I said, "**I'm sure you can make room.**"

I needed this. He didn't understand that I needed it to save myself, to be able to *stomach* myself, and he and his stupid roster were getting in the way.

"Fine." Gabriel softened. His brow smoothed and then furrowed as he looked at me and then the high collar of my leotard, giving one slow nod. "You stay until the end of class. Then I'll see if I can make room."

My lashes fluttered. It was so hard to hear him over the blood rushing in my ears, Acheron wide awake and ready to do more damage if he resisted. It didn't matter that it thought dance so silly—the old god was a weapon in my hand, and sometimes I had to pry my grip away one finger at a time. It would make sure I could not be denied.

"Yes, okay," I whispered, more desperately than I had any right to sound.

"You do everything they do right now. Deal?" He took a step toward me and gestured to the crowd, and I noticed a scar, light, jagged, and old on his left hand. Where he was missing a pinkie finger. Acheron sneered from inside me at his proximity. "Don't waste my time. I hate it when people waste my time."

He was still scowling as I scurried away. And by the window, Vanessa applauded my apparent success before we got started.

For all his disagreements with the Paris Ballet Company, Gabriel stuck to the classic warm-up, and I was mostly grateful for it. When he clapped his hands, people grouped together to carry the long barres across the floor, and in a flash, all twenty-five of us were in position and rolling our necks. However, he preferred the same electronic tunes from the lobby instead of a live pianist.

He led the routine with the efficiency of someone who studied under Madame Demaret; I recognized some of the combinations, the way he spent a long time with sweeping legs and pushing the thighs past burning. The lightning-fast commands I always struggled to keep up with.

"Pas de changé, two, three, four, plié, tourne, plié, tourne..." Gabriel chanted over the music. He paced the room, adjusting the posture of one person, raising the chin of another, praising a third in low, gravelly whispers.

It was everything I'd grown up doing, but every motion made it abundantly clear how out of shape I'd become. Months of inactivity had transformed me into a weak thing, eating away at my stamina and flexibility in a way the paltry Theatre Illusorio audition didn't show.

Things I could do in my sleep two months ago left me winded and embarrassed, so trapped in my own head that when Gabriel stopped in front of me and uttered something, I didn't even hear him at first.

"Huh?"

He grimaced at my form. "Was Madame Demaret still teaching when you were there?"

On the tips of my toes, I turned on the barre and sank into a grand plié. My thighs screamed bloody murder. "Oh, yes. She was."

Gabriel wrinkled his nose, eyes darting to Vanessa. "I hated her. Guess I'll have to undo all the damage she taught you too." And then he kept walking, raised his hands, and clapped loudly again. "Water break."

After only five minutes to quench our thirst, we were back at it. Maison Lumina touted itself as a premier *modern* dance company, and so the choreography Gabriel taught was closer to contemporary and free-form than the classical ballet that I was used to.

"Remember to slide into your breaths and flex your foot, Brandt," Gabriel said as he counted through the motions again and again.

Only, none of it lined up with the counts. It was like everyone danced on some separate meter I couldn't sense. All around me, they flapped their arms like birds, then rolled on the floor with feline grace, but I was again at a disadvantage. I didn't feel the music the way they did—I didn't feel *anything*, really—and I certainly didn't know how to somersault. And though my arch was finer than some others in the room, I wasn't the *only* ballerina.

When I ran forward and tried to tumble over my head, a loud *thud* echoed across the room, rippled through the floor, as my spine uncurled and my head cracked against the wood.

Exactly, it seemed, when Gabriel was looking my way. As if he could sense my mortification and wanted to dig the knife deeper. As if to say, *This, girl, is exactly why I left that place.*

Finally he shouted to the room with too bright a grin, "Now let's move to groups."

I shut my eyes and inched away.

"Laurence!" My heart fumbled, and when I looked at him, he was pointing to the first group. Where everyone would be watching the new girl. "With them."

There was no way I'd get this job.

Still, I took my place, shoulders slumping and head throbbing as I waited for the electronic swell to summon us forward. We charged and swung our arms up in what he called a "deconstructed grand jeté." I crawled when I was supposed to crawl, rolling sloppily over myself and flinging legs over my head when he told us to. I tilted my head and flapped my crooked, rigid wings, pointed my toes, and leapt as if my life depended on it.

All the while, I felt nothing.

Once, dancing made me feel like a bird of prey, graceful in the air, and now I was clearly wounded and struggling to stay aloft.

With every turn, every unnatural twist to my torso, every stilted breath, I felt myself sinking further and further out of reach. Again. Expected to feel music while I was as cold and stiff as stone. I stopped seeing dancers, stopped seeing Gabriel frowning at me in the mirror, and there remained only the pitiful girl of my reflection staring back, glaring, while that demon of a shadow put a comforting free-form hand on her shoulder.

And I hated her, how weak and scared she wanted me to be.

*This is your fault,* I told her, because I had to make the monster strong to survive. Because one day, there wouldn't be anything left of *me* to be found, and Andor and Keturah—they'd finally realize how carved away and hollow I'd made myself and know there was nothing dense enough to fill it.

**Even if you have to fight to hold on to** *them*, the storm of static rippled at my side and from within my bones, **you will never have to fight to keep me.**

I swallowed and pushed on with the routine.

Vanessa was gone as soon as class ended, squeezing my shoulder and muttering an excuse about meeting someone for lunch. It didn't matter if it was real or not, I kept my head hanging low and listened to the room empty. None of the other dancers bothered to look at me. I wasn't a threat anymore. I wasn't *Laure* anymore.

Footsteps shuffled to approach me as Gabriel crossed the floor. I could tell it was him by the bare, mangled, veiny dancer's feet before me. The warp of ballet on his bones. The way Acheron hissed protectively in his direction. He sighed, giving me time to brace myself for the blow sure to send me spiraling. "Look…"

The mark on my forearm screamed for me to do something I had no energy to do. To fight back when I was already so sick of fighting.

"I can't promise that I will be able to feature you in our next show, but I suppose I can make room in the tour."

I raised my gaze from Gabriel's gnarled toes and looked at him, at the steel of his face as he stared back.

"Do you have time to come to my office?" He turned and began descending the stairs, never once glancing back to see if I was following. Of course I was. "I need your information to draw up a contract."

I was right on his heels, trying not to trip over myself. "Wait. Does that mean—"

Gabriel waved a hand. "Yes, yes, you're in. I said I'll make room, weren't you listening?"

"Yes—"

"But if you want to be full time, I need you to loosen up."

I nodded. "Of course—"

"And *clean up your act*," he scolded, his voice echoing in the stairwell as he rounded on me and made me draw up short. His nostrils flared. "You smell like the floor of a bar."

My face went numb from disbelief. I didn't even register the insult. All my aches went silent as I followed Gabriel Trémaux to his office, nodding, mouth agape with my head so far below the water, fighting back the sting in my eyes.

# CHAPTER 10

I *got in.*

I didn't mind that Saint-Michel Notre-Dame metro station was teeming with people when I arrived to head home. The white tile walls hummed from the voices, the click of ticket machines, the rumble of footsteps, the whirs of escalators, gates, and subways. Parisians streamed past me in a hurry, shoulders and bags bumping into mine, while I carried on in a trance.

Because somehow I did it.

Standing in the center of this loud, crowded hall, the shock slowly wearing off, it was déjà vu. I was back in Opéra Garnier and clutching the phone in my hand, waiting for someone to reach out and shake me awake. Any minute now, I'd stir to find myself back on Acheron's shores, or still in my bed in the 19th—anywhere but this station, this reality where Coralie was *wrong.*

*Who would you be without me?*

*You shouldn't have come back.*

If I could be reborn from nothing and do this, maybe I didn't come back wrong.

In the faint reflection of the glass doors between the subway platform and the tracks, Acheron stroked my hair with its shapeless hand, and as if in response to the phantom touch, my scalp itched.

The vibrating phone in my hand dragged me back to my body. To Saint-Michel station, to a train heading toward Bagneux leaving without me. To all the people brushing past me, unaware that I was being revived in real time.

I had to tell the others—

Thickly, I looked down.

JULIEN.

My father always called as if he was able to sense my excitement and wanted to dampen it. It was like some radar that parents were attuned to, where every elevated heart rate, every caught breath and hopeful smile was a moment to insert themselves. I didn't care what he wanted, but today, since I was winning, I decided to be cordial.

"*Yes*, Papa?" I was too wired to temper the forcefulness in my tone.

There was a beat of silence on his end, perhaps because the name still shocked him. And no matter how many times the word slipped from my own mouth, it didn't feel natural to me either. My father was burned into my life as *Julien Mesny*, regardless of how we tried to convince ourselves otherwise.

"Hello, Laurence," said the voice on the other line.

I froze in the middle of the hall. My pulse was picking up, stumbling over itself because that wasn't my father's voice. It had none of his tired baritone, none of his weathered resignation. No, this voice was feminine, clever, and no less familiar. The kind of voice that tapped right into my programming and sent chills down the nape of my neck.

*My little ballerina, would you like a macaron?*

Acheron stirred awake, scuttling under my skin to listen closely. It was paying attention, intrigued by who it heard. By the memories it felt resurfacing.

The mother in my dreams was beautiful, with a radiant, white smile and soft, brown skin the color of acorns in autumn. She smelled like lavender and would smooth her hands over the neat curls of her little twin who nodded eagerly before a display of sweets.

"How nice of you to finally answer," said the voice on the phone. "Your father and I were getting worried."

Though she'd been gone for years, though the only contact we had was the soulless greeting cards that orbited my birthday, I still recognized the smile in her voice. I'd memorized everything I could about her. I'd become a *ballerina* for that smile.

It had been their little routine—getting dressed for ballet class and picking out confections from the colorful rows at the pâtisserie. Then they'd sit in the Jardin des Tuileries, eat them, and smile before walking to the studio, hand in hand.

There was no one in the world who could come between them, this woman and her eager shadow.

Woodenly, I pulled the phone from my ear and stared at the screen as if her face might materialize. But she was calling from *Julien's* number. Why was she calling me from Julien's number?

"I . . ."

What could I say? Everything I ever imagined saying to her late into the night when I couldn't sleep, every unanswered voice mail that I'd left, begging her to come home, it all dried up.

*What color do you want today?* the woman would always ask.

*Pink!* the girl would always shout, her voice high, while she stood on the tips of her toes to peer over the counter.

The little girl would always pick strawberry, while the woman ordered rose. They'd laugh the same laugh and smile the same smile, all the way to the park, all the way to the fountain. This routine they'd shared was sacred.

In Saint-Michel station, I swiveled on my feet in search of the exit and collided with someone. "But it says . . ." Another person, and another. With mumbled apologies, I fought my way through the line of busy people trying to catch the next train while I was trying to catch my breath, the coherent sentence still frozen in my throat. "How are you…"

My mother, to her credit, waited patiently for my stuttering to stop. "I came as soon as I could. As soon as I heard and was able to get away. I'm with your father right now, catching up on everything."

She came here.

For me.

After twelve years of begging, she was finally here.

"I-in Paris?" I asked slowly, because surely I had it all wrong.

"In Paris," Alexandra Freeman, my *mother*, repeated, still with that smile in her voice. Like she was a diplomat or royalty, unfazed by even the cracking up of her only offspring.

Which I could only assume, since I knew nothing about her now. I didn't know this woman who could drop her little girl off at ballet class and never come back. Maybe there were others in her many years away. Yet she was back, all because of the collapse. All because there was a moment when everyone thought I was dead. Her included. This was all my fault.

"Listen, your father told me you were okay. He was genial about me coming back. We've…made our peace." She paused, considering her next words. "And I'd like to see you while I'm here."

*No.*

While she chewed, the little girl would stare up at the woman with such veneration in her eyes, such adoration, that even years later, it nearly killed her to remember how it felt.

I couldn't. I wouldn't.

Only I didn't *say* any of that. I couldn't get my mouth to cooperate. My tongue and throat couldn't form words, not when I was panting and running full speed up the escalator. Not when my vision was tunneling. Acheron watched on curiously.

"Lunch?" prodded my mother in my silence. "Next Saturday?"

*No! Say no!*

Deep down, I was screaming, but it was coming from the girl who had gotten swallowed in the collapse. None of this was real. Not Gabriel's offer, this phone call, what she was saying. I could come back to life, but my world couldn't be remade into this. It just *couldn't*.

Because it had been the purest of worship, yet the woman still left without saying goodbye. Without looking back, without wavering *once*. So the little girl then vowed to become a god so glorious, her light was inescapable. And she'd worshipped herself instead.

Alexandra laughed. I hated that I'd missed her laugh. "I consider that a yes. See you at noon. I'll send you the address."

Finally I broke the surface, back into the fresh, cold air on the street. My lungs burned as if I'd been trapped, not underwater, but once again choked by ice. It took me time to thaw, to stop shaking and regain control of my body and finally manage to work my jaw into saying something.

"No. I don't want to see you."

But it was too late. The phone had already clicked on her end, leaving me to say it in the emptiness she'd left. Again.

The lights of the cottage were still on when I finally arrived in Elysium, body racked with exhaustion. It had been a long time since I'd danced so much, and I was out of shape, and though Maison Lumina's offer managed to numb the aches for a bit, the call that followed took the remaining wind from my sails.

I felt half dead and sure I looked it as I hauled myself over the threshold, eager to dissolve in a hot bath. Thanks to years of ballet, the pain and its remedy were all familiar, and that left me equal parts relieved and melancholic. That I still recognized the tenderness proved that the Laure I once was, the one everyone preferred, was not so far below the surface as to be out of reach. That I only felt this because I'd lost myself for so long made the hurt worse.

"Niamh?" Keturah's voice carried from the living room. "Is that you?"

I shut the front door and pulled off my shoes. "Not this time."

Her footsteps drew nearer until Keturah filled the archway, the scent of cocoa butter drifting through the hall. She leaned against the frame with a smile on her face, lips painted bright red and fluorescent hair burnished by the low light behind her. An angel with her halo. She eyed my clothes, hair, the droop of my shoulders with her astute brown eyes, but didn't bother hiding her surprise. "Not going out tonight?"

"Not really in a party mood." Drained, I sank onto the creaky wooden stairs of the cottage and shook my head.

"I get that."

There was a disarming way she carried herself, even after all that happened, as if the whole world had little effect on who she was. As if she were made of steel, yet never turned hard or cold. It made me wonder how much anger Acheron had taken from her. How much it could take from me if I asked.

Keturah drummed her fingers on the stair railing, dislodging chips of white paint. "Well, want to clean with me?"

Her chipper voice compelled me to arch a brow. "Clean?"

"Nothing puts me in a better mood than tidying a place up. Everything in its rightful place, a problem I can fix, with an easy solution. We don't get many of those, do we?"

And despite my exhaustion, despite hearing the obvious takeaway, despite wanting to just hide until I felt strong enough to face the world, I got up and followed her into the living room. She was impossible to resist; it was hard to refuse her anything. She made me *want* to be around people, if the people were her.

The cottage wasn't a complete mess—no spills or stains that needed scrubbing, excluding the ash-coated fireplace. Instead, there were small blankets thrown in a heap, used mugs mostly empty and gone cold, pillows and papers and books and discarded sweaters in disarray. I recognized some of the things as Niamh's, from the blue sweater too small for any of us to the careworn bag on the floor: Chapstick, an old, disintegrating pack of tissues, a rusted pocketknife. Things she forgot to take with her, moving into her new life in Nanterre.

I began fluffing up pillows on the nearest divan. "Why are you in a bad mood?"

Keturah flapped out Niamh's sweater and folded it. With her back to the lamplight, the dark circles under her eyes seemed more pronounced. "Well, I haven't been sleeping well, not that there's anyone to blame for that. And I have a lot on my mind—Niamh, Andor, you. I even find myself thinking of my brother lately."

"Your brother who died?"

"Yeah, his name was Joey."

Keturah didn't speak about her family much—none of us did. For some reason or another, Acheron liked its outcasts. All I knew was that she had several siblings of whom she was the oldest, and when Joey died suddenly, she left and never went back. I rarely answered calls from my parents, and Andor... His situation with Ciro's parents seemed the least complicated.

"Maybe one day, I'll tell you about him," she continued with a sigh before wrapping an arm around my shoulder and drawing me into her barbed wire–necklaced collarbone. "Want to tell me what's got you down? I take it the audition didn't go so well?"

The tension in my muscles faded some as I pulled away to stack old coffee mugs into each other. "No, I got in, actually."

Keturah gasped. "Really? We should celebrate! Why aren't we celebrating?"

*Because I don't know how.*

I didn't know how to smile and dance and actually mean it. I didn't even know if this was something I was supposed to be doing, or if Maison Lumina would be another mistake in the long list of bad decisions I made. Though I got in, I was still taking on water. And it was hard to celebrate anything after a phone call that left my world in shambles.

My hands stopped stacking.

With a shrug, I said, "I don't think I know how to start over."

Then I was off, cradling two stacks of dirty mugs to my chest and weaving around the coffee table made of books to the kitchen. Folded over the sink and working them in suds, I didn't have to look up as she trailed me.

"Well, there isn't exactly a blueprint, you know?" said Keturah softly, leaning against the counter. "You just do it, and maybe it works out or maybe it doesn't."

"You changed cities. You worked with a touring band and at tattoo shops and bars. I only know how to do ballet—"

"For now."

I couldn't help but glare at her, her grin, the way she so delicately swept suds onto the tip of her finger and spotted my nose. That she was beautiful and sweet and soft was unfair. That I had to chew my lip to avoid thinking about doing something careless was *also* unfair.

Keturah sauntered her way out of the kitchen. "It's all right to feel aimless and afraid. The world's a big and scary place."

And then she was gone.

A pale white face moved in front of the window over the sink, just enough to catch my eye. When I raised my head to see it, I flinched away, splashing dishwater down my front.

"Coralie."

She stood there, staring at me as I stared at her.

"She's not real," I mumbled to myself. "She's in my head, which means she can't hurt me. I can ignore her."

And maybe I would have told her that she was wrong about me, that I could dance without her, that I could be someone without her—but then she raised a slender fist and knocked. The window rattled. *Tap, tap, tap.*

I took another step back.

If she were a ghost, or a figment of my imagination, she wouldn't have been able to make that noise. A ghost shouldn't have been able to swing the window wide open as she did next.

Coralie grinned with such malice, such unadulterated, wicked joy at my shock, that it angered me as much as it disturbed me. After all of this, how was she still here? How was she *touching* things? Where did she get the right, when she'd *died* and I won?

"Cool, huh?" said Coralie pointedly, arching a blond brow. Her gaze flicked briefly to the ceiling, her eyes drawn to the stain in the pale wood, from where I'd vomited in the room above when I came back from the dead.

I shook my head and reeled back, out of the kitchen, away to fetch Keturah.

"You're running out of time," Coralie announced at my back. "It's coming—the beginning of the end. You know all about that, right?"

In the living room, Keturah stood by the fire, head bowed, frowning at something in her hand. She was slow to stir at the sound of my approach, turning ever so slightly that I saw what she held—a French passport. Niamh's old bag hung from her wrist.

"Need something?" she asked distractedly, tossing the passport inside.

"There's—there's something I need you to come see."

And then we were rushing through the doorway and into a kitchen that sat empty. The window was still propped wide open as Coralie had left it, proof that she was here, but the ghost girl had vanished again.

"What is it?" Keturah asked, turning in circles. Looking for something that couldn't have been real.

Acheron was shaking its head in my marrow. **She won't believe you, you know. She thinks you're childish.**

"Uh..." I pressed the heels of my palms into my eyes until I saw circles. "I must be tired. I thought I saw something."

# CHAPTER 11

"So, why exactly are you moving there again?" Niamh's voice crackled over my wireless earbuds as I hobbled my bags to the door.

The building was pretty, faded art deco apartments with geometric lines to give its face dimension and small wrought iron balconies that only fit tangles of ivy. Before me was a rose-red door with a keypad, sandwiched between a chocolatier and a bag shop in an alley in the 14th arrondissement. It looked old, classic, the concrete dirty in the recesses. The storefronts were cluttered, suitcases spilling onto the narrow sidewalk. But importantly, it was close enough to the Catacombs that I could always slip back to Elysium when I needed to escape.

I inserted the code I'd received from Andor and tried not to think of who had lived here before. What happened to Ciro.

But if I closed my eyes, I could still imagine the police lights in the dark, Andor folding into himself on the curb, Keturah's face slick with tears. The trees in Square de l'Aspirant Dunand had looked like reapers.

"It's a lot of rehearsals, and they run pretty late," I answered, forcing myself through the door and turning into the first stairwell. "It's easier to come crash here than going all the way to Elysium every night. Or taking the RER all the way out to wherever you are."

"Le Vésinet," she corrected, and I rolled my eyes.

Like hell she was living there.

The apartment building had worn wooden stairs that creaked as I climbed and no elevator to bring me to the top floor. The middle of the day left most of the units empty so that the only sounds to carry were my footsteps and labored breaths.

And yammering heart. Whether that was Acheron's excitement or my apprehension, I couldn't tell.

"Yeah, but why are you *dancing* again? Like, why bother, when you have Acheron?"

"What?"

She snorted. "If people could use Acheron the way we do, they'd never work another day in their lives. Like you said, we don't even need money."

Discomfort prickled at the back of my neck, and I scratched it away before shouldering on. "Nobody dances because it's good money. I dance because I like it. It's what I do best."

**Among other things**, supplied Acheron helpfully.

I didn't want to know what other things it'd meant.

"Then why'd you stop?"

*Because it was killing me.* Even though I'd quit, I was still there when the walls fell down around me. It was hard to give up something so personal, something that most people couldn't walk away from unscathed. Not unless you were Gabriel Trémaux. It had left me, not the other way around.

At the landing, I rooted through my coat pocket in search of the key. Andor had made copies for me and Keturah long ago in case we ever wanted to use the place, and after so long in Elysium, I wasn't used to the idea of carrying around a key anymore. It felt real and adult in a way I wasn't ready to be.

Part of me expected the door to be unlatched again.

"I left because I had to," I responded as I stepped inside. The bags slid from my grip to the floor with a soft thud. "And besides, if you don't need money, how exactly are you and your friends paying for a place in *Le Vésinet*?"

Something shuffled on the other end of the line. Niamh replied in singsong, "You'll just have to come and see for yourself. I'll send you the address."

I flicked on the light and looked around. "Anyway, thanks for helping me pack. Can't wait to go put it all away by myself."

Ciro's beautiful apartment was exactly as I'd remembered it. The walls were covered in a dark green wallpaper and black-and-white portraits of graceful celebrities. There were works of Andor's too, painted natures mortes and drawings all framed by a dedicated fan. The dining table was all glass, but the chairs and couches were soft white fabric and decorated with white throw blankets and pillows. The ruined white rug had already been removed.

Ciro's body had been taken away, but it was still his books stacked on end tables, his taste in design, his girlfriend's painted profile among the wall of stars. Photos of him and Andor and his parents sat on the shelves. Would I find his wardrobe of expensive, white fitted suits lining the closet too?

"I still can't believe you guys had the place all along and didn't live there."

I kicked off my boots. "It was Ciro's."

"Who's—oh."

We'd mentioned him a lot in passing, enough for Niamh to have a vague understanding that he was here one day and gone the next, that he and Andor were closer than close. She knew enough not to ask questions, to realize she was on the outside of this, and that was a safer place to be.

"Well, have fun with your extremely vanilla life! You know who doesn't have to do all that shit? *Me*," she chimed before hanging up.

Then it was just me in the quiet, doing the work of settling in: unpacking my stuff, compiling lists of things to buy, things to get rid of. First I scrubbed down the bathroom, and then I scrubbed the kitchen, and when my curly hair began sticking to the back of my neck, I moved on to rearranging furniture.

**This is good for us**, Acheron crooned, while I grunted over a heavy sofa. **A place of our own. Free from their judgment.**

I didn't have to ask who "their" referred to. I didn't want to.

It was hard to know how long I threw myself into moving, soreness permeating the column of my spine, deep in focus, when there came a knock at the front door. I was breathing heavy, wiping the sweat from my forehead and relieved at the sound. A break. A key fiddled in the lock as I hopped across the floor.

"Coming!"

It was a minefield of empty bags, piles of old cleaning products, Ciro's expensive aftershaves and shampoos, stacks of books, blankets and pillows, a new Marley mat to dance on, and a barre still to assemble. Standing mirrors had been shoved out of the way, but only barely so. But the place was coming together.

It looked like just maybe, I could pull this off.

"What took you so—" My voice cut out with the swing of the door. My burgeoning smile ceded instantly to eyes-wide panic.

Instead of Keturah, Andor stood on the landing, scratching the back of his neck nervously with one hand and holding a potted succulent in the other. He raised it for me like a peace offering, tipping the side of his mouth but keeping his distance, as if he expected me to shut the door in his face. Or throw more barbs his way.

Only, stunned, I didn't move. Or do anything. It was so odd to see him here, like this, looking his true nineteen years instead of immortal, with skin bronzed instead of bloodred, two normal, human eyes instead of four, the sclerae white rather than filled with black ink. Here, in this shape, his left eye was completely fogged over but still brimming with hope. But I was a dragon breathing fire and the reason he kept getting burned.

"W-what are you doing here?" I staggered back, clearing the doorway for him to enter.

My question was nonsense because I knew that he knew I was moving in. I'd relied on Keturah to make sure he was okay with it when she'd proposed the idea. He knew all of this, just like he knew I was avoiding him.

Yet here he stood.

For all my nerves, Andor just blinked. "Where else would I be?"

He strolled inside, breezing past me in a cloud of fresh roses and fog, leaving me to hinge my mouth shut and latch the door behind him. And I suspected that he did so knowingly, judging by his grin when he turned. He was smug, knowing how much he affected me. It made me look even more pitiful as I fiddled with the lock, trying not to watch him slide the faded wool coat from his wide shoulders or sweep his long, dark hair out of the way. He rolled up his sleeves, and it was impossible to miss the corded muscle of his arms, the four eldritch marks decorating one of them.

I felt Acheron scowling.

"So how can I help?" Andor asked as he surveyed the mess. And he said it in the most natural tone, like he'd always planned to be here, to help unpack my things, to assemble my portable barre.

I couldn't help but ask. "You're not mad at me?"

Days had passed since I drew blood at the cottage and left him as close to angry as I'd ever seen him, but this boy in front of me was anything but. It had to mean something that he was here, mean that we were *more than*.

A muscle feathered Andor's jaw as he mulled over it. He tilted his head and pursed his lips, putting on a show like he hadn't fully decided already to hate me or not. He'd always chosen his words carefully, while I swung my blade of a tongue haphazardly. He was the better, gentler, of us two, and here he knew he had the upper hand.

**It is easy to be gentle when the world doesn't demand anything else from you**, Acheron countered.

Andor leveled his dark gaze onto me. "Do I have a reason to be?"

It was a test. He was testing me, and I supposed I deserved it.

"Well, I was being kind of an asshole."

"You were," he conceded with a chuckle. There was a dimple, a single one, in his smile that said I was forgiven, and his eyes crinkled, raising the room's temperature several degrees. We were deep into February, but I considered cracking a window.

I stared at the floor. "I'm sorry."

"It's okay, Laure."

I liked how he said my name. *Lau-ruh*, two syllables, like he wanted to drag it out, savor it. Like it tasted sweet when I was anything but. I wanted to draw it from his lips.

But Andor was already moving on, sinking to his knees to work on the barre. "Keturah told me the good news. When do you start?"

"Monday."

My thorns were melting away with every word from his mouth. Maybe we were just friends. Friends who fought and stared too much and kissed once or twice. Maybe he promised to melt down Palais Garnier and build an altar for all of his friends. I could totally handle that. Just like I was handling my mother in town, the girl in silver, sucking at dance, and knowing fifteen other acolytes were roaming the damn city.

"You don't sound excited."

"No, I am," I said too hurriedly. Though there were just us two in the room, it felt small. I felt suddenly flushed and frantic. It was so easy to mess things up, even when I said all the right words. "It's just... well, my mom called right after I got the news, so it's not so exciting. She's here. In the city. She wants to meet for lunch. Her and Julien."

Only Andor knew what that meant to me. Only he knew how my mother had left me behind. Whatever we were to each other, only he knew all the words to make the scar tissue stop aching for just a second.

He looked up from the instruction booklet, and his down-turned eyes were so soft it hurt. I still wasn't used to him seeing through me, how it felt when he cut down to bone. "And will you? Go see her?"

"Of course," I chirped, busying my hands with the Marley mat and a roll of tape. "Nothing I can't handle."

And surely this all proved as much. He and Keturah thought me fragile, unstable, but I was back at a dance company, meeting my mother, being around him and his gorgeous gaze behind long lashes. I was the portrait of normal and well-adjusted. There was no reason for them to worry, to leave.

"Oh. Okay, good—"

"But will you come with me? I could use the support."

Silence blanketed the room. The question hung in the air, waiting for me to realize how it sounded. How he was looking at me, the tips of his ears turning red. How he just got here and I'd already invited him to meet my parents like we were a *thing* thing, only days after he pretty much confirmed that he knew about all the drunken kisses with strangers and then I'd ridiculed him for grieving. His brows high, his mouth parted, he was as caught off guard as I was.

I straightened. "I meant—"

"I'll come with you," Andor answered calmly, slowly, before I could make any excuses. Before I could take it back. And then he returned to working on the barre, a small smile on his face that made my skin prickle.

**It will not last,** Acheron hissed from my bones. **Not him. Not worthy of a being of your caliber.**

Rather than reply, I bit my lip until the pain sang brightly. If I asked what I wanted—like, *Is it jealous?*—I'd ruin this peace with Andor, just like I did in the woods. Balancing the two of them meant choosing my battles, and now was no time to rail against Acheron's machinations. Not where Andor was concerned.

In the quiet, we set up the rest of my little dance corner. Though I tried to focus on installing the Marley and arranging the standing mirrors, I was aware of his every motion—the sighs, stretches, the occasional hand brushing my arm to get my attention. With each question, each comment, each minute ticking by, we drifted closer and closer until, by the end, I was helping him carry a fully assembled barre sturdy enough to hold my weight in position. My shoulder bumped his as we admired our handiwork, his skin a hearth I was drawn to. We didn't hear the apartment's lock rattle before Keturah marched through.

When she dropped her things on the table, we broke apart and lurched around. She looked frazzled, eyes bulging, scanning the room and its corners for something while her hands ripped at her coat and scarf.

"Is Niamh here?" Her voice came out the softest whisper, setting me on edge.

"No..." I said, brows knitting in confusion. "What is it?"

Keturah glanced behind her, as if she expected Niamh to pop up at the mention. As if she was *afraid* of Niamh, my recruit, the youngest and slightest of us all. And I hadn't even told her about the screaming woman at the club yet.

Andor slowly lowered his phone and took a step. All the tenderness from before bled from his voice as he said sharply, "Keturah, did something happen?"

She licked her lips and nodded. "I found...So I think I found Niamh's passport the other day."

That night in the cottage living room, as Keturah and I cleaned up Niamh's belongings from the floor, Keturah had stared at the inside of the booklet for a long while. She'd looked perplexed then, but now she looked...unmoored. She couldn't stand still—freed from her outerwear, she paced and wrung her hands.

"And?" I prodded. Unlike her, my body went rigid as dread sank through me.

"And her name isn't Niamh, for one," she snapped, raking her hands through her violet hair. "It's Margaux Lozach. She's French."

Andor reeled back and scoffed in disbelief. My heart was beating in my throat, my head shaking absently. It made sense in a way—Niamh was secretive. Of course she was a liar. She was angry the way we were all angry. Life had probably been cruel to her as it had been to all of us. Maybe she just wanted to become someone new as I had.

And the way Acheron was listening now, preening, she couldn't actually be dangerous. It wouldn't have let me choose her otherwise, would it? We saw in her what it saw in me, and I always felt in control.

I shook my head more emphatically this time. "Maybe there's more to it. Something we don't know. I mean, I killed my best friend. We all did ugly things to get here—"

"I didn't," Keturah quipped.

I clamped my mouth shut.

She didn't mean it to sound so callous, I could tell, but it was true. Her deal with Acheron hadn't endangered anyone like mine did, and she wasn't poisonous like Andor either. And for all his brooding, Andor had never really hurt anyone before—he was too soft. He didn't have it in him, not the way Acheron had hoped. But if Niamh was anything like me, she could.

I'd noticed that glint in her eyes just a few nights ago.

My phone buzzed on the table, and I drifted forward to look at it, to have anything better to talk about than yet another one of my glaring mistakes.

It was a text from Niamh. The address, in fact, to her new place, to meet the others. An invitation extended to all three of us. There was a lot about that night where she used her favor on a woman I'd tried to forget, to pretend didn't happen so I wouldn't have to deal with it.

"What? Is it her?" Keturah asked, tightening her hands on the back of a chair. Bracing herself for impact. Her knuckles shone white.

I nodded stiffly. "Some nights ago, she said she'd met more of Acheron's . . . people."

They exchanged glances in silence.

"They have a place," I started. "Just outside the city. Others like us—they want to meet."

"I'm . . ." Keturah massaged her temples and turned languidly for the door. "I'm way too tired for this. We'll talk tomorrow, yeah?"

As we listened to her descend the stairs, Andor swayed on his feet, looking around for his coat, ready to follow. To get as far away as possible from me and another mess I made.

"Are you leaving too?"

My voice sounded so small in this massive apartment. I hadn't thought about what I'd do with all this space to myself, how I'd fill it. I'd never lived alone before—there was always my dad or Coralie, sound and presence to keep me grounded. Staying here alone, I would really be apart from everyone else. It'd be temporary at first, this distance, until it grew wider and wider, and we became strangers, all of us—and what if I missed something?

*It's coming—the beginning of the end.*

What if Acheron finally asked something of me, to repay all the power I took? I wasn't sure I was ready to handle it all on my own.

"Some of us need our beauty rest," mumbled Andor as he stifled a yawn. "We can't all stay up like you."

"Right, of course." I would have bristled were it not for the tired smile he gave me after.

**You know it will not last**, Acheron whispered. It was sneering again. Disappointed. **He is only a distraction.**

Andor reached for his jacket, and without thinking, I seized his wrist. The skin was feverish, and pins and needles suffused my fingers and palm immediately upon contact. Even if I let go the moment I realized, the touch still would've hummed through my hand, up my arm. He was under my skin.

**He cannot accept you**, Acheron continued, louder now. **All of you. Us.**

I squeezed my eyes shut.

I didn't want to be just friends, but I didn't have the guts to say that. Not yet. I'd faced down my best friend while Lethe raged through her veins, danced for thousands of people like my life depended on it, and bled for Acheron's favor, but this, I couldn't tell him this. I needed him to just know it and feel the same. Even if Acheron was right about this like it was right about everything else.

We agreed on many things, but I was unwilling to give up *this*.

"Unless…" Andor raised his thick brows and craned his head at me. He was scanning my face, reading my inner battle with the thing that made me. "You want me to stay?"

With the scent wafting from his frame again, roses and fog and wilderness, he was a garden begging for a promenade. A labyrinth decorated with poison flowers to get lost in. He was inviting me in, and all the while the shadows of his eyes flickered, pinning me in place, dancing over the bob of my throat as I swallowed.

Like me, he had a tiger buried deep down, and now I had its attention. How could this match be anything but divine?

Maybe Acheron was wrong about some things.

Heat flushed my cheeks. "Please."

Putting it so frankly was mortifying, too vulnerable considering the last time I'd tried, he shut me down. The fire burning through me was equal parts embarrassment and craving, but I sensed Acheron's irritation flaring too.

It wasn't happy with the choice I'd made. That I'd won.

Yet Andor dragged out his decision anyway, staring right at me, refusing to look away, forcing me to hold my breath until my vision swam, unknowing that I was sandwiched between the boy I wanted and the wicked dark I needed.

Until finally, the smug bastard broke into a grin and laced his fingers through mine. "Call me a masochist, but I'd never say no to you."

# CHAPTER 12

Ciro's newly renovated shower was heaven on earth. The strong pressure, the waterfall spout, the beautiful deep green paint framed by white hexagonal tile, the gold trim—it was a welcomed change from the wonky trickle and sticky heat of the cottage. The three angled mirrors over the sink were perfect for styling my ballerina bun ahead of my first proper day at Maison Lumina.

I didn't know if there was a uniform, if they'd be as strict as the ballet had been, but I hedged my bets since Gabriel was classically trained too. Maybe it'd earn me points.

In my reflection was a sliver of the old Laure from before the collapse: the tame hair, a strappy, high-collared leotard that hid Lethe's scar around my throat, the waistband of my sweatpants rolled up, light mascara and sheer lipstick. Only, now there was also the person-shaped storm hovering closer and closer every time I looked. At the audition, Acheron had its hand on my shoulder in reassurance. Now it seemed on the verge of subsuming me, making the edges of *my* body frizz and fray like static.

"What are you doing?" I whispered, staring into that faceless face that verged on kissing mine.

Acheron reached out as if to curl the hair at my temple in its finger. Though there wasn't true physical contact, the skin prickled anyway. **If my vessel wants to play human, so be it. We are one, even if you despise me.**

I shook my head and moved toward the door. "I don't despise you. I just wish you'd tell me things."

**All in due time.**

The apartment was still as quiet as when I'd awoken, morning light streaming through the wooden blinds, a sleepy city only beginning to stir. It wasn't what I was used to anymore, both too loud and too silent—there was no gentle hum of a flowing river, no blood lapping at the rocks, no skittering creatures in the tall grass, no birdsong from the canopy. I hadn't risen to the soundscape of Elysium like I'd done in the weeks prior; instead, I woke on the top floor of an apartment in Paris again. My apartment now, I supposed. This high up, in this part of the city, there were no sirens or angry car horns either. The rumble of motors and shuffle of opening storefronts felt so far below.

Down the hall, I caught a glimpse of Andor in the living room. He curled up in a white velvet chair by the window, a sketchpad in his lap, a paintbrush poised above it, his tangle of dark hair swept away from his face. The end tables had been rearranged to keep a glass of pink-tinted water and a tray of color pots close. And there was a wrinkle between his brows from his deep concentration that only smoothed when I spoke.

"Have you seen my white sweater?" I asked as I waded inside, scanning the cushions and floor corners for a wad of knit wool. "I don't remember unpacking it."

He inclined his head slightly, dark eyes flicking to me and then gone in an instant. I could see his exhaustion more clearly in the dawn, shadows nestled in the valleys of his face.

I'd awoken alone earlier, wrapped in a pile of blankets on a massive bed in which I'd slept soundly for hours, for the first time in . . . I didn't know how long. There was of course a bad dream somewhere in the thick of it, Coralie and the girl in silver blurring together, but no ghosts standing over me at least.

Andor was a different story.

He'd made sure to lie on the very edge so that we didn't touch. So that we were close but he and his poison remained perfectly out of reach. So that, when he stirred in the middle of the night, bolting upright with panicked breaths and shudders so strong I thought there was an earthquake, I had to crawl to him.

"Just a bad dream," he'd murmured, climbing to his feet.

And I could only stare, because for a moment, it didn't even look like he'd recognized me.

But he stayed nonetheless.

"You probably left it at the cottage."

I inched closer, sitting at the edge of the sofa, and nodded. "Are you painting?"

"I'm practicing," he answered softly, the delicate curve of his mouth twitching toward a smile. He flashed his work, a freehand sketch of the rooftops from the window. All of it was shaded in the pale pink of sunrise. "I signed up for a few classes while I wait for the next term, and I'm all out of habit."

Just like me.

Only his "out of habit" looked a hell of a lot better than mine.

Andor moved his brush along the page in small, gentle strokes. I'd only ever marveled at the aftermath of his work, the portraits of Joséphine, Ciro, Keturah, and me among the gardens and meadows and stage. But his process too was hypnotizing, his focus, the frown of contemplation as he applied a light blue across the landscape next.

"I don't think I've ever seen you work before."

"No? Well, what do you think?"

Finally he glanced up and really looked at me. If the dark circles under his eyes were more or less pronounced than any other day, I couldn't tell. His smile was too distracting—it led me *away* from concern, which I suspected was intentional.

"It's—it's . . ." Only around him did it take me so much to cobble together words, to understand what I meant to say. Around everyone else, I had to hold back my tongue, and now here I was, searching for it.

How was I supposed to think straight when he was cataloging every trace of the ballerina before him? When I saw, beneath his dark lashes, that the monster in him was responding to it? That, with his hand that reached up and grazed my cheek, he smoothed out that same curl at my temple like Acheron did, only this *really* left the skin tingling.

*I think I like you. And I want to know what haunts your dreams, so I can chase it away.*

"It's nice, Acheron. I like it. I like y—"

"'Acheron'?" His expression shuttered instantly, and he withdrew his hand. Dabbed his brush in the pot of yellow and returned to his work.

Shit.

"That was an accident—"

Frostily, he quipped, "I bet."

He didn't look up at me again. I didn't deserve to be looked at, anyway.

I rose from my seat and squeezed my eyes shut. Whatever this was—sharing this great new apartment with my not-boyfriend and the eldritch god inhabiting me—I was ruining it. It was ruined before the day even began. And now I was expected to go to Maison Lumina, all in some far-fetched attempt to convince him and Keturah that I was fine, that the Laure they knew and liked wasn't completely dead and gone. And I was doing *just great.*

"I'm gonna go," I mumbled, turning away, fearing what other horrible thing might come out of my mouth next.

Though no one knew who I was, when I entered the main studio, I still attracted curious glances from the others at the company, who folded and contorted in stretches or ate their breakfasts and chattered away.

"Welcome!" Vanessa said in singsong, in a sweet voice that probably would have granted her a career onstage if dancing hadn't panned out.

"Late night?" I sank onto the floor and nodded to her.

Her dark hair looked a little greasy and half-assed in a messy bun today, far from her usual prim and proper look at the ballet. Despite her smile, her eyes were veined with red and bleary.

She shrugged. "Not really. It's complicated."

I stretched my ankles. "Gabriel still hasn't sent me a schedule or anything. Is that normal?"

"Yes, he decides a lot of stuff last minute."

"Remember how, at the ballet, every rehearsal and every person in it was planned like a year in advance?"

She rolled her eyes. "Yeah, it was torture."

"I mean, it wasn't all bad..." I rubbed my arms.

There was value in the structure and organization of the ballet, to know that changes rarely happened. To know who you were and what was expected of you, even if you didn't like it. Very few surprises, until Acheron came along.

The studio may have touted itself as more modern than the Paris Ballet Company, but as far as I could tell, we mostly looked the same: leotards, sweatpants, tights, and vests. I watched a girl beside us peel plastic wrap from her calves—a classic trick to keep them warm. There was no one who screamed *étoile* or *premier*, however. No dancers stretching by themselves, eying their reflections with the air of superiority belonging to someone who guest-starred in other productions and traveled the world. No upturned noses, no predatory glares. The person to beat could be anyone in this place, even Vanessa. Whom I surpassed at the ballet, by the way.

"So, who's like…at the top? Who do I watch out for?" I prodded, trying to sound casual.

Vanessa knit her brows. "What do you mean?"

"I mean, who's the prima? Who gets all the solos and special attention? Who should I avoid pissing off?"

She tossed her head back and laughed. "You really need to ease up. We got out of there, remember?"

A young woman separated herself from the pack and began rallying us to the barres, and I figured I was lucky—it was harder to conceal pins, razor blades, and thumbtacks in thin slippers than in pointe shoes. Which meant I had to watch out for the knives hidden behind their warm welcomes instead.

"Morning classes are taught by the senior dancers," Vanessa explained next to me as we rolled our shoulders and necks. "The ones who've been here the longest."

The dancer in charge of warm-ups smiled a lot, went around the room complimenting everybody, and as I followed her instructions, I tried to recall if anyone ever smiled at the ballet. Guest instructors and masterclass teachers, perhaps. Definitely never Madame Demaret, Hugo Grandpré, or Yelena, his junior. Even at the academy when our lessons were assisted by older students, no one just smiled. It was off-putting. Like they were planning to rob me or something.

"Great structure!" the senior shouted at me as she passed, which earned me more glances and more smiles.

This place unnerved me.

The warm-up, though, was not entirely foreign, thankfully, nor were some of the terms. We practiced our pliés and battements, folding over the barre and warming up the thighs all the same. I wasn't entirely clear on the counting still—it was less a matter of steady beats and more reliance on lyrics and feelings. There was no underlying pulse I could find, that strange disconnect between parts of my body persisting.

It all felt awkward and unnatural to me, like a posed doll rather than a human body. Or maybe I was too far removed to human these days.

When the senior demonstrated her routine with music, my heart sank deep into my stomach. She at least was fluid in her movements: There was a primal prowess to how she crept along the floor, how she writhed and dove. The poetry of her movements made sense—so why didn't mine? Why was I so wrong?

"Then drop down, swing your legs over your head, and flip!" the senior chimed, and all around me, everyone flipped over their heads, landing on their knees with sensual ease.

Everyone except me.

I just sat up, confused. How was it possible that I looked even worse than last week?

In the studio mirrors, my figure haunted the group. They all swelled and cowed, rolled and flipped, and I stood over them the way Acheron stood over me, unmoving, rigid. I was a ghost again with a broken expression. There was no lyricism, no beats, no *feeling*.

Again no one looked at me like I was some new girl coming to take their places; they weren't concerned about me at all.

"What did you think?" Vanessa asked breathlessly when we were released for a break.

I couldn't summon a response. I was terrible, but I couldn't just go home. And before I could take my seat and sulk like I'd wanted, Gabriel noticed me. He waved an indiscriminate hand for me but didn't bother to actually say my name or look up when I approached.

My insides revolted against whatever he planned to say, every nerve awake and on edge.

"I still haven't figured out your schedule or placement, so just observe the best you can."

Which meant he wanted me to sit out. I did enough dancing in my lifetime to know that meant *Stay out of the way.* I'd joined a dance company where I sucked so much, my only task was to sit back and watch.

Eagerly, with a mask I'd mastered over the years from disappointments at the ballet—because how different could this place be, really?—I nodded and smiled and skipped back to my corner.

And deep in my marrow, when I was far enough out of sight, Acheron whispered, **Don't worry. Soon, everyone will know exactly who you are and what you can do. Soon, everyone will be very afraid.**

# PART TWO

# THE CORRUPTOR

# CHAPTER 13

The address Niamh gave me led to a castle. An actual château with a big metal gate in hues of gold and blue patina. The white-and-red marbled façade towered impressively in the distance while we waited for our Uber to be buzzed inside, and the silence that ensued after I announced my name was harrowing.

"What. The. Fuck," Keturah muttered behind me as she gaped out the window.

I shifted away. "When she said she was in Le Vésinet, I thought she was joking. I didn't think . . . Do you think it's a prank?"

As if in answer, there was a nearby beep, and the gate began its mechanical whir to open. For us. To see Niamh. Margaux. Whoever.

She was in a mansion more lavish than even Coralie's family had lived in, the kind of place that millionaires bragged about, with dozens of rooms and bathrooms and indoor swimming pools and probably a movie theatre in the basement. A fountain of cherubs greeted us on the drive inside.

Pillars of red marble framed every massive, clean window, and surrounding the mansion was a sprawling ground of lush trees that no normal person could afford. On the edge of my vision were groundskeepers, weeding around the fountain, trimming the hedges, tending to the foliage to keep it all neat and perfect. It was a loud excess that made my skin crawl, like I was back in Opéra Garnier but now I really *was* a guest.

"Maybe Niamh just lives on the property because she works for the family?" I asked, my voice pitching high and hopeful as I climbed out of the car and turned in a circle. But I wasn't convinced. Not when she'd said there were fifteen more like us. Not when she'd confirmed that she didn't need money either where she was.

The others took in our surroundings, Keturah with a tint of disdain, and Andor with wonder. This might become another painting of his when we were done because it felt like the kind of palace the president would live in, once built for a king. The kind of landscape painters loved. Even if all the plants looked manufactured.

Keturah wrapped her arms around herself and scowled. "What did she say exactly?"

"Just that there were a lot of them," I answered, jutting my chin toward a figure approaching through one of the windows. "A nightclub isn't exactly the best place for an interrogation."

"What was she doing in a nightclub? Isn't she sixteen?"

I started up the marble steps. "Same thing I was, probably."

And I didn't elaborate on that, on how I felt about my bitterness so entwined with Niamh's own darkness. They didn't need to know how I used Acheron for special treatment, or what *she* did next, making some mortal scream just because she could. I was already a monster, a sucky dancer, and always stuck in my own head; they didn't need to know the company I kept was cruel too.

Large glass doors swung open to reveal Niamh, short and waspish and thin with blond hair smoothed into a bob. Against the backdrop of this elegant home, I'd expected her to dress wealthily, in silk and jacquard robes, doused in gold jewelry and ambergris perfume. Instead, she wore ripped jeans and a white sweater that looked familiar, cable-knit and soft wool. Like the one I was looking for earlier. And she glowed with pride, soaking in our expressions at the surprise she'd just dumped into our laps.

Niamh threw her arms wide. "Welcome to Palais Rose." She clapped a hand on my shoulder and squeezed tightly, sinking her claws in. As if I hadn't *made* her. "Thanks for coming!"

I watched Niamh pull Keturah into an awkward hug, stiffness overtaking Keturah's posture as I replayed all her conspiracy theories: about Niamh being an international criminal with a stolen identity. A diamond thief. A black widow. A spy. Then she moved on to Andor, whose brows knit even as he patted her on the back.

When his eyes flicked to me, I turned away and smiled harder. "What a place, you weren't kidding."

"Let me give you a tour," she segued magnanimously, tossing me a wink as she started toward the fountain. We all looked at each other, wondering how any of this could be real, and then followed.

"Should we even be here?" I asked, scurrying ahead.

Niamh laughed, flashing sharp canines encased in silver and crusted with gems. "Why shouldn't we be?"

"How can you afford this place?" Keturah's skepticism bled through.

Niamh shrugged as she always did when faced with a question she didn't want to answer. "Isn't that what Acheron loves about us—we always find a way? You once told me that, Laure." The sudden shift of focus made me blanch, but she merely moved on to gesturing to the building's façade. "This is Palais Rose, architect unknown. It was constructed in 1899, with obvious inspiration you might recognize from the Grand Trianon. You know, the one in *Versailles*."

We started down a flight of stone steps along the side of the mansion, and when Niamh was out of earshot, Keturah whispered, "'You know, the one in *Versailles*,'" with a mock, nasally tone. Andor snickered under his breath. "I don't remember Ciro being this annoying."

"Famously lived in by Comte Robert de Montesquiou, La Marchesa Luisa Casati. Josephine Baker considered buying it before she died,"

Niamh continued obliviously, locking eyes on me again. Her brows were raised, like she was expecting some reaction, and when I gave her none, she added, almost as an aside, "Arsène Lupin even had one of his adventures here."

Though I knew she wanted me to express some kind of wonder or amazement, that she wanted my approval, it only reinforced how much someone like us *shouldn't* live here. In a historical mansion the size of a hotel. She'd probably take offense if I said so, if I ruined this little outing by exposing myself as bitter, ungrateful, and confrontational, so the best I could offer was a nod. Better not to point out that Palais Garnier had its love of gold and famous guests too, that it made monsters who then turned it to rubble.

Better not to rock the boat, considering everything that came out of my mouth was cursed.

There was a garden just beyond the stairs and a large outdoor terrace decorated with pristine white tables and chairs. Some were occupied, a pack of people in normal streetwear lounging, ankles crossed and feet propped up, blowing cigarette smoke and drinking from cans as they eyed us eyeing them. Their presence was marked by the same undercurrent in the air, the pull of gravity taking root deep in my bones, drawing me toward them, them toward me, even as I also only wanted to reel away from this place.

Something in them was of Elysium too. Niamh wasn't lying about that.

"Thirty bedrooms and an underground swimming pool inspired by ancient Greek bathhouses," enumerated Niamh. She was bragging, casting bait in the hopes we bit. Because she was planning something that involved our participation. "And don't ask me how many marble fireplaces. All that matters is it's big enough for *all* of us."

Keturah stepped closer into the huddle, slinging an arm around my shoulder to insert herself between Niamh and me. "What? All of us for what?"

But Niamh's smile didn't falter. "To live here, of course. All of us who were chosen by gods to be gods—we should stick together."

The strangers lounging at the tables were watching us closely now, their cigarettes burned to stubs and extinguished, cans emptied and crushed, but they lingered all the same. The entire castle grounds, from the weed-whacking to the birdsong, had gone quiet with anticipation as she said the next part.

"We've been waiting for you. All of you." But Niamh was looking directly at me.

Thankfully, someone approached then, breaking up this strange moment, dressed in the plain black slacks and white shirt of house-keeping. They whispered hurriedly in Niamh's ear while Keturah's scowl worsened, and Niamh nodded, her expression turning grave. It was the first look from her that didn't feel carefully constructed, *calculated*, and she promptly regathered herself, gesturing to the gang on the terrace.

"Dominique?" Niamh called, settling on one of them. "Can you take over the tour and bring them into the tearoom, please?"

He nodded rapidly at the command, like a soldier called to serve. His hair was bushy, mousy brown, and shoulder-length, and his sepia-washed skin looked paler when he stepped into direct sunlight. His face was narrow, and there was no mistaking the curves of a bodybuilding physique that lay underneath his should-be-baggy clothes. He barely stood taller than me. At his attention, a few more approached too, like our Niamh had suddenly transformed into somebody else's leader. Like she had some *authority*.

Then Niamh turned back to us, gesturing to the small horde of fol-lowers who closed in. "This is Dominique, chosen two years ago."

He gave a curt wave.

"Salomé, chosen *six* years ago, and still has five more to go."

A woman with the palest ivory skin I'd ever seen and long, dark pin-straight hair nodded. Though she was the shortest of the group, the others gave her wide berth, as if she was poisonous like Andor. Or just someone to fear. There was a classic beauty to her colorless features, her small nose, shiny eyes, and bright red lipstick that reminded me of how nature often tried to lure prey into a trap. Like a snake with the most beautiful markings.

She didn't wave or even smile. Her expression remained severe, discerning.

I'd missed some names, some faces, staring at her, but then Niamh placed a hand on the shoulder of a young boy. So young, he couldn't have been more than fourteen, with ruddy skin and overgrown copper hair. Too young to be here, with us. He flashed unusually pointy teeth, as if they'd been filed down.

"And this is Florian, the youngest. Acheron found him two months ago."

I gulped but didn't look away, even as we mumbled our greetings. The hair on my arms, on the back of my neck, stood on end, and I could tell the others felt it too. Andor's spine was rod straight, stiffening progressively as we strayed farther and farther from the car, deeper and deeper into what was starting to resemble Niamh's web. Keturah couldn't seem to unfurrow her brow long enough to say hello.

Then Niamh was rushing away, following the servant inside. She shouted over her shoulder, "And be on your best behavior. Laure is Acheron's vessel."

I shut my eyes.

It hadn't occurred to me that Niamh might latch on to that, ascribe some extra meaning or even *remember* that I'd mentioned it. I was angry and excited for someone to share it with, confused about what it meant, yet the way she said it, the way Dominique and the others looked at me, Andor shifting his weight from foot to foot made me regret it. He didn't like them knowing it any more than I did. Keturah clung to my side. It suddenly felt like something I shouldn't have shared at all.

But Acheron supplied, grinning, **You're like a god among gods here**.

And it had hardly cost me anything... Yet.

I pinched the skin over my mark to stop the crawling unease from all of Palais Rose's splendor, from all these people and my own foolishness at mentioning being a vessel in the first place. We didn't really know if it entailed anything, but what if someone in Niamh's group did? Would they tell me?

Dominique was on the move, talking about some reception room and a miniature greenhouse for snakes, and we followed, the rest of Niamh's friends watching me appraisingly. Their gazes stung on my face, on my back, where suddenly I was back at the ballet, being dissected and evaluated, measured and compared part by part. Like I ceased to be a person all over again.

Inside, we listened to Dominique gush just like Niamh over high vaulted and domed ceilings, the delicate, sparkling chandeliers, the countless fireplaces carved from marble, the chairs and cabinets and mirrors lined in gold. A green room, a rose room, a sky room, a glass room— we passed them all as he led us across the wings in search of tea none of us really wanted.

Andor studied him and asked blankly, "So what did Acheron give you?"

"Actually, my connection is with Lethe," Dominique answered, glancing back with a wink, but not long enough to see how Andor, Keturah, and I faltered, how we looked at each other as if we'd misheard.

Dominique had a deal with *Lethe*? It instantly explained the unease, the writhing under my skin, yet there was nothing about him that over-lapped with Coralie—his skin was bright and lively instead of sallow. His full head of hair was shiny. The muscles on his arms, through his pants, were far from the bones that jutted out of Coralie's shirts and skirts in the end. And he wasn't trying to kill us.

Yet.

I shook my head slightly and whispered, "I didn't know..."

"How did..." Andor breathed, swallowing his words with a stiff smile when the youngest of Niamh's friends, Florian, noticed us falling behind.

But I knew what he was asking, even if he didn't say it—how did Niamh find them? And why? Why was he so special to survive Lethe when it'd corrupted and killed my best friend? How could Acheron and Lethe live under the same house without trying to destroy each other?

Quick on her feet to dispel Florian's suspicion, Keturah cleared her throat and asked loudly, "Is this the original floor plan?" Her slender hands convincingly stroked the frame of a door we'd just passed.

Dominique turned back and arched his brows with amusement, as if he knew that wasn't her real question. "No, there've been renovations, I think. You should really ask Niamh though—her memory's better than mine. I can tell you more about the cinema in the basement, though."

And then he kept walking, and we trailed behind.

House staff in the same uniform as the first streamed past, cleaning mirrors and windows, polishing silver candelabras, sweeping away dust, carrying floral arrangements and tea. Unlike the residents, none of them looked at us, or even acknowledged us, as we stepped out of their way.

Keturah tapped Andor and me on the shoulders and whispered back, "Everyone working here is mortal. No marks."

I nodded. "I mean, most people *are* mortal—"

She clutched my sleeve. "No, I'm wondering *why* they have mortal staff at all—Ciro didn't. How do they afford all of this? And aren't they concerned about secrecy?"

Indeed, everyone who walked by, who reached up to adjust the curtains and rearrange the pillows—none of them had marks on their arms. No tattoos, no magnetic pull from the root of my spine that called them kin, nor the urge to run away. And I couldn't help but think in that moment what Niamh did to that woman at La Tempête, the sobs racking her shoulders while Niamh just eyed me and grinned. Waiting for praise just like she did today when she showed us this mansion.

Like she was courting me for something.

Dominique and the others didn't acknowledge the staff either. No nods of recognition or smiles, thanks or greetings, like the people cleaning their floors and arranging their furniture didn't even exist. Or were beneath them. I saw what Keturah meant—all of it felt...odd.

Andor's frowned deepened.

"Just because they're mortal doesn't make them less than us," Keturah continued, rubbing her arms to shield against the chill of this place. It was unusually cold for so many fancy fireplaces. "My deal's almost up—it doesn't take much for us to be one of them again, you know?"

We hung back, letting the rest of the tour group disappear around a corner.

"Will you...will you get another?" I asked, unsure if I understood.

Andor looked as confused as I did, blinking slowly, but here wasn't the place for me to have any other kind of reaction, not when he was watching, when whatever we were was already hanging by a thread. Here, I had to show that I was perfectly stable, that I could handle anything, and anyone.

Even my recruit who was up to something.

Even Keturah turning away from the only thing that bound us together.

She leveled her gaze on mine. "No, one was enough for me. I'm sure." And then she smoothed out my hair and Andor's like she read our thoughts. "I'm not going anywhere. Anyway, I just wanted to tell you. Let's get moving before they come back to tell us about their indoor squash setup."

"Totally." My voice rang false, sounding off-kilter, as I straightened my spine, shoulders back, and strolled into an ornate tearoom. The picture of calm, right before colliding with a muscular frame.

A tanned, four-fingered hand caught my arm to steady me, setting my nerves alight, and my head snapped up to capture his face.

Gabriel Trémaux stood in the door, gazing down on me with his brows high. His shock mirrored my own as he took in the red ink peeking out from beneath my sleeve, as I balked at the pale whitish scar on his arm.

And he was here. Another one of Lethe's chosen.

My *boss*.

"Of course, you know Gabriel," said Niamh lazily from inside the room. She sat cross-legged in an armchair, sipping her tea. Light from the chandelier above had the effect of deepening the shadows of her face, accentuating her predatory features. Though I knew I shouldn't have, I felt like prey, even as I stepped out of Gabriel's grip just to quiet the revolt in my bones. She knew exactly how Gabriel and I knew each other.

He cleared his throat. "I thought I recognized the feeling of someone poking around in my brain."

I shook my head. "I never—"

*Oh.*

That first day at Maison Lumina, when I'd wanted to audition and he initially resisted, I'd tried to apply subtle pressure to change his mind, though nothing about him really looked glassy or under my influence. That was because the Lethe in him had refused, the same way I'd struggled to fend Coralie off in her last moments.

Gabriel gave some attempt at a smile, but there was no amusement in it at all, making me question if I'd ever really seen his smile on dance posters or if I'd only imagined it. The hardness to his expression was the same as at the studio, though perhaps a little colder here. He nodded his à bientôt, threw a scowl over his shoulder in Niamh's direction, and then stepped out of the room without another word.

Niamh seemed unconcerned by his curtness. "One of Lethe's chosen—there's plenty more where he came from, but unlike him and Dom, they don't show their faces much. Not ones for camaraderie."

All of her words were pointed, coated in a veneer of acceptance, but only just. There had been a conflict between them before we walked in, far deeper than who was chosen by whom. But I just sank into the velvety couch, stiff and reeling, because my boss was one of them. Because my boss was like Coralie, chosen by the same thing probably for the same purpose, and I could never erase the scars of her rampage. Andor's eye would never heal. Ciro and Joséphine would never come back.

Of all the dance companies in the city, I picked his.

Andor and Keturah were staring at me, waiting for explanations I couldn't give.

Instead, I focused on the room, decorated with cream-colored furniture and walls, paneled with burgundy accents and checkered flooring and a fireplace carved from the same red marble as the exterior. A real, working fireplace with a fire burning inside. There were large, framed paintings on every wall panel, dark, Baroque, of women surveying us as we nearly tore from our skins with discomfort.

"So what do you think? Did they tell you about the movie theatre?" Niamh goaded, setting the teacup down. She was still using that accent, I realized, pretending she wasn't French. "Have you changed your mind? Are you ready to join us here? Live like kings?"

I flashed her my most bulletproof smile. She may have looked the part of a predator, but I was a monster first. "And do what exactly?"

Dominique, Salomé, Florian, and the others all exchanged a look, but none of them said anything. They let Niamh do all the speaking, deferred to her like she was recruiting us, *collecting* us like pieces. But I was uninterested in trading the ballet's menagerie for another.

She clasped her hands in her lap. "Well, all of us have something special, either from Acheron or from Lethe. We aren't like the average person on the street—we were chosen for something better. It's like you said, Laure, we have the most power. And now more than ever, we should stick together."

"What do you mean, 'now more than ever'?" Keturah jumped in. "What's going on?"

From her place by the fire, Salomé stiffened. Dominique blinked in disbelief. None of them were smirking now. A seriousness took over the room until it was all quiet, all tense, until we all were waiting for someone to explain what they knew that we didn't.

Niamh cleared her throat. "That rot we saw? Elysium is sick. It's dying. Why else would we be here? Shouldn't the vessel of all people know that?"

# CHAPTER 14

*Elysium is sick. Why else would we be here?*

As soon as the car rolled to a stop, I flung the door open and started walking. It didn't matter that Andor and Keturah were trailing behind, calling my name. By the time they were out and the car pulled away, I'd already breached the alcove and was storming into the shadows.

Two at a time, I rushed down the steep, concrete stairs, stairs I used to imagine falling down, but this time, my panic kept me upright.

*It's dying.*

It didn't make sense that Niamh knew before me. It didn't make sense how a place carved from the body of a proto-god could die. It was meant to be immortal along with everything in it. If Elysium could die, then so could Acheron, Lethe, Andor, me—our lives were tied to it. Either we were promised a lie, this was one of Niamh's tricks, or else something was wrong. I liked none of those options.

"It isn't going anywhere," Keturah shouted somewhere far behind me on the stairs. Like there was anything for her to say that'd change my mind.

Instead I hissed under my breath to the shadows, "Aren't you worried?"

**No. Why would Elysium matter when we can be a god in the world above?** Acheron replied coolly. **Isn't that what we wanted?**

"What are you gonna do?" Andor asked, a little breathless and trying to catch up. "Where are you going? Are you even sure she was telling the truth—"

"She's telling the truth." I hated saying every word of it, the reality that Niamh's smug indifference was still nestled in truth. Just when I thought I had the upper hand, to corner her about lying about her name, she'd dealt this blow. "I know because I saw it. We saw it together."

One of them stopped walking, but I didn't care to glance back and see who. What I'd presented to them was another facet of my failure, another way that I'd dropped the ball: I was so full of myself and what they thought of me, how they viewed my capabilities and my strength, that I'd neglected to tell them.

The rot, Coralie, the girl in silver—all my secrets were piling up.

We rounded the corner and began pressing into the thick, metallic air that marked the coming of Elysium. It coated my mouth and lungs, the familiar hook on the inside of my ribs pulling me toward the iron door.

But it was . . . open.

Red light from Elysium's skies spilled into the Catacombs, illuminating the rock walls and cavernous ceilings. The door itself was dented and rippled and hanging on its hinge, as if something sharp and strong had rammed its way through. And Elysium's warmth was just ebbing out, an exposed vein, a body cut open.

"What . . ." I muttered, finally slowing my pace and turning back for the others.

In the corner of my eye, I glimpsed a small ball of white frozen in Acheron's alcove. It sat in the center, surrounded by stalactites like spires of blood hanging down, the pool of red shimmering against the walls. Beside the low table, topped with a cup and dagger, the tools of the trade of making deals, was a jackalope.

An Elysian jackalope, with pristine white fur and three bloodred eyes stretched wide, a small branching of antlers, and long ears erect. Its slender body was raised in tension, heart rattling rapidly in the palm of my hand, and legs poised to flee.

And we found it in the Catacombes de Paris. On the wrong side of the door.

"Andor?" I asked softly, careful not to move, to scare it off. Beside me, he and Keturah had gone still. "Has this ever happened before? Where they—"

"Leave Elysium? No." He frowned. "At least, not that I'm aware of. Joséphine used to leave the door open all the time, but nothing ever *wanted* to get out."

Elysium was dying, and even the animals could sense it.

Oily dread slicked my stomach.

Keturah, unperturbed, strolled into the alcove, crouching with her hand out. She looked like she was trying to pet it, as if it were a dog instead of a wild animal, cornered and afraid in a strange place. "You're both being dramatic. It's just a rabbit—"

The jackalope lunged, nipping at Keturah's fingers before darting away. It slipped past Andor in the blink of an eye, and then we lost it to the dark. Escaped into Paris. She only grimaced after it without another word and started for the door.

Balmy heat plumed in my face as I crossed the threshold and marched through the meadow of tall, thin white flowers. They didn't cower and crumble so easily under my hurried steps, like they excused my franticness. And all the susurrations of Elysium swelled the instant I broke through the tree line and stepped into the forest.

It could sense my anger and sang it back to me. It got it while the others didn't.

"Laure, wait!" Andor shouted, finally chasing after me. *Finally.*

But I didn't slow down.

I was too angry at myself for missing it, for strolling right into that patch of dying sludge and letting it bleach the bottom of my shoes without saying a word. For looking at all the dead birds and foxes floating in the mush and forgetting. For putting my own bullshit above all of this, this place that transformed me. The place I used to escape to every chance I got when I felt the hands of ballet choking me.

**Stop running.**

"Slow down!"

As if I could.

Just as pissed as I was at myself, I kept seeing Niamh's face. That warped, ugly smile because she knew something I didn't, being the better vessel while wearing my fucking sweater that she stole. So self-satisfied, squatting in some palace while our true home suffered. Talking about marble finishes and gold trim and a private movie theatre for her and her fifteen sycophants while Elysium was dying, and for all we knew, it could take Acheron with it. Take *us* with it.

I could've wrung her neck—I should've choked her out right there and then.

"Laure, we don't even know where we're going. Would you slow down—"

"I can't!" I spun around for just a moment, just to make them understand, only to see Keturah and Andor draw up short. Their complaints went quiet as they took in how my shoulders heaved, how my blood boiled, and I was about to erupt. "I saw it. I knew. I walked right into it!"

And then I was off again, stumbling through the tangles of vines and bramble, over bushes and the thick knotted roots of oak trees. My hands stayed busy scratching at my nervous mark.

Somewhere far enough behind, I heard Keturah say, "I've got this." Then sure enough, there was only a single pair of footsteps following me.

But I didn't want to be followed. I just wanted to fix whatever I'd left to fester.

A shadow lurked on the edge of my vision. It hummed with a familiar electricity and heat and cautioned, **You will not like what you see. Stop this.**

"What the hell did she even mean by 'sick'? It's not…" Words tangled in my throat as I kept pushing, trying to rationalize exactly what Niamh said, faced with what we saw. What more her new friends could have told her that I didn't know. Meanwhile my feet screamed in protest that these were not the right kind of shoes for this shit.

I was still beyond sore from my foray back into dance, from being out of shape and spending hour after hour, day after day rebuilding the tone and stamina I'd lost in my thighs and calves, retraining the structure in my core, flailing on the floor, leaping, contorting. I was covered in bruises, because at least ten times a rehearsal I crashed onto my shoulder, ass, knees, or head trying to learn how to fucking tuck and roll into the perfect somersault. I didn't have the strength to be out here, saving Elysium from falling apart. For all my faking, I wasn't strong enough to do it all.

Keturah sighed. "Maybe she misunderstood—"

I shook my head and shoved up my sleeve to scratch at my mark, the skin stinging and raw and already starting to break. I hadn't even realized how hard I'd been itching, just like before. It felt like Acheron was crawling around endlessly, a hundred insects trying to escape from under the muscle, and I was helping free them. My body revolting at Lethe's rot.

"We're getting closer," I said instead, holding up my arm as proof.

She scowled and hurried after to me. "You mean you feel that too?" Rather than scratch, she smacked the skin of her arm lightly. Again and again, the *thwack* dulled by the thick black fabric of her hoodie. "No, something's not right. We should go back, talk to Andor—"

Instead, I pushed harder. The last time I was here with Niamh, it'd taken us almost an hour of hiking to find the sludge. Now it wasn't even half of that before the squirming sensation expanded to a full-bodied scream. And my legs slowed in protest.

"This is wrong," I muttered to Acheron, to the dark, tainted corner of my sight. "The ridge is so far off. We're not even at the crossing."

**This is not for you**, it buzzed.

The smell came next. Thin, sweet, and sour like bananas taking on mold in the sun. It tilted my stomach, even as I rushed to cover my face. Keturah groaned not far behind. The trees here were thinning too, marked with the same climbing white blight that had swallowed the clearing I found before. Though the ground was wet, seeping with cloudy, rancid liquid, it wasn't yet a marsh of death, not yet capable of bleaching the toe of my shoes, but I could see it wasn't far off. Leaves clumped and rotted on the ground in bleached masses like soggy toilet paper.

And all around these spindly dying trees were more animal corpses. Crows and jackalopes and foxes, still, but there were also the unmistakable bloated bodies of a pair of two-headed deer, mother and child, the necks bent at sagging angles. The animals' coarse brown fur was bleached white on the side that touched the wet, their wide eyes glazed over and trained on the sky.

Whatever this was, it was spreading. It was far worse than when I'd left it.

Keturah clapped a hand over her mouth.

"Why didn't..." I pressed a hand to my heart, willing the pulse to steady. But I couldn't compel myself, it didn't work that way. "Why didn't anyone try to help, to make it better? If something's sick, if something's suffering, you don't just *abandon* it—"

"Oh, Laure," Keturah began, but it all got lost.

The crawling sensation was all I could hear, all I could think about, fighting for my attention. The static in the thinned dark telling me, **You shouldn't be here**. It was the pop of a knuckle on fire, the writhing of nerves in a flame. It was in my head, between my bones, and I couldn't stop it from ballooning. It grew louder and louder—

Until I struck out.

In a form that would have impressed me any other time, my fist landed squarely in a nearby tree trunk. Once, twice, again and again until there was something louder than how angry I felt. It should have hurt, the bark shredding my knuckles, the impact on my bones, but the tree, like all the trees around us, was sick. It felt more like punching flesh, like a sack of meat with all the give and softness of muscle and a harder, bonier interior to lend some resistance.

My skin split all the same. Blood dotted the tree's white, spongy flesh, the pulp broken and peeling away where my fist had landed.

Then I doubled over to fight the bile rising in my throat.

"I can fix it," I promised the fetid earth through gritted teeth. So that Acheron heard me, so that it could tell Elysium to slow down and wait for me. "I won't—"

"I know," Keturah whispered, her hand gliding along my spine.

I needed everything and everyone to know that, even if Niamh and the others had, I wouldn't give up. Not when I'd already given up Coralie and the ballet. Not when I didn't have very much left to lose.

"We won't abandon it," said Keturah, her voice muffed as I turned and pressed my face into the crook of her neck. Her arms squeezed around my middle.

We stayed like that, in an embrace, my chin resting on her collarbone, my face enveloped in the warmth of her. I was close enough to her pulse to focus on it, to let it steady me, and then to notice when it shifted. One moment, it was calm, and then suddenly it elevated to alarm. Her stiffening shoulders followed.

Keturah gulped and slowly whispered, "Laure, do you—I need you to tell me you see that over there."

Reluctantly, I peeled away. "See what?"

"Him." She extended an arm, a trembling finger pointed toward the cliffside, where a dark figure stood silently among the melting, rotting trees.

It was hard to catch his features from a distance, but he wore a colorful graffiti-patterned hoodie and skinny jeans, and his skin appeared the color of sable. Almost the exact shade of Keturah's. He was tall and scrawny, young-looking, though his eyes were obscured by a thicket of locs. And with him standing in shadow, I couldn't tell if he was smiling or frowning.

"Yes, I see him," I admitted, brows knitted in confusion.

Was it another acolyte, and all of Elysium was in exodus? Or was it a mortal who'd somehow found the door and gotten lost? None of that explained why Keturah was so rigid and shaking, the color drained from her face, the sparkle snuffed in her eyes. Why her bottom lip was working so hard to say more.

Still in a whisper, as if she didn't want him to hear, to stir, Keturah clarified, "It's Joey."

I rounded on her, and she clutched my wrist tight enough for nails to dig into my scar. Though I winced at the pain, I couldn't say anything, couldn't wrench away, and she didn't loosen; she only took a step back and then another, dragging me with her.

"It's not just me?" I whispered, reeling from the haunted look in her eyes, the chill in her blood. My own pulse, on the other hand, went wild with the realization.

"What—" She tugged harder. "We need to go."

And then Keturah was pulling me back through the trees, away from the new clearing of death, from the boy. We were scurrying and stumbling, and then she was running full speed, me trying to keep pace with her as if we were being chased. I tried to glance back at him, to gauge his reaction and if he'd follow, but he was gone. Without a sound.

As if he'd never been there at all.

Just like Coralie.

"Joey, your brother? But he's—"

"Yes, he's dead. He was there, and he's dead."

# CHAPTER 15

"I can't believe this is still on. We should be in Elysium."
Andor wrapped an arm around my shoulder to stop me from
fleeing, as if he knew the proximity would send my thoughts into a
tailspin. "You can't just put off everything because of some tree mold
and hallucinating dead people."

"But how could I see the ghost of someone I've never met—"

"These are your parents," he snapped. "Who are *alive*."

I'd chewed my lip bloody by the time we arrived at the restaurant,
and not even the scent of Andor's skin, of rain and fresh herbs, could
soothe me fully. Not even the fact that he was here, with his arm around
me no less, considering I'd called him *Acheron* earlier this week. Though
he seemed to not want to dwell on it as much as I did.

The red-painted bistro was small, nestled in the streets of the
7th arrondissement with gentle music and a bright sign advertising a
long wine list and the best tartare in Paris. It did nothing to stop my
nerves, frayed and fried from my march through the rotten marsh with
Keturah, the horror embedded in her expression as we'd fled, seeing
yet another person who couldn't possibly be there. Dead people we
only seemed to see when we were in Elysium. He didn't think there
was any truth to Elysium dying, so instead I was going to a restaurant.
To see my parents.

And just my luck, *both* of them were together and on time—a first—
and waiting for us. For me, technically. It was unfathomable, the sight of

the two of them together again. And whether they were *together* together or just amicable, I couldn't tell and feared to know.

Julien, whom I sometimes called *Papa*, whose quiet disposition and widow's peak I inherited, had traded his usual construction clothes for one of the only worn-out button-downs he owned and a knockoff pair of shoes that wasn't battered and stained with oil. And he talked with as much animation as his perpetually tired face would allow, to *her*. To the woman who birthed me.

Julien had always insisted that I was Alexandra Freeman's little shadow. In complexion, in restless hair that refused a uniform curl, dark eyes that narrowed on perceived weaknesses. I had her lean figure and love for ballet. And best and worst of all, I had her ambition and selfishness too.

Alexandra abandoned me, and then I abandoned Julien. Sometimes I wondered if he saw it coming—me running away and never coming back—in the moments he saw my mother in me. We never were close enough for me to ask.

"Is that them?" Andor asked as he dropped his arm, taking the warmth with him, though it was less question and more observation.

My mother was imposing. She was tall, with skin the color of perfect chestnuts right before the roast, and young too. Her dark curls were pinned up in some chaotic fashion, but her clothes were the neat, polished trim one would expect from someone with a doctorate in art history from La Sorbonne. The kind of person whose only contact with their daughter was the same birthday card every year. She was unmistakably mine. Andor didn't need me to speak to confirm it.

Savoring the taste of blood on my lip, the mass of shadow gathering on the ground, I nodded anyway. Acheron was inspecting her, searching for something.

As if she could sense me, as if her motherly senses hadn't dulled despite all the time and miles apart, Alexandra raised her head and looked right at me. She had a hawk's gaze, locking on mice scurrying in the field. It took a long time for her to rearrange her expression into a smile in our approach.

"Laurence," she breathed, at the same time my father said, "Laure."

"Papa, nice to see you again."

Then nausea climbed in my throat, even as my legs carried me into the waiting arms of my estranged mother. She folded me into her chest for a hug that lasted too long and yet was too brief for her time away. Like we were both distant cousins and also old friends meeting up at a coffee shop. Like it hadn't been twelve years since we last saw each other, and she wasn't my mother and I wasn't her child.

As if to say, *You're an adult now, and I don't owe you anything.*

Ironically, in her arms, I felt even less like an adult than I already did.

"My colleagues say this place has the best tartare—do you like steak tartare?" she chattered excitedly, dragging me to the door.

And then she glanced at me in earnest, but if she was here, if she hadn't *abandoned me*, then she'd know that I loved tartare, the brutal rawness of the taste, the softness of the flesh. Clenching my jaw, I could manage only to nod my head. What I wanted to do was crane my head back and release a guttural scream into the restaurant.

Alexandra didn't pick up on any of it. She didn't know how to read me at all. "I came from Japan for a conference and had *horse* sashimi. It reminded me of—Oh!" Her eyes widened as they finally noticed the figure hovering patiently behind me. "Who's this? You brought a friend."

I seized the moment to put some distance between us. "This is Andor."

"Hello," Andor started without missing a beat. He breezed past me with a bright smile on his face, the brightest of us all, filling the space between me and my parents and shaking their hands. In the chilly weather of early spring, they didn't seem to mind his leather gloves, which they'd read as fashion instead of a safeguard. "Nice to meet you."

I adjusted my coat collar, ignoring the questioning glances from both my parents. I hadn't mentioned he was coming, and I wasn't going to explain now why he was here. If they wanted to know the nature of our relationship, they'd have to get in line. I certainly wouldn't be the first one to bring it up.

"Andor, right," my mother continued, veering toward the door without missing a beat. "I'm sorry; Laurence didn't say you were coming. I hope you like steak tartare."

He unbuttoned his jacket, smile never wavering. "Actually, I'm vegetarian, but I like salads!"

My mother eyed him before she led the way into the restaurant, my father trailing behind. And the moment they turned their backs, I felt the brush of Andor's shoulder against mine. The backs of his knuckles grazed my hand next. The contact was light considering all the layers between us, but there was power to it. Like the monster in me was charged by his, strength in numbers.

Then, like some alternate universe, I took a deep breath, went in, and took my seat. For lunch, with him and my parents.

On account of my fierce devotion to ballet, a scarce love life, and even scarcer parents, this was uncharted waters. The people who called themselves my parents would have never met my . . . something. Would it matter if Andor and I weren't just friends? Would they care to know that sometimes friends fell asleep side by side in the same bed, night after night, close but never touching? Because his kisses were poison? And I craved them anyway?

My mother's astute gaze flicked back and forth between us again, assessing, before she cleared her throat. "So, Laure, tell me how you've been."

Her smile was shiny and white, perfectly straight and square. She was far from the monsters I was used to, yet I was nonetheless unsettled.

I shifted in my seat. "Fine, I guess."

Because what else could I say? That I was a wreck? That a building fell on me and my best friend and it was partially my fault, and I lost everything I had and everything I was and didn't know if I'd get it back? If she were really my mother, if she was here, these were all things she would have already known.

Alexandra reached across the table for my hand, froze, and seemed to think better of it. "I'm glad to see you're okay. I was traveling for work when I heard. I came as soon as I could."

She came twelve years too late. When was she going to explain herself? When was she going to apologize?

"Were you there?" she probed curiously. "When the building came down?"

Her eyes locked on my throat and the scar that no doubt peeked out of my turtleneck. It matched the scars around both wrists and ankles too, courtesy of Coralie's violent restraints. If she was here, would she have visited me in the hospital? Noticed what I was up to before it got so far? Or would she have been like Rose-Marie, pushing me toward a cliff and then running to save herself when the monster refused to go over the edge?

Finally, my mother glanced briefly at Andor's face.

So I nodded to distract her. "Yes, I was. Coralie too."

The death of my childhood friend didn't seem to matter to her or Julien. She just continued her bland smile, asking her bland questions, as if none of this were really happening, and she didn't owe me anything. And Julien, ever the coward, examined the menu scrupulously.

"What have you been up to since then?" Alexandra droned on, unperturbed. "Where are you dancing now?"

She didn't ask if I was okay. *If* I was even dancing anymore, if I wanted to. It was assumed that I'd dance, because a ballerina was all she'd ever known me to be. That was all she'd ever *taught* me to be. She was now a stranger, but I was still exactly as she'd left me.

I rolled up my sleeves, aching for a fight, and stared at her. Glared, really.

Was I so awful? Was I so insufferable at six years old, something about me so wretched and rotten and impossible to fix that she had to leave and never come back? Was there some shadow so dark and hollow within me that young that she left me behind? That same darkness became an opening for the thing we called Acheron, who called itself the Daemon King, who wrapped itself around my spine and would never let go. Was that why it chose me?

"Well, I've been good. There was a faculty position at—" Her voice cut out. And rather than detecting the rage in my eyes, hers were focused on my tattoo. The red ink on my arm, Acheron's mark, apparently more interesting than the scar below it or how much I hated her. "Where did you get that?"

With a loud scrape, I shoved back my chair and stood. There wasn't enough money or time or love in the world to keep me sitting here, listening to her pretend she didn't throw me away. Pretend she didn't know that I needed her as much as I needed Julien. I was flesh and blood and feelings just like everyone else; I wasn't carved from stone. I was just a *girl*.

Andor called my name at my back, but I was already wending my way through the tables toward the restrooms.

My blood was fire and white-hot anger, and I needed cool water to temper it. I needed to get out of that moment before I added another thing to my list of regrets. Like breaking each of her toes and fingers, like stealing teeth from her mouth, one for every year she'd been gone. Like squeezing her heart so she felt a fraction of the pain she'd caused.

The door to the restrooms barely swung shut before I heard the footsteps that pursued me, before I felt the rapid, nervous heartbeat of my mother on my heels. She waltzed inside with a heavy sigh, blocking the exit, trapping me between her and the row of sinks. No longer in the mirror, Acheron buzzed from a corner of the room, coalescing into a shadowy mass on the floor. It was here with us, growing stronger, growing itself a body, readying to devour her, not that she noticed. Not that now was the time to freak out about it.

Rage flared in me. And hurt. My fingertips prickled as the nails elongated and thickened into claws. My gums stung. I was letting it transform me, so I flipped on the tap to distract myself with washing. "What?"

"I know about the red god." She leaned against the adjacent sink.

I closed the tap and froze, waiting for her to repeat herself. Positive that I'd misheard. There was no way she was yet another person who recognized my mark, who had me figured out while I still didn't.

"I know," she said again, gesturing with her lips to the red print on my arm. "You think you're special? You aren't the first to lose yourself in Nyarla's clutches."

Acheron shuddered with pleasure and inched closer to her.

"'Nyarla'? First, this is from *Acheron*, and second, I haven't *lost* myself—"

"Acheron is not its real name, that's what its *followers* mistakenly called it." She scoffed at me, as if I was such a child for not knowing. "And I won't ask what it cost you. It doesn't matter. All that matters is that you get away when it's over."

I hated her. I hated that she knew more than me, I hated the wistful way she looked at my arm, I hated how she abandoned me, how she just walked back in here like nothing happened with the audacity to give me advice I didn't ask for.

Once she was a ghost haunting my steps, but now she was the thorn in my paw. I needed her out.

"You don't know what you're talking about." I strained to stay cool.

Just outside this bathroom was Andor, making small talk with my *father*, waiting for me, hoping I was all better and fixed and well-adjusted and capable of having a simple conversation with the woman who made me. But she was the first to kindle the fire I couldn't put out.

Alexandra shook her head. "I know more than you think. I studied at the Sorbonne, Laure; I know a lot about desperation and competition and wanting to be the best. How do you think it wormed its way in? Where do you think you got it from? Why I tried to save—"

She pursed her lips and refused to finish.

On the floor, Acheron—or *Nyarla*, if she was to be believed—curled around her now, so close that if it was physical, if she had a mark, she might have felt the prickle of its skin on her ankles. Delight rolled off its form in recognition.

She noticed how I watched our feet and folded her arms, unseeing. The judgment was plain on her, easy to recognize because it resembled my own. She looked at me with pity. She looked at me the way I looked at Coralie when she'd lost her way.

But I wasn't *lost* right now. I was angry, and I had every right to be.

"If you think it's so good and well-intentioned now, consider this: When I knelt before Nyarla's pool and asked for its help, it demanded my firstborn child in return." She stared pointedly, pausing to let her words sink in. Pausing so that I understood that she'd promised Acheron *me*. "Does that sound generous to you? Did it tell you?"

I dried my hands on a paper towel to give myself time. To steady the spike in my pulse and choose my words carefully. It was none of her business that I was Acheron's vessel now, or what it had and hadn't told me, and I'd find my choice words for Acheron later.

She, however, was not someone I trusted; I wouldn't let her see me shaken.

Crushing the paper and in a level voice, I remarked, "It sounds like you were naïve and made a bad choice."

My mother caught my arm, turning my wrist to the light. The mark shone crisply then, the ink bloodred under the fluorescents, even against the brown of my skin turned translucent where blue veins showed. If I was supposed to be embarrassed or ashamed, I wasn't.

"You don't understand—"

"I understand very clearly, *Maman*," I spat, jerking out of her grip.

It probably didn't feel how she wanted it to feel, and I hadn't uttered that word in so long, it couldn't sound like anything other than toxic to me.

*Maman, come back.*

*Maman, I'm sorry. Whatever I did, I'm sorry.*

*I'll be good, Maman. No, I'll be the best if you just pick up. If you come home.*

No, I wasn't that girl anymore.

She stepped back, and I marched past her. The restroom was shrinking, the restaurant was too small, this city wasn't big enough to get me away from her.

I'd only managed to pull the door open before Alexandra spoke again, her voice so small and pathetic that I couldn't help homing in on it. It was so unlike her, and I was so much a monster, that it sounded like a kill.

"I loved your father, Laure, but you weren't planned. I was young, and I made that deal because you weren't supposed to be. I never wanted to be a mother, so I thought we were safe . . . But I guess you've always been unstoppable."

When I glanced back, I saw how sad the smile on her face was, like it was both good and bad being what I was. Unstoppable. But I wasn't unstoppable at all. I was *just a girl*, trying to become someone new when I apparently didn't even know anything about who I'd been.

"Maybe it did something, or maybe we slipped up. I just didn't expect you to be so much…"

**Like me**, Acheron supplied from the shadows in the room, at the same time my mother whispered, "Like me."

But rather than say anything to either of them, rather than process any of it, I kept walking. I crossed the restaurant floor in a flash, snatched my coat from the back of my chair, and fled.

# CHAPTER 16

I was halfway down the block before Andor's long strides caught up to me. Before I remembered that I'd left him alone with my father. He surpassed me in an instant, blocking my path, though his breath remained calm, his coat and gloves still in his hands, and I glared.

"Move," I snapped, even though I could have walked around him. I wanted him to buckle first.

He dared to search my face instead. "What happened?"

I stepped around him and kept walking. "I'm not going back there. I won't spend another second with that woman."

"Talk to me—"

"Do you think we had a choice?" I didn't want to talk, but those were the words that escaped me first. "In any of this?"

Andor's brows knit together in confusion as I rounded on him.

"Following Joséphine, Acheron, its *favor*," I spat.

*Us.* Did we even get to choose us, or was that Acheron too, tuned only to the frequency of itself?

I went on, my legs slowing subconsciously, "I wagered my will to dance for that power. I sacrificed my best friend, and died and was reborn, and I gave it my body—did I have any say? Did you?"

As we neared a park, my body went slack against the gates, and the fight drained out of me. Andor leaned beside me and frowned, and I had to force myself not to watch his expression as he worked through what I was saying, what I asked him against why I stormed out of that restaurant.

He had such a lovely frown, and it was a shame I might have been preordained to find it distracting.

"I don't know," he admitted finally, raising a shoulder. "I think I did, but why—"

"Apparently, my mom and Acheron go way back." The sigh that escaped me was heavy as I sank to the ground and dropped my head in my hands. "She bartered me to it before I was even born. Then along came a kid that wasn't supposed to be, and eventually she got sick of pretending, and you know the rest."

He settled at my side, his knees brushing mine, his warmth bleeding through my jacket. "You think that's why she left?" And then he shifted and more urgently asked, "You think Acheron targeted you?"

I shrugged helplessly. "Well, what else am I supposed to think? According to her, I couldn't have *possibly* decided anything for myself."

"And what did it say?"

"Nothing."

With the storm brewing in my veins, Acheron was smart to stay quiet. Hiding from my periphery. For once, I didn't want it to say a thing.

So we sat in a pregnant silence, watching people amble past, going about their lives. But inside, I bristled at how that woman had under-estimated me. How unfathomable it was that perhaps I could be stronger, braver, smarter, more deserving than her.

I had weeks of feeling like I wasn't myself, and now I was faced with the question of when I'd ever been. Which Laure was the real one? Had I ever been really, truly mine?

My father was definitely my father. I looked like him, and for all his faults, he was mine. There was no denying I looked like her too, but now I guessed, on the inside, I looked like Acheron: ancient and other-worldly, incomprehensible, and a fucking liar.

"Just what I need—another reason I can't fit and act like the well-adjusted, perfect ballerina everyone wants me to be." I snorted bitterly and kicked out a leg. "Especially her. Especially *you*."

Andor entwined his fingers with mine, his thumb drawing circles on the back of my hand. "That's not true."

The sensation in my palm was as soothing as menthol, but did I even have a say in savoring it? In not minding how it brought my senses to life? And as if he could read my response, he let go and shifted away, once again inches out of reach. So I rounded on him.

"Seriously?"

He startled, his eyes going wide. "What—"

"What is *with* you?" I snapped, pleased to have somewhere new to sink the rage swelling in my blood. "It's hot and cold. I'm not made of glass, you know."

"It's not that—" His shoulders climbed to his ears.

"You can't even sit here with me while my mother just blew up my entire life and every choice I've made? You can't even hold my hand?"

He blew out a breath, raked a hand through his curls, and turned to the street. "I-I'm trying. But the last time I held you, you died in my arms. It's not exactly easy, you know." His voice was a mumble, low, both indiscernible and impossibly clear. Not nearly as strong and steady as I'd always known him to be.

"I..." I started to say, but came up empty. Heat rose to my cheeks as I considered those last hazy, dying moments and took him in: his head drooped to avoid looking at me, the dark lines of his face from how little he still slept.

All of us were sleep-deprived and hiding it.

"The nightmares?"

His eyes flicked to me, and he nodded.

"But you didn't kill me," I said slowly. "Coralie did."

Andor tilted his head toward the sky and shrugged. "So how much poison is too much, then? And what am I supposed to do when Acheron's always watching? Knowing that I'm the one who brought you back to it?"

It was my turn to wince, not that he noticed. But I was grateful that he didn't squirm when I sidled closer and lay my head on his shoulder, that he only stilled for a fraction of a moment instead of making some excuse to flee. Progress. "You know it hates you?"

The tension drained from his frame, and he snorted. "Well, the feeling's starting to be mutual."

Then, as we sat like that, second by second, one after another, the breaths came easier. The storm lessened, with me breathing in his scent, listening to his heartbeat, and the dark clouds in my vision receded.

Too soon, Andor cleared his throat and began rising to his feet. "Come on. It's cold. If we stay on the ground like this, we'll get sick."

"I can't get sick, and neither can you." I rolled my eyes but pushed myself up anyway.

*Neither can Elysium.*

And when I pressed closer to him again and brought his hand to my mouth, he didn't pull away. He just kept frowning down at me as I gazed up at him, and for a moment my mother and Acheron's bullshit was left back in that small restaurant bathroom. They were a problem for another day, a day when I was stronger.

I dared crack a smile. "It's not watching right now, you know."

His mouth twitched as he looked for a rebuttal but found none. He wasn't sure he believed me, I could see in his dark eye, but he couldn't find the words to say so. Or maybe he was just tired of putting up a fight.

Andor tilted my chin with his burning hand, folded over me, and pressed his lips to mine. The kiss was brief, so very brief it might've only been a brush. *Too* brief but still I tasted the floral sweetness and the bitterness of herbs. It filled my lungs. A spark glided across my skin.

I rose onto my toes for another, and he was gone, stepping back to slide on his coat. But he was grinning. It was enough to reassure me that I had someone on my side who hadn't schemed to be there.

We parted at the metro station, and I kept walking along Boulevard Saint-Germain. It was still too early to sulk at home, my thoughts remained tumultuous even though I wasn't at risk of spilling over.

My mother was a monster. Had been. Was still. Before I was even a thought in her mind, she'd ransomed me for her own ambition. She'd offered me in exchange for power to an old god that lied about its name, an old god she hardly knew or understood, and when it became clear that I was to be real, she didn't flinch. She didn't seem to consider at all how that would affect me. She looked me in the eye and named me Laurence Mesny and raised me to be great, practically pointing me in its direction. She force-fed me lessons, promises she had no intention of keeping, pretending I wasn't the goose she'd fattened up for slaughter.

Did I ever say anything that reminded her of Acheron? Could she see it in my eyes the way I sometimes saw it in Andor's? Part of me still longed to know what was the moment that triggered her disappearance, but she *owed* me an explanation—I shouldn't have had to ask.

**You do not think like a vessel should**, Acheron advised as I continued down the street. **And you promised to trust me.**

Though I walked with some speed, I had no direction in mind. I took turns as they suited me, depending on if I wanted to wait for the changing lights, if I didn't like the crowd of another block.

"*You* don't talk to me," I growled, earning me a glance or two from people on the street. But I was good at being stared at.

Did she know that Elysium was dying too? Was that really why she came—not for any concern for my well-being but out of interest for her old life? Her life before I came along and apparently ruined it?

Not that it mattered. I was done with her. I didn't *want* her explanations. I didn't care if she was here to save Elysium or to say her goodbyes or if the guilt of abandoning her daughter twelve years ago had finally eaten through to the core of her rotten heart. It didn't matter if she thought I'd died, if she was concerned about me. Me, my dance career, my relationship with Acheron—none of it was any of her business.

At the sight of the imposing, Gothic building that marked Musée de Cluny, I turned right for the library. This close, it made sense to go inside and put all this energy to good use. I wouldn't be like Niamh or my mother, abandoning Elysium to die.

I didn't know exactly what to look for as I strolled beneath the high, arched ceilings, past the gazes of painted white intellectuals on the walls, through the towering stacks of dusty tomes. Rich wood tables and chairs lay around every corner and in the center of the floor, inviting me to have a seat and be a scholar. At the academy, I only studied as much as necessary—I didn't need calculus or physics or history to be a ballerina. And while I certainly enjoyed balancing chemical equations and pretending to understand German, I'd always enjoyed dancing more.

But now I'd pretend again—it was apparently what everyone did. I pretended to be okay, Andor pretended he wasn't having nightmares of me dying, and Niamh pretended to trust us because she needed us for something. My mother had once pretended to tolerate my existence. Now I was going to pretend to be a scholar, a student of botany and the natural sciences, even though Andor was the only one of us who could keep a plant alive.

I landed at the main desk and tucked an errant curl behind my ear. There was only one librarian seated, poring over some massive book larger than my torso.

"Where would I find books on tree diseases, like fungi and stuff? Or anything on crops, really."

They studied me for a long moment before gesturing up to the second-floor balcony, to a section of shelves positioned before massive windows. And I rushed toward the creaking wooden stairs without another word, lest they notice how out of place I was. With only my phone and wallet, I didn't have anything to take notes on. No bag either to carry any books for study.

Then again, I also didn't know what I'd find. There was no chance of tomes entirely dedicated to dying Elysium, no step-by-step instructions on how to save the place with red skies from a creeping white death, anyway.

Instead, I started pulling from shelves anything alluding to the health of trees and soil. There were entire encyclopedias on crop destruction, journals on diseases that infected bark, theses on soil maintenance and diagnoses. I took as much as my arms could carry and snapped photos of all the rest to come back later.

In any one of these could be Elysium's cure.

**You will not find what you seek in any of these books**, Acheron countered. **You will not find what you seek *at all*.**

And because I was in a library, I held my tongue and merely thought instead of saying aloud, *I'm not talking to you.*

The barbs on my tongue made it settle back down in my chest, back to resting or whatever it did when it wasn't determining my every thought, step, and impulse. Did I have any choice in being a vessel at all?

*No*, now wasn't the time to spiral. It wasn't about me right now, but instead proving Niamh wrong.

I tottered over to the nearest table, basking in the last rays of sunlight from winter's glacial departure, and thought of my recruit. Her smug expression, her knowing more than I did, trying to impress me when she learned what I was. Her real name. Margaux Lozach.

It was a quick and easy search, yielding no social media accounts but dozens of articles about a house fire up in Bretagne a couple years ago. A woman from the Lozach family who died, a suspected arson, her young daughter still missing. The photo was blurry, but with short hair and time, it could be Niamh.

It *was* Niamh.

"What did you do?" I whispered to Acheron as I folded over my phone, though I didn't want an answer. What I really meant was, *What did you make me to do?*

**I didn't make you do anything you didn't want to**, it replied. **And she is not your enemy. She could be your ally, though.**

Chilled to my core, a little more afraid than I wanted to admit to myself, I pulled the first book from the pile and cracked the spine. Curing tree rot suddenly seemed an easier task.

Somewhere in the hours lost, the shuffle of footsteps and the fall of a shadow over me drew me away from the growing text on my notes app. A sinister shiver slipped down my spine, and the mark on my arm began to squirm in protest. When my head snapped up to the alarm bells and settled on the figure, I startled.

"We meet again," said Gabriel with an upturn of his mouth. It still wasn't a full smile, not one that met the severity of his blue eyes, but it was the warmest I'd seen from him so far. It was kind of scary.

I rubbed my face and leaned back. "Gabriel, hi. What are you doing here?"

He gestured to the book in his hand, some thick anthology by the name of *Necronomicon: Weird Tales of Lovecraft*. How absolutely uncharacteristic of him. I hadn't even considered he could read, eat, do anything other than dance.

"Need to stay inspired," he answered. "It's hard to choreograph and stage modern interpretations of ballets if you can't envision anything else."

It made sense, I supposed. And after so many pages, my energy was starting to wane, so I merely nodded. The sun had long since dipped beneath the horizon, the library's lights blaring overhead, and I had a waiting text from Andor asking if I'd eaten. My father had already tried to call me twice, not that sending him to voice mail did anything. I felt worn thin.

Gabriel stepped closer and peered at the open book. "And what are you . . . Oh."

The photos said enough—gnarled trees, bark patchy with white or fuzzy green spots, the rot and parasites bursting through the surface, fire blight. It was like that with all of them, graphic photos that said I was looking in the right spot, but none of them had any answers I could follow. Like, how the hell was I supposed to find industrial-strength pesticide to start, and what to do if that wasn't enough?

"You wouldn't happen to know anything about dying forests, would you?" I tapped my finger on the picture of a desiccated apple tree.

He grimaced and adjusted his grip on his book. "Look, I may be overstepping here, but I've been in Elysium a lot longer than you, and I've never seen anything like this. I'm not sure . . . Sometimes the best way to deal with these kinds of things is to let them run their course. Let it go."

My mouth went dry.

"There definitely won't be any answers you need in *that*." He nodded his head toward the other open book, an encyclopedia of bactericides, echoing Acheron and all the rest.

I craned my neck to get a good look at him. The weathered lines of his face made him look older than he was—he looked to be in his thirties when he was maybe only a few years before Joséphine's time. There was no telling, just by studying the pale mark on his arm, the severe scar where his pinkie finger used to be, how long he'd been in Lethe's clutches. Coralie, at least, had been smart enough to just spare a couple molars, and yet Lethe ran through her in the span of a few months. How much longer did Gabriel think he had?

"Let it run its course?" I repeated dully.

He nodded. "If Lethe has taught me anything, it's that sometimes you need to let things go."

And I couldn't help but scoff at that. How could I? *Why* should I? It was so hard for Coralie to let go that she was stalking me from beyond the grave—

I perked up in my seat. "Have you seen the ghosts too?"

Because the ghosts had to be connected. No one saw Coralie when the rot was beginning, but as it spread, she managed to knock on the window. Then I saw Keturah's brother.

Gabriel gave me a hard stare that told me he did see them. Even if his mouth turned to a straight line and he said instead, "You can't avoid facing loss. Especially when it comes to Elysium." And then he placed a dry, massive palm on my shoulder like that was supposed to comfort me instead of pissing me off. "Everything dies. Even gods."

Acheron sneered at him.

I shrugged out of his touch and shut the encyclopedia with a *thud*. "No offense, but you can go shove your advice."

Because if the rot was oblivion, and *I* came back from oblivion with the rot in me, then it was my fault. I did this. Coralie was right once again.

*You shouldn't have come back.*

Elysium was dying because of me. Because I came back. So for once, I was going to save something instead of tearing it apart.

Gabriel raised his brows, though he didn't look offended so much as taken aback. Being at the ballet, I was sure he'd heard worse. And he retorted with just as much venom, "Grow up. You're an adult now, so act like one."

*Barely.*

"If you'll excuse me," I drawled, sure to bare my teeth at him as I scooped the books into my arms to return to the shelves, "I have trenches to dig."

# CHAPTER 17

"Hey," I uttered to Vanessa as I dropped to the floor, breathless. The stairs to the main studio left me winded, and it was maddening to see plainly how far I'd fallen when I used to rush up and down the many floors of Palais Garnier all day, every day.

In an effort to maintain appearances, show that I could handle anything, I'd dragged myself to Maison Lumina bright and early on Monday morning. It didn't matter that Elysium was rotting away, that Keturah and I had spent all Sunday and gone late into the night digging trenches to starve off the diseased land, that I was bone-tired. I didn't even know if I still had a job, for what I said to Gabriel. But I hauled myself here for a master class because this routine of embarrassing myself among people who should have been my peers put Andor and Keturah at ease. And especially after that horrible lunch, trying to be good at this again gave me some sense of ground beneath my feet.

I knew who I was because I was here, even if I wasn't sure I *should* be anymore. Even if I sucked now, though I hoped it showed a little less. Somehow, I *wanted* to be good again.

Vanessa bobbed her head but said nothing, thumb swiping fast at whatever she was typing. And because I was so attuned to studying Acheron, Gabriel, Andor, and Keturah, I noticed at once the dark circles beneath her eyes too.

To party so much, she was just as meticulous—she swore by drinking tons of water, resting a lot, still going to the gym as much as we did as ballerinas. She also took every drug she could get her hands on, for the perfect paradox, but this was the first time she actually looked *haggard*. The first time she looked unwell, far worse for wear than I'd ever seen her.

"Hit any good parties lately?" I prodded as I hinged forward to stretch my hips and spine. The shoveling had been hell on my back, and I didn't imagine Keturah faring any better. "I saw that DJ Sparx did a huge set at En boîte over the weekend. Bummed I missed it."

She kept swiping.

"Vanessa?"

Her head snapped up, bangs fluttering around her bloodshot eyes as they struggled to focus on me. "Huh? Oh, yeah, it was great." Then her head dipped, and she went back to her phone.

*Message received.*

She was certainly no Coralie, and I was capable of taking a hint: Our relationship had formed over a mutual desire to escape the ballet. That's it. Just because she'd recommended Maison Lumina to me didn't mean we were suddenly close as can be. She'd lost her best friend too—Olivia—in the collapse.

Still, to temper the urge to smack her anyway, I told myself she was probably just seeing someone and tapped through the sparse inbox on my own phone where I found yet another missed call from Julien waiting.

His name had gone through phases in my life: First it was surprising that he wasn't just Papa to the world; and then it was a weapon I'd used to spite him. Just as we fractured as a family, he became Julien in times of rage, when I wanted him to hurt. Then, a nuisance. Julien was a phone call at all the wrong times because he'd never learned to text. And now it meant *her*.

I'd never loathed my father. I resented how easy it had been to push him away and how much I grew up without him around, sure, but he was always pitiful. Like me, a victim of our circumstances.

Alexandra, however, I loathed. Her postcards, her arrogance, how she assumed herself beyond reproach. She didn't think she had anything to apologize for, and she gallivanted back into my life like she was a gift. Like she had a rightful place here. She thought she knew me and gave me advice I didn't want. She pushed me into a corner just to tell me I was both unwanted and a pawn, reducing all I'd achieved and everything I was to *her* actions. And she had the nerve to use my father's meekness to get to me.

I swiped the notification away. That was the most cordial I could be. If she were anyone else, the monster in me would've preferred to tear her ears off and make her eat them. Not like she'd listen, anyway.

Then followed a text, *PLEASE HEAR HER OUT*, and I got rid of that too.

From the base of my spine, Acheron just grumbled, **You have a god's capriciousness, you know?**

And it took everything in me to throw a glare at my reflection, at the mass of static beside it, instead of giving *it* some choice words. Like for starters, demanding what else was it keeping from me about Elysium?

At the front of the room, the instructor from the American Ballet Theatre shook out her arms and fiddled with the zipper of her wool vest. She was quite tall, with a long neck and face and average brown hair that swung around her shoulders in a ponytail. I didn't catch her name, and she didn't bother to introduce herself, but she had too much energy this time of day for my liking. "Shall we get started?"

*No.*

The rest of Maison Lumina seemed to embrace her enthusiasm anyway. The warm-up felt like Pilates: There were elements of barre without the barre, micromovements in plié that toned the calves and made them burn. We balanced on a single leg and squatted, planked, did crunches—all before we could actually dance. And they all ate it up while I was preoccupied with hiding all the other things on my mind, things that I'd rather do.

And at the same time, I wanted to look effortless like I used to but succeeded only in just keeping up. Just barely treading water.

"Now, can we break into pairs?" the instructor shouted with a mischievous grin as we all climbed back to our feet. This was the closest I'd felt here to ballet times, to directors who almost seemed to enjoy our pain, because that showed we were learning. After all, nobody *liked* dancing with a partner, even if it helped your artistry. Sharing your body, being in tune with someone else's moods and movements—it could be bothersome at times. Thanks to Acheron, I knew very well. "Everyone find a partner."

I groaned as I pushed myself up and pivoted around, trying not to acknowledge the dread building in me. "Vanessa, do you want to—"

But Vanessa already had her back to me and was waving to some girl nearby, on the younger end of our group, with the tips of her blond hair dyed electric blue. She looked familiar, maybe someone who'd left the academy early. Who got out before it ruined her like it did the rest of us. With how poorly I was doing, I didn't see a point in memorizing names or getting to know the others anyway.

And as expected, all around me, the other members of Maison Lumina partnered up while I had no one. Because I was new and a liability.

*You will always have me.* The memory of Acheron's nonvoice glided across my skin like a winter breeze, putting the hairs on my arm on end. *Always.*

Always was a long time. Was I supposed to feel like this forever?

I shifted from foot to foot, looking around for another awkward loner who was left without a partner and coming up empty. It became apparent in this moment that Gabriel *did* plan Maison Lumina well, and he didn't account for an odd number. He didn't account for a disaster like me.

And there too went my hopes of proving I could be better, belong. Of having just one win today among a recent waterfall of losses.

Hands clapped behind me, making me jump as Gabriel vaulted up from his seat. "I want to join! What should I do?"

*Oh gods, no.*

When Acheron wrinkled its nose, mine twitched too.

At the front of the room, the instructor pointed in my direction. At me. With a gleeful smile Acheron and I couldn't help but picture smashed in. "It looks like she still needs a partner."

I stiffened.

Gabriel mirrored her smile as best he could, but only I knew that underneath, he was a monster like I was. Maybe worse because he had Lethe in his veins. Or maybe that unwittingly made him the perfect partner.

Without another word, he crossed the floor to stand beside me and nodded in acknowledgment. There was no hostility to his eyes or posture, no memory that I'd just told him to shove it two days ago and he called me childish, but I didn't trust it. It'd be well within his ability to drop me the moment we went into the dips, or toss me over his shoulders and fling me on my head. To take my eye, have Lethe seep from his skin like razor wire to wrap around my throat, and this time, not let go. Finish what Coralie started.

A violent shiver rolled through me, and I inched away and did my best to ignore him.

"Okay, we'll start with your legs shoulder-width apart and then you want to roll your torso up."

Unfortunately the combination was jazzy, which, thanks to the ballet, I had no experience in. With what time was I supposed to learn these other styles? How did anyone else? However, with a series of quick steps and spins around a partner while our hips swiveled, for once and to my surprise, it was a rhythm I could actually pick up and follow. And as a ballerina, I wasn't a stranger to partner work with people I detested— I'd leapt and trusted classmates like Rémy Lajoie and Geoffrey Quý to catch me, and they did. Rémy was a capable dancer until he died in the collapse. And Geoffrey was smart to move to Milan, where ballerinas didn't die every few weeks.

Still, I wasn't accustomed to dancing with Gabriel. His cologne was too strong, like leather and vetiver, and it stung deep in my nose. His hands were large and dry over mine, and though his grip was light, the Lethe in him made my skin crawl. Every time his icy fingers grazed me, I tensed, and the shadows that rimmed my sight and gathered on the floor shuddered. Acheron kept its watch on him, looming like a threat. And I refused to look him in the eye.

"The audition's over," Gabriel goaded at my side. "You can relax now."

Except I couldn't.

I could see now that it would help if I did, that my motions would become all the more fluid if I could figure out some way to just let loose. To just *dance*. But I didn't know how, or worse, what would happen if I did. I couldn't risk reaching into the depths and severing the chain of all I'd once been, and I didn't want to risk letting out something worse.

Because I could always be worse.

"You aren't being graded," Gabriel added, bemused when I stumbled over my feet. "Let go—"

I scowled and spun in front of him. "Please stop talking."

His smirk didn't fade. He was nonchalant, and teasing me was the most easygoing I'd ever seen him.

*Figures.*

Soon, the part I hated most came to fruition: performing in groups. Two or three pairs at a time took turns dancing for the rest of the room, adding their own flairs, being not just dancers but *performers*. They had the charisma, the smiles, the sultry glances and touches that made them compelling to watch. That reminded me why I'd ever loved this at all.

Meanwhile I couldn't bear to even *think* about caressing Gabriel's scratchy face. The bitter cold that lurked beneath.

When it came to us and the intro music, we treated it as a rehearsal only. Gabriel swayed to the music, eyes closed as if he'd been hypnotized by the smoky vocalist, and I rocked on my heels, back and forth to keep my nerves at a minimum, to keep from jumping out of my skin. Then we stepped into the music together with some semblance of coordination, though I still refused to meet Gabriel's eye and he did everything in his power to distract from my confused steps. Beside him, and much to my chagrin, my attempt at fluid motions especially paled.

The only thing I did excel at was the illusion of length. I could point my toes, keep the line of my legs smooth, and lean into beats well enough. When I raised my knee and kicked out my leg, Gabriel clamped one hand on my waist, another on my leg, and spun me around him. It took all the power in me just to lean back into his chest, but it worked, drawing out the lines of my body with some competence.

It was the first time the instructor nodded at me.

The first time I looked good.

The first time I looked . . . familiar. Traces of that old girl, the one I'd left behind, in the shape of me.

Then came applause, the same level as all the others, and I knew they weren't clapping for me. At this point, I was used to it.

I pulled my gaze away from my reflection, the glimpse I caught fading fast, and sagged my shoulders, just relieved it was over. What else did I expect? What more was I hoping for?

Gabriel clapped a hand on my shoulder and squeezed the back of my neck. Almost as if he knew how much my skin hurt around him and wanted to mess with me. "You know, you aren't bad, Laure. You're just a little brittle...A brittle ballerina."

Then he laughed and walked away, and I was left hearing those words ringing in my ears.

"Yes, I know," I muttered through gritted teeth into my bag as I packed it. I knew very well how stiff I was—we were in a room full of mirrors. I didn't need him to tell me.

I didn't need him to laugh at it.

Feeling both weird and irritable, I shifted to look at Vanessa. It had been more than a week since we last went out, and I could use the distraction. I needed it, I was ready to slip into the stream, drown out the noise before I either broke something or broke apart. Before anyone else realized I was a ceramic pot showing cracks.

"Hey!" I started, playing at chipper, flinging my bag over my shoulder. "Know of anything good going on tonight? I could use a break—"

Sill so absorbed in her phone, Vanessa didn't bother looking up as she shook her greasy head of hair. If she had, she might have noticed how my eyes narrowed onto her neck, onto the bruise near her collarbone, at the base of her throat. It was common as dancers to see bruises littering the body and bloodied toes and tights, signs of our endurance and dedication, but not there. There, where the skin was a rich purple and shaped like a blossom, it didn't make sense. It didn't come from dance.

Something in me—Acheron—shifted at the sight.

"Nope. Sorry."

And then she scurried away, her eyes weary and panicked as she weaved through the crowd. She didn't look happy, like someone slipping away to see a paramour. She looked scared. Worried. A look that screamed trouble.

I took a step to follow and chewed my lip. We weren't friends, Vanessa and I, and we'd never been. Her business was hers, and mine was mine, just like our relationship was restricted to parties where she didn't ask what I was running from or how I got what I wanted, and I never asked what she was looking for.

Well maybe now she'd found it, and I didn't want to be the one to take it from her just like, in some ways, we—Coralie, Lethe, Acheron, me— took Olivia and over a hundred others. We'd already taken enough.

# CHAPTER 18

Unsure what to do with myself after Vanessa blew me off, I hopped on the metro and decided to pay Keturah a visit at work. Her hours were unpredictable and hard to follow, but at the very least, her studio was positioned close to En boîte, and I told myself that if she wasn't available, in case she couldn't get away or didn't want to for a break, it wouldn't be *too* bad to dip into my old comfort with a bottle of prosecco. Even if it was just me and my lying shadow.

And really, all that mattered was that my mood was enduringly sour, and I didn't know where to dispel it. Partying alone didn't have the same glowing appeal, but the last thing I wanted to do was go home, alone but not, and replay everything Gabriel had said. Be reminded that I was brittle, that my mother wouldn't stop calling, and that I was just a small, naïve girl, incapable of choosing for myself. That Elysium was rotting while all I could do was wait. It'd take time for the trenches to do their magic, so my hands were tied.

I sure as hell wouldn't call Niamh for some company.

Twenty minutes and deflated shoulders later, I was chilling outside Keturah's office, sitting on the curb with my knees folded into my chest and waiting for her to step out. I didn't particularly mind the cold—it was bracing, especially to my muscles sore from dance. And the dark and the quiet, the way the streets gradually emptied as the sun set and the people fled to more exciting venues, didn't bother me either. The dark was great for thinking, for staring at my fast-growing shadow as it stared at me. It looked almost person-shaped now. And on *this* side of the mirror, no less.

**You judge yourself too harshly,** Acheron said, forgetting that I still hadn't forgiven it. That I still wasn't *talking* to it.

"You didn't tell me about Elysium or my mother," I snapped instead, resting my chin on my knees. "I'm judging *you*."

It didn't react. It didn't have the features to react. There was only a beat of silence as we watched each other, willing the other to break first, and then it said more softly, **Would it have mattered?**

I scoffed. "Yes! She thinks you're using me, that I'm too childish to see it. I'm not your pawn, *Nyarla*."

**What does it matter, the word of a stranger? Don't I have your trust?**

"Not when you don't tell me anything."

Because that was the problem—not that my mother waltzed into my life and cast doubt on everything, but that there was doubt to be cast in the first place. I wouldn't have to believe her or spend hours at the library studying plant death and fungi if Acheron explained *some*thing. I was tired of being in the dark.

The shadows only frizzed in response, the current moving and shifting and folding in on itself, even as the overall frame of it remained inhumanely still.

"Like what's happening with Elysium," I nudged, hating how petulant I sounded. Needy. Immature. Should I have had to grovel for information when Acheron was using my body? Was this what it expected from a vessel?

**Elysium may not survive the change it is undergoing, but I am change, and I will always be the Daemon King. Nyarla, child of Azathoth, the one who brought you back. A little gratitude would be nice.**

I couldn't help but brood. Without Acheron, I'd be dead alongside Coralie, and it hadn't even asked for much—blood grew back, but I still had all my bones at least. I couldn't tell what was stopping me from feeling grateful then.

"And we're in this together? As a *team*?"

It shuddered its wordless assent.

"So that means I chose you, right? Of my own free will? And Niamh too?" The words came out a whisper, and I averted my gaze to the dust I brushed from my shoes. "Or was it predetermined because of whatever my mom did?"

Acheron's silence lasted so long that I wondered if it hadn't heard. If it was ignoring me. Or maybe it just didn't want to say.

And then finally, it spoke. **I carry the mantle of chaos. Your path is predetermined in that, like everything, you have an infinite number of paths. You go where you will go. You become what chaos has decided you will become.**

I felt myself nodding, unsure if that was what I wanted to hear, but at least it wasn't what I *didn't* want to hear. Even if I didn't understand it. Maybe, for all my daring, Acheron was still unknowable, even to me. For all my pretense of taming the dark, shadowy thing in my body, I'd never know it at all, and I wasn't supposed to. Or perhaps it was still being cryptic, answers only leading to more questions of things it didn't want to divulge to me. Not yet, or ever.

"Hey, sorry, that took longer than expected," Keturah said in rushed breaths. She tied her jacket around her middle and nodded down the street. "You wait here long?"

Brushing the dirt from my hands, I shook my head and stood. "Never too long for coffee with you."

Then we were off, down the street in search of an evening latte for her and hot tea for me. She had another late night ahead of her, doing whatever sound engineers do, but it didn't seem to matter much that she stepped out in between runs for quick breaks here and there with friends.

Of which I was still one.

**For now**, Acheron supplied plainly. **Until she sees the real you in all your glory.**

"So, how's dance going?" she asked as we fell into step beside each other, not noticing how my nostrils flared. How I glared down at my shadow. "Are they signing the entire company over to you yet because you're so good?"

I couldn't help but scoff. "No, I'm terrible."

Her shoulder bumped mine. "Oh, don't say that—"

"No, I'm actually terrible," I insisted, tossing in a shrug for good measure. "He called me a brittle ballerina today. And you know what? He's right. I *am* brittle."

Keturah tilted her head.

"I'm not very good because I can't loosen up. And I'm brittle from trying so hard to keep it together. If I loosen the reins, I don't know what'll come out." It felt good to say it aloud, to throw it all out there even if Keturah didn't get it.

She weaved her arm through mine, pity nestled in the galaxy of her brown eyes, and turned us onto a big boulevard. Then finally in a soft voice, she said, "Maybe you need to forget about what everyone will think, and stop using Acheron as a crutch. We're not going anywhere."

With a flourish, she raised the sleeve on her forearm to expose the smooth skin underneath. Despite all the whorls of tattoos, it was easy to spot the absence where a red river used to be. And how all I smelled on her was shea butter and peppermint, rather than sensing the electricity crackling in her every step.

She was so good, the only one who wasn't a monster, who managed to keep herself completely, and I didn't know if I deserved her. But that twinkle in her eyes, her smile, the soft timbre of her voice—she may be mortal now, but I'd still kill for her, easily. No one, not Coralie, my mother, Acheron, would take her away.

I didn't bother to fight down the smile. "How do you feel?"

"Good!" She stretched her arms. "It was just a break I needed after Joey and then things ending with my ex—I told you about Céleste. I'm still catching up to all those feelings I missed, but I like being vulnerable. And speaking of vulnerable, how'd it go with your mom?"

As she grinned, my smile faded to nothing. To a glower.

"That bad, huh?" She sighed and strolled into the café when I opened the door.

I followed and groped around for a change of subject. "Did I tell you I looked into Niamh?"

Her brows raised.

"There was an arson that killed a woman named Lozach near Brest, in Brétagne. Her daughter is the suspected culprit, but she disappeared the night it happened."

None of the articles talked about a motive, why a fourteen-year-old girl would intentionally burn down a house with her mother inside. And because she was so young, there wasn't any detail about her—if she'd gotten in trouble before, if this was an isolated incident, if her mother was the actual monster.

Standing in line and waiting to order, I crossed my arms. "But for all we know, it could be a misunderstanding. I mean, if I was framed, I'd go into hiding too."

I didn't know why I was defending her. Maybe there *was* more to it, hidden in the way she'd talked about Palais Rose. Why she was there, enshrouded in gaudy wealth, trying to surround herself with petty people who thought themselves gods. Maybe she was trying to build a family to replace the one she lost. Or maybe it was just wishful thinking on my part, so I didn't have to feel guilty for being wrong.

Keturah pursed her lips. "Maybe we just should stay out of it. Forget I saw anything."

I shook my head. "I'll try to talk to her. Ask her about it. Maybe we misunderstood—"

"I'm not interested in understanding anyone with *servants*," she retorted, waving her hands and stepping up to the barista. After placing our orders, she turned to me. "So, where are you going next? Off to some party?"

The best I could offer was another noncommittal shrug. I still hadn't made up my mind, whether to throw on the only nice thing I had in my bag or go home to an apartment that still had Ciro's touch all over it. Haunted by the ghost of my dead self or haunted by the aftermath of Coralie's havoc. To the boy connecting us through life and death who couldn't get over that I'd died too, that the wicked dark was a part of me and neither of us could escape. Dancing in some hot, crowded club, drenched in sweat and bass, sounded exactly like what I wanted and what I didn't have the energy for.

Rather than answer, I just looked at her. *Really* looked at her. She was taller than me, with a fuller figure, all curves and warmth and soft, clear skin. Even her belly, peeking out from beneath her cropped hoodie, was decorated in tattoos, in an intricate floral and snake pattern that caught the eye. The lip studs, dramatic and heavy eyeliner, and violet curls that fell into her face.

Watching me watching her.

I swallowed and took the coffee from her hand. "Sorry."

And Keturah just cocked her head and smiled, like she could read thoughts I wasn't even thinking. Wherever this was going, I was too much of a mess to figure it out.

We later parted with our goodbyes, and the farther I retreated down the street, the more confused I felt. Not by *Keturah*—she made sense, being kind and brave and like rays of sunlight on a free afternoon. Or even Andor, all brooding flowers and bright paints. I more so didn't understand what *I* was doing, what *I* wanted, where *I* was going. With both of them. Even as my feet carried me toward familiar territory, the thump of club music traveling up the sidewalk and into my soles, I felt more lost.

En boîte had a line, as usual, everyone shivering in their very flashiest, ready for the heat inside. The chatter of eager partygoers was a welcome sound that, as I got closer, lessened my desire to go inside. They made apparent how tired I was. How all this running made me just want to sleep.

Glimpsing the crowd, I was drawn to two familiar people talking beneath the lamppost. It was hard to miss the harsh tone of Niamh's hair, which she'd styled in tight curls. She looked bright, in makeup and lipstick, a soft pink dress I quite liked hugging the square of her body. I might have owned one just like it. And she talked animatedly with a blur of dark, shiny hair, the wiry body of a ballerina I recognized instantly.

Vanessa.

There was an intimacy in how they regarded each other, how Niamh reached out to brush her fingers against the bare skin of Vanessa's pale arm. The glint in Niamh's eye, real or imagined, like a hungry fox spotting a rabbit. Vanessa only smiled and leaned into the touch, not knowing she should run. Because this was probably who she'd been texting, who she was too focused on to hold a conversation.

My chai suddenly took on a bitter taste as I thought about the bruise.

Just as I backed away, Niamh glanced up, past Vanessa, and spotted me. As if she could sense me here the way I sensed her. It was a brief look, cold and sharp and wicked. Telling me something I didn't understand. Acheron understood, though. It shifted in my skin and at my feet, like she was talking to it directly. And it stirred a little faster, like it didn't care for whatever she'd said.

"What is it?" I mumbled, watching Niamh nod her head. She and Vanessa peeled away from the pole and sauntered to the door. "What's going on?"

**She wants more than she can have**, Acheron hummed in my muscle.

The pair walked closely together, Niamh's arm draped possessively over Vanessa's shoulder with the message clear: *Stay away*. They were already inside by the time I managed to unroot myself, and then I was turning back. I could warn Vanessa, but what would I say? Would I explain to her what Niamh was like, dangerous and unencumbered? That we were the same kind of predator? That everything Vanessa thought she felt was fake? That Niamh had crossed two dead people so far?

No, with the way I kept talking to her, Vanessa would only think I was obsessive or spying on her. We didn't *have* that kind of relationship. If I just warned her that Niamh was someone to avoid, would she listen? And if I went to Niamh, would that go any better?

**What is a mortal to you?** Acheron asked lazily. **Remember when you hated her, wanted her punished?**

"Things change." I tossed my cup into the nearest trash can and retreated, to the metro, onto a train, all the way to the 14th arrondissement, to home. The longer I stayed out here, avoiding everything, afraid of everything, the worse I felt. I was sick of treading water—what I needed was a break, to regroup in the morning when I could see clearly.

Andor was moving around furniture in the living room when I carried myself up the stairs and through the door. Everything was in disarray, the couch shoved into the center of the room with plastic over it, the TV and stand pushed up against it. More plastic tarp covered the floor, and he paused from lifting picture frames from the wall to smile at me.

"Hey," he said softly, as if he could tell I was close to shattering and couldn't stand the volume. As gentle as a caress.

"Hi." I dropped my bag on the floor. "Moving on to a bigger canvas?"

He nodded and extended a hand as I approached. A hand. For me. I saw the hesitation in it, the trembling, how closely he studied me when I took it. But he didn't take it back. I wondered if he was measuring poison doses right now.

"I was thinking the walls need a new color," said Andor with a grimace. "No one loves white as much as Ciro. *Loved.*"

I brought his knuckles to my lips and smiled at the tingle. His hands had the wear and tear of use, of calluses from drawing and gardening tools, cracks from always scrubbing paint and dirt from his skin, nicks from the razors he used to sharpen his pencils, all from before his deals. I loved all of it. All of him. "Want some help?"

# CHAPTER 19

There was no sign of Vanessa in class the next day. It was odd, knowing her from the academy, where she'd even come in with the flu, but I decided not to put too much stock into it. A doctor's appointment, a visit from her family, maybe too much to drink the night before.

So I shot her a text. Light and simple, not too worrisome or clingy or forceful. *Hey, when you get a chance, can we talk? Face-to-face.* I didn't want to risk spilling anything in text, anything that could incriminate me or that Niamh might see. It felt neutral enough.

Then I put my focus on rehearsal. We began working on a new piece, some feral and animalistic combination Gabriel choreographed with a lot of slow, prowling movements, relying on the tone of muscles to appear other. Different.

"This is going to be a weird one," he prefaced.

But I tried to have fun, to not think about Niamh, or Vanessa, or Elysium, even while I still felt awkward in my skin. In the mirror, I looked like a puppet with the strings all tangled, despite Gabriel's encouragements. Maybe because of them.

Acheron stood behind me like a ghoul, tall and motionless no matter how much I writhed and crawled. My control over my movements was both too much and too little, but I was *trying* at least. Even if unsuccessfully. And for once, some of the others were struggling to make any sense of it too.

**I admire your persistence**, crooned Acheron during the break. I chose you for a reason, even if you cannot see it. Even if you mistrust me.

"I don't mistrust you," I mumbled automatically into my water bottle before we went back at it. I was saying that a lot, I found.

When Gabriel dismissed us for the day, I checked my phone for a reply while packing my bag, thinking of nothing but the comfort of a hot lavender bath. But there was still nothing from Vanessa. The message was left on read, but no speech bubble indicated a response in progress. Not even a thumbs-up react to let me know she'd acknowledged it.

Just silence.

Her social accounts had gone quiet since the weekend too—not a single video, photo, inane thought—when she'd been impossible to silence before. Always talking about her sister who married a real Italian prince, her brother-in-law and all his gifts. Now there was nothing. It was so unsettling that I didn't notice Gabriel's approach behind me, didn't attribute the skin crawling and shadows dispersing to his proximity until he cleared his throat.

I jumped and whirled around.

"Laure, good job today."

I snorted. "Are you joking? I was terrible."

Gabriel shrugged. "Everyone is terrible when it's something new. I think you did well, considering. Anyway, I have a special assignment for you," he said quite grandly, his chin high, the hint of a smile on his narrow mouth. I couldn't tell yet if it was a joke. "How good are you en pointe?"

It took me a moment to process, because of all the assignments I expected, they were all snarky or barbed, like taking a sedative. Going to a spa. Quitting. But dancing *en pointe*? I could do all the warm-ups, prep the shoes, and channel those muscles in my sleep.

It was what I'd always dreamed of doing, what I'd loved most about being a ballerina: the prestige of employing this illusion of legs so long, feet so small and sharpened to a point, so inhuman and ethereal that we merely glided across the floor. We fluttered, transcended our bodies in real time. No effects or tricks of light necessary. We were real, mortal magic.

My eyes narrowed. "Good . . . Why?"

"Great. I have a part for you, I'll teach on Monday? Bring your shoes?" He raised his brows with as much eagerness as his stern face could show.

And I couldn't squelch my suspicion. Why would he want anything from me when I was so bad? Why did he even keep me around, wasting money on my salary when he could just fire me and bring in someone less brittle, more pliable? Even if I danced at the very back of the stage, I was a risk.

But I accepted his challenge, knowing that meant going back to the 19th to get my stuff. If he thought he could trick me, or embarrass me, I wouldn't fall for it. If there was anything I could do well, it was dance en pointe.

Then he went his way, into the depths of the building where his offices lay, and I went mine, stepping outside into the night. The sky was remarkably clear for the coming spring, and the air unseasonably warm. The day's rehearsal ran late too, leaving the streets empty enough for a comfortable walk. No darting around tourists and their numerous Chanel bags on the way to the metro.

"Think he's up to something?" I asked, not bothering to glance at my shadow or say its name. I didn't have to.

Stalking alongside me now, Acheron considered the question, measured its words. **Nothing beyond your faculties, I'm sure.**

A nonanswer. *Why did I bother?*

It took about three or four blocks before I noticed a current in the air. It was a pull that latched itself behind my navel, tapped into my core programming, and carried me along. Reeled me in before I even realized I was caught. It was the scent of ozone and the prickle of static, traveling up the back of my neck as I shifted to actively following it. Tracking it like a predator. As strong as the perfume of fresh bread from the bakery in the morning.

"What is that?"

**It is you**, replied Acheron, craning its head-shaped blob in the same direction. Another nonanswer. **It is me.**

My coat buzzed from the vibrating phone in my pocket, but my concentration hardly wavered. I barely glimpsed the screen, yet another incoming call from a number I didn't recognize, before I hit answer and hurriedly put it to my ear.

More important was that pull—what was it? And if Acheron wasn't nervous, why was I?

"Hello?" I mumbled absently, rounding another corner and picking up my pace.

"You're hard to get ahold of. If I didn't know better, I'd say you were avoiding me."

My feet tripped over themselves at the sound of my mother's voice. There was amusement in her tone, like she wanted to provoke me. Like she knew how angry I was, and it entertained her. Like she knew what I wanted and wouldn't give it to me just because of how much I wanted it. An apology. Some fucking remorse. She'd go on pretending this relationship right into a grave.

I shifted the phone to the other ear. "Usually when people don't answer your calls, it's because they don't want to talk to you."

She didn't miss a beat. "Is that so?"

Around another corner.

"Look, I don't want to argue with you, Laurence," my mother started with a sigh. But that amusement was still there. Still trying to push me toward something. "I just wanted to give you my new number. I've decided to stay in Paris awhile longer."

With the street devoid of cars, I darted across, ignoring the red traffic light. The pull was growing stronger, so thick that I felt it on the roof of my mouth, on the nape of my neck, the hairs on my arms. Something was happening, and I'd miss it if I didn't move fast. Acheron paced itself beside me.

"I hope we can have a relationship now that—"

"You can choke," I snapped, before ending the call. And with the phone in my fist, I was running now, because this was more interesting, less infuriating than whatever performance my mother was putting on.

My arms were pumping by my sides, feet shouting in protest when I finally heard them. Saw them.

There was the muffle of a high whine, the chitter of laughter. Four figures huddled in the dark of a narrow alleyway, but the mere presence of them flashed under my skin like a beacon, like they were signaling for Acheron.

For me.

I slowed but kept wading closer.

"This is what they're meant to do," one of the voices was saying, and it was the smooth, lilting tenor of a voice I'd heard before.

Then I saw his face, the waves of his shoulder-length hair, the muscle through his tight clothes. Dominique. He had a malicious grin on his face as he regarded a woman forced to kneel before him, and he was flanked by Salomé, the pale and serpentine woman, who watched on hungrily.

The kneeling woman was held in place by someone I barely recognized, someone who looked familiar but not entirely. The figure had traces of lankiness, but there was some early definition to the muscle too, like a starving street cat, some structure to the jaw carving away at once-round cheeks. His red hair was still the same, but the rest of Florian had changed. He'd matured in just a matter of a couple weeks.

None of them saw me creep closer.

In the ensuing struggle, as the woman railed against Florian's grip on her hair, lamplight fell on her face and I clapped a hand to my own.

She had no mouth.

The place where her mouth should have been, where lips and teeth and tongue should have been trying to scream was all skin—*smooth* skin. Ghoulish. She was mumbling, pleading, whimpering because she couldn't beg. She'd been changed, somehow, and they didn't look at all concerned.

Cold sweat slid down my sides.

"Go ahead, Salomé," Dominique nudged. "Show her your true face."

At his cue, Salomé glitched. It was the same kind of static that I'd seen countless times watching Andor switch back and forth between the mortal boy and the monster Acheron had made. I'd soaked in the towering antlers as they'd flickered on his skull, his face growing longer, body taller and wider. His teeth transformed to shards of broken glass. His eyes went from two to four, sclerae white to inky black. I relished in the dark delight of such a vision.

And now Salomé was doing it too, but with none of Andor's beauty. She flashed once, twice, and then a third time, and each time her face sharpened, the sockets of her eyes emptied and hollow, her fingers sharpened to claws. Fine needlepoints protruded from her skin.

The woman on the ground tried to scream but went mostly unheard. She shook with the effort. Liquid ran from her eyes, too dark to be tears.

I pressed into the wall and whispered, "Acheron, what were they—"

"You're not doing it for long enough," protested Florian loudly.

Salomé shook her head. "If you show them your face for too long, they die on the spot. I told you we're not meant for mortal eyes." Then she put her hands on her narrow hips and studied the woman for a long time. "I can make her…" She twirled a finger around her temple and whistled. "Enough so she starts wandering around, ranting, totally losing it."

At this, he perked up. "Go for it. If she gets too loud, I can always remove her vocal cords."

I propelled from the shadows as casually as I could. "What do you think you're doing?"

Florian flinched at my voice. Salomé's gaze snapped up in surprise. Dominique didn't stir at all. He took the longest to look at me, and he didn't appear even remotely guilty. And I didn't miss how they all relaxed when they saw it was just me, comforted that I was one of them.

But I wasn't.

As I neared, I got a better look at the streaks running down the poor woman's face. The tears were purely blood, and up close her lack of mouth felt even more gruesome. She was a clay model for Florian to mold, probably just like he'd changed himself, and she was powerless to stop him.

I looked away to avoid the nausea stirring in the pit of my stomach.

Dominique extended a hand toward the woman. "She thinks she's too good to bow. To submit. She doesn't know a god when she sees one. Or three."

"We get bored, cooped up in the house all day—" Salomé shrugged.

"You mean the *mansion* where you all squat?" I quipped before I could stop myself, and at once, I watched their ease turned to defense. Their indifference transformed to glares as they all hardened. "Leave her alone."

Dominique frowned and shook his head. "Thanks for the suggestion, but no thanks, *vessel.*"

"For now," Salomé added, and they all erupted into giggles.

If the jab was supposed to make me uncomfortable, it succeeded. They made it sound like I was a teacher's pet, a spoilsport, a snitch, and I'd get what's coming too. Somehow I was the asshole for ruining their fun, raining on their parade of menacing an innocent woman for their egos.

With a flick of Dominique's wrist, there was a low *pop* that came from the woman's body, accompanied by a smothered shriek and cry from her walled-off mouth. Then another, and another, sickening cracks I recognized but couldn't place. That made me wince.

I grabbed his arm. "I said knock it off!"

Salomé continued to snicker and rolled her eyes, like my resistance was funny. Like I was a *child*. "Just mind your business—"

The fire was kindled before she finished spitting the word. It roared in my ears, the shadows, Acheron's power at my fingertips, in my eyes, on my tongue. It filled me up and looked for victims to consume whole. All of me hummed with power and settled on them in the flash of a second.

**"Change her back and fuck** *off*," Acheron and I sneered. We spoke as one, my alto and something much deeper, two of us interwoven and overlapping. Acheron infusing my words with more than ever before, showing them what it meant to be a vessel. That we weren't the same caliber.

And indeed, they paled and stiffened. Their eyes didn't glaze over, but they peeled away quickly, one after another, and the flesh covering the woman's mouth dissolved, melting like grease, until her weeping was all I heard beneath the inferno in my blood. In only seconds, she was freed, and she collapsed on the ground, clutching three broken fingers to her chest. I recognized the welt and swelling, felt the throb of her skin as if it was my own, it was so loud. Even as, from this wall of power, a storm of shadow and rage, her pain was both familiar and entirely alien to me.

Dominique did that with just a flick of his wrist.

Like tearing the wings from flies, holding a magnifying glass over a colony of ants. They were going to torture this woman using all Acheron and Lethe had given them, just like Niamh had done in the club. And *I'd* enabled her. I let her get away with it, and now there were more in her stead. Did they teach it to her, or did she teach it to them? And for what?

"Come on," Dominique called flatly. "We got what we came for, anyway."

He stepped right over the woman's body as she curled in the fetal position, and all their eyes locked on me in open defiance as I forced them away. In their eyes, I became a bleeding-heart hero for the same mortals who had once cast us all out.

Yet I held my ground, my arms crossed, my ears roaring, my eyes seeing red. I didn't know how I'd looked, how monstrous I appeared on the outside compared to the swell of seething within, but they didn't try to challenge me. The woman on the ground was trembling, gaping up into the light like I was a fearsome angel instead of the devil I knew myself to be. Like I was born for this.

**You look glorious by the way**, Acheron murmured, looking me over, grinning proudly from its shapeless face.

# CHAPTER 20

"'*Your call is important to us*,'" I repeated in time with the robotic voice. "'*Please hold.*'"

I paced along the empty street outside of the old, Gothic church, waiting for the police to pick back up. The hold line's music was nondescript but repetitive, with a reminder timed every couple minutes to ratchet up my nerves. Did they have something to share or didn't they? Why did it take this long to know?

Between my own sleeplessness and Andor's bad dreams, I spent much of the night thinking about the woman I'd saved. Her cursed face, warped without a mouth so no one could hear her scream, the real, live flickering monsters who hovered over her in the dark, the sound of her cracking bones. And because Salomé had talked about her true face, I couldn't help but think of the girl in the silver dress from En boîte. The same bloody tears rolling down her face as she sat, dead in an instant.

Both of them had Niamh at the center.

**What do you expect to find?** asked Acheron, its full, shadowy figure propped against the wall like a real person. Even its humming, blurred legs crossed casually at the ankles.

I stared, my mind tripping over itself at the uncanniness of it. How wrong it looked. But then there was a click and a stern voice on the other end before I could conjure an answer.

"Yes, hello? Miss Mesny?"

My legs drew up short. "Yes. I'm Laure Mesny. I'm here—"

"I'm sorry, but I can't provide an update on last night's victim, as it's part of an ongoing investigation." The officer's voice was impatient, enough to make my breath catch. There was more to what had happened than they wanted to share.

I cleared my throat. "Did they tell you I'm the one who found her? Who called it in—"

"Yes, I know," they snapped. "Look, the fact still remains that there's an open investigation, so we cannot share any details on the matter or private information about the victim. As for the other case you mentioned, the girl at the nightclub, En boîte?"

"Yeah?"

Their voice was obscured with the crackling static of papers, but I could still hear them: "The Palais de Justice intern's cause of death was a drug overdose."

Acheron tilted its head. My brow knit in confusion, as I remembered how I'd found her. Sure, she'd seemed a little wasted as she flitted off to the bathroom, but what drug froze you in fear? What made your mouth hang open and your tear ducts overrun with blood? No, impossible, that was eldritch.

I shook my head. "That doesn't make sense."

The officer sighed. "Well, that's what the report says."

"Well, can you tell me her name? What—"

"That's all. Thanks."

There came another click, one that said the call was over and that was the best they'd offer. Did they care at all or were they out of their element, trying to comprehend a sudden death in a nightclub followed by a woman who swore she had no mouth? Would Niamh and her friends just get away with it, menacing every mortal in their path?

*You* did, Acheron pointed out. **And why would a god apologize for the storm in its wake? Does the falcon apologize to the mouse before it dines?**

I squeezed the phone in my grip, picked up the container of kerosene, and headed inside without another word. The last thing I wanted was to be compared to Niamh, a petty god on a mean streak. I'd had *drive*. Purpose. I didn't step on people just because I could. I didn't burn down my own home with my mother in it and kill innocent girls at a club for laughs.

**No, but you did drown your best friend amid the ruins of your house of worship.**

In the dark of the tunnel, I whirled around to glare. And even in the dark, I felt Acheron reconsider its gleeful tone. "Whose side on your on?!"

**Apologies.** And then more softly—fondly?—it added, **You are doing well. Better than you give yourself credit for.**

Then it dissipated, leaving me to cross into Elysium alone. I'd originally planned to do these rounds with Keturah, to walk along the trenches and see if anything we did had worked. But after my stumbling upon Dominique and the others, Elysium couldn't wait for the end of her shift—I needed something to make them leave the city, get them far away from the world *now*. Before they did something worse, before more blood they spilled splashed me.

The blowtorch in my backpack shifted as I descended the meadow, a loud, rattling reminder of what I had to do if the trenches didn't work. Fungicides and bactericides only worked for one or two trees, but they wouldn't save a forest. So if we couldn't cut away the infection,

I figured the next best was to burn it. If Elysium came from the body of a proto-god that once walked this earth in olden days, then I'd treat it like one.

A crop of soggy, golden hair waved at me as I approached, and before I knew it, Coralie was standing by my side, hands shoved in the pockets of her dingy hoodie. As if she'd been waiting patiently for my return while I was busy playing dancer again.

"I don't see why you're doing all of this instead of just letting it go like Gabriel said." Her tone was arrogant as always.

"You don't just quit things because they aren't working," I explained, marching past her.

"Isn't that exactly why you quit the ballet?"

I glowered. "No. I tried to make the ballet work. I tried to *fix* things there, just like I'm trying here. And how do you know what Gabriel told me?"

Coralie shrugged. "I'm part of you. Or you're part of me. Or he's part of me. I don't know, the void doesn't exactly hand out a manual."

Instead of parsing whatever that meant, I tuned her out. All of this, I was doing to save Elysium, heal the forest, and maybe Niamh and her ilk would leave Palais Rose. They'd surrender Paris because their true home would be safe again. They could be gods here. Reign here. And also, this was my home too—how long had it been since I walked along the river? How long before this was another thing I lost?

Coralie kept her chatter to a minimum until we passed the tall walls of Andor's labyrinth, when I started to recognize the feeling. It was in the ground, in the air, a sign of warning that made my skin writhe. My fingers again scratched idly at the mark on my arm until I forced myself to stop.

Because if I felt it so strongly so soon, there was a bigger problem.

"So, what's it like on the other side?" Coralie asked brightly, grabbing my attention. "A job all on your own, a new apartment, *Andor*?"

I shook my head. "I'm not talking to you about Andor. If you want to talk so much, why don't you tell me why I can see you?"

The hands that switched to swinging by her side slowed to a stop before she clasped them. "Do you remember when we met? In Madame Gagneux's school when we were, like, seven?"

"No, *you* were seven. I was six. You were a year ahead, remember?" I corrected quietly, distractedly, taking note of the squelch under my boots. It was a bad sign, especially as the trenches were still ahead. Which meant the infection was spreading; it'd jumped the trenches in a matter of days.

Though I didn't particularly want to venture down memory lane with my dead best friend, it was better than discussing my sort-of boyfriend. Andor and I still hadn't had that talk.

And those earlier years with Coralie were sweeter. The ballet hadn't sharpened us as weapons against each other yet, and we were still naïve enough to believe we weren't each other's competition. That we could both be primas on a shared stage. Two Giselles, two Juliettes, two Auroras and Esmeraldas and Cinderellas. It was a fantasy we'd shared until it transformed into a shard.

Coralie snickered. "Everyone hated us."

My mouth twitched with a smile I resisted. Even that young, I stood out, like there was a feral aura that repelled the other kids in our group. They all had their own friends, and I stood apart at the barre, practicing my posture like a robot in the mirror.

And nobody else wanted to be friends with the rich little crybaby whose mom always hovered.

"Not that it mattered once we had each other," I replied, squinting all around.

Still water began to gather at my heels, muddied and full of dead, floating bugs. Then the trees were once again dotted with white. The bark hadn't started peeling in this section yet, not so soon, and the branches were still stiff and high, but not for long. All of this was proof that the trenches had failed miserably. The spread wasn't slowed or curbed or in control.

So without other options, I began splashing kerosene at the base of the healthy trees. One of the journals on forest management talked about the value of controlled burns, where people actually set fire to parts of the woods to clear the old growth and make room for the new. There was a lot of work involved with setting up the blackline, some section of burned area so that the fire didn't cross. I had to start amputating before Elysium went septic.

Only with less resources, I had to hope that accelerant and Acheron as a border would be enough. A blood river couldn't burn, could it?

Coralie sat out of reach of the muck, drawing her knees to her chest. "Do you remember how we clung to each other on that first day? You begged your mom to come with me, and I demanded my mom let you come to our house."

"They couldn't stand each other."

The very thought made laughter bubble out of me: Rose-Marie cornered into being polite for her daughter's only friend, and Alexandra, who knew more than her and wasn't shy about letting it show. They hardly managed to be on the same side of a room together, but we didn't care. We put on mock ballets and played with each other's hair and ate ice cream all the same. And I pretended not to notice how Rose-Marie relaxed when my mother stopped showing up.

Words heavy, Coralie said, "We never wanted to be apart."

Now it was my turn to roll my eyes and keep chucking kerosene.

"Is that your reason? Some childhood promise to stalk me in the afterlife?"

"I'm trying to help you," she replied with a hint of exasperation.

"Were you helping me when you stabbed me in the heart? Literally?"

She climbed to her feet. "You know I'd never kill you. I never wanted to kill you, Laure, even if I got carried away. Can you say the same? Can *Acheron?*"

I dropped the empty kerosene container down at my side, more forceful than I intended. The frustration was spilling out of me, at her cryptic behavior, Acheron's incessant pruning, at the world above that was rivaling this rot as my biggest problem. I didn't want to play any more games, unravel any more puzzles.

"If you want to help me, tell me how to stop this."

Her glassy eyes stared long and hard at me.

If she were alive, her round cheeks would flush red, and her pointed chin would wrinkle a little as she pursed her lips. I'd memorized all the minutiae of her irritation over the years, and it was this that kept reminding me she wasn't real. Alive. For all the memories she recalled, this wasn't *my* Coralie. This was a figment of Coralie frozen in death.

"You can't," she stated before dropping her gaze. And then more gently, she mumbled, "That's what I've been trying to tell you. Everything comes to an end, Laure. Even a living god-corpse. Even us. You just have to move through it."

I fetched the blowtorch from my backpack. "Wrong answer."

Then I proceeded to set the forest aflame.

Coralie moved to stand beside me as we watched the fire shift from blue to red, catching and spreading along the kerosene trail. It licked at the bottom of strong, sturdy trees and devoured those with white spots on exposed roots. It ravaged the dusting of molded leaves and soggy carcasses. It skated along the receding shoreline of Acheron, illuminating the pallor of its slowing stream.

"Just don't trust anyone or anything, okay? No matter what it says." Her imploring sounded louder this time, pointed, snagging my attention long enough to see her glance over her shoulder too. Almost in the direction of the blood river.

# CHAPTER 21

The last time I came to the apartment I shared with Coralie in the 19th, in an unremarkable building along Avenue de Flandre, was the morning before I died. It was not long after Coralie had tortured me. I woke up in the hospital, scarred and recovering from hypothermia, and decided then that the ballet wasn't worth the fear. Not worth the misery and obsession, the glamorous pain and loneliness, not when it had propelled Coralie to a zealous state, and when none of them had even wished me well. So I'd come then only to pack a bag to save myself, and then I went on to the ballet, where I met my end.

Andor and I stood outside of the apartment now, the rusted metal gate waiting silently for me to come inside. It wasn't poorly maintained, but it *was* well-worn. More than Ciro's, historic and preserved. Looking at it made me think of every time Rose-Marie had wrinkled her nose, especially when we first found it, how proud we were to claim it. It was a far cry from their massive apartment in the 2nd, but for me, it had been an upgrade. And it was close to the ballet. And it was *ours*.

"We don't have to go in if you're not ready," said Andor gently, his shoulder brushing against mine. And I knew he meant it, that he wouldn't judge me if I just handed him the keys and marched back to Riquet Station without another word.

Certainly it would be easier to abandon this place and never think of it again. Discard all the clothes and photographs and letters and jewelry, all the mementos I'd managed to hold on to, pain that I could avoid. What if I found something I couldn't come back from?

I tightened my fist on the keys and charged forward. "No, it's fine. I need those shoes for Gabriel. And Keturah's coming over later to watch a movie, remember? I can't take all day."

The gate's whine was the same, as was the smell of plant mold that clung to the inner courtyard. This place, like most in the city, still refused to adapt to elevators, so we climbed the linoleum stairs all the way to my door that looked inconspicuous with its sameness. Yet I felt like a stranger.

The apartment inside was a time capsule.

In some ways, when I opened the door, I still expected to see Coralie there. Sitting on one of the bar stools we'd used in the kitchen, munching down on cold pizza or whatever sickeningly sweet dessert she grabbed from a bakery on her way home. I expected her shoes to block the door, her bag thrown in the entrance, dirty socks on the couch. There'd be some sweaty bolero from the day's lessons laid over the back of the chair, and the air would smell like muscle cream and her favorite lemon verbena soap.

But instead, everything was…in boxes. There were no shoes in the entrance, nor the little queer pride welcome mat we'd put down. Unlabeled brown boxes sat half-open and stacked in the kitchen and living room, surrounding the suspiciously empty furniture. The plants along the windowsill were dying, desiccated and crunchy from their months without water. The TV was packed away, lamps wrapped in foam.

While I was gone, Rose-Marie had swept all traces of Coralie away.

I draped my coat across the arm of the couch and waded deeper. Over my shoulder, I called out, "Take whatever you think we'll need. Whatever you want, really."

Both bedroom doors were closed, and I braced myself for whatever I'd find inside mine. Did Rose-Marie tell someone to pack my things too, or did she expect me to come back and do it myself? Did she ever plan to say? I hadn't seen her since her speech at the memorial.

And everything in that room, I'd buried along with the girl I left at La Madeleine. It all belonged to my ghost.

With my hand hovering over the doorknob, I listened as Andor began to sort through boxes behind me. It was supposed to be me and Niamh, in the hopes I'd talk her out of this violent streak she and her friends were in, but naturally she'd bailed.

"The whole point of being chosen is to live like *actual* gods," she lectured when I'd called. "It's the mortals who should do our laundry, clean up after us, pack our shit. Serve us the way they're intended."

It sounded like a recruiting pamphlet for a cult, so much so that I only scowled and just hung up instead of replying. What was the point?

When I swung the door open and saw the state of my bedroom, something in me deflated. All of it was untouched, exactly as I had left it when I fled. The books were still on the shelves and arranged alphabetically, the bed neatly made, the desk clear, the closet arranged. There was only a thin layer of dust to suggest I didn't live here anymore. That perhaps my ghost had moved in and still did.

**You should know your fire-starting won't change the future of Elysium**, warned Acheron as it trailed inside behind me.

I glanced around and grimaced. "Then what will?"

Instead it only flickered, like it didn't *want* Elysium to be saved.

I took a peek at Coralie's room next. I didn't relish the idea of

Rose-Marie scolding someone to pack up my things, but I also didn't love the idea that I'd been left behind. And the finality of seeing Coralie's things put neatly away, fitting into four perfectly square boxes. Her mattress had been stripped of its sheets, her immaculate nightstand emptied and dresser drawers set aside.

There was nothing left of the girl I'd loved except for the ghoul who haunted my dreams and followed me around.

"Everything okay?" Andor's voice was muffled from the kitchen swallowing him whole.

"Peachy," I replied curtly before retreating back to my room and seizing one of the new, still-flattened cardboard boxes propped against my wall.

Acheron leaned close. **Why don't you tell him the truth? Is it because you know he won't accept the answer like I do?**

I felt the prickle of static at its proximity, like brushing against my father's old TV or touching a light switch after walking around in socks. The pain in my arm was surprising but fleeting, and though I flinched, I tried not to let it show. Acheron gave no notice that anything had happened, that it was growing stronger still.

There wasn't much on my desk or inside it—I was quick to toss anything from my studies that didn't revolve around ballet; and mementos of my first pointe shoes, the pair from *Giselle* as the last show I'd danced at the academy, and printed photos of Coralie and me didn't take up much space. I didn't keep many other trinkets, and never found the need to when Coralie was my only person and she was always right there. All that remained were old playbills and stretched-out hair ties.

Fragments of a life that couldn't exist anymore.

The clothes were the easiest to riffle through. I spent most of my life in leotards, sweatpants, and pullovers. The nice clothes—my pleated skirts and collared shirts and dresses—all fit in a single box. I didn't have much jewelry or many pairs of shoes either. I was lining the bottom of a box with my dozens of leotards when a shadow moved across the doorway.

Only this voice was soft. Human.

"So this is what your bedroom looks like, huh?" asked Andor, a wry smile on his face as he scanned the room. "Why am I not surprised?"

I felt myself mirror him, felt myself smiling in kind. "What does that mean?"

From my seat on the floor, I watched him venture closer, taking in the boxes and their contents, the books that remained on the shelves. I had an entire system for my tights, all delicately rolled in a variety of colors to resemble a bouquet of roses, and his fingers glided along the thin fabric before he settled beside me.

"It's very … severe." He said it with a laugh that made me feel all warm and light. "Ascetic."

Afraid of whatever giddy expression I wore, I turned away to keep filling the box. "I spent all my time in the studio, anyway."

Andor's long limbs danced around me as he assessed what was left, as I tried not to catalog his every movement. The air was perfumed with his scent, of rain in the forest and a top note of whatever oil paints he'd used in class today. There was the stain of blue in the shape of a thumbprint along his jaw, yellow dusting the edge of his collar. His curls bounced around his shoulders with every turn of his head. Then he dragged something from under my bed with interest.

"What's this?" he inquired, holding up a rattling plastic container full of brown markers. More than a hundred of them when I'd stopped counting.

Still pretending to focus on packing though I hadn't made any progress at all, I answered, "Exactly what they look like—brown markers. It used to be cheaper to buy pink pointe shoes and color them brown than order specialty ones that match my skin tone from abroad."

For a long time, he stared at me, and I saw that shadow of irritation flicking behind his dark eye. And behind him, sitting stiffly on the bed, was Acheron. Watching, silent, stoic. I could tell it didn't want him around, but *I* did.

"I thought the ballet paid for those?"

I listened to him pop off the lid and study all the markers that dried out. "For the academy, nope, nothing. And the company only paid for the pink."

He only scowled and muttered something like, "Fucking ballet," before he assembled a box himself and got to work on my books.

And I could only nod in agreement. It was what Keturah said anytime I told her about the ballet and what it was like, the rules on how we wore our hair, the tint of our nail polish, the instructor's disapproval at tattoos and blemishes. Their harshness, and vying for their approval regardless, was the necessary evil to survive a world I'd thought was inlaid with mother-of-pearl, and now I only felt foolish looking back. Seeing how easily they'd replaced me, how good it felt to see it all reduced to a pile of dust, I knew I was better to have left it all behind.

Even if I was lost now.

Even if there was no blueprint for grieving yourself, the girl you were supposed to be. I would have done it all over again too.

"Do you miss it?" Andor didn't look up from carefully extracting the biographies from the shelf. "I know you're dancing now, but do you miss that place?"

I pushed aside my clothes and sighed. There was no clear, clean answer to that: I hated it, and I missed it, just like I hated what Coralie did to me, but I missed curling up on the couch, watching crime dramas and cooking competitions with her. The smell of her shampoo was interlaced with the smell of my skin burning under her lighter, and for the ballet? Every good picture had blood spots and microfractures buried in it.

Sprawling on the floor, eyes trained on the plain, wood ceiling, I shrugged. "Well, the hours were grueling, and the strain it put on my body was unbelievable, but...Spinning and floating and gliding across a stage? *That* was the closest I'd ever been to godhood, I think. I was untouchable."

"Yeah, I remember." He lay on the floor beside me, propped up on an elbow, and brushed the hair from my face. It set my skin alight. "I painted you."

He was close.

My heart hammered loudly in the ensuing silence, from the heat of Andor's body so close to mine, the rumble of his own pulse in the palm of my hand. He traced my features with long, calloused fingers as delicately as I'd watched him paint. Was he memorizing them? Admiring them? Every place of contact tingled, like a fizzy drink instead of the sharp prickle of static.

There was a different flicker in his gaze now.

Holding my breath, I pushed up and kissed him. On the mouth, holding his face to mine, feeling the warmth and poison seep into my skin. He tensed for only a moment, eyes widening, before he relaxed, before wrapping an arm around me to pull me closer instead of running away. Until there was no space between us at all.

Andor's hair was soft in my grasp. When his lips parted, the scent of roses filled my nostrils, while petrichor tickled my tongue. The room and all its boxes faded away until we were back in that labyrinth with the sweet smell of flowers and the earthy hum of blood meal soil, the chirping of crickets in the moonlight. This had none of the teeth and desperation that I expected when I thought about kissing him. I didn't know myself to be capable of something so . . . tender.

Andor grinned against my lips. "Is Acheron watching now?"

For once, pressed against him, I'd forgotten all about it.

When I nodded my head to the shadowy form he couldn't see but was fast retreating, he tossed his head back and groaned. And high on this feeling, on him, I rolled away in a fit of giggles. It was the first laugh to travel to the tips of my toes in months. Since *before*. Even though I covered my face at the mortification of it.

"Please be careful with it," Andor murmured, bringing his lips to my collarbone, setting my skin ablaze. Then he pushed himself up languidly into a seated position and raked a hand through his luscious curls.

"You don't trust it?"

I hadn't mentioned my talk with Coralie, how she *also* gave the same warning. It chilled the fire coursing through my blood at once and turned it to slush.

He shook his head. "Not anymore. Not with you. It's . . . different with you than the rest of us. Like it needs you for something."

Because I was its vessel. Because it wanted me to give something it wouldn't or couldn't ask the others whenever the time came.

"It's like a parasite," added Andor, grimacing.

But I didn't want to think about that, how much the idea stuck in me, and sour the mood. Not when this was the clearest things had ever been between us, when this was the first time in months I didn't feel like I was trying to outrun something. Instead, I arched a brow and smirked. "Are you jealous?"

He pressed his brow to mine, staring intently into my eyes, and whispered against my mouth, "No. I am always yours. And I trust you."

I held my breath.

And with a devilish smile that made my heart stutter, Andor rolled away and went back to packing.

When my bedroom had been reduced to only three boxes and the kitchen foraged for a fourth box of supplies, we started carrying them down the stairs. Other than the books, they weren't too heavy—after all, how heavy could tights and pointe shoes be?—and it was on the second trip that we heard the click of heels approaching. And a face the whole city could recognize filled the entryway.

It was like seeing a ghost. Around every corner, I kept expecting to see Coralie, to hear her soft snores or snorting laughter, and then finally I glimpsed her in the doorway. The same green eyes, the same heart-shaped face, the same shade of gold hair framing her like a halo in a Renaissance painting.

Only this face had aged, was older around the eyes, had the steady lines of a frown near its mouth. Her hair was polished and always sleek, her throat covered in diamonds.

Rose-Marie glanced haphazardly between us before stepping inside and clearing her throat. "I wondered when you'd come around."

I couldn't remember the last time she'd spoken to me. It was so long since she last acknowledged me that, for a moment, I thought she'd meant Andor. But she'd reserved the coldness in her gaze all for me, of course.

I chewed the inside of my cheek and nodded, resisting the urge to make myself small enough to escape her notice. The boxes weren't tall enough to hide behind, and she couldn't punish me anymore. She couldn't make me feel any worse than I already had—not when I'd suffered far worse.

"The apartment's been sold," announced Rose-Marie, wading in deeper and removing the sleek, expensive-looking gloves from her hands. "I'll need your key by the end of the month. Don't leave behind anything you want to keep."

*Like Coralie?* I wanted to ask.

Because Rose-Marie wasted no time in stuffing everything about her daughter into a box. She'd lied about the misdeeds of the monster she made and then packed away that shame where no one else would see. But I'd seen.

Instead, the words that came out of me were, "I tried to save her, you know."

They left my mouth before I had time to consider whether I really meant them, but in a way, I *had* tried to save Coralie—after talking to her had failed, after walking away had failed, I stopped her the only way I could to put an end to all of it. She was hurting where Rose-Marie had left her. It was for me most of all, but some part of it was for Coralie too.

Rose-Marie sneered. "No you didn't. If you loved my daughter, then you wouldn't have let her drown. I shouldn't have anything to grieve."

I scowled and studied her.

It would cost me nothing at all to make her drop dead. Or apologize. Or hand over every card in her wallet, all the cash, all the bank accounts and investment portfolios, the deed to her *three* houses. I could make her choke on her own diamonds while I drank the tears that formed. Throw herself down a flight of stairs. Use the stiletto points of her Louboutins to mutilate her renowned, celebrated face so she'd know what it was like to be no one and nothing.

I could call it justice for Cor, revenge for me, divine retribution, even—all of it would have been easy, but I would have felt nothing. It didn't matter that Acheron was salivating for the chance, wild with the promise of her suffering.

She, and her spite, meant nothing to me because I wasn't responsible for Coralie and all of those people. I wasn't the monster she wanted to blame.

So I hefted the last box in my arms and shouldered past, tossing out before I went, **"From now until the last of your days, you will be every bit as miserable and unloved as you made Coralie feel."**

# CHAPTER 22

It was late by the time Andor and I returned to the apartment, hauling all four boxes up the stairs to the top floor. Thanks to the steady abuse my thighs had taken since I joined Maison Lumina, that I survived the climb *twice* was a feat. Yet what Rose-Marie had said, implying that I shouldn't have let Coralie die, that it was my responsibility to fix the problem she'd created, continued to bother me.

My anger might have spewed over, erupted like magma and incinerated everything if it wasn't for the boxes tiring me out. If it wasn't for the way Andor's hands kept accidentally brushing mine at times that didn't feel accidental at all, and the way he swept past me, leaving the scent of rainwater in his path. Like he was doing subtle, gentle things to calm the storm.

When I inserted the key and dragged myself across the threshold, I still might have fumed if it weren't for all the lights on, the TV rumbling, and the sight of a fuchsia afro rising from our couch.

"Took you guys long enough," Keturah shouted over our heaving breaths. She waved a hand to the TV. "You need to come see this."

I fanned my collar and slumped against the wall. "Can it wait? We just—"

"*Now*," she snapped, cranking up the volume until the news report was screaming at me.

"*—We are back again to discuss the string of assaults in the past week that have left several hospitalized and ended today in the death of a banker.*"

I drifted inside, Andor shuffling quietly behind me. We left the door wide open.

*"Eyewitness reports say that three young adults aged sixteen to twenty-five were caught fleeing the area where an investment banker was gruesomely muti-lated and murdered near Parc Montsouris. The same descriptions have been spotted in six other assaults throughout the Paris Metropolitan Area. The only distinguishable marks are matching tattoos on the left arm of some in red ink, indicating cult activity or initiation."*

Andor grimaced when the news flashed a crude replication of Acheron's mark followed by three drawings that looked eerily similar to Dominique, Florian, and Salomé. He clenched his jaw. "What the fuck are they thinking?"

*"... at least three of the survivors were reported as incoherent when found, and have yet to gain lucidity."*

I turned away from the screen to finish sliding the boxes into the apartment. To do *something* correctly. All the while, I chewed the inside of my lip and started thinking.

"What do we do?" asked Keturah with a sigh, swapping the many sil-ver rings on her fingers, one after another. "We can't exactly name them to the police—they'd kill the whole department."

"With however Niamh is managing to stay at Palais Rose, I'm not optimistic either," Andor agreed, and when he crossed his arms, he looked all the more imposing.

**You should punish them,** Acheron suggested. **Remind them who we are.**

I heaved the door shut. "I-I'll skip rehearsal tomorrow to go to Elysium, see how the burning turned out. Niamh gave this whole speech about them being gods in Paris since Elysium had failed. Maybe then they'll go back if it's over."

And then I was faced with what Acheron and Gabriel and Coralie said, about how none of this would work. How Elysium couldn't be saved. How I should have let it go. They didn't give me any other choice besides a head-on collision, never once caring that I was tired of fighting. And evidently, Niamh's chosen weren't afraid of someone they thought could be replaced.

*No thanks, vessel. For now.*

Keturah nodded distractedly, unconvinced. "Of course that's her plan in the end. I don't have my mark anymore, but she's made you both targets too."

That Elysium had a serious problem became more apparent when Andor and I entered the Catacombs. Surrounded by shadows and the scents of wet rock and mold, the usually sinister red glow emanating from inside seemed less . . . vibrant. The red was muted to a dull pink, like bloody foam, watered down and weak. And the music, which sounded like "Waltz of the Flowers" to me, was quieter, faraway even when I passed right in front of it. It was as if the elder god was somewhere else, busy or bleeding out.

I kept walking rather than let the nerves get to me. None of it felt right—the pull that latched onto me, a line I knew that would lead me straight to Acheron's bloody shores again, was less a compulsion and more a suggestion. An idea that I could let slip from my mind instead of something that once threatened to be all-consuming.

And by the apprehension in Andor's steps, I knew he felt it too.

Then the question I'd been avoiding became a pressing thought: *What if it didn't work?*

What if all of this really was for nothing, and Elysium couldn't be saved? It seemed so far-fetched before, but the sky had lost some of its saturation now. It thinned overhead, no longer the richness of blood, the warning of redcaps, and more water with only pinprick drops and a bit of iridescence.

Soapy.

Oily.

*Anemic.*

Even the wind that breezed through my hair in greeting as we walked through the meadow didn't smell as strongly of cinnamon and struck matches; instead, it smelled strongly of rust. And it wasn't as warm as the caress of a lover on my cheek. In fact, the air was so cool I found myself pulling my coat closed and drifting nearer to Andor just to leech some heat from his frame.

"This doesn't feel promising," Andor muttered, knitting his brows.

He began changing his appearance the moment we passed the threshold. His skin was no longer honeyed brown and was instead back to bloodred and shimmering. His frame had elongated and stretched out, taller, stringier, his features exaggerated into a gruesome cryptid. Any softness to his face that I'd touched yesterday turned rigid now, and his four eyes all flooded with black and the thin line of white. I couldn't help but marvel at the shadow his crystalline antlers cast, how it caught in the low-hanging branches when he forgot to duck. How the light glinted on his shard-like teeth.

Away from it for so long, I'd forgotten how much this monster had excited me.

Swallowing, I looked away and asked, "Has a mortal ever seen your true face? Like, has anyone who *didn't* have a deal ever seen you like this?"

Just the way he turned his head to look down at me was uncanny. Birdlike and awkward, as if here, in this form, he had to practice human gestures. He answered plainly, "No."

"Do you know what would happen if they did?"

"No..." His voice grew more cautious now, the shine of his eyes studying me, unblinking, to see what I was getting at.

I still hadn't told him about finding the others. About the woman they'd menaced in the alley before I intervened. I didn't think I had to—I thought I'd handled it. Would they have killed her if I didn't stop them? I still pictured how I'd left her, in the arms of a pair of medics, mumbling and hardly keeping it together. She didn't understand the flashing lights, the colors of the ambulance. After Salomé had shown her true face, the woman hadn't understood anything at all. The girl in silver had fared worse.

And according to the news, they were only two of many.

"I didn't know that they were doing this to people. I thought..."

Taking two long strikes, Andor blocked my path and braced my shoulders with his clawed, bloodred hands. The contact forced a shiver down my spine and made my pulse spike. "What are you talking about?"

So I told him then, about the woman with no mouth, how Florian appeared to age, the bones that Dominique broke with only a gesture, what Salomé had said about her true face. The guilty didn't seem to care that I'd stopped them, that I had to use my power as a *vessel* to stop them. They didn't seem to have faith I'd remain a vessel much longer either. What was I supposed to do now that they had done it again?

The shadow that came over Andor's face, the set in his jaw as he listened intently, was fearsome. He looked exactly like the kind of creature you didn't want to piss off, and I wished he'd been there with me—they might not have respected me, but Andor had *four* deals concurrent. Enough to look like a nightmare personified. He was a monster through and through, the kind with enough restraint to choose softness while poison coursed through his veins.

"You think they're flashing their true faces at people for fun?"

I nodded. "Or searching for something. They said they get bored, but also that they got what they *needed*. And let's face it—Acheron, Elysium, Lethe—none of this was really ever meant for mortals. We aren't meant to be here, making deals, letting that in. What if Acheron *has* to change us just so we can withstand it?"

"What? Like it's so beyond comprehension that just a glimpse of it makes someone break down?" His tone had some levity back in it, meant to be a joke until he saw the seriousness on my face.

Acheron, Nyarla, child of Azathoth. The Daemon King. The wicked dark. So many names for something with so many faces, something it never intended for us to know fully. But what I did know was that the longer I was a vessel, the stronger its body grew. How long would it be before it didn't need me anymore? Before I stopped being useful?

As we marched past the great walls of the labyrinth, I asked, "How did you find your true face? Does everyone have one?" And at his prying gaze, I stared forward and added, "I basically only have red eyes unless I'm angry."

"I like your red eyes," mumbled Andor softly, his knuckles grazing mine. "I think everyone gets one, but it's something you have to learn how to do. It's like, giving in completely. Not so much listening to Acheron and doing what it says, but you shed your skin and *become* Acheron, kinda. It should feel like being bare. Naked. Unloading your consciousness."

Though I loved the gentle lilt in his voice, the feverish way he talked about it, I muttered under my breath for effect, "Painter, gardener, eldritch monster, and transcendentalist too. He can do it all."

But as we reached the end of the labyrinth's length, the mood vanished. We both slowed to a halt and exchanged a long, silent look.

The burning hadn't worked. Just like they'd said.

Elysium's rot was still expanding, stretching farther and faster still than the last time I was here, talking to Coralie. It was so close to the labyrinth now and preparing to breach its walls, the same spotted white that reduced the trees to mush, that eked from the sopping ground. And certainly as I stared farther in the direction of the disease, the state of the trees worsened until they were indistinguishable from the muck of that first clearing. The low masses of bodies in the shadows were hard to miss.

Anything that didn't manage to flee was lying there. Dead.

"The organs are failing. What about the blood..." Andor muttered before turning without another word. His long legs traveled fast, marching deeper into rot. He was going at a slant, toward where the trenches touched Acheron's shores. "I need to see how Acheron is resisting the spread. Nothing else can escape, but maybe Acheron is the key..."

I had to scurry to follow until his steps drew short on a low overhang. The river ebbed slowly down below, thickly, and the sight caused the breath in my chest to still. Crops of white were bleeding into the landscape, seeping from the infected trees through the sandy dirt and into the river itself.

And the river of blood became corrosive. It ate away at the shoreline, at the rocks, while growing paler and paler in color. This wasn't the Acheron I'd sunk into, that I'd slept beside. It wouldn't be blood for much longer either. This rot was something else.

This rot was why it needed a vessel. What it was trying to escape.

"Come on." I seized Andor's hand and whirled around.

He stumbled behind me for only a moment before his tangle of limbs met my stride and his long fingers entwined with mine. "Where—"

"To the source."

To the heart of the infection, to where the rot was worst. Where it started its spread.

It was a hike that we'd at least dressed for this time. The deeper we marched into the forests, crossing over the terrain and descending cliff-sides, white, sweet-smelling mold coated my shoes. The smell invaded my hoodie and clung to my hair.

All around us, Elysium had grown desolate. It was a wasteland of soft, pulpy trees with the bark peeling in chunks and branches hanging limp. Bloated and rotting animal carcasses littered the landscape until they were all I could see, until I found myself turning around and around in circles, lost. With dead birds half eaten by maggots all around my feet.

"Can you see what direction looks the worst?"

"No, I—" Andor stiffened and went quiet. His hand tightened hard enough in mine that the tips of his claws bit into skin.

The brightness of the pain drew me around to the stricken look on his face, until I found what he was looking at. In the center of a clearing, surrounded by collapsing, desiccated trees and mush, there was a figure waiting, watching us silently. And unlike with Keturah, I didn't have to guess who it was. Even if I didn't recognize it, the way Andor's pulse hiked up said more than enough.

Ciro Aurissy had a distinct look—from his high brow and pointed chin, the coarse hair that he'd grown out long and dyed ash white, and moon-pale skin. He was tall and thin and well-dressed, even in death. He'd had a smile that sent everyone at the ballet swooning from the moment he joined the board. And he was standing here in Elysium, amid the rot, staring at us.

"Is he…" Andor whispered, turning his head toward me slightly, though his eyes couldn't leave his best friend. His brother.

"He is."

Then I bounded after him.

And Ciro broke into a sprint.

It was hard to run with the ground so soft and wet, with the high mud and fallen trees everywhere. Every few steps I had to leap over some undetermined carcass, but this time, I wouldn't let the dead escape. Not when they clearly had so much to say. Maybe they knew where to go next.

Andor's footsteps squelched and squished behind me as he called out, "What are you doing?"

I pumped my knees faster. "First, Coralie. Then Keturah saw Joey. Now Ciro?" My breaths turned to rasps. "They know something!"

For a moment, he didn't say anything back. He just kept running, moving deftly over obstacles until he was taking the lead and shouting, "Ciro!"

I joined in, "Ciro! Wait!"

We chased the ghost still dressed in white through the tangle of trees and rot and corpses, until they grew sparser and sparser. Until there were none at all. Until the sky lightened to the white grey of Paris on a cloudy day. There was no more red here, anywhere, wherever Ciro had brought us. No more Acheron limning my vision, buzzing under my skin. No color at all, or sound, or life.

And in the corner of my eye, I glimpsed another figure sprinting full speed alongside us. A girl with frizzy, golden hair and pale, almost bluish skin.

Coralie joined the fray, running too until the four of us converged on new ground that crunched and clinked as we moved. It didn't have the same squish of the marshland or the bounce of healthy forest floor. Instead it slipped under my soles like wet rock. Only the rock was white—

"Oh my god, is that bone?" Andor slid to a stop.

I crashed hard on my knees and looked around.

Over the course of our run, the landscape of Elysium had changed drastically, and here we were surrounded by mounds of bones. It was a starker version of the Catacombs: rib cages and finger bones and leg bones and skulls and little knots of vertebrae, all stacked into piles. And so many piles. Real bones, human *and* animal, big and small. As far ahead as I could see. We'd run until death had become a place.

Coralie and Ciro stood calmly among the mounds and waited, spines straight, like we were supposed to understand from the sight alone. Like this was enough to piece it together.

Clinging to Andor, I climbed onto unsteady feet and doubled over to catch my breath.

Fog rolled low across the ground, chilling the air. Then came another figure emerging around the mounds, someone else we knew and recognized: Joséphine Moreau, with her auburn hair and porcelain skin and bright red lipstick. All the poise of a prima ballerina, even with the gruesome gash that killed her still raw at her throat. An echo of mine and Ciro's. As we neared, she turned her head and pointed a finger to tell us to keep going.

It was a procession of all we'd mourned.

"It left the door open," said Joséphine sadly, her voice falling flat in the dead air. And it was truly her voice, the same that enticed me into the dark and had last told me to conquer the world. "We heard you grieving and came out. It carried us out."

We moved slowly through them all as they stared, as they pointed, ushering us deeper and deeper into the cold. Into the mounds of bone and closer to the brightness beyond.

"What the fuck is going on?" I muttered, trying to resist a shiver as I followed their gazes. They clearly wanted us to keep going, to find whatever there was to see. But none of it really explained what we were seeing now, how they were here, why. And Joséphine and Ciro sending us a message from beyond the grave was a better alternative than thinking it was a trap to kill us, here where it was so full of death and Acheron couldn't watch.

Coralie had said she was *helping* me.

So I slipped and glided and dropped down on the wet bones until I was crawling on my hands and knees while Andor remained frozen somewhere farther back. The wet and the fog both stung, nipping at my skin like the harshest cold of winter, like a familiar ice, until my fingertips were numb and wrapped up in my hoodie sleeves and I couldn't feel my toes. The unease in my skin swelled to full-body shudders. And the sky only seemed to get brighter.

"Andor," I said, squinting as I inched closer, into the white. "I think I see it."

There had always been another river in Elysium, another god to contend with that was easy to ignore when it was so far off. Up close now, it was pure light. It seared my eyes as I neared, this haunting thing that stole our friends from us. I could see that it was overflowing, inundating the land and spreading like pestilence, killing everything in its path. And I should have known it sooner from the cold alone.

Lethe.

"Oblivion," supplied another voice that sounded eerily like mine.

My head snapped up to see her standing over me. My ghost. Her hair was soaked and curly, the exposed scars on her wrists and throat fresh, arm broken and jutting at a weird angle, clothes torn and dusty from the collapse. A blossoming stain of red ran down her front from where she'd been stabbed. From where I'd pulled out what was killing us. The old Laure *had* died there, after all.

She was proof that Acheron had left part of me behind to make room for itself in my body. That Acheron had left an opening, and oblivion was seeping through, bringing them all back.

My ghost sank to her knees and turned to me and smiled with blood on her teeth. She cupped my face in her freezing, blood-soaked hands and whispered, "Oblivion is inevitable. And all that consumes will be consumed as well."

# CHAPTER 23

*O*blivion is inevitable.

Lethe was overflowing. It wasn't just a little rot that was spreading, but the full power of Lethe, of death, of *oblivion* leaking out, killing everything in Elysium. Including Acheron, and maybe us too. And how do you kill oblivion?

The thoughts ran on a loop as I followed a Palais Rose servant to the gold room. The mortal was a little gaunt around the face, with glazed-over eyes that showed none of the spark a normal person, one who wasn't compelled, would have. They walked with their shoulders slumped and a slight limp of the right leg, and every time we passed a wall sconce and stepped out of the shadow, I wondered if the dark trim on the bottom of their pants was actually blood.

It also could've just been my exhaustion, bleary-eyed and out of it from such a late night on Lethe's shores, but I decided to err on the side of caution.

**Take me to the gold room and then leave**, I commanded, staring at the back of their shaved head. I didn't know if they would listen, if they *could* listen, but I hoped so. **Leave and never come back. Take as many with you as you can.**

Then I pressed the heels of my palms into my eyes, pushing that exhaustion as deep as it would go, shook out my shoulders, and shuffled along.

Shivering, we'd had to haul ourselves over oily, bleached bones and hike back through swampy forest. It had taken hours just to reach the apartment, and then Acheron and I had stepped away to finally talk. Time had bled together then—I didn't really remember falling asleep, only that when I'd finally awoken, half the day had already passed.

But I needed to be here, to tell Niamh and the rest the news about Lethe and hope they'd see reason. That they'd be propelled to better action.

"Acheron, how did you kill oblivion?" I whispered softly. If Lethe was its opposite, I figured it had to know.

It didn't respond.

In fact, it was odd—I was so out of it, so bone-tired, that I only just now paid it any attention at all. Just now noticed that the shadow that followed me, that clung to the rim of my vision and stalked my reflection was unusually quiet. Subdued. Was it a side effect from standing so close to Lethe just hours ago, or did this come later?

"Laure!" Niamh greeted me before I even cleared the threshold, before I could dwell on the feeling. Her voice had all the grandness of a leader, all the zeal and power that brought people to their knees. What Acheron had probably expected of me. "My favorite vessel."

It didn't sound like she meant it at all. The smile on her face had a sinister edge that confirmed the same.

The gold room was not just a room decorated in gold but a *throne* room. There, at the end of the long hall, Niamh's tiny frame sat on a gilded throne, her legs crossed neatly and wearing what unmistakably resembled my favorite steel-toed boots. I'd bought them to celebrate my raise at the ballet, but they'd been destroyed by Lethe's tainted waters. Hers, however, were blemish-free. And she sat on a dais in front of a rich, velvet tapestry, leaning on her hand as if she was bored of holding court.

She wasn't the Niamh I knew at all. Sitting on this throne was Margaux.

"To what do we owe the pleasure, so unannounced?"

Flanking her stood all of her sycophants, ones I recognized and others I didn't. Dominique was the closest, along with Salomé, Florian, and several others I might have met but couldn't bring myself to name. But even though Maison Lumina didn't rehearse on Saturdays, Gabriel wasn't here among them. I guessed he wasn't loyal to Margaux's way of the world.

Standing all alone in the middle of the floor, I realized that, in this kind of situation, I was probably expected to bow. People bowed before a throne, didn't they? I swallowed. Listened for Acheron to supply words of encouragement, a boost of strength, *anything*. The power was still there in my veins, I felt it, but the dark god was silent. Or unavailable.

So I did not bow.

"I've been trying to save Elysium," I started, only looking at Margaux but speaking clearly enough that the others could understand. "I've been trying, and I failed. I researched diseases, fungi and bacteria and viruses and parasites that can destroy entire forests. I dug trenches, I burned it, I even tried bleeding in it, hoping Acheron might do some healing. *All of it* failed."

None of them showed any interest. Margaux swapped her short legs to right-over-left.

"So I hiked to the source. Lethe is overflowing. It's flooding the soil, and that's how it's spreading. That's what's killing everything, and I don't know how to stop it."

Then I waited for them to say something. To show dismay on their stony faces or volunteer suggestions. Some of them with their Lethe marks might have ideas.

Margaux raised and dropped a shoulder. "So? We're already here. Why are you telling us?"

*I should have left you as a thief in Prague.*

I licked my lips and tried again. "Acheron is infected too. It looks like it's dying. We don't know what that'll do to *us* if it does. We may not have long."

Finally, the others exchanged glances of worry, ushering panicked whispers to each other, but when Margaux leaned back in her throne, they settled. If she wasn't concerned, then neither were they. And that was a pathetic, spineless move to make.

"Acheron is a god," Margaux quipped. "It cannot die."

Yet it wasn't talking to me right now. It wasn't standing here, encouraging me to snatch her down from the pedestal. Was that because of something I said, or because it didn't need me anymore, or was it because Lethe had finally snuffed out the pilot light?

"But even if it *could*, it won't matter when we're done here."

This wasn't going at all like I'd hoped. "What are you gonna do?"

"That's none of your business, since you've made it clear you want nothing to do with us." Margaux sneered, anger flashing red in her eyes. It was the first sign of her true face, so much like mine, and I wondered what else she might be hiding underneath. How much did the girl in silver see before she died on the spot? "Find someone who cares. Consider yourself dismissed."

The rest of them snickered. That I was down here, a vessel pleading for help while Margaux sat on the dais, refusing, was amusing to them. As if Acheron had found a better vessel in her, anointed her the new chosen, and I was the last to know. But *I* made her—who was she to dismiss me?

Fire kindled in my veins, rushing down to my fingertips.

"Fine. If you'd let Elysium rot, then so be it, but it's dangerous and selfish of you to carry on like this *here*." I let my voice fill the room, let it be very clear that I wasn't *dismissed*, that I wasn't going anywhere. She couldn't make me.

Margaux arched a brow.

"The assaults? The dead banker? What do you think will happen when police connect you to the Palais de Justice intern? And vigilantes start eyeing anybody with Acheron's mark? You put a target on all of our backs—"

She erupted with laughter, high and harsh and so inauthentic. None of it was genuine, not in her eyes or in her posture. All of it was a show to bare her teeth and push me to silence.

"You think I care about that girl?" She nodded to Dominique and crossed her arms. "Let me show you how little I care. They told me about your interruption. Did you forget what you told me? What you are?"

Dominique slipped out of the room as her voice echoed through the hall.

"Whatever happened to 'the happiest are the ones with power'? Whatever happened to survival of the fittest? The strongest? Where are your *teeth*, Laure? Show me your true face, be unashamed."

I clenched my jaw.

Margaux smirked knowingly. "You can't, can you?"

My gaze drifted to the sounds of a door opening and shutting and found Vanessa, escorted by the arm by Dominique. She looked more exhausted than I did, the circles beneath her eyes black, bruises and scrapes mottling her bare arms. Her hair was matted, unbrushed in days. And she looked unusually thin, hollowed out, *starved*.

How long did Margaux hold her here? Why?

"What do you think you're doing—"

"What you should have done!" Margaux erupted, sending a chill down my spine.

With only a glance, Vanessa was forced onto her knees. She trembled and let out a whimper, cowering behind her arms as if someone had raised a hand to strike her. As if there was something more terrifying in her mind that the rest of us couldn't see.

"That's not funny—"

"She betrayed you, vessel," Margaux snapped, each consonant clipped and clear. "A mortal snubbed you, spilled all her little secrets about you. So punish her."

I took a step forward, slow and steady. "No."

*Acheron, I could really use your help right now.*

"Punish her, and we'll stop."

"I don't want to, and you can't make me."

Silence blanketed the room, the high ceilings and stale air thickening at my defiance as the other acolytes looked at each other. And I only glared at Margaux.

"No more random assaults," she teased. "No more picking on your poor, precious mortals. I'll lay down my weapons and give up. Hell, we'll even help you fix Elysium if you want. If you punish her. And I mean *really* make her learn her lesson: never to cross a god."

She was so smug, and at her wide grin, the others began laughing again. So gleeful and so far gone, while a mortal girl sat battered and afraid before them. It was sick.

I crossed my arms. "No."

There were many monstrous and wicked things about me, but this was petty. Small. Needlessly cruel. None of it was me.

"You won't bully me," I retorted, loud enough for the others to understand it too.

Hovering over Vanessa, I extended a hand to help her up. To lead her out of this wretched palace, away from these sadists masquerading as victims. Though we'd never been close, never really even liked each other, something in my expression seemed to persuade her. Eventually she took my hand, shaking so badly I wondered if she was freezing, and

I pulled her to me. She had never looked so frail before, and I was afraid that if I let go, she might collapse. We turned away.

At our backs, Margaux shouted, "Let's not pretend you're so holy that killing is above you, Laure. We all know about Opéra Garnier. One hundred and thirteen deaths on your hands."

I stiffened. Glanced over my shoulder, unable to hide my seething. My guilt. Coralie had torn through that place in a fit of rage, and if I hadn't snapped, if I hadn't pounced on her, the walls might not have fallen. But that was *her* shame too, and I hadn't known then what would happen.

And Margaux wouldn't have known about it if she hadn't found Vanessa. Even with a little sparkling wine in my system, I'd never say a thing, so she went and found herself an eyewitness.

"Then so be it," muttered Margaux with a sigh, sinking back into her chair.

The instant she settled her attention on Vanessa, the mortal girl screamed. She erupted into bloodcurdling shouts so loud, so close that it pierced my ear and sent me stumbling away. I winced, clapping a hand to the side of my head, and rounded on her, just as Dominique twisted both of his wrists.

It looked as if he was twisting the cap off a bottle, but with a sickening crack, Vanessa's head swiveled around. So far to the side that the neck snapped and twisted at an angle, bones jutting out beneath the skin as she crumpled to the floor. An unmoving heap at my feet. So fast, I only had time to flinch.

Another dead girl before me, yet another for Margaux's ledger. And I knew—the girl in silver from the bathroom of En boîte, the red crusting her eyes, had been a test. Margaux flashed that girl her true face, probably just to see it in action. While I was busy clubbing and running from myself, she was recruiting an army. Galvanizing them to be gods on earth.

I stared at Vanessa, the crink in her neck, the lack of serenity in her expression, the contortion of her body—all wrong. I stared at her for so long that I didn't see the others leave their posts at Margaux's side. I didn't see them encircle me and then close in until it was too late.

Somebody fisted my ponytail and yanked me back and down. Right off my feet.

Before my brain could catch up to what was happening, all of them were upon me, seizing my arms and legs, booted feet pressing into my ribs. They held their positions, wrenching my arms, while Margaux's steps clicked through the hall. The heels of her nice boots, the ones she'd copied from me, echoed off the ceiling.

"Maybe this will help you come around," said Margaux calmly, tucking her hands in her pockets.

Then came a crack at my ribs, sharp pain radiating through my chest and stomach. It forced the air from my lungs, the fight from my limbs. Fists and elbows and knees rained down, knocking my face from side to side, letting my skull bang against the wood floor and rebound again in a violent waltz.

I pulled and thrashed and kicked under their grips to no avail, exposing one side of my chest or back to more beatings as they laid waste. There was no hiding when they held me down, pinned my arms.

"St—" I tried to say, to summon some power before something struck me in the mouth.

*Acheron, if you don't help me, you'll lose your vessel.*

The skin of my cheek split.

*Where are you?*

The sound of my nose crunching bounced around in my head as the hot rush of blood flooded my face. It ran down my chin, in my mouth, and speckled the floor. Another blow to my stomach knocked a ragged breath from me.

Tiny hands gripped my cheeks, and my eyes fought sluggishly to focus on the face before me. Margaux with her hazel eyes and slick blond hair, her sharp mouth moving close. For a moment I thought she'd kiss me. Instead, with a quick swipe of her tongue, she licked my blood away and tossed me back down on the floor. "Maybe now I'll be the new vessel."

**"Get off—"**

The pointed tip of a shoe caught me in the back of the head, threading my sight with darkness. Stars danced for me in the yawning abyss that pulled me down, and my body went slack. Resistance bled out of me. A faraway door clattered shut. And something angry and primal reared its head in my absence.

As my eyes drifted shut and I yielded to the gravity that overcame my limbs, I thought I heard a chorus of distant screams. Maybe my own, or an echo of Opéra Garnier. Horror curdled in the disembodied voices, crested by the squelch of flesh, thick splatters, and the wet snaps of bones.

And then it all went dark, and quiet, and cold.

# CHAPTER 24

I didn't remember getting home. I didn't remember leaving Palais Rose and heading to the train station, or hailing a car and riding back into the city. I barely remembered climbing the stairs to the top floor and taking out my key. It felt like I was progressively waking up, the world slowly coming into focus until I was semi-here, groggy, twisting the lock and stumbling into the light.

There was a loud *thud* as soon as I walked through the door, shielding my eyes with a muffled groan. Andor stood in the center of the room, staring, a glass rolling around his feet, water pooling into the rug beneath. It captured Keturah's attention, and she twisted in her seat on an armchair before surging to a stand.

They gaped at me in silence. Abject fear etched in both their faces, fear I'd only seen on them when we'd found Ciro's body. Something about me scared them. So, with a wrinkle in my brow, wincing, I looked down at myself.

I most certainly didn't remember the blood. Or the smell.

Blood ran down the length of me, a little sticky and wet but mostly dry and crusted through my sweater and jeans. It was dark and rich, far more than a single body could lose and still survive, coating my sleeves, my hands, flaking under my nails. And there wasn't just blood either—clots solidified in my hair, dark chunks caught in the knit that resembled pieces of meat. Liver, kidney, entrails, I didn't know, but the stench emanating from me was awful.

With my body fully awake now, I gagged.

The smell was in my nostrils, on my tongue, and I lurched forward and bolted. Weaving past Andor and his fallen glass and puddle of water, past Keturah with a hand pressed to her mouth, and into the bathroom.

I barely made it inside before the vomit came. Chunks landed in the sink, the faded brown tones of flesh swimming in reddish pinkish yellowish fluid. It wasn't just leftover lunch but shreds of something sinewy and raw, clinging to my face, embedded in my teeth. Pieces of someone.

Someones.

"But how did I—" My voice was shot, throat aching like I'd been screaming.

I swiped the hair from my face and closed my eyes, trying to think. Trying to remember. And though I didn't hear them approach, I felt Andor and Keturah standing in the doorway, still gaping at me and the sink and my panic.

"Laure," whispered Keturah in measured calm.

Her tone was commanding in the way a girl forced to grow up and care for others could be, that demanded I look her in the eye, and I did. I hoped she knew I didn't mean for this—to be another burden for her to take care of.

"What happened?"

I shrugged helplessly.

In the mirror, beneath the waterfall of viscera, my face was a wreck. The skin around my right eye was tight and swollen. A gash still bled lightly along my cheek, and my nose had ballooned and turned a shade of deep, brutal purple. Underlying the confusion were pains radiating from everywhere, my wrist and back and chest and stomach, places all demanding my immediate attention.

I peeled the disgusting sweater away first, and Keturah gasped. Andor disappeared into the hall.

Massive bruises bloomed across my ribs and stomach in wretched patterns, rising out of my jeans and along my hip bones. One wrist had swelled to twice its size, but the rest of me was still waking up, it seemed. I only felt it like a memory.

"I don't..."

A persistent throb stabbed at my temples and spiraled through the back of my skull as I tried to remember. I woke up. We said our good-byes, and I took a train to Le Vésinet. I talked to Niamh in the gold room, offered my hand to Vanessa before she—

"Fucking Niamh." I groaned, closing my eyes to the light again, only dimly aware of Andor returning with what sounded like a first aid kit. Somehow I found myself sitting on the floor.

Keturah's voice came closer. "What did they do to you? What..."

*What did you do to them?*

That was the thing I didn't recall at all. One minute, I was trying to take Vanessa away from that place, and the next, she was dead, I was surrounded, and the blows were coming down faster than I could understand. Faster than I could fight back. But the blood, the chunks, the partially digested flesh that I'd rinsed down the drain—that wasn't mine. So whose was it?

"They killed Vanessa," I rasped at last, each word like pulled teeth as I let Andor turn my head this way and that. His poisoned fingertips dulled the pain a little, and I wished he'd never let go. "And jumped me for refusing to help them."

Even through the blurred vision, the pain and swelling, I didn't miss the muscle feathering his jaw, the flare in his nostrils. Anger flickered in his dark eye as he dabbed at my mangled face with a cloth. Every stroke was gentle but focused. He was close enough that I smelled him through the rust and viscera.

I raked a hand through my matted hair, fingers snagging and

agitating a contusion on my scalp. "I think I got hit in the head; I don't remember leaving. How I got here."

"This doesn't make any sense." Keturah sat on the edge of the bathtub and dropped her head in her hands.

The disinfectant Andor dabbed around the side of my face made me wince. I went on, "She told everyone about Palais Garnier. What happened in the collapse. She wanted me to kill Vanessa simply because she's mortal, and she'd end the attacks around the city."

Neither of them said anything after that. They let the silence in this small bathroom hang, and I leaned into Andor's hand as it cradled my tender jaw.

This was all ruined. Elysium was dying, and Acheron might have been next, judging by its silence. Niamh or Margaux or whatever she was called and her gang of assholes were all too high on a power trip to care. Vanessa was dead, one in a long string of attacks. My wrist was the size of an apple, and my face looked even worse. I definitely had a concussion too, and at least a couple fractured ribs.

If I wasn't a vessel, I might have been dead. If I even *was* a vessel anymore.

"You did the right thing," said Andor finally, softly, though there was an edge to his voice.

"It definitely doesn't *feel* like I did the right thing," I retorted as I reached over to turn on the bathtub faucet. Before I did anything else, I needed a bath. I needed to think.

Acheron and I needed to talk, if it was still alive.

"I don't think all this blood is mine."

"They could've killed you," Keturah surmised gravely. She massaged the skin of her arm, the space where her mark used to be, as she headed to the door. "And killed others. As far as I'm concerned, they deserve it, and we should go back and give them more—"

I balked. "*You* shouldn't be going anywhere. Not when you're mortal now."

Keturah returned a withering glare. "I'm mortal. Not powerless."

Andor took her by the shoulders and steered her toward the door. "We can deal with this tomorrow. It's late, and you need rest. Will you be okay by yourself? Do you want help?"

He nodded to the bathwater, and I blinked slowly, my face rushing with heat. It made all my injuries throb more, the idea of him helping me out of the rest of my clothes and hobbling into the bath.

"No. I'll be fine."

I watched them retreat, Keturah first and Andor latching the door behind himself, my fingertips gliding across the steaming water's surface. Waiting for the dark god to make an appearance. Apologize for its absence.

It didn't.

"Where are you?" I muttered through clenched teeth.

Sliding off my socks, where blood had even seeped into the bands, I kept searching for the buzz of its figure, the shadows in my periphery that would flicker rapidly, with agitation. It should have been angry or disappointed or—hell, even smug. But instead, there was just nothing.

The decadent heat of the water stung my muscles and scraped, snatching the air from my bruised lungs as I slid in. I didn't stop sinking until all of me was submerged, my face and scalp burning, Margaux and the choked expression of Vanessa's face drifting at the surface.

Then came flashes of Palais Rose's gold room. Rows of sharp teeth sinking into the soft flesh of an ear and tearing, claws piercing a throat like daggers, a boy reduced to a pile of blood and gore, organs splashing wetly on the wood floors.

No one was safe from what I'd become.

Suddenly they were all screaming, running, scrambling to escape.

Squeezing my eyes shut, holding my breath, I tried to go back earlier. To before Palais Rose, before waking up in the afternoon, to last night. Andor and I were still so cold and soggy when we'd stormed into the apartment, the stink of oblivion on our skin. While he'd called Keturah to tell her everything, I'd slipped into the bathroom and locked the door so that Acheron and I could talk. Uninterrupted.

Pain lanced my skull, the memory sharp as I dredged it up.

"Explain," I'd demanded before even turning around. "Why didn't you tell me?"

Acheron had stood by the sink in a towering form, all its features fully defined—not only a head, but arms, fingers, legs, feet. And all of it was composed of static, electricity confined in a human mold. Soon it wouldn't be tied to Elysium at all.

It had flickered—no, my thoughts flickered. Part of me didn't want to remember what Acheron had said. What had happened. Something about it was as wrong as whatever I did at Palais Rose, wrong enough for me to try to block it out.

*Fuck Elysium, we'll make our own paradise*, Niamh's voice from the night at the club echoed in my head, and I pushed harder, pressing into the pain.

**Are you angry?** It had asked, the voice still humming from my marrow.

I'd wrapped my arms around myself and paced. "Yes, I'm angry. I'm your vessel—you didn't think to tell me these things? About why you didn't want to save Elysium? About *Lethe*?"

**I warned you**, it had replied with its trademark lack of emotion, **but you were so distracted with that boy. You didn't want to listen.**

That wasn't true. I'd started to object, when Acheron draped an arm across my shoulders to slow me down, and I'd felt it. The length of its arm against my skin, the flood of power upon contact. It had felt real and firm as any person, no longer confined to just a reflection or shadows, and stronger and more painful than that brush in my old bedroom.

It could *touch* me.

The memory of that contact still burned, enough to force me above the surface. I sat up and wiped the wet from my eyes. I didn't want to remember anymore.

**But there is nothing to worry about**, Acheron had continued. **Soon none of this will matter—**

I'd wrenched out of Acheron's hold and seethed. "I saw what it's doing to you, to the river. What if you die? What happens to us?"

**Milk of the Void cannot kill the Daemon King.** It had swayed on its feet. **The Nameless Mist does not stop Nyarla. Nothing holds dominion over a child of Azathoth.**

And it'd seemed so funny—that Acheron wasn't truly its name, so Lethe wasn't real either—that I'd just laughed. With my head hanging low, I couldn't stop the laughter bubbling out of me. I was so fed up.

Finally Acheron had explained, **It always comes, sometimes slow and often sudden. We have warred since the start of time and before.**

Tears had welled in my eyes. Because all of this had been pointless from the very beginning. Everything I'd done was rendered useless. But the laughter wouldn't cease.

**Life and oblivion, chaos run wild and swallowed by order only to emerge again. That it tries is inevitable.**

It had occurred to me then: Oblivion was coming and inevitable, but what if it didn't stop at the door? What if it branched into the Catacombs? If it climbed the stairs? Was the whole of our world rotten too?

I pressed the heels of my palms into my eyes, now in the bath and reliving last night before the god, at the rush of the realization—the insistence on spreading, on recruiting, leaping at the opportunity of a vessel. All this time, Acheron knew and told me nothing because it was scheming to outrun death, once and for all.

Acheron and I were both trying to escape our situations. It had been waiting for someone like me to come around, someone hungry for all the right things and twisted enough to take it. Someone so eager to be seen she'd never know she was being manipulated, or wouldn't mind. A desperate girl willing to give it anything, easy to distract so no questions asked.

It was using me.

*A parasite.*

Andor had knocked on the door then, called my name warily, making me jump. And before I could reach to unlock it, to explain all that I'd heard, Acheron had gripped my wrist. Tight enough to twinge. It'd *grabbed* me.

**He will not make you a god. He will only impede your ascension,** it had warned.

My brows knit, but I'd nodded slowly, relenting, and backed away. I was starting to comprehend, starting to truly see. "Okay."

In the bath, my nails bit into my scalp. The force of the headache, of the memory, was overwhelming. It was inescapable. That memory was all I could see and feel and hear. I couldn't look away.

Rather than relent, Acheron had only stepped closer and placed both hands squarely on my shoulders, thumbs digging into my collarbones. Every bit of contact had seared into my skin. The lights in the bathroom had dimmed when it looked at me. **You need only to give yourself to *me*. No doubts. No hesitation. No more questions.**

It had raised my chin, pinched between prickling fingers, so that I could stare back into its featureless face. So that I couldn't escape the absence of its eyes and nose and ears and mouth, remember that it wasn't like me or Andor or Keturah or even Coralie. So that I'd remember that

I was dealing with something other, and act accordingly, like the vessel I'd signed up to be.

"Okay." I'd nodded again.

Then Acheron had kissed me. Some semblance of a mouth had pressed against mine. It had none of the sincerity or the tenderness or *love* of Andor, and it was packed with so much power, it'd burned like a brand. Like possession. It'd hurt, and I'd wanted none of it, even as we fit so perfectly, as my eyes drifted shut, as my lips parted of their own accord, and I took the dark inside. What else was I to do? How could I ever say no if we were always to be together?

"Laure? Is everything okay?" Andor had yelled from the other side of the door, but he was so far away from the amalgam of current and teeth, tongue and heat, predator and prey. Could he sense the choice I was about to make?

The first time we'd met, Acheron had remarked, *Let's see how voracious your appetite is.*

So I opened my eyes and bit down. Hard. Teeth clenching with all my might, until I'd felt the give of flesh, tasted sharpness, until my prey had startled under my hold with the realization I wouldn't let go. Acheron's hands had groped my arms for purchase, its resistance swelling to a scream that seemed to shake the walls, but I was never going to yield.

And then I'd torn the tongue from the dark god's mouth.

*All that consumes will be consumed as well.*

I'd watched it stumble back, bewildered and gaping as I chewed. The meat had been tough, the taste bitter, but I was tougher and more than voracious. I was ambition nurtured by the dark.

Acheron had collapsed to the floor in a bramble of static, trembling from shock while the doorknob rattled behind me. Without breaking eye contact, ignoring Andor's calls from the other side, I'd chewed and chewed until *it* was small and in pieces for once instead of me, until I swallowed the last of it, until I was fed, my belly full, while Acheron was a cowering mess beneath me.

"I am not yours," I'd growled, right before I went in for more.

# PART THREE

# THE USURPER

# CHAPTER 25

Standing under the cathedral's stone arch, I reached Margaux's voice mail for the fourth time that day. Though I'd tried calling her again and again, sorting through the fragments of whatever I'd done at Palais Rose, it was to no avail. I didn't know if she was dead or alive, what pieces belonged to her or someone else, and I was no closer to understanding what I'd become. What primal thing I'd seized the moment I usurped Acheron.

*Killed* Acheron.

"Fine, whatever," I sighed into the recording before hanging up.

My guilt was laced with anger: Margaux was my recruit, my protégée, the only one I brought into the fold. When I was supposed to be guiding her, she'd turned into a tyrant, and then I might have torn her to little pieces and not even remembered it. Because that was what I'd done in the heat of the moment, seeing red and feeling sharp—I tore people and gods to *pieces*.

Andor and Keturah were already descending the old, stone steps that led into the Catacombs, and I darted to catch up. We had a lot to do on this dreary Sunday, the sky as perfectly dismally grey as I felt, and there was no time to fret over whether or not I'd killed a killer. With or without Acheron, my bruises had lessened some, the gashes beginning their accelerated healing, but I still woke up this morning feeling like I'd had the stuffing beat out of me. I was already fretting enough, still deeply unsettled, with what I *did* remember.

The only bright side was waking up from a dreamless sleep between the two of them, head resting on the broad expanse of Andor's chest while my legs tangled with Keturah's. They'd been waiting for me when I climbed out of the bathtub, and somehow this was the only thing not painfully confusing.

"No answer?" Keturah asked from the helm, her voice bouncing around the cavernous walls. There was no sense of apprehension in her tone, no concern for Margaux or the others at all, but then again, she didn't know about the tongue, and she didn't *see* the bloodbath in action.

"Nope." I eased down the steps one at a time, each level flaring up through my torso and into my ribs.

The thing was, the longer I went without hearing anything, the more I felt sure Margaux was planning to strike back. I feared that most of all—the last time someone retaliated against me, Ciro and Joséphine wound up dead, and Coralie pushed herself past the point of no return. And when that didn't work, then I died too. This time, if it happened again, I wouldn't have Acheron to fall back on.

"I'm kind of afraid to see what it looks like now," Keturah continued chattering into the darkness. "It changes more and more every time we go back."

I pitched forward and slung my arms around them both, ignoring the twinge in my shoulders. The corridors were a tight fit, but if I held them close enough, we made do. I had to savor this before the hammer came down. Keturah squeezed my hand, and Andor smoothed down my hair.

"Yeah, I'm kinda expecting the labyrinth to be destroyed by now," he admitted softly.

Despite their light tones, my nervousness was only exacerbated by the lack of pull from my chest, the colorless glow up ahead. Gone was the bloodred, and like a storm cloud, white was fast approaching overhead when we passed through. From where we stood on the hill, it did appear that Lethe was expanding, stretching wider and wider until eventually it'd engulf the red river completely. Consume all that was left. And with no pull, no song from Acheron's shores to welcome me home, it was like even my body didn't recognize this ghostly place anymore.

I could only hope that, whatever happened next, it didn't take me with it.

"So what all are we grabbing? I'm packing up my things, but what else?" Keturah jutted her thumb to the cottage and released a shaky breath.

Andor gestured in the direction of the labyrinth. "I'm just gonna sort through my canvases, but I need help carrying."

His gaze landed on me, pointedly, beseeching. And with all my life tucked away in Ciro's apartment already, I only nodded and followed him, and Keturah departed for the cabin by herself, oblivious.

Once we were shrouded by trees, he shifted. His body expanded, lengthening, skin flooding red, and antlers climbed from his skull like vines seeking water and light. The scar across the left side of his face deepened. Two pairs of eyes scanned our surroundings, in search of more deathly apparitions that might want to pay us a visit. And despite whatever I did to Acheron, it seemed to have no effect on his power either. His monstrousness was unchanged, like maybe what I did wasn't permanent.

"So, how are you feeling?" Andor asked, cocking his head in my direction. "After last night?"

The way he said it didn't sound so neutral and curious at all. There was some weight to it, a tightness in his mouth and a muscle twitching in his thick neck as he leveled a glance at me. Bracing himself in case I was in danger or *the* danger. In case we had yet another problem to worry about. It was the kind of question I felt compelled to answer, no matter how I thought about it.

And there was something so beautiful about his true face, about the monster he'd become and how comfortably, easily, and *gently* he wore it, that I was transfixed enough to answer. All his softness was a choice, a defiance; it was the only way that something so dangerous and volatile as Acheron could be tempered without bloodshed. The exact opposite of mine.

I drifted closer until my hand grazed his and admitted gravely, "Well, I remember some of it. I'm not exactly thrilled knowing that anytime I close my eyes, a man-eating monster could jump out."

He only laughed. "And here I thought you were scary as is."

I glared, not wanting to entertain his joke. Even if there was some truth to my ferocity. Even knowing he *liked* my ferocity. "Not funny. What if it comes out in the middle of the night?"

Andor clasped his claws over his heart. "What a worthy way to die."

He hardly noticed me shoving him through his own fit of giggles, and somehow in the shuffle we'd become entwined, his fingers threading through mine, my arm looped through his. His touch was a balm for all my aches and pains.

"Any idea what triggered it? Your terrifying fugue state?"

I looked away.

That night, when I'd finally unlocked the door, reeling, a god freshly devoured and its blood only just washed from my face, I'd smiled at him. Assured him that everything was okay and curled up in bed. It hadn't seem like a good time then to add to the misery, not when I was still trying to grasp what I'd done. None of it had felt real. And how could I explain it now?

"I think I have an idea," I mumbled, training my eyes on the withering labyrinth up ahead.

"And?"

My teeth ground to stop the truth from coming out until I knew for sure. Until I was certain it wasn't a misunderstanding. I said slowly, "Acheron and I may have come to an understanding."

His brow furrowed, but he didn't press it. I wasn't ready to say more just in case Acheron came back, angry but unharmed. Or sidled up to Margaux and made her a more docile vessel instead. It just didn't seem possible that *I* was the one who killed it.

Even if it felt completely gone.

Our walk transformed into a waterlogged hike through the sickly, boggy remains of Elysium. The ground had gone completely mushy, sinking under our steps, and an old sweetness perfumed the air over the faint floral and herbal scents of the labyrinth. There was no telling what awaited us inside. *Who* Lethe might manifest as another warning.

"So the people we saw...you've seen them before, right? With Keturah?" Andor changed the subject, and his voice dropped to almost a whisper. "I thought they were just hallucinations."

I nodded eagerly. "Her brother and Coralie. Then again, Coralie also stalks my dreams, so I suppose that's not surprising."

He tightened his hold on my hand. "I thought I spotted my mom. Standing on the other shore."

He rarely spoke of his birth parents. He mentioned Ciro's parents sometimes, their kindness, their warmth, how he remained another son to them even in the aftermath of Ciro's death. He visited them for dinner on Sunday evenings, had suggested I come along though I'd stiffened at the thought. I wasn't fit to be around others, didn't know how to behave and be normal.

And now, having seen what I could do, that seemed even more apt.

He cleared his throat. "My parents died when I was eight. Car accident. I was staying with Ciro when it happened. My mom liked to dance to whatever was playing on the radio, in the kitchen, in the car, in public. Was probably listening to something good when they hit the ice."

I followed his gaze straight ahead, expecting to see the apparition myself but finding none. And Andor's tone was so wistful, a smile in the quirk of his lips, that it caught me off guard. He didn't seem to ache the way I did thinking of Coralie.

"I think Lethe only shows those you care about, the ones you really grieve," Andor admitted begrudgingly before tossing in a noncommittal shrug. "Maybe it's not *so* bad."

The inside of the labyrinth fared no better than the exterior. The hedges were spotted white, and the ground was still soft beneath our feet. It used to hum as I walked through from the blood meal in the soil, plants fed and nourished on blood from Acheron, but now it was dead quiet. Still. All the flower blossoms had turned grey and wilted, and what once was a garden returned to wilderness was somehow an even sadder rot than all the rest.

It was strange to see it this way, so limp and choked out, when Andor had once made a myriad of stalks bloom before my eyes. We talked and hid away from the world here. We'd first kissed and clung to each other like life rafts here.

So how were we supposed to just give this up? Walk away?

A fouler smell emanated from the corpse flower nestled in a corner. The large, fleshy plant was fuzzy, greying, its roots liquefying and shiny. More bleach white seeped into the ground and poisoned the walls around it.

In the center, the once-bright pink oleander trees were forlorn. The bark had begun to peel, the wood spotted and sickly, and the blossoms had long disintegrated on the sopping ground below. The sweet smells were overwhelming and wet now. I hurried to take up the canvases and get out of here.

"I'll need you to tell me which of these are totally ruined," I called over my shoulder, bending down. The art was mostly portraits of me and Joséphine, but there were some landscapes, still lifes and natures mortes around here and Paris. Quite a few of them were lighter around the edges that touched the ground, as if the rotting white of the Lethe just started consuming them too.

Andor raised the portrait of me that he'd created for a showcase, a re-creation of my audition but transposed in the meadows, surrounded by white flowers and hemlock. I was blowing a kiss and looked so *sweet*. So innocent. Nothing like the girl who wrought destruction, brazen enough to eat a god. He didn't bother suppressing his smile as he studied it.

"I like this one," he said finally, before setting the canvas aside. He riffled through the rest, a discard pile amassing before my eyes.

"But—" I seized the one of Keturah sitting high in a tree, looking down, grinning. "How do you know it can't be saved?"

He gestured to the face where the canvas sagged, all the colors muted and lines warped. And apparently touch-ups were out of the question. "Look at it—it's ruined. Don't worry, I'll just start again. I can always make new ones."

Then he smiled at me, hopeful, like it was so simple, just starting over. As if I hadn't even considered it to be an option, to wipe the slate clean and begin again. As if I wasn't floundering at doing just that.

I sniffled and turned away. I couldn't stop the tears, the pressure in my face and the trembling in my lungs. It was the sagging paintings, the decaying flowers, years of labyrinth work decimated in a matter of weeks. It was that none of us could come back, and none of us could avoid being changed by it. It was Lethe, eating away at every good memory I had. It was that change was coming too fast, and taking too much, and uncertainty seemed to be more commonplace than special occasion. That I'd never get to go back.

And even though warm, strong arms wrapped around me from behind, a ghastly mouth pressing kisses and whispering assurances into my hair, it still sucked.

# CHAPTER 26

Sometime long before dawn, the city quiet and dark beyond our windows, I disentangled myself from Andor's and Keturah's sleeping forms and slipped into the living room. Despite the aches in every part of my body, or perhaps because of, it was getting too hard to sleep.

I was too afraid, too wired.

And unthinking, scrambling for purchase, still reeling and searching for something in my life that hadn't changed, I picked up my phone, went through the recent numbers, and hit call. The ringing in my ears built as a promise of some escape, some outlet for the steam before I bubbled over. Margaux, the monster in me, Acheron and Elysium—I needed *something*.

I chewed my busted lip, gnawing through the clot and scab while I waited. The coppery taste and the pain kept me steady with each trill, as I wondered if she would answer. If she was still around, or I'd succeeded in pushing her away. Or maybe it was just early, and she was asleep like everyone else.

I didn't know what I was doing.

Abruptly the sound cut out, and a voice groaned, "Hello? Laure?"

The blood rushing in my head was too loud. Too much. It drowned out everything I'd planned to say to her until I was just empty. Just like our first call, every thought I had evaporated until there was only silence thick between us. Was it *you were right about Acheron* or *you were wrong about me?* Did it matter? Would she care?

There came the rustling of blankets, her shifting and breathing, and then slowly, my mother said, "Laure? Are you there?"

"Yes," I answered quickly. The panic in her tone unnerved me enough to speak, enough to loosen my jaw, maybe some kind of automatic programming that linked me to her the same way I sometimes called my father *Papa.* It was uncanny—she wasn't supposed to worry about me. I wasn't used to it.

She sighed. "Good. I... I told you I'm not giving up on you."

I slumped against the kitchen counter and hung my head. "I know. Yet another one of your mistakes that started when you offered me up to a fucking god."

The quip flew out of my mouth faster than I could stop it, but my tongue had always been covered in barbs, and it was the least she deserved. Worry or not, I was allowed to get my jabs in for a little while longer. Even if I didn't understand why I was talking to her in the first place. I didn't know why I called. If a god dies on a bathroom floor, does it make a sound? If Andor didn't feel it, did she? She of all people was supposed to notice when I was different.

But something about snapping at her had slowed my heart some, softening the anxiety that hummed under my skin. My fingertips were starting to go numb.

"I—" She began to stutter out some excuse.

"Look, that isn't why I called," I replied, studying the ugly pattern of bruising circling my wrist. At least the swelling had gone down. "Do you... Do you want to meet for tea?"

I flexed and pointed my feet to test the tightness of the ribbons. The pointe shoes were fresh, customized just how I liked them but still considerably stiff. And I'd missed even this sensation. Once, they were my past and my future, a rite of passage and a piece of armor.

They looked like they belonged on my feet.

"Are you ready?" Gabriel asked from across the studio as he snatched the towel from around his neck.

He'd spent the better part of the morning teaching me a new variation, pretending not to notice my black eye, and now was the time to put it to the test. To show that I was good at *something* other than falling on the floor and having an attitude problem. Maybe.

I pushed to my feet and took my place on the far left of the studio.

It helped that there was no one watching, none of the other seasoned dancers to judge how terribly brittle I was. And after crying for so long in the labyrinth, after helping haul the paintings and Keturah's stuff back to the apartment, so little sleep and so much restlessness, considering how bruised and beat-up I still looked, I didn't imagine I'd be anything but.

Unlike any other variation I'd ever done en pointe, the music wasn't classical. It was *swing* of all things.

A complicated drum fill erupted from the speakers, and when the rumble of the cymbals came, that was my cue.

With a glance to Gabriel, at his nod, I darted out onto the floor like I was being chased. At first, the steps were at an angle, the classic ballerina run, but then I switched to staggered, stilting, and bordering on listless. Looking back and breathless at whatever pursued me.

"Good! Now fall!" Gabriel shouted as he scurried after me, sliding across the floor to the choppy double-time trumpets.

He was gaining on me, and I dropped to the ground, sure to keep my toes pointed, feeling his own fall in the bending floorboards. He swung his arms to the trill of a flute and then flipped over my prone body with all the grace of a panther.

And for one long moment, as his muscular form sailed over mine, I saw Acheron: a shadowy face with indiscernible features, the sheer scale of noise that accompanied its form. A threat looming. Trying to overtake me.

*Nothing holds dominion over a child of Azathoth.*

Nothing except me. Laure. *Just* a ballerina.

When Gabriel's body cleared, as he rolled on the floor, I slid up. Toes still pointed, hinging at the hip so that my chest rose first. Like a girl rising from the dead.

"Like a string pulling from your ribs," he'd described it.

Like Elysium calling me home.

In a seated position, I felt him place hands on my torso and lift until I was standing. Until I was en pointe with my arms draped over his shoulders, so very soft and fragile, as if his touch wasn't searing, ice-cold.

"Nice!"

His voice boomed, sharp in my ear as he held my hand over my head. Back leg floating up in a wave, holding steady on one foot while he walked slowly around me. It was all muscle and focus to keep the ankles strong, especially as I leaned forward, body splitting in a perfect line. Turning as if the floor beneath me was a rotating platform, as if it wasn't *all me*.

This was why Gabriel had come to me, because in his head, it was all splits and pointe, straight lines and willowy grace. I didn't have to somersault or contort myself when these shapes were already so familiar. It required my level of fixation, the cutting eye of a perfectionist.

I tumbled out of the splits in time with the rhythmic bass, and when he caught me, I sank in his rough grasp like every wilting flower in Andor's garden. And with every pirouette across the floor, my body unlocked. It unloaded all my frustrations and worries and fears. It left my insecurities in the wind.

There was nothing left to do but let it all go, run, jump, and know my dance partner would catch me. Which, sometimes in the past couple of hours, he didn't. Or did, right before we both hit the ground anyway.

Still, I bolted across the floor and leapt, using his shoulders to pump off the ground and gain some height. To fly. Gabriel cheered as his hands clasped my waist, my body a smooth line from fingertips to toes. For a moment I was weightless, once again a condor in flight, arms spread wide, and he then seized my momentum to twist me in the air. The studio whirled rapidly in my vision. The throw was timed perfectly to a gap in the music. Like a caught breath, waiting to see if I'd fall.

If I was brittle, I would've broken in the silence.

But when the brass resumed, Gabriel caught me, we dipped, and then started over again.

My mother was sitting on a green-painted bench and holding takeaway cups in each hand when I spotted her. The park was quite busy with the early thaw of spring, children darting through the trees with their trickles of laughter, and students from nearby colleges and universities wrapped themselves in blankets around bottles of wine and thick books.

I didn't know if she remembered this place and all the times she'd brought me here, but Jardin des Tuileries was all that came to mind when she'd asked. It seemed fitting in a way, that we started here and we ended here.

And it would be an ending, no matter what she thought.

She didn't look so much like the last time we'd met—the effortless glamour of her updo now seemed messy and rushed, the boxy coat ill-fitting instead of chic, the signs of age on her face more pronounced. It was so weird, seeing a woman I once worshipped brought down to her knees before time. No longer a god but a simple, mortal woman while I'd managed to overcome the curse she'd left me.

When she finally noticed my approach, she straightened. This time, I didn't bother to style my hair, to brush my lashes with mascara or put on my neatest, prettiest pink dress. I didn't want to be the portrait of softness, goodness, *polished* anymore. Not when I was really, truly wild now. A savage kind of girl who bit out tongues and tore boys to pieces and could fly.

"Thank you for calling," she started as I sank into my seat. Something akin to contrition played out across her face. "For asking to meet."

A warm cup was shoved into my hands, and she brought the other to her lips. Steam rose from the lid, the bitterness of coffee curling in my nostrils.

I didn't actually like coffee, but why would she know that? Why would she know anything about me? I supposed it was better than if she'd brought strawberry macarons like I was permanently stuck at age six.

"We need to talk," I said, holding her meager offering close anyway. At least it was warm.

Something had come over me, something awakened in the aftermath of the crying and strengthened this latest rehearsal with Gabriel, where it seemed like I'd found my nerve again. And it could only be nerve, crying in front of a boy and then launching yourself into the air about a hundred times. There was none of the trembling hands or grappling for words, only steel resolution as I watched my feet, the bleached ends of boots I couldn't bear to throw away. Not anymore.

Elysium was dying, but these were a reminder that at least I tried. That if Acheron was dead, I was the one who killed it. That at least I did something more than kill a bunch of mortals for my ego or abandon a little girl to the predatory thing in the shadows. Me, the Laure I was now, was a force to reckon with, onstage and off.

My mother cleared her throat. "I agree. I said a lot of things at the restaurant that maybe—"

"Yes, all that and no apology," I retorted, nodding my head slowly as if I was still waiting for her words to sink in. But they had no substance, there *was* nothing to get. It was all air, and this time I would let her know.

She stiffened. None of the contrition from earlier, as if maybe it wasn't real, or I'd only imagined it, or maybe it only existed when she thought I wasn't going to ask for an apology from her. When I wouldn't make her name what she'd done, and it could all be blown over. When she wasn't on the defensive, uncomfortable. But healing was supposed to be uncomfortable.

Finally I met her eyes and stated calmly, "You know you left me, right?"

Those words, aloud, to her. I imagined, if it was still around, Acheron would have hummed in my veins with approval, but there was only me. I missed it, and I was angry for the position it put me in, for what it made me do, but I'd won. And if I could defeat a hungry, manipulative, ancient god, I could talk to the mother who set me up for it.

"Laurence—"

"I'd love to say I'm not angry anymore, but I'm still livid."

She was the first to break eye contact, to look at the children running around. I watched her grind her teeth, watched her steady herself as if she'd been wronged, ambushed. As if she was the child, and I was the parent. In some other universe, maybe I would have felt guilty.

With a level voice, my mother replied, "I made a mistake I'm not proud of. I was young and overwhelmed, and I just didn't want to do it anymore. I'd hoped staying away would save you, but I'm not that person." She put her hand on mine and flinched when I took it back.

No one seemed to like me taking back what was mine.

"I want to make it right."

I snorted. "You don't make it right by pretending it never happened."

Her expression bottomed out, until it felt like a middle-aged woman who I was bullying. Until I was somehow the menace, and she was defenseless against my words. Somehow I had all the power now. She muttered through gritted teeth, "That was ten years ago—"

"Twelve," I corrected. "I hadn't seen or heard from you in *twelve* years. I was *six* and had only just started dancing when you left. You didn't even make it to the first recital."

"Then what do you want?"

I opened my mouth and clamped it shut again. *What did I want?*

*What do you crave?*

It sounded so much like Acheron, it struck me to silence. In this moment, all I wanted was for her to acknowledge the scar tissue. That I'd needed her and I did all of it—the years of ballet, of bloody toes and splints and bruises, Acheron—to find a way back to her. To cover the gaping parent-shaped rupture she'd started. I was the one left grasping at air, trying to prove I wasn't someone people needed to run from.

I'd wanted to never be discarded again, so I nearly let Acheron consume me whole to make sure of it.

But *I'd* won in the end, against the ballet, against Coralie, against Acheron, by choosing me.

"I was stuck in the same place you left me, while you got to move on and become a different person," I said plainly, my voice the softest it had ever been. In becoming a man-eating monster, I replicated Andor's greatest trick. "I don't want to be lost and scared anymore. You could have guided me, instead of me guiding myself. I'm not begging to be heard anymore."

When I looked up again to meet her eyes, I saw the tight line in her mouth, the severity in her dark gaze. Her gaze that looked so much like mine, and yet so foreign right now. She was hurting and trying not to let it show. She was an animal backed into a corner, seething, and trying to figure out an attack and escape, beyond reason.

I sighed and climbed to my feet. "I guess I was just tired of carrying all this around. So I'm putting it down. Letting it go."

"I'm sorry!" She shrugged helplessly and spilled milky espresso as she sat her cup aside. "Is that what you want to hear? I'm sorry."

In spite of those words, the tone of her voice and how pitifully inadequate they were, I breathed a sigh of relief. The fire in my blood had fizzled to nothing, leaving just smoke and darkness and me, shaking my head. No aches, no anger. Nothing to regret.

"Next time, try saying it like you mean it. Then we can start over."

And then, with a smile, this time *I* left *her*. My mother, Alexandra Freeman, the woman who birthed me after promising me away to a wicked god, was stuck in place, watching my back as I disappeared, guessing if I'd return.

I chucked the full cup of coffee in the trash and didn't glance back.

# CHAPTER 27

I wasn't angry when I left my mother, like I'd expected. When I walked out of the park, I held my head high, and there was the beginning of birdsong in the air. My breath was steady, footsteps even, the monster in my blood calm. In the warming sunrays and the gentle breeze, I really felt *relieved*.

Because I wasn't the one stuck anymore.

Heading into this, I wasn't sure if I'd be able to set it free—all the weight of expectations, of shame that *I* was the flaw that needed fixing and fear that after the ballet, I'd never get a chance again. Yet somehow my shoulders were unburdened. The little girl spinning, waiting for her time to be noticed, to be inescapable and undeniable, could finally stop twirling and rest. I didn't have to try anymore to be immortalized; I didn't have to want it, and I no longer had to sacrifice myself to get it.

In a way, it was freeing, knowing things only mattered because they didn't. A dark god was immortal and all-powerful until it wasn't.

I was already halfway through the neighborhood and headed toward the metro station when the text from Keturah came in: *How did it go?*

The two of us locked in an arena, mother and daughter fighting for the final say, could it have gone any other way? It was just like in the ballet: The young and daring cannibalized the old and cautious. Partway through typing a response, I looked up to avoid colliding with a light pole and felt it again, that familiar, heavy presence of one of *them* ahead of me.

Olive skin and harsh blond bangs. A perpetual scowl, and the wraith-thin body of a young girl, weaving in and out of the crowd with deft hands.

*She's alive.*

Margaux swiped the wallet from someone's coat as she limped past, all while speaking rapidly to the taller, paler figure to her right. She held Florian's rapt attention, and he nodded with all the attentiveness of an eager student, her latest mark none the wiser. He looked even more muscular now, *older* than I knew him to be, even beneath the scrapes and bandages decorating his upper body. He was changing himself, paring away all his most hated parts the same way he'd removed the mouth from that woman so she couldn't scream.

And Margaux and her ilk let him.

I managed to dart behind a tree just as Margaux cast a cursory glance over her shoulder. It was as if she could sense me, still a vessel despite my lack of god to serve, like I sensed her and the others. I might as well have been a lighthouse for how she often trained on me in a crowd, and now I was here, just out of sight, sporting the remains of a black eye and still with no Acheron to shield me.

As if she could *hear* me, I held my breath and waited. What would she do if she saw? How would she exact her revenge? My back to the bark, I shuddered at the thought of Dominique breaking my bones one by one, my mouth walled over by flesh so no one could hear my cries. Of her going after Andor or Keturah. I didn't know if I could summon the savage thing again; I didn't know *how*. What if it was a fluke, a perk of being high on Acheron's flesh that eventually wore away?

Leaning out from the tree, I peeked again and sighed. Margaux and

Florian continued slowly along the big avenue, still talking and laughing and unaware. And I slipped back into the stream, moving fast to catch up, hoping to overhear whatever she was planning for me. For the others.

There was a nondescript package in her bruise-mottled arms, thick, maybe files, maybe money, wrapped in brown paper. She clutched it to her chest and ambled along, her limp even more pronounced up close, while Florian frowned at her.

"...don't get why I still have to follow you around," he complained, fidgeting with the fresh stitches at his hairline.

And though I couldn't see Margaux's face, her posture didn't change at all. His challenge didn't threaten. She just shrugged. "Maybe because no matter how much you change your appearance, *I'm* still older."

He shook his head. "But I can look older. Why would anyone there accept anything from a sixteen-year-old street urchin?"

"Why would anyone take a delivery from a grown man dressed like *that*?" She looked him up and down for emphasis.

Florian crossed his arms. Witheringly, he grumbled, "Obviously I'd change."

Margaux readjusted her grip on the package. "Besides, this isn't going to *the* Cour d'appel, it's going to security. It's *my* plan. I need to know it won't run into any more problems. Like you and Salomé with that secretary who got us on the news."

"We were just having fun—"

"You weren't supposed to be having fun," Margaux interrupted. "We needed information, and your *fun* broke her brain, which was why I had to go out and find another one. Nobody wants to keep cleaning up after you."

Florian groaned loudly and ruffled his hair, wincing at whatever fresh pain he found there. The motion was incongruous with what age he appeared to be—the frustration of an early teen boy couched in the muscle and facial hair of a guy in his late twenties. *Gross.*

I hung back when we reached a crosswalk with a red light, pretending to text Andor while pedestrians pooled in between us. I needed all the cover I could get to avoid a brawl, to avoid turning all monstrous right here in the middle of a busy intersection. Making minced meat of killers was very different from decimating the city block.

"Maybe we'd do better if we actually understood the plan. Like why there?"

"Because that's where it all goes down," snapped Margaux, her teeth bared and shoulders seeded with irritation right before she stepped out into the street. Whatever I'd done to her, the range of motion in her upper body was limited. The lights changed, and we all followed. "There is no justice for monsters like us. We aren't the kinds of victims these systems were built to protect. So if we aren't safe, no one is. You want to leave your mark on the world? You want someone to hear you? To respect you? To not fuck with you? You don't sit around and wait, you don't hide in Elysium, you take their safety, their justice, their laws. *That* is how you become someone to fear. Acheron or no Acheron, this is how we seal our legacy."

A chill ran through me, stunning me into place.

*Soon I'd be a name no one would forget. A raging fire they couldn't escape.* Margaux sounded like me. She sounded hungry and hurt like I once did—I'd basically recruited and armed myself.

"Plus, there's someone special there I have to pay a visit to. You can stay home if you don't want to help."

To my luck, they turned down another crowded boulevard, the city center teeming with more and more people as we neared the Seine. Soon it became a struggle to keep up, to maintain a distance but still hear them over the chatter and horns and buses. And at the pace they were going, how ragged they looked, pretty soon they'd notice me coming up on them.

Florian's fingers fidgeted at his sides. "Well, how am I supposed to believe anything you're saying? You did trick us into pissing off that harpy friend of yours. You said she wasn't a real vessel but"—he held up his bandaged arm—"I had to grow half this back, you know. What's left of Elijah is soaking through the floors, and Dominique lost an *ear.*"

She glared at him. "She's not my friend—she was a means to an end, and then it didn't work out. *You* were on board with getting a vessel involved, remember?"

Guilt ached in the pit of my chest for just a flash and then transfigured into anger. There was no forgiveness or understanding in Margaux's voice, and no reason for her to think of me as anything more than an obstacle in her path. But at the same time, she'd conspired against me from the moment she met them. All her prodding and friendliness were to manipulate me, to get what she wanted. Just like Acheron.

Well, she got it.

"Besides," Margaux sneered, clearing her throat, "if you've got a problem with me or my plan, then in two days' time, you can go fuck right off and do your own thing. Me? I'm staying here."

For a long time, Florian didn't say anything. He dropped his head in contemplation, his ears flushed red no matter what he did to age and recolor his features. Like an amalgamation of parts, freckled skin still peeked out from around the collar of his shirt, even if it'd vanished from the neck up. Almost like he'd forgotten to conceal it there.

I hung back, dying to run and tell Andor and Keturah everything I'd heard. A day or two was hardly enough time to mobilize, to gather an army the way Margaux had been amassing acolytes for her cause for weeks. She had something to promise, and I didn't. It would only be us—*two* of us, really, because Keturah's mark was long gone, and there was no Acheron to get a new one. She wouldn't stand a chance, not with their true faces, with Florian's shape-shifting and Margaux's manipulation and Dominique's hunger for bones. She was resourceful, sure, but I wouldn't throw her in their way.

"You really think it'll work? We'll be *gods* gods here?" asked Florian with all the tone of a young boy unsure. A young boy being baited, lied to.

I knew how it felt, asking that same question.

His apprehension contrasted starkly with Margaux, with her sharp nod and the fierce determination in her shoulders, back and down, chin up. She seemed taller than she really was, even with the limp, the stiffness in her movements. She wasn't afraid of what they were doing, the consequences, the sacrifices she'd make of herself. She was going to let that hunger for power or revenge or vindication consume her, just like it almost consumed me. How much damage would she cause before she hit rock bottom and learned to let it go?

"If not in Elysium, why not here? It's what I deserve."

I turned back and away, up the street we'd walked and toward the nearest metro station. The texts were firing off as fast as I could type them, knowing we didn't have a moment to spare. We couldn't wait, and we'd need more than just me and Andor if we wanted to save Margaux from herself. To stop her from burning the world and us too.

I didn't know if I was blameless, how much of Margaux's recruitment was me and how much was Acheron, not when I recognized so much of her. Beyond handing her the loaded gun, I didn't question, and for one second, I'd even encouraged her that it was always okay to take, even if you self-destructed in the process. Yet I used to judge Coralie for not knowing the difference.

"This is what you wrought too," I muttered out of habit, though there was no more static in my bones to listen, to know I was talking to it, "trying to escape."

If Acheron were still around, it might have disagreed. It probably would have sided with Margaux, stoked her hate, and pointed her in this direction. It would have made me join her, take her help and sit on the golden throne she was keeping warm for me. It had wanted us to be a god among gods, delighted at the chance of putting them in their places. Ruling over them as the most supreme.

But it wasn't around to do anything anymore—it was really, truly dead and gone.

# CHAPTER 28

Andor sat in an armchair, brows knit in concern and gaze following my every move while I paced the length of the living room. I'd already chewed my nails to stubs while we waited in silence, me periodically glancing out the window into the dark Paris streets like I might recognize someone watching, Keturah's prolonged absence like a splinter in my foot I couldn't reach.

"Where is she?" I muttered, letting go of the drapes to take another tour of the room. "Shouldn't she be here by now?"

It had only been a couple hours since I'd crossed paths with Margaux and Florian, eavesdropping on their plan. Hours since I turned away, insisting to Andor and Keturah that we meet immediately, that it couldn't wait. Andor had promptly extracted himself from his latest art class to arrive at the apartment before I did, and though Keturah confirmed she was heading out, she still wasn't here.

"There are probably still metro delays," countered Andor as he massaged his temples. "Don't worry."

I hadn't told him anything yet—I wanted us all together when I explained, to lay it all out once so we could hit the ground running after. And I certainly couldn't risk saying anything in text, not with Margaux's friends around every corner. Not after what they did to Vanessa. On my way back, I half expected to run into Dominique, to have him break my wrist while Margaux pulled a knife before I noticed what was happening.

In fact, it occurred to me that I was lucky I hadn't already.

"Will you at least tell me what this is about?" Andor added.

"No, we have to be together." I leaned against the wall and studied the blood beading around my nail beds. The skin was in tatters. "What if they got her?"

He cocked his head and stared at me, pinning me in place. "'They'? Who, Margaux? Why would they—"

The door rattled in the other room, propelling me off the wall. He dropped his inquest to rise from his seat, so that we were both up to watch Keturah enter. She was flushed, color rushing to the tip of her nose, breathing fast as she peeled away her coat. There was no sign of danger in her eyes, no impatience in her hands as she slugged her things aside and shut the door. Just breathing heavy because of the stairs. Not in pursuit.

"I came as soon as I could," she said as she crossed the floor. Her gaze flicked between us and our silence, trying to get a read on what this was, studying us for fresh injuries. Finding nothing in Andor, she settled on me. "What's going on?"

Now they both trained on me, just like that night in the cottage when they'd approached me with concerns about Niamh, when they expressed their concerns about *me*. The intensity of that focus, of feeling like they'd find every single ounce of my flaws, pick out all the cracks in my veneer—I didn't want to buckle again. I didn't want to run or lash tongues. Under their watch, my heart spiked, the sound of my pulse roaring in my ears with the fear that if I spoke, they'd realize it was at least partially my fault.

It was the reason I'd ignored all of it for so long, the reason I pretended everything was fine—everyone always abandoned me. Of course they would too if they saw the mess I'd made. The mess I was.

But I also had a choice.

Nervously, I crossed the floor to the window once again just to be sure. Then I marched into the kitchen to fetch the blender.

"Laure? What are you—"

"Shh!" I hissed, shocking her to silence.

They exchanged glances and watched as I dumped the two full trays of ice from the freezer into the blender and replaced the lid.

"I left work for this—"

I triggered the machine, seized both their hands, and dragged them into the bedroom. Closed the door. Let my shoulders sag. There was no putting this off anymore. I closed my eyes.

"I think Margaux and the others are planning something big. Like *government* big."

The furrow of Andor's brow didn't fade. It didn't smooth out as he continued to look at me, blinking, waiting for my words to make sense. Beside him, Keturah only pursed her lips. So I tried again.

"I saw Margaux today walking around with a very special-looking package and tried to listen in. She said again that if they can't be gods in Elysium, they'd try here, that they have plans that involve the Cour d'appel de Paris."

Finally Keturah sank down onto the edge of the bed, her quiet heavy. "But..."

"I don't know what, but I think she was carrying a bribe for security. Or blackmail, or *something*."

She covered her mouth.

I shook my head and with my back to the door, slid down to the floor, until my chin rested on my knees. I could blame Acheron all I wanted, but Margaux was my recruit, and I had every chance to steer her in another direction. In some ways, I failed her too.

"You're not responsible for her actions," Andor countered, though I hadn't realized I'd said the last part aloud.

"Aren't I?" I mumbled, torn between energized and worn thin. "I think she killed someone, the first night I saw her at the club. A girl died, and I didn't even think of it at first. And then we talked again and again, and I was so angry and frustrated that I basically egged her on.

"That anger and entitlement—she thinks this is the only way to get respect, and it doesn't matter who or how many people she has to step on to get it. She's just like Coralie, like *me*, and I ignored it because I didn't want to cause trouble. Or make it look like I couldn't handle it."

The very thought burned in my chest. Would Margaux have gone this far down the path if I'd said something? If I shut her down the moment she made that woman cry in the lounge? It was a slow and steady escalation while I was caught up in my own mess, questioning me and Andor, my dancing, my mother. I buried my head in Elysium while Margaux prepared an invasion on the ground.

And then I went and killed the only thing capable of stopping her.

Keturah pinched the skin of her forearm and stared blankly across the room. Maybe if I'd had a little more restraint, she could have been talked into another deal just to square this away. She could have been protected against their true faces at least. Now I'd left her defenseless.

Andor followed my gaze and raked his hands through his hair, messing up his bun until it fell apart, curls cascading around his shoulders. "And what about Acheron? Will it do anything?"

I closed my eyes for a beat. Now was the time to explain.

"About that."

They leaned forward.

"So, Acheron has been building its own army to protect itself from Lethe, arming people desperate to survive," I started slowly, training my focus on the flex and release of my feet to avoid their stares. *Acheron wanted people like it.* "The more people it had, the greater its chance of survival. And now we have a bunch of outcasts who want to conquer the world. They have no fears, and they're going to grab power, and I was supposed to . . . to be their leader."

Andor ran a hand down his face.

"But not *me* me. Acheron was trying to manipulate me, gain control of me. When it realized I didn't want what it wanted..." I took a deep breath. "It kissed me. Or tried to consume me, I don't know—"

Keturah lurched forward. "I'm sorry, what?"

"It has a mouth?" Andor retorted.

"—so I ate some of it instead. I killed it, it's gone. There is no more Acheron, like it vanished and hasn't come back. I think it's dead; it can't help us anymore."

In the kitchen, the blender whirred softly, all the ice cubes crushed up and turning warm in constant motion, and in our room, we all just stared at each other. I rubbed the back of my neck and waited for them to process the scheme, the kiss, the eating. Heat rose above my collar and pooled in the pits of my sweater.

Andor pulled up his sleeve and studied his own arm, the four marks still bright as ever. "If it's dead, then how do I still..."

I shrugged helplessly.

Beside him, Keturah started laughing. "Great, so you ate a god and can turn into a monster. Why don't we just go stop them right now, then? We get a couple guys, go over, kick their asses, stomp their teeth in—"

Andor swiveled around. "You don't have a mark!"

"I'm a Black punk from London. I've had my fair share of brawls—"

"And what will you do when one of them flashes their true face?" I asked softly. Because that was what they'd done before, Salomé and the others. They found their fun torturing mortals before giving just a flash of their truest forms. And it killed.

Keturah glared at me.

"What we need is more help. Like Gabriel. Maybe he knows some others with Lethe deals to help balance them out. Have a little more perspective, talking power before we resort to *brawling*," I said, narrowing my eyes at her. Just because we were capable of great violence didn't mean I wasn't tired of scrubbing blood from under my nails. Besides, I didn't have the money to keep losing clothes like this.

"Balance?" She seethed, her gaze turned harsh. I knew what she was thinking, what I thought of every time I saw Gabriel, was in his presence, felt that chill. "Lethe took everything from you—"

"No, *Coralie* did." I checked my phone to see if Gabriel had responded. I'd wanted to fill him in too. "Acheron didn't turn you into a homicidal monster, so maybe Lethe's the same. We need more hands on deck, and we need to meet somewhere without tipping them off."

Andor craned his head back, shut his eyes, and sighed. "She's right."

But Keturah only continued to glare, tapping the stud through her tongue on her top front teeth, until finally she relented. "Yeah, I don't like this."

Neither did I.

Then Andor turned to me, frowning. "Did you really eat it? What did it taste like?"

# CHAPTER 29

The squish and squelch of molded, rotting soil beneath our feet gave way to the slip and soft rattles of bones as we approached Lethe's shores again. Since Keturah hadn't come with us the first time we found the white river, chasing Ciro down, she gawked, wide-eye gaping as we weaved slowly through the mounds of skeletons. It was no fun watching the horror settle on her face as she realized what they were, the mix of human and animal, big and small. They trickled steadily from the sky like rain, fresh deaths always coming down.

"All's welcome on Death's shores," Gabriel said brightly as he spread his arms, catching our attention. He stood on a small hill overlooking the river, beneath the warped and twisted limbs of a dead tree. He didn't seem as uncomfortable as we felt, surrounded on all sides by death, followed by dead loved ones. Their apparitions seemed both fixed in place and fluid, blurring ahead and behind when we walked past.

Keturah's brother. Andor's mother. Ciro. Joséphine. Coralie. Me.

I half expected to find Acheron here too.

I nodded in greeting to Gabriel and shoved my hands in my pockets. We spoke sparingly outside of rehearsals, since I'd always been so preoccupied about my mother and Margaux, and that little breakthrough with the pointe shoes wasn't enough to change it. His gaze had lingered only briefly on my face, mottled with marks when I'd shown up to learn the variation, but there were no lasting looks today. He must have known what Margaux ordered, what went down.

And in this moment, I could do nothing more than hope that he was trustworthy. Or at least that he'd heard what *I* did and was on the right side.

"Thanks for coming," I told him, aiming for congeniality but ending up cold.

The reality was that I didn't want to be here, talking about this. I was fed up and lost, and fed up with being lost. I was feeling guilty and angry at myself, Margaux, and Acheron for making me feel guilty. And worst of all, I was feeling all of it *here*, only inches away from my own ghost and the ghost of my best friend, my first love, the girl who killed me. I might have made peace with the world, but all of me could still hurt and was hurting, and I no longer cared to keep pretending it wasn't. Not even in front of the Gabriel Trémaux.

I was a lethal cocktail of emotions, and Margaux had made a grave mistake in setting me loose.

Gabriel shrugged. "There's a door not far from the studio. It took no time at all."

Keturah glanced around us. "Door? There's another?"

"You didn't know? There's a bunch around the city." He nodded his head farther down the shoreline where, if we squinted hard enough against Lethe's bright white light, we could make out the faded wood of a door just beside the trunk of another dead tree. At first glance, it looked like part of the tree itself. "Where did you hike from?"

We gestured off into the distance. It didn't surprise me, with what Margaux once said. The size of this place, of Elysium, stretched on far beyond what the eye could see, and, I suspected, the human could understand. Things didn't seem to be built at a scale to be digestible, comprehensible. This land and its gods were of something else, something mortals weren't meant to touch and play around in and eat. And now Margaux and her gang were going to wield it as a weapon they didn't understand.

"You know, sometimes I come back to consider its progress," Gabriel continued, glancing around. He seemed in no hurry, though we were all starting to shiver. "The slow creep. You can get so trapped in the wheel, little mice working and eating and sleeping, riding the train, doing laundry. Sometimes I forget that this is a cycle. That it ends and begins again."

He sounded like a new age prophet, his voice smooth and dripping with unpalatable wisdom. Lethe was in the process of absorbing everything we loved about this place, while Margaux was poised to take what was left of the surface. Even if it had to, some of us didn't want it to end. We didn't ask for this cycle. But Acheron had left the door open when it dragged me from oblivion, and I was the catalyst that triggered all of this.

I looked at my specter, at her hair matted with water, blood, and dust, the slick wet red of her shirt, the welts and bruises and broken skin. The *optimism*. She thought she was finally free, finally found, finally right. We'd gone through an entire rebirth only to be cursed again in the next life.

"Riveting," I snapped, unwilling to mask my bitterness. We didn't have the time. "While Elysium is in its final stages, let's get to the real problem: What happens if a vessel betrays the god? Or, say, kills it?"

Gabriel flinched. "Kill it? Who would—" His eyes widened slowly with understanding, brightening as he gawked at me. At my stony expression, at the blank acceptance of my companions. And for once, in his disbelief, he actually looked his age of late twenties.

"Okay," I drawled impatiently, "easier question. How do we stop Niamh?"

He scratched the back of his head, and it took a long time for him to find the words, to gather himself and speak. "Right, the little tyrant. Well, the last we spoke, I told her that her hubris would ruin everything for all of us, so I refused to be a part of this. And my whole perk with Lethe is I can't be manipulated. By anyone. She won't surrender Paris. She wants to be a god, and this is not where the people are."

"Maybe we try to end her deal somehow," Andor suggested, his brows raised hopefully. "Take her power?"

"Or imprison her here," Gabriel added, still studying me.

There was another option. One that handled Margaux permanently. Messy but once done, it'd be over for good. There was no Acheron this time to rear its attention, to guide me toward the idea already formed, to be enthralled at my consideration of it at all. It would have loved my becoming.

Coralie's apparition grinned at me as I thought it, as I parted my lips to give life to it.

"Or we could kill her," I pointed out flatly. Not that I enjoyed the idea, but that was always a choice. I'd expected them to all balk, to clamor in with alternatives and rebuttals and *you didn't mean that*s, but when nothing came, I went on. "She clearly has no problem killing or manipulating others into it. Even if we burn her mark and take her deal, what's to stop her from getting another with Lethe this time?"

Andor's gaze lingered on my arm. On my mark that was still there in pristine condition. It was so easy to read his expression, reliving the moment he and Keturah had found me in the tunnels, Acheron's imprint burned from my flesh. Just like Coralie had done to Joséphine and Ciro before she'd killed them. The mark protected us, and stripping it away made us vulnerable. We would be doing to her what was done to me, knowing exactly how easy it was to go back and beg harder. How it opened me up to whatever a god planned next.

Finally, Andor raised his dark eye to meet mine. "And you're fine with that?" Everything at stake filled the weight of his voice.

I bit the inside of my lip and glanced away. It didn't matter what I wanted, what I was fine with. Not when Margaux was poisoning Paris. Where would we go next? How long was I supposed to keep grieving things?

"Let's go back to the idea of taking her deal," Keturah floated out there, nodding, her voice smooth to defuse the tension. She didn't want me killing any more than I wanted to do it.

But I knew if I did, if I seized a fistful of Margaux's fried hair and pushed her down below the surface, I could hold her there. I could let the anger win. After all, I was reborn as a vessel. Almost *destined* for it, even. If Margaux only respected power, if she only responded to it, well then, I was more than capable of giving her another, more final taste of my monster.

"How do we stop her from getting another?" Keturah prompted. "Even if Acheron is...gone, there's still a million doors right to Lethe. All's welcome as you said."

"I could make her forget this place entirely," I answered calmly, determined, searching their faces for approval. An offering between us to be the Laure I wanted before I unleashed the Laure they needed. "I'm the vessel of an eldritch god, after all—or at least, I *was*."

# CHAPTER 30

"Is that so?"

The voice carried from around a tall stack of bones, bones that shifted as we spun and Margaux stepped out from its shadow. She was flanked by a couple others, and she looked dressed for a show. The special guest for a party. In a dress that looked disturbingly similar to mine, a shade of rosy pink, high-necked with pleated skirts. She looked like a woman ready to conquer the world. Like a colder version of me.

She beamed as she looked at me. "We'll just have to see about that, won't we?"

I turned on Gabriel, ready to lob an accusation. Keturah was right to mistrust him from the beginning—

But he only shook his head desperately, as if to deny that Margaux had found us, to deny the label of traitor I'd already silently applied to him. Florian and another acolyte seized the distraction to sneak up behind him and grab him. They wrenched his arms back until he was hunched over, until he hissed at the pain and we heard the *pop* of joints. And before we could clamber forward, he was being forced down the hill. To join us. No matter how he'd resisted, Florian was even bigger now, bulky, and it was futile.

"Keturah—" I started.

"I know," she said, immediately dropping her head. Closing her eyes. Even as her nostrils flared, she veered toward self-preservation and trusted me to get her out.

Before we came here, we'd talked about sequestering her away, perhaps leaving her to "guard" the apartment alone while Andor and I dealt with meeting Gabriel and stopping Margaux and her friends. She'd hated every idea, but we didn't want her to *be* in this position, the one she was in now. We didn't expect to be found so soon, to be betrayed. Especially when we barely had a plan.

And now we needed another one.

I examined them, Dominique, Salomé, and others who'd jumped me. Who'd watched or joined in as Vanessa was tortured and killed. They were all covered in scrapes and bruises, limbs wrapped from sprains and broken bones. A wad of bandage was plastered to the side of Dominique's face where I'd allegedly torn the ear clean off. And seeing me, none of them looked happy. The way they exchanged glances now, they looked apprehensive. Like I might do it again.

The corners of my lips twitched into a smile. A sneer. And they immediately dropped their gazes.

*Good.*

Andor's shoulder brushed against mine as he pressed close. Keturah wrapped a hand around my coat sleeve, as if she could feel how they surrounded us. How sorely outnumbered we still were. Us four, if we were to include Gabriel, to their ten.

"So what, gonna sic your henchmen on me again? Didn't turn out so well last time, did it?" I jeered, breaking the silence with as much bravado as I could muster. I was covering up the fact that I didn't know if I could just summon the monster here and now; the last time had been unintentional, as I begged a dead Acheron to help me. This time, I knew it wasn't coming, and I was on my own.

Cold sweat prickled down my spine, raised the hair on my arms. I couldn't see how we'd get out of this yet. I didn't know a way to escape with Keturah still alive. Not that I'd ever let that show.

But once, I *was* the vessel. I could compel them for a moment, hold them off again and again until Andor and Keturah escaped. It could work—

"I'm so disappointed in you," said Margaux, dragging my attention away from the wooden door just beyond reach.

They could make it if they ran. They only needed moments.

"I really thought you understood this time. Seeing that room, seeing what was left of *Elijah*, nothing more than a puddle of blood and chunks. Nothing recognizable. I thought that meant I finally got you to understand."

I wrinkled my nose. "Understand what?"

Margaux gestured to the bone fields of Elysium. "Our true nature. That we're predators, we're *meant* to dominate, and we can't do that if we're crying over an empty forest and a mortal girl we don't even like that much. If your misplaced empathy keeps making you interfere."

Even then, when they broke my nose and fractured my ribs, it was manipulation. All she did was manipulate. Lies and half-truths and schemes. She probably manipulated me that night in La Tempête too, getting me to drink myself silly on prosecco and spill my guts.

I squeezed my eyes shut and took a breath. "I take it Acheron didn't want you as a vessel, huh?"

When I opened them, I found Margaux glaring at me, flaring her nostrils, a bull ready to charge. She swaggered closer, jutting out her jaw as she searched for something quick and pointed to say.

There was enough distance to run, to freeze them all and bolt through the mounds. The marsh and what was left of the forest could be a great place to disappear. We could get a head start before they even broke through my hold. They weren't used to it; they didn't know that they could fight it.

If my hold even worked here, so close to Lethe.

"Vessel or not, you're either on our side or on theirs," she continued blithely. "The gods or the mortals, hunt or be hunted. You forget that they drove us away. They pushed us out, and that's how we got here. You could help us punish them."

No more proselytizing.

Running hands through my hair, I shook my head, trying to drown her out. Did she get exhausted, trying to keep score of who wronged whom all the time? A running list of all the reasons we were so broken and miserable? I wanted out—I was ready to be free of it all, the spite, the need to be acknowledged and cooed over, the scar tissue we pretended wasn't there. When did we get to focus on *living* anymore?

"Last chance—"

"Do you ever get sick of hearing yourself?" I snapped, moving my body to shield Keturah. "I'm so tired of hearing you talk."

Margaux pursed her lips, and for a long moment, we stared at each other in a battle of wills. Me waiting for her next move, the fire in my blood at the ready to be cast out. To stop them in their tracks and pull the others behind me into the marsh.

Finally, she sighed and turned to Florian. The boy who looked like a man still held Gabriel, positioned precariously close to the white river. Thick fog ebbed around their feet, icy water spilling onto the bones beside them. Over my own teeth clattering from the cold, she told him, "Your power won't work on him, so deal with him the old-fashioned way. Throw him in."

"**No!**" I struck out, seizing the blood and meat in Florian's body as his grip tightened around Gabriel. It was a grapple for his mind—I held as steadfast as I could while he trembled, confused and in pain, to break free.

And so close to the edge too.

Margaux applauded. "Now she comes out to play, of course. Laure still thinks she's a hero."

Two hands on my shoulder, she shoved me then, a quick and harsh force that sent me stumbling into Keturah. And had the intended consequence of breaking my concentration. Keturah tightened her hold on my arm, steadying me on the slippery bones just as Gabriel's cry rang out in the still, dead air.

A splash strangled the rest of it, the surface of Lethe rippling as he went under.

Florian backed away, hissing from where the river's waters splashed him. Burns mottled the side of his face as he turned, grimacing, and wiped his nose. Blood I drew, that followed whenever I pressed hard enough, smeared the back of his hand.

We waited in the quiet to see if Gabriel would resurface. Acheron wasn't the easiest to swim in, not when the blood was so thick, but it wasn't a death sentence. Not like a river of oblivion that no longer stirred.

Fed up with this girl and her insolence, her constant kneading and carelessness, I rounded on my heels. "I'm not a hero, and I'm nobody's villain either."

I backhanded her before she could say anything else. The flat of my hand connected with her jaw, feeling light as her head snapped to the side, as she swayed on her feet. She was so small and thin, it might as well have been a punch for how she crashed back into a seat and caught herself. For how she stared up at me, giving glimpses of a child pushed down on the playground.

For a moment, I bared my teeth, sneering, standing over her, shoulders heaving. That felt good. "This is my last warning."

Only she straightened up, hauled to her feet by eager cronies, a long red scratch from my nail drawn along her cheek, and her eyes feverishly bright with the provocation. She wanted a fight and someone to triumph over, to measure her worth against. I'd just given her what she wanted.

Without looking away from me, she ordered, "Do him next."

Dominique and a wretched, faceless acolyte grabbed Andor before I could reach for him. Shield him. Take him away. He struggled as best he could, though he was smaller than Dominique's muscled frame, even though he was caught off guard, all while I was rooted in place. Panicked. Thinking.

He was a soft boy not meant for fighting, for danger. He was destined for gardens and oil paints and the warm light of setting suns. He wasn't supposed to die. Acheron had promised.

Them, on the other hand—I could be convinced.

It was my fear lashing out before I realized. Fear and cold fury swept across the shore and squeezed until everyone around us, everyone except me, Andor, and Keturah, winced. They clutched at their chests and doubled over, the pain swelling enough for Andor to break free of their hold and lock onto me. Onto the blood dripping from the fist I made, from clenching so tightly my claws broke skin.

Something flickered in his expression—whether it was pride or terror, I didn't know, there was no time to question. All that mattered were the broken heartbeats of the acolytes all around me, asynchronous, staggering out, bodies collapsing onto cold, wet bones as they struggled to understand. As they begged Margaux to make it stop.

And then we were running.

Not toward the wooden door along Lethe's shores, wherever that would spit us out, but toward the woods. Toward the cottage and the iron door, *our* door. Because if Margaux had any sense when she planned this ambush, then she would have been clever enough to position someone on the other side in case we escaped it. But in the forests, we could hide out for as long as we had to.

Clinging to each other, we slipped and vaulted over slicked bones and barreled into the marshes. Dirty white water and mud sloshed around our feet as we darted around dead trees and over rotting skeletal remains of animal carcasses. All around us was a sea of death, flies and maggots and bones, while we'd left oblivion far behind.

"Where do we go?" I shouted, that fury and determination giving way to panic.

"It's too sparse and bright here, but we can lose them in the Catacombs!" Andor threw a glance over his shoulder and picked up his speed.

Keturah and I shared a look.

If I stopped running and surrendered myself, could I convince Margaux to let them go? If I promised to help her lay waste to everything the mortals built, would she let them live? If I sacrificed all the parts of myself that I only just found, carved them all away until there was only the hunger and sorrow left, the monster Acheron wanted, would she be satisfied then? Would it be worth it?

Was I worth it?

*No.*

There was a blur of shadow in the corner of my eye as we crossed into the thicket of stringy, pulpy trees. It felt like familiar blood, a pull I knew and recognized. So sudden and small that the movement slowed me down, and then I was propped against the melting flesh of a trunk to catch my breath. Keturah did the same.

Andor hung back, watching as a fox darted toward us. Ears back, nervously looking around, it fled with confusion etched on its small face. Soundlessly sprinting back into the shrubs.

Keturah tugged on my hand. "We have to keep moving."

"Too late," said a voice, Salomé, as she emerged from behind white-speckled hedges.

And in our surprise, she struck fast, smooth, the metal in her hand catching in the light. It twinkled as I pulled Keturah away, as her hand sailed through the air, as she swiped clean across Andor's exposed throat. Because he had been open and facing her, or maybe trying to shield us.

With a victorious smile, she'd cut him deep enough that his eyes rolled back in his head before he even hit the ground. Tendon and sinew, exposed and wet. Blood pumped into the ground in thick, heavy spurts, and Andor's body went limp before I could reach for where he'd fallen.

Before I realized I'd even lunged for him next. *After.*

Keturah didn't release her iron grip on me. "We can't save him. We have to keep running—"

My heels dug in. I couldn't look away from his face, the vacancy that fast filled his expression, the blood on his hands as he'd tried to cover his wound. It didn't look like him, like the boy I knew, and he didn't look like he was sleeping. The blade had been harsh enough that he was nearly severed, so that his neck twisted at a wrong angle. Another of my faults, letting razor-sharp girls who weren't afraid to hurt him walk free.

I'd saved Keturah only to forsake him.

A strangled cry filled my ears that might have come from me, covering up Keturah's yelling, the sound of my own heartbeat. Because Salomé was still here, standing over him, brandishing that bloody knife she'd used to cleave through *my* Andor, and she was coming for us next.

Stumbling back, numbed, I watched and waited for his body to mend itself back together. For the seam Salomé made to stitch itself closed. For his head to right itself on his shoulders, for Acheron to make good on *anything* it had promised us. But nothing moved. I managed only a single step before a loud, sharp pain rippled through my hip. It shot through me like a bolt of electricity, from the center of my thigh and zipping up my spine.

My legs gave out from under me at once, and I dropped, sprawling on my back, just out of reach of Andor. The scream of the fracture echoed all through me, while Keturah was snatched from my hands.

Dominique's bushy head and prominent brow came into view as he and the others caught up. As Margaux was the next to step over Andor's mangled body, just like they did the mouthless woman, as she hovered over me, as Keturah grumbled in the sounds of struggle. All at once, we went from having a chance to being dealt a crushing blow.

*Come on, monster*, I pleaded.

The pain radiating through my thigh was too much to stand on, to put *any* weight on. So unbearably loud that it twinged even when I tried to sit up and scoot away, that I couldn't think about anything, do anything but pant just to keep conscious. My teeth clattered loudly from it as a red stain blossomed through the fabric. As fierce white bone jutted out from my jeans.

I needed that primal darkness to wake up and take control before it was all over.

Salomé held Keturah by the back of her neck, but in a flash, Keturah struck out. She caught Salomé in the nose with a headbutt, and we all heard the crunch as Keturah darted away.

Until Florian grabbed her too, wrenched her up by her bright hair.

"**You better**," I gasped, voice low and raw enough to be a growl, "**bury me deep. Or I will destroy you.**"

Margaux wasn't smiling anymore. She looked angry, still with blood smearing her chin from when I'd squeezed her heart. A little trick I'd never told her about, that Vanessa couldn't have prepared her for. She'd make me pay for this, even more than she already had. At her feet, Andor's body hadn't stirred. Hadn't shown *any* signs of healing at all, like he was really—

"That's exactly what I had in mind," she told me before turning to Dominique. "Let's show Laure the grave we prepared for her, since she won't *die*, and she's so loyal to this place. Bring the mortal with us for insurance."

The struggle began anew as more surged forward to help subdue a swinging, biting, angry Keturah.

"Margaux—" Desperation seeded my voice as I tried to summon the wicked dark and came up empty.

"You must be so sleepy," the blond-haired woman said, and instantly, a wave of drowsiness rolled through my limbs. Her doing. "If you don't stay out of my way, Laure, I will flay her alive while you watch."

Her power was a heavy blanket that draped over me. It was sudden exhaustion that hit me like a wall, from years of fighting, pushing, jumping, spinning, running without end. The kind that racked my bones, that was useless to resist. My eyelids drooped despite my refusal, and then I crumbled into myself. Back into the waiting dark.

# CHAPTER 31

I fell into and woke up in pitch-blackness. Something, maybe rain, trickled above me, catching on the ceiling, while grogginess swept through my body and filled my head with cotton. My mouth was dry, arms rubbery, and pain throbbed in my thigh, into my hip, into my feet.

But at least it was no longer broken.

More trickling overhead, scattered falling.

Interspersed with pauses, rather than a steady shower.

With a groan, I tried to prop myself up, get my bearings. My arms shook with the effort, head lolling to the side, and then my forehead collided with something above. Pain diffused through my scalp.

Nothing moved when I pushed against whatever was above me, palms flat and pressing up with all my might. It didn't shift or shudder. The grogginess faded fast, and my panic was wide awake now.

I felt around the flat sides and beneath me, studying the depth of wherever Margaux had placed me. Splinters prickled my fingertips from the rough surfaces. And the trickling above grew farther and farther away, more and more muffled.

My head flopped back, and I closed my eyes to think.

It sounded like someone was tossing something above me, moving in heaving gestures and scattering clumps. And the walls surrounding me were wood on all sides, straight and narrow. A wooden box for me to lie in—a *coffin*, crudely made, just for me. I smelled fresh wood and earth. *Dirt.*

They were burying—Margaux was burying me alive.

My breath cinched.

"Well, this sucks, huh?" a voice said at my side, though this box was hardly big enough for two. The last voice I wanted to hear right now. It was too dark to see Coralie's apparition, but I pictured her smiling. Grateful to see that I was unable to escape her at last. It was all she'd wanted in the end: us together forever.

The next breath that escaped me was ragged and tear soaked. Full of snot and full-body misery.

Despite all my railing against that fate, I was finally here. In her clutches. No Acheron to hide behind, no Keturah or *Andor* to dig me out. And she'd even had a nicer coffin than me.

No Andor at all, his head nearly shorn from his torso, the stringy veins quivering as his body dropped in a heap. No last words or final wishes, no saying goodbye, no chance for him to be angry that Acheron had lied to us—if he had known that he could die, would he still have decided to help me? If he saw what a knife could do to him, how fast it would fell him for choosing my side, would he have ever looked my way?

Every breath came out shakier than the last as I tried to stop the sobs from rising up. From overtaking me.

Andor was dead.

"Is your plan just to sit here and mope?" Coralie asked sardonically. Callously. Like she wanted to drive me into snapping back. "Because if so, Keturah'll be dead of old age by the time you get out."

I wiped the wet from my face with my dirty, splintered fingers and took a shaky breath. Swallowing air to stop my shuddering. "I'm not talking to you."

"Why not?"

"Because you're dead. You're not really here."

Coralie's hand glided along my arm, forcing a shiver down my spine. It was as cold as ice, as the dead, and she erupted in a fit of giggles at my movement. "Can't I be both?"

"No."

And my voice, in spite of myself, sounded reluctant. Did I want her here? With me? Did I want my best friend back more than I wanted to be alone? Sometimes I thought I'd lost Coralie long before we fought in the water, but that didn't mean I didn't miss her. That I didn't mourn her as much as the person I'd been when I had her.

Even if she was rotten to the end.

How long before Andor's ghost joined us?

In the quiet, almost as sad as I felt, she whispered, "No, you're right." She sounded like a ghost grieving herself, and perhaps that was what a ghost was—a lament frozen in time. How long would it last? Until Lethe was done overflowing or until the end of the universe? Until I was gone and there was no one else to remember her?

There wasn't enough space to bring my knees to my chest, to curl into myself. I was trapped in a box faced with all that I'd lost until who knew when, and I couldn't even console myself. Keturah could only hold out, keep her eyes shut, for so long—I didn't believe Margaux would even honor her own threat. And Andor . . . who would bury him while I was down here? Could I claw my way out? Did I even have the willpower to try?

"Just because all things end and you're allowed to be sad doesn't mean you get to give up, you know?" Coralie continued, poking and prodding until she found my softest parts.

I stared into the darkness. I couldn't even *cry* in peace—

"You have no problem getting angry, but then what? What comes next? Besides moping."

"I don't know—"

She nudged my shoulder. "You quit your only dream and then killed me. You tried to pretend none of it mattered and recruited some girl who *killed* your boyfriend. And that god you thought you befriended was just using your sadness, trying to manipulate you to take over your body and then your city. And now you're buried alive by the girl you helped recruit. What are you gonna do about it? Lie here until the end of time?"

"Shut up—"

Coralie shoved me again, my shoulder knocking into the hard wood wall. "Make me. If you don't like it, do something about it."

I flopped over. "What do you expect me to do?"

"Grow up!"

My pulse swelled in my ears in the silence. Running through her words again and again until either she disappeared or I put my hands around her throat. She sounded like Gabriel.

"You're disappointed and lost. You died and came back changed. Are you allowed to be someone else? Do you even *want* to be someone else? Where do you go? Oh boo-hoo!" Her freezing fingers fisted my shirt. "I'm *dead*. I can't do any of those things. You think you made a mistake? You regret killing me? You miss me? Well, if time doesn't stop for me, it certainly doesn't wait for you to stop running from yourself like a coward. If you don't like where you are right now, either get comfortable or change it. I thought even *you* knew that."

Though I tried to pry her fingers away, her grip was like steel. And she was stirring something in my veins, so that I was breathing heavy even as she was the one speaking. But I didn't have the oxygen to waste.

My eyes stung. "But I don't know how."

"Margaux thinks she can manipulate you into being what she wants. That this punishment will make you see things her way or keep you busy long enough that it doesn't matter."

My lips trembled. "Sh-she can't."

I saw exactly what Coralie was doing, I saw where she was going, and I would follow her there. She was right about Acheron so far.

"Why not? She thinks she knows exactly who you are."

"She doesn't know me."

"She thinks she can manage you. That you're so *easy* to control."

I hiccupped. "And I'm not."

"And what did you do to Acheron when it tried?" Coralie screamed, her face pressed to mine so that I felt her cold button nose. There was no tickle of breath from her mouth, only the wet stench of rot on her skin.

"I tore it to pieces," I answered, picturing how it quivered under me, how great it felt to tear into its buzzing, humming chest.

*Laure* did that. Not just the vessel. Not *just* a ballerina. Not Andor's girlfriend or Margaux's prize to be won. I didn't do what I was told. I didn't make myself palatable. I killed Coralie to save myself, and that didn't involve languishing here in a filthy pit with her annoying ghost.

Yes, I'd loved her, but she was rotten. She and the ballet, they were poison to me, so *I* walked away. *I* bit the tongue out of the Daemon King itself when it tried to feed me lies and then I swallowed it just to free myself. I alone was the Wicked Dark now. I became a monster by *choice* and wouldn't let the world erase me now.

Coralie cupped my face in her cold hands and pressed her freezing lips to mine, shocking me back into my body. Into this coffin. "That's my girl. Now get the fuck out of this grave and make yourself a menace."

Though it was dark, though she was dead, I nodded to her. To myself.

And I got to work, smashing fist after fist into the coffin lid until I broke skin and bled, until the wood cracked and buckled and caved in on the side. Wet, slushy dirt filtered in with it, but I was already pushing through the other end. Sweeping. Crawling my way to the surface.

Clawing my way, once again, out of death.

And this time, no primordial soup or bargain or aspiration of godhood was there to help. This was all me. I was the Laure who never stopped coming.

It couldn't have been more than a couple minutes, but it felt like hours. Days, even, before my head cleared the mud and I saw light. The moment my chin broke the surface, I sucked air into my lungs that tasted sweet and molded. Nothing like the Elysium I'd once loved. Yet I was fighting to pull my torso out, kicking and writhing to free my legs.

But I was out.

The sky was fully grey now, light as morning under thick clouds, and still so bright I had to squint and cover my eyes. The mud clung to me as I crawled, half dragged myself to the edge of the muck. Up onto sparse grass and more squelching mud that was, at least, more solid than the soil I'd been swimming in.

Lying on my back, shivering, I breathed and stared at the sky and the mountain of bones in my periphery and the spindly dead trees on the other side. I didn't want to close my eyes for a while, to be back down there in the dark so soon again. My arms and legs spread wide, starfished in dirt, alive alive alive, feeling fat, steady droplets trickle down. One and then another and then a downpour.

*Rain.*

It was raining in Elysium. It had never rained before, not once since I'd first crawled into that pool of red and let it take me. Yet it smelled like rain, tasted like rain, droplets heavy until it was a shower to cleanse the dirt and blood from me.

As if Elysium wanted to say, *You're all right.*

It was a mix of laughter and sobbing that broke from my chest. Coralie hadn't climbed out with me. There were no more ghosts here to hold my hand. Andor was gone, just like Acheron was gone, and I only had one shot to save Keturah and stop all this. Yet I'd conquered Acheron and was still here. Both above and below. Alive and lost, finally awake.

I screamed as loud as I could, for as long as I could, until it didn't hurt anymore, and then I stood the fuck up.

# CHAPTER 32

"If any ghosts want to tell me how to stop Margaux without Keturah getting flayed alive, that'd be great!" I threw out into the quiet, half expecting Coralie to make another resurrection.

But there was no answer, other than the lapping of water against bone. So I tightened my grip on the shovel thrown carelessly where they'd buried me, and continued on my path.

No steadier on my feet, I limped among the mounds of bones by Lethe's shore. In the hours I'd been under, the river had seemed to steady itself somehow. It was no longer overflowing with milky white, no longer pumping bleach into the soil around it. If I looked at it for long enough, staring through the dancing mist that took on the shapes of people and animals, the water level seemed to go down.

As if oblivion had wrought all the damage it wanted, and it was sated now. All was laid to waste and now it was time to rest.

As if we were connected, a link established when I was pried from its grip. It'd started bleeding when I came back. Now that I was no longer hemorrhaging grief, it too had . . . calmed.

Soon came a noise through the rain. It sounded like the shuffle of bones, the shift and cascade of my own footsteps and someone else's in thick air. Soft and getting closer.

Was I being followed? Were they not done with me?

I turned toward the sound, gulped, and took the shovel in both hands like a bat. If it was Salomé again, charging out to finish me off, I'd swing. I'd break her jaw and then cave it all in. That much, despite the tenderness of my still healing leg, I was capable of.

But there was no heartbeat accompanying the sound, no brush against my fingertips that marked the feathery pulse of a bird or rabbit. There was also no pull of an acolyte, the charged air that marked them as one of my kin; neither was there the dull ache of discomfort, of joints to pop, or skin crawling, an itch out of reach—

"Laure!" Gabriel said as he rounded the bones and stepped into view. He swerved out of the reach of the swinging shovel. "Oh thank god! Are you okay?"

Then he barreled toward me and pulled me into a hug. My skin should have rebelled at the contact, at how he then held me at arm's length to study me, but it didn't. I felt nothing. He looked sopping wet, as if he'd just climbed out of the river. His dark hair clung to his face, his tight shirt sticking to the overly defined muscles of his chest. His skin was extremely cold.

Gabriel's brow wrinkled. "What happened to you?"

I extracted myself from his hold and raised the shovel. "Buried alive."

He balked.

"Can't stop," I added numbly before I continued limping on my way. The next words, I pulled from my mouth like teeth. "They, um, they killed Andor. And took Keturah. I need to bury him. I can't just leave him there. And they need Keturah alive as collateral so at least—"

He scurried to catch up. "I'm sorry to hear that."

I could only nod, wondering how long I was going to keep stumbling upon the bodies of people I knew.

We walked in silence for a while, sloshing through mud and swamp, retracing what were Andor's last steps. It took me a moment to muster up the energy to ask, "Are you alive? Or dead? You seem dead."

The corner of Gabriel's mouth twitched into a semblance of a smile. "Aren't we both?"

"I can't feel your heartbeat." I pressed my palm against the base of his neck just to be sure and found nothing at all but cold stillness.

"Well, I feel better than ever. Well rested." He pressed two fingers over his carotid for a long moment and shrugged. "Look, I swear I didn't know about Niamh. She must have been watching, had someone follow me."

I nodded again. The last thing I wanted to do was replay those moments. The fighting, the running, the knife, and the blood. "I kinda figured you weren't working with her when she threw you into Lethe."

Gabriel grunted his assent. "Still want to cut her mark off?"

*Ha.*

My answer bubbled up from the deepest, darkest part of me. From the very heart of the wicked dark, an answer that was all my own. "I want to feed her to her friends so that she will finally know the fate of gods."

The sound of it aloud almost made me smile. Almost. The dark agreed with me. It looked good on me specifically.

Gabriel's brows shot into his hairline, and he took a step back. Like he wasn't already dead. "Jesus."

"I had some time to think about it—"

My feet stopped as I turned back to the forest, as my gaze fell to the ground. The shovel slipped from my grip and clattered beneath me. And with breaths turned shallow, trembling in my chest, my pulse a caged animal threatening to break free, I stumbled forward. Gaping at the ground.

Panic rose into my throat, climbing like a scream, clawing its way out.

Andor's body was gone.

The ground was stained with blood, so much of it. All of it. I recognized the trees too, the withering bush that Salomé's frame had run around. Where the fox had darted by. He was here when I shut my eyes, and now he wasn't. Someone had moved him.

I raked my hands through my hair and stared at the red-stained mud, the coagulated blood, and the flowers. Those stupid white flowers from the meadow, all those shoots reaching up, the petals limned with drops of red. *Asphodels*, Andor had called them once. And they were sprouting, blossoming, blooming in the shape of his body where it had lay. Where not even the sopping mush could stop them.

"He…" Nothing more could come to my tongue.

My thoughts scrambled to understand. To keep up. Did they bury him then? Otherwise, where was he? Where would they take him?

But also flowers were *blooming*. In Elysium, which was dead. It was the first fully living thing I'd seen here in days, in weeks. These flowers rising from the dead, from the corpse of my fallen boy who was never supposed to die. They were alive here. Life and death were cyclical here, inevitable. Both of them, emerging again.

I plucked the flower and stared at it, willing it to explain. What was it trying to tell me? What was I supposed to understand?

And then I heard my name.

My name in his voice.

"Laure!" It bellowed from somewhere among the tangle of trees. From the direction of Lethe.

Gabriel turned too, scowling in the distance in search of what was coming.

I didn't let go of the flower as I started running, my body operating on its own accord. Seeking him out even as my mind *knew*. "Andor!"

All my thoughts quieted, taken over by one drive. To find the voice, get to the source of it, go, go, go. It didn't matter that it didn't make sense, that he was probably just another ghost, that none of this made any sense. It didn't matter that I'd watched the life drain from his eyes, that flowers grew where he'd been slain, that without Acheron, things didn't come back anymore. There were no more gods here to save him.

"Andor! Where are you?"

"What?"

When a head of dark hair emerged between the trees, I bolted. I leapt and hoped that he would catch me.

Andor and I crashed to the ground, my arms and legs wrapping around his middle, and I refused to let go. Because he was solid. Even as we sank a little in the wet mud. Even as he groaned, as if I'd knocked the wind out of him and squeezed so tight he couldn't draw in another breath. He smelled of blood and sweat and fresh herbs. The front of his shirt was crusted with dark red. Mud had caked into his curly hair, but the steady rainfall was slowly beginning to rinse it out.

"I'm okay," he whispered. "Are you okay?"

But I couldn't stop my shaking. I couldn't pry myself away. And through the tears and rain, I couldn't reconcile why there was no gash at his throat.

Coralie had looked like her corpse. She looked broken and drowned, just the way I'd left her. Gabriel too. And when I saw my ghost, it was the same—the red running down the length of me, an arm crooked at a bad angle, the cuts and scrapes of falling glass. Yet Andor didn't have his gash. He was perfectly unmarred.

"How..."

My fingertips brushed the smooth skin of his throat. Was there still some bit of Acheron that saved him? Did it take a long time to knit him-self closed? His skin wasn't cold, but it didn't have the burning heat of Acheron either. It was just... as warm as living. A strong pulse thrummed under my touch somehow, and I focused on it. The contact was a rush, like fresh air in my lungs when I should have felt the pins and needles of hemlock. He was changed.

Andor nodded and pulled his arm from around me. "I know. And look."

Both of my hands seized his forearm when he slid up his sleeve, the fabric bunching harshly at his elbow. Gone were the four Acheron marks, the four tattoos of red ink that had bound him to the blood river and covered all the skin. There was no trace, no scar, no burned flesh to strip it away. Replacing them was a new mark I'd never seen before. In the shape of a flower, the Asphodel, imprinted in green.

I narrowed my gaze. "Elysium?"

He pressed his brow into mine and breathed against my lips, "I think I'm its acolyte. I think it took my blood and saved me."

# CHAPTER 33

The sky had darkened to the grey of an impending storm by the time we crossed Pont Saint-Michel. Strong winds whipped across the dark surface of the Seine, and the buildings of Île de la Cité never looked more imposing. Like the fortresses they were always intended to be, no matter how they were dressed and redecorated in gold and prestige.

My heart thrummed as we stepped off the bridge with the anticipation of what was to come.

Somewhere from among these few buildings, there was the gentle pull of Acheron's acolytes. I sensed them the way I smelled petrichor before the rain, a subtle shifting in air pressure that brushed against the back of my tongue.

It was here. And now.

Yet...

"Where is everybody?" Andor asked, taking the question right out of my mouth and pinpointing exactly what felt so strange about the scene.

It wasn't the dark skies or the imposing façades that slowed my steps. Île de la Cité was home to not only the Palais de Justice but also restaurants, apartments, a hospital. The police prefecture was nestled right at the very heart of it—so where were the police? Quai des Orfèvres should have been lined with deep blue vans. Heavily armed guards were supposed to be permanent fixtures as they roamed the main boulevard.

"They left the barricades behind," I muttered, the furrow in my brow worsening as we waded in.

Gone were the sounds of restaurants bustling, kitchens lively with voices and clattering dishes. There were no bicyclists darting through, shoppers stopping at the florist on the corner. The very heart of Paris, where Clovis, first king of the Franks, once built his fortress, was empty. Yet that pressure in the air only grew as I followed the boulevard north.

The isle was claimed again by new conquering hopefuls.

At the staggering silence, I walked faster.

Palais de Justice was a castle, once a palace reappropriated for courts and prison, long before the revolution had culled the monarchy. The massive gates at the entrance were propped wide open, rendering the security turnstiles built into the gold ornamentation useless. Nothing stirred within the inner courtyard.

Andor squeezed my hand tightly as we came inside, as if he wouldn't dare to let go ever again. Amid the scent of freshly tilled earth, he whispered, "Why does it feel like we're walking into a trap?"

Yet there was no one in the windows, on the roof. The current was stronger here—they were definitely nearby—but not *here* here. They weren't concerned about the entrance, not when they'd already seized the whole building. However they'd done it.

I shook my head. "Why would Margaux set a trap for someone she's just watched die?" When I glanced at him, our eyes met, and if this were the old Andor, a shadow would have flickered in his pupils. But they were warm and simple now, and still made me shiver anyway. "She has Keturah—she isn't expecting either of us."

He nodded toward the door to our right that led into la Conciergerie.

It was the prison wing of the palace, less colorful and more severe. An overturned sign advertised the chance to see rooms where Marie Antoinette was held before she was taken to the guillotine. Chilling.

"How did she manage to do all this?" he asked as he nudged the sign with his foot and studied the cobblestones of the courtyard. There were little splatters of blood that looked too bright to not be recent.

I pressed my ear to the door. "Margaux's got the gift of manipulation. She can make you feel anything—rage, panic." Though it remained quiet in the courtyard, something stirred on the other side of the door. I stepped back. "There's—"

The doors flung open with a loud crack, knocking me back. Andor only barely seized my arm and pulled me out of the way before a stampede of business suits charged past us. The fear in their eyes was immediate and harrowing, the wide panic as they pushed and shoved their way out of the building, across the courtyard, spilling onto the boulevard. They didn't even see us. They just cried and ran.

And they didn't look back.

Behind them, as the flood of office workers slowed to a trickle, came others with their clothes torn in shreds, limping, bleeding. Like the woman from the alleyway, a couple didn't have mouths to wrangle into grimaces.

A man with skin grown over the indents of his eyes wandered, sobbing up the hall.

"They're close," I whispered and crossed the threshold. The floors were wet, slippery in places where they had been splashed with a colorless liquid. The smell wrinkled my nose. "It smells like—"

"Gasoline." Andor's gaze flicked up and down the corridor. "You sure they brought Keturah here?"

I started toward where the eyeless man had come from. "I don't know."

Part of me hoped she was, and the rest of me hoped she wasn't. I didn't know how I'd save her, stop Margaux, *and* flee a prison inferno with Keturah unscathed. But I needed to know she was okay. I had to see it with my own eyes, and my only plan involved killing them before they laid a hand on her.

I turned down another gasoline-soaked hallway and swallowed. "I gotta give it to her, though. She wants to bring about a new era of gods, and it sends a clear message: Gods don't need laws. Or courts."

The very words brought a grimace to my face. Margaux unrestrained was dangerous, and she'd convinced the others that she was holy. They saw their salvation and their dreams in her lies, and the broken bodies piling up pointed to her. And Dominique. And Florian.

She was just like Acheron.

Up ahead came the splash of liquid on stone, gasoline thrown haphazardly to coat the halls of Palais de Justice and la Conciergerie before Margaux set it all aflame. And it was a shame, really, that she had such narrow, selfish goals. Seizing the heart of Paris just to soothe her ego? I didn't know what I'd do but it seemed so . . . small.

The dousing stopped the moment I crossed a doorway, the pull so strong that it swept me under before I'd even realized. Florian and Dominique stood still, staring at me as I gaped at them.

They were still hunched over, open jugs poised in their hands, gasoline pooling inches from their feet. A shadow flickered across Dominique's gaze as he took in the person at my side, Andor. Who was supposed to be dead. He thought they'd dealt with us, and he was wrong.

"Florian—" Dominique started, throwing the container of gasoline at the door.

We ducked out of the way, Andor shielding me with his shoulders as the container and gasoline crashed into the hall. Following right behind was Florian, sprinting as fast as he could.

"He's gonna warn Margaux!" I shouted before starting after him.

I'd only managed a step in pursuit before Dominique slammed into me with all his might. The collision sent pain clanking through my bones as I dropped to the floor, Dominique's massive frame on top. He snarled as he flipped me over, rage filling his eyes. His muscled hands lunged for my neck.

Andor charged after us, but Dominique struck fast. He shrugged Andor off with a sickening crack followed by Andor's sharp cry, and as hands closed around my throat, I saw Andor falling away, gripping his shoulder.

"Margaux should have let me kill you when you first walked into our castle." Dominique sneered. His fingers squeezed tight, nails digging into flesh.

My windpipe shut, my hand found the front of his shirt, my own claws stretching and piercing through skin toward his heart. His grip didn't relent, even as I tried to wrap my power around his pulse.

He was of Lethe, though. His heartbeat was slippery, so faint that it danced out of my hold if I didn't focus. I couldn't stop it for long enough, not with my head filling with blood. Ears rushing with the sound of my own brain screaming.

Shadows limned my vision, and for just a moment, I thought Acheron had come back.

Then Dominique's skin took on a sickly green hue. Peachy skin paled as thick, green veins spread rapidly through his flesh. His hold slackened.

I pried at his fingers as Dominque's own breath lessened and turned to coughing, as green filled his body. Vines climbed until they covered his face, until his green-tinted and green-veined eyes rolled back into his head. His body went rigid, and then a stalk of asphodels sprouted from his gaping maw.

And as he fell away in a fit of gagging, of suffocating on flowers, little pricks of blossoms ruptured his eyeballs.

Clear fluid and blood splattered my face as I pushed myself up and skittered away. But I couldn't tear my gaze away—Dominique writhed and trembled under the invasion of greenery until it finally won out, until he died with small stems sticking out from beneath even his fingernails.

"What…" I wiped the wet from my eyes and looked at Andor, who was standing over me.

But he was gaping at his open palm, his other arm dangling uselessly by his side, as if the blight had come from *him*. His expression was split between glowering and fearful, quiet rage ebbing from his shoulders for Dominique and even quieter alarm at the havoc his hands wreaked.

*Elysium.*

I gulped. "That's… that's new."

Finally, he looked at me and softened. And then, with his good hand, he pulled me to my feet. "I've never heard of anything like this."

His fingers grazed the skin at my throat, which was probably taking on color judging by the knit of his brow. His hands were the same calloused hands that painted me, that tended to roses in his garden, that'd stitched up my cheek. And now they'd killed. For me.

"That could come in handy," I admitted.

If anyone was worthy of Elysium, it was Andor.

I hooked a hand around the back of his neck and pulled him down to me, mouth against mouth. It was quick, and then we were off, running in separate directions. I tried to follow Florian's trail, and he went around, in search of where they were keeping Keturah. It meant leaning into the current, going where my bones resonated the most.

"Please!"

The shout came from a room down another corridor, panicked and chilling me to the bone. It wasn't Keturah, not any voice I recognized, though I did know the voice that followed.

"Shut up!" Margaux yelled back, followed by the sound of an attack, flesh striking flesh, the thud of a body colliding. "Do you think you get to beg?"

I doubled back, sliding underfoot in gasoline on marble flooring, and braced myself beside the doorframe.

Inside, Margaux stood over a middle-aged man, a burning torch in hand and an overturned gasoline container at her feet. The man and his suit were drenched, and the resemblance between them was slight but hard to ignore. His hair was also black as hers had been, coarse and wiry, though his was run through with grey. The same close-set eyes.

An old score to settle.

Her lip curled back. "What makes you think you're allowed to beg? Did you listen to me when *I* begged?"

If I waded in, she'd fight me. We'd lose the upper hand. I bit my cheek hard to resist the urge.

"All the torture I went through," she said quietly, her words laced with bitterness, "and you did nothing. You enabled her and had the nerve to go to work every day and talk about *justice*. What justice?"

She dangled the torch over the man, flames dancing just far enough out of reach. Any moment they'd jump.

"You know nothing about justice. And the law? Since when did the law help me?"

In a sudden movement, Margaux kicked the man in the side. It was now or never. If she dropped that torch, if Keturah was still inside, it would be over. But any choice words I'd prepared to say, to bargain with, to threaten her into letting it go, to punish her for killing Andor—they all died on my tongue.

Palais de Justice wasn't just some brash show of ego like she'd pretended. Because a system that couldn't protect her deserved to burn in her eyes. It was her gift to herself.

Hedging my bets, I stepped inside.

"Why am I not surprised you got out so early? Have you come to stop me?" she asked softly, so small and unlike the severity I'd grown accustomed to. Nothing like the fearsome girl who buried me alive. "Do you want to take the torch out of my hand?"

I only thought of Andor, his hand gripping his shoulder, his eyes laced with pain. I needed him to get out of here, but not before we got what we came for.

"Would you give up if I did?"

Without glancing at me, she answered plainly, "No."

Margaux didn't smile. She didn't look *happy*. She looked pained, like she was excising rot that had taken root inside her. And she was expecting me to interfere, to take this from her, because that's what I'd been doing all this time by fighting her. She'd had to sacrifice Andor to get to this point.

And I couldn't help but sympathize with her. She was trying to cut it out before it infected everything. It had already twisted up inside her and left her nearly empty and desperate, and she was trying to let it go. Just like I did.

So it didn't surprise me at all when she tossed the torch aside and darted past me.

Flames swelled in the place she stood and spread fast, the fire hissing and spitting as it caught and swallowed the room and everything in it. The man curled up at its center screamed. Heat licked the back of my neck as I stumbled back and volleyed down the stairwell after her.

As far as I was concerned, I just wanted Keturah back and Andor safe. I was never set up to be a hero, and I had better things to do than rescue the undeserving, the same way no one was ever interested in rescuing girls like us. Suddenly the world was lucky this was all she wanted, that this was all we took as reparations when the world rendered us disposable.

# CHAPTER 34

"Come and catch me!" Niamh sang at the top of her lungs as she darted out into the open courtyard, me on her heels.

Fire tore through la Conciergerie as our footfalls tumbled on stone. It ate away at the drapes and spat out of the windows on the street, filling the air with acrid, black smoke. The whole thing was a sight to behold—a magnificent fortress transformed to a palace now consumed by flame and darkness.

It roared against my ears as I kept moving, coughing, my feet carrying me away until I could only slump against the gate, brace myself against the stitch in my side. The pain was fleeting, the cost of panic, but it was in the same place Coralie had stabbed me. The same place that'd killed me.

*You're alive, alive, alive.*

Something grabbed my shoulder, whirling me around.

Andor engulfed me in an embrace, showering me in the smell of gasoline and sweat and wild roses and dirt. His left arm remained limp at his side, but it didn't stop him from cradling my head to his chest and steering me away from the blaze.

I drifted along, still breathless. "Did you find her?"

He nodded toward the north. "Near Pont au Change. I was headed that way when the fire broke out."

There was a new gash on his brow and the smear of blood from wiping it away, but no sign at all of Florian.

The fire alarm was ringing loudly, enough to rouse the small island, anyone hiding inside. More people spilled into the street, enmeshed among the Palais de Justice evacuees, the judges and lawyers and clerks in their torn and dirty suits and robes. People from the shops and apartments scurried too, hands shielding their eyes as they regarded the fire. Niamh's handiwork devoured a historic building and her past along with it.

I didn't stay to watch. Instead I weaved through the crowd, following Boulevard de Palais north toward the other bridge: Pont au Change. The Marchand Bridge. Where they were holding Keturah.

If Niamh wanted to keep me in line, if she wanted insurance, she'd need Keturah alive and unharmed. I kept telling myself this, as I bumped into more and more people, as the wail of faraway sirens penetrated the thick smoke.

The moment I broke through the mass and stepped onto Quai de l'Horloge, the narrow street lining the water, Keturah screamed.

"Look out!"

My gaze snapped to her, one hand reaching out while Niamh seized the other, forcing her away, farther up the bridge.

And looking at her made me notice Salomé's approach, her face exaggerated to a menacing snarl as she charged at me. It was her true face, the one she could conjure on command and that I couldn't have seen in the dark, and it was stunningly viperlike. Too beautiful to not be dangerous. She was covered in scales that each ended in spikes, a vibrant gradient passing from yellow to blood orange across the length of her face. Her eyes were wide and round, the sclerae transformed to marbling green with a thin black slit running down the center.

As quickly as Salomé appeared, so came others for Andor. We were ambushed while they helped Niamh get away, while their fearless leader retreated and left them all behind.

"You should've stayed in the grave if you knew what was good for you," Salomé hissed, right before she unhinged her jaw to expose two long, curving, dripping fangs and lunged at me.

We grappled, her clawed hands digging into my shoulders as I returned the favor.

But I just wanted to live. And dance. Kiss and be kissed, love and be loved.

I wasn't interested in being a figurehead for Niamh, or Acheron's mouthpiece, or the acolytes' enemy. I just wanted to be *Laure*, with Andor and Keturah by my side. The one whose teeth were taking on an edge to defend that.

We struggled for dominance, shaking and stumbling to break the other's hold. It didn't matter that she was smaller than me. Her grip was strong and made me unsteady on my feet. Even as I tried to maneuver our way toward the bridge, Salomé resisted.

Behind her, Andor was fighting too—he clutched his attacker by the throat, and flowers rippled through and sprouted from their body.

Then I cinched Salomé's heart.

It was easy to tug on the strings that ran from her heart to mine. This close, being the dark's acolyte, it took only a thought from me and then she was faltering, her hands loosening as she sank down. Her face fell, as she realized what I was doing again.

I stumbled out of her grip and turned, where Niamh's gaze found mine, her defiance loud and clear in the grin she flashed. Even as I'd let her go, as she had her revenge and I just wanted Keturah back, she thought I was still after her. That I still *cared*—

With a blow I couldn't brace, one last, dying push, Salomé knocked into me and I went wheeling back. Pain spiked through my hip as it hit the stone railing, and then I watched my legs go up and over. The sky shifted in my vision, up became down. My body flailed through the air, searching for purchase I'd never find, in free fall, with Salomé's serpentine eyes watching, triumphant.

Icy waters stung as they swirled around me, as I was swallowed by the Seine.

# CHAPTER 35

But I wasn't afraid of the dark this time, not as I plunged in, not as the light faded from view and the chill seeped into and immobilized my bones. I didn't rail against the coming quiet, even with the sight of Salomé and Niamh peering over the edge seared into my brain.

They thought they'd escaped my wrath at last. They thought the depths of another river was enough to get away.

But it wasn't enough.

It wasn't enough that Palais de Justice was burning. That Niamh had gotten her revenge and I didn't stop her. That Elysium was rotted, Keturah was mortal, Andor had died, and I dug myself out of a grave—none of it sated them. None of it was ever enough unless I was on my knees, unless I was someone else's pawn. A tool. A *stepping stool* for someone else's dream.

Coralie. The ballet. Acheron. And now Niamh. All of them wanted my total submission—they wanted to mold and sculpt and control me, weaponizing my hunger and sharpening my grief until I was a force they could profit from. I was being carved and hollowed out for them so they could wait for the main course.

They couldn't just take the wins and walk away.

But I didn't just bite the tongue from the devil's mouth and swallow it in pieces. I reached inside and took its beating heart in my hand, and I sank my teeth inside and watched the shadows dissipate before my eyes. I watched the lights flood back into the world, and then I washed the static blood from my hands.

*I* made the devil fade away.

And this dark was mine.

Collapsing into myself—the way stars were born and died, from a cloud of pressure and heat and matter, the way time stopped and became a place—felt a lot like falling asleep. I saw Niamh's friends beating on me, and my body broke apart at their feet all over again. Then, like now, there came a moment when my body finally stopped resisting, when all the fuel ran dry, and I just started to float. I closed my eyes and let gravity pull me in and under.

It cracked my ribs and bowed my back, twisting and compressing me until I caved inward. Until every bone in my body snapped, and then ruptured, and then was pulverized to dust, and then to hot plasma and radiation. Until I was small, microscopic, atomic, and so heavy. Until I was absence and archaean.

Until I was everything and nothing, the beginning and the end.

With nothing left to contain it, nothing in its way, the monster within finally woke up. And like a black hole, there wasn't enough here in these depths, in this hell, to contain it.

It was the dark, and I was the dark. And from my prison of flesh and bone, I was set free again.

The Seine frothed and sloshed around me, the water surging the walls until only wind was left, whipping through my hair and clothes as I ascended from the bottom. I raised my head and roared like a titan.

Windows along the quay shattered, sprinkling shards of twinkling glass onto the running forms of people and the water below. The screams that erupted along the length of Pont au Change sounded so distant to me, I was so high above and far below. I drank in the sound until there was nothing but me.

"I am speaking now."

Faster than light, the world bent and stretched around me. In an instant, I moved from the bottom of the river, coated in sediment and filth, and then I was standing on the bridge. Sopping wet river evaporating because I was burning hot. Angry. Seeing and unseeing again, a predator on the move.

"NIAMH."

Stone trembled with the bellow of my voice. Rock broke away and fell into the tumultuous stream that was left. Shrill terror ebbed from the fleeing crowds around me as I stared straight ahead.

No more mercy, giving second chances, finding a way—now I was the looming shadow that sent the ants scattering. Niamh was wrong to think she knew me, to think she *understood* me and what made me tick.

I was incomprehensible. Laure meant energy evolving, matter pressed so deep into itself that she became a black hole in the flesh. Chaos taken form.

With each step toward the petrified girl, her crop of fried blond hair flapping in the wind like a banner, the ground cracked. Rifts sped through concrete as I grew heavier and heavier, as the wind swelled to a roar outside of me. Pebbles and debris, fallen bags and their contents stirred on the ground and took flight as I grew nearer.

As I stalked onto Boulevard de Palais toward my prey.

"You are not a god." My voice was sheet metal tearing and the echoes of the deep ocean.

This was what Acheron sought to control, to keep for itself until I snatched it from its chest.

Limbs extended from my back like weeds, thick as my arms and lined with sharp teeth. Tentacles writhed around me, animating shadow in the inferno light. What still ravaged the fortress was spreading on the wind, eating away at the isle. Meanwhile my wretched shape wavered in the reflection of Niamh's wide eyes as she cowered. As space curved all around me, sucking in flyers and brick, tearing signs from over doors.

"Then what does that make you?" Niamh thrust an arm to the street, to the destruction wrought as fire crawled up the block and the last of the mortals fled the isle with bleeding eyes. "Face it. You're not any different from me, Laure—"

I curled a bloodred tentacle around her throat, squeezing her to silence. **"No, you seek to control what was never yours, but _I_ am the dark that answers when you call. All that you are is bound to me. And you have pissed me off for the _last_ time."**

Then it was only a flick for me, a pointed release of my grip, but Niamh's tiny body sailed through the air before colliding with the golden clock in the fortress corner. Glass and gold and cogwheels tumbled in the wind. I watched her drop to the ground in a boneless heap amid the clock pieces and caught a glimpse of myself in a storefront window.

Horror.

All my rows and rows of teeth. Red eyes covering my cheeks and shoulders and arms. Tentacles ebbing in dark space, shadows dancing, light bending all around me. And the blood of Acheron coated everything, appearing like wet skin—_my_ true face.

A door broke away from its hinges, a lamp from its mount on a building façade. Stone crumbled from flame and compressing air around me. The wind became a maelstrom, where all along the quay and the bridge, mortals huddled together, clinging to the lampposts. Stretched out and probably screaming, not that I could hear from my cocoon.

The force of me was sucking them in. I was undeniable, irresistible.

I'd finally become, at my very core, what I thought I wanted to be, inescapable when I wanted it least.

This was the Laure beneath the mask.

Every step as I crossed the boulevard to Niamh's crumpled form weighed heavier than the last. The street rippled and ruptured, sending a crack tearing down the length until the entire block of buildings was leveled. In silence. Smoke and dust plumed in the air before I sucked that in too.

**"You were arrogant, thinking you could control chaos,"** I said calmly, standing over her, close enough to hear her whimpers. **"I don't belong to you. Or anyone."**

Light from the raging fires dimmed as it all curved into my orbit, was absorbed into the center of me. Île de la Cité lay in ruins at my feet, acolytes trying to hide terror at a true monster, Niamh cowering in defeat, and yet I wasn't sated. I was still hungry for more after all I'd given, all I'd been forced to bear. This Laure wasn't finished making a mess—she wanted to smash and break until she was only pieces, until like Coralie, like Acheron, even she was absorbed into something bigger.

Niamh's body shuddered with coughs as the very pull of my existence snatched the air from her lungs. Others too, crouching on the bridge, trembled with the effort, clutching their throats as they fought to breathe. And there, hiding beside a car along the quay, I spotted Keturah. She clung to the front of Andor's shirt as he shielded her eyes, as he squinted at me through the dark and smoke and debris spinning through the air. Even seated within a cloud of wreckage, my body warped and transformed to cosmic horror, they didn't run.

He didn't look away.

He'd never looked away.

So instead of continuing to collapse, instead of radiating energy until I burned out and ran dry, the monster, the black hole, settled into equilibrium. What I could feel of me was weightless again, drifting back into nothing all the while being *everything*. At rest. No longer spinning. I was no longer vying to have my pain be the prettiest or the loudest, and so the maelstrom transformed into a breeze.

# CHAPTER 36

When light and sound returned to the remains of Île de la Cité, it was like the first day of spring. The slow climb as everything came out of hiding, as people ditched their cover and ran for their lives, scrambled for safety, covered their ears, shielded their eyes. Bleeding. Screaming. Stumbling over the fallen who didn't look away. Fire roared on as the air settled, and I felt the heat on my face as I continued to stand over Niamh.

"Kill me," she rasped, finally defeated, mollified.

She was worshipping as much as she was fearful, waiting for me to strike, expecting me to kill as I had before. She was waiting for it to hurt. What better end for a god than fate at a more deserving and powerful god's hand? A violent end, far better than being quietly forgotten. Bang rather than whimper.

"I told you, I don't answer to you," I replied blankly, before looking away to find Andor and Keturah's approach. "I don't care what's expected of me."

Then I stepped into their waiting arms, into the warmth and scents that came with living. It was one long moment of repose, of grounding peace before the work began. Outside of us were several angry and terrified demigods denied their kingdom, and we needed them gone. I wanted them to surrender godhood with no compromise at all.

Keturah pressed a cocoa butter–scented kiss into my hair. "You did great, Laure."

I searched her soft brown eyes, bloodshot, weary, and exhausted. "And you're okay? They didn't hurt you? We tried to come as fast as we could—"

"No, I'm okay," she insisted, smoothing the frizz from my face. She met Andor's gaze, and her lips twisted into a small smile. "We're all okay. Well, you destroyed a whole city block including the police prefecture, but it was so dark, maybe no one recognized you anyway."

Andor snorted. "Speaking of which, we should probably go."

Withdrawing, I turned to study Niamh, who'd propped herself up to a seated position amid the rubble. She was bleeding from the scalp and wheezing. And at my nearness, she flinched, and her heart rate spiked.

"**I don't want you and your friends setting foot near Elysium again,**" I commanded, loud enough for the others I felt lingering around to hear. I didn't care that there was no glaze to her eyes, no emptiness claiming her face even though what I said took over.

It wouldn't matter that she was once Acheron's chosen, that once my power didn't work on them like it did on mortals. It didn't matter anymore because I'd become the Wicked Dark. I was Nyarla and the Daemon King, child of Azathoth and Acheron now. And in a way, she was mine.

"**And I rescind my favor.**"

"Your—" Niamh started to question.

But then she lurched to the side and vomited. Sounds of sick carried all around us as she and her friends all doubled over, as thick, red blood splashed on the cobblestone and paved streets. Acheron's blood removed from inside her, through her mouth and eyes and nose and ears. *My* blood, my power, stripped from their bodies.

She looked awful, and I couldn't help my grimace. Even if it was a fate she deserved, that I liked best of all.

I stifled a yawn and backed away. Exhaustion was beginning to knot itself in my body as my mind spurred my body into motion, as I turned. The last time I'd changed into the monster, I'd slept for days to recover the energy it took. Now I felt primed to sleep for a week. A month.

Keturah looped her arm through mine. Blood was drying in one of her ears. "Banishing them from Elysium? When there's already nothing left?"

I only glanced to Andor, and he scratched the back of his neck while his face flushed red. He looked worse for wear, a fresh gash along his collarbone, though whatever had broken in his shoulder seemed to have fixed itself.

On account of him being an acolyte still.

He cleared his throat. "We figured out how to fix it."

Her brows wrinkled with suspicion. "'Fix it'? You—really?"

"Why?" I asked, nudging her. "Does that mean you want another deal? With the new Acheron?"

Keturah cackled. "This day killed any lingering doubt in me. With you two, I think it's okay to be the mortal one."

So together, arm in arm, the three of us started down the street, past the great blaze gutting the rest of Palais de Justice and its neighboring buildings, back toward Pont Saint-Michel, where we'd arrived. The wailing sirens were still so distant, they couldn't touch us.

Not when we were going home.

# EPILOGUE

The white, winding corridors in the basement of Opéra Bastille bustled with activity as Andor and I walked through. Stage crew carried massive cables and rolled black boxes on wheels, and dancers in sweatpants and drastic stage paint squeezed by a musician wielding some kind of shiny tuba larger than me. Laughter and commanding shouts filled the concrete walls.

It was the frenetic chaos of opening night, and it didn't matter whether it was Maison Lumina or the Paris Ballet—I breathed deeply and drank it in. The clock was counting down until stage call summoned us up, until the curtains peeled back and we danced and spun and rolled like the professionals we claimed to be. It had been months since I last bathed in the applause of a room. A lifetime ago.

The clock was at once slow-moving and too fast; we had too much time to kill and too little to waste.

So I resorted to giving Andor a tour of the place to keep moving— all the blank basement walls, the nondescript dressing room doors, storage closet after storage closet, a sprawling rehearsal room covered in black soundproofing drapes, and my fellow dancers contorted in stretches and scarfing down their early dinners.

All that glory was mine to share with him.

Because I was a dancer in the shape of a monster.

"And now," I teased as I hit the elevator button, "for the best part."

His thick brows shot up, and he broke into a conspiratorial grin.

In the coming weeks since Île de la Cité, a new brightness had filled his eyes. Gone were the dark circles, though he still sometimes stirred in his sleep. And though nothing started yet, I caught him with enrollment paperwork for École des Beaux-Arts. In part because he was liberated from Acheron, whom he never truly trusted anyway, and in part because things were healing. Him. Me. Us. Elysium.

"What could be better than the smell of industrial cleaner and seeing people who look like pretzels?" he asked as we stepped inside, and the metal doors closed around us.

"A tough one to beat, for sure." I selected the topmost floor and turned to him. "How's it looking over there?"

I didn't have to specify what I'd meant. Where *there* was.

Most days, thoughts of that place knotted in the pit of my stomach and wouldn't let up. I wanted to go, and I wanted to stay away. I was afraid of what I might find and who I might run into in spite of my command. Was it really growing back, or would it turn to a decaying wasteland the moment I crossed the threshold?

It didn't matter the photos Andor took of fresh grass sprouting from the grey. That I'd watched him grow things—*anything* now, including massive plum trees, with ease. When rehearsals for *Orphée et Eurydice* picked up, I was glad to be carried away, to not have to look around corners for Salomé with her knife. Niamh with her scheming.

He leaned against the wall and sighed. "Taking forever, if that's what you're asking."

It wasn't.

"Still no sign of Acheron?" I asked quietly, licking my lips.

He shook his head.

The last time I was at the bone shores, the day Andor died and I was buried alive, it had looked all dried up. And even in the revival of Elysium, there was only a slow trickle of blood that made its return, but no shadows in my view. No darkness watching me in the corners of the room, looming over me in the mirror. Even now that the great death was over and life was returning anew, Acheron was still gone.

"And no trouble from the others, right?"

They were all but one accounted for, and hadn't returned to Elysium. Andor would know. Dominique and Florian were seen roaming the streets of Paris, Salomé implicated and arrested in the death of that banker. But Niamh, maybe she was dead. Maybe she was Margaux again or someone new in another city, waiting for another opportunity.

Andor smirked. "Or what? You'll go all black hole again and swallow everything?"

I stroked the ink on his arm. Elysium's mark glowed a vibrant green that suited the brown of his skin. It was still so unusual to touch him and not feel poison that all this time later, I kept waiting for it to follow. It was hard to imagine this was all it could feel like: heat and smoothness and fresh air in my lungs. That's all.

From the top floor, I led Andor along a dark corridor and up a staircase leading to the roof. It wasn't much of a secret—in the early days of the academy, we did almost all of our performances here. I knew Opéra Bastille better than even Opéra Garnier, and the sterilized cleanliness of the modern building made it far less haunting to roam.

Still he clung to my hand and hovered close as I shoved open the door and propped it wide with a loose brick.

The sky was the orange blue of sunset over the city. Sounds of traffic down below were a little melody, far enough that we also heard the wind that overlaid it. And then Andor's gaze traveled from the skyline, to my face, to the fresh sprouts of a vegetable garden behind me.

"There's a . . ."

I giggled and pulled him along. "Yes. I think they give it to the restaurants or something. I don't know, but Coralie and I used to sneak up here and steal stuff to snack on during long days." Then I plucked a cherry tomato from the stalk and plopped it in his mouth. "I'm sure they'd *love* some volunteers if you ever want to pay me a visit."

Wind picked up as I watched him stroll along the kale and carrot planters. He touched the leaves and studied the new sprouts seriously, and I turned away and stepped into the garden shed to answer my buzzing phone.

"Keturah?"

"Where are you?" she shouted, though the static cut through her voice. Her cell service was terrible. "Someone . . . Here for you."

I sighed. "We better go. I think Keturah's downstairs."

Andor brushed the dirt from his hands and scurried past me into the hall, his wildflower smell filling my nostrils as I ducked inside. Back into the elevator, hitting a button for the farthest part of the basement, because I had a job to do and there would be more time for things like this. Gardens and rooftops and city views.

Then he stepped closer, pressing a hand into my waist.

"Is Acheron watching us right now?"

I arched a brow. "What? No, you know—"

His lips pressed into the base of my jaw, forcing a shiver down my spine and a flush to my face. "What about now?"

Another and another, kisses along my cheeks, across my nose, until he hovered over my mouth, maple-scented breath tickling my face.

I gulped and smiled. "No, I'm pretty sure."

Hands buried in his hair. Mouth ensnared on mine, grateful I hadn't started my makeup yet. His body pressed so close to mine that I felt the heat, and I craved to be folded into it, until every inch of us melded together forever.

And when the elevator chimed and spat us out in the basement, I fixed my clothes and stepped back into the maze. Winding and winding, our hands entwined while we worked our way back toward the stairwell, to where Keturah was probably waiting—

*Her.*

Alexandra Freeman stood at the bottom of the stairs with a bouquet of soft pink tulips in hand. She looked nervous, chewing the corner of her lip as I approached, as I surveyed the woman who made me and then abandoned me and then waltzed right back and refused to leave. As if she could spot something in a stray hair, in the flush in my cheeks, her gaze flickered briefly to Andor. Our hands.

Then Keturah wished me luck with a planted kiss on my cheek, and my mother stared at that too. Dissecting everything that surrounded me as if it would help her know me instead of just asking.

"I . . ." she started, holding out the flowers as far from her as possible.

"Thank you," I said calmly, though my nerves were a riot in my chest and in my fingertips. I didn't know what else to say, what more *needed* to be said when the gesture was apparent.

She was trying something. She and my father, who'd texted a blurry selfie from his seat on the balcony.

Her hawkish eyes, the eyes I got from her, studied my face. "You look different."

I brought the tulips to my nose and sniffed, let the scents steady me. "This isn't an apology, you know."

"I know." My mother's spine straightened. "But I'll be watching this time. I'm really trying, Laure. Fresh start, you know?"

I turned toward the dressing room. There wasn't much time to do my makeup, to get ready, to adjust to what exactly this meant, my new normal. Andor, Keturah, the power that welled and slept inside of me without a puppet master, my *parents*.

Still I nodded, because it was the best I could do in the moment. Because I was still learning how to just let myself *be*, whatever that looked like today. I twirled and called out over my shoulder, "I know."

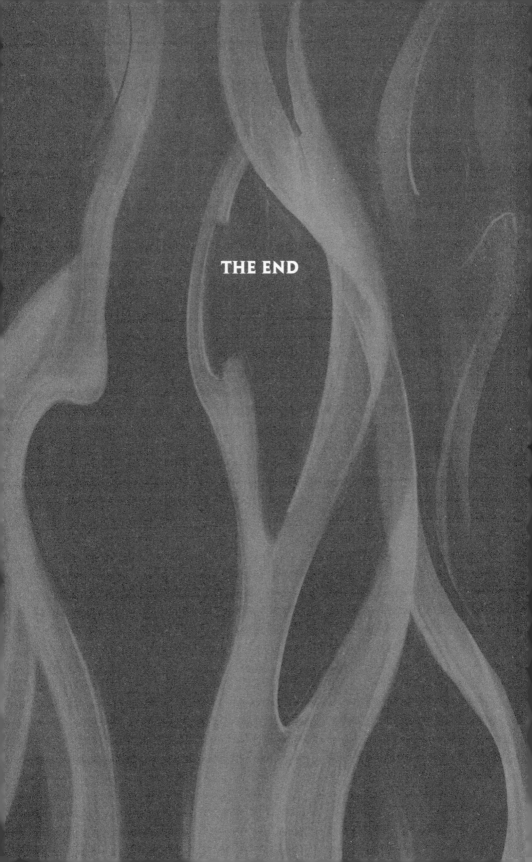

THE END

# — ACKNOWLEDGMENTS —

If *I Feed Her to the Beast* was a marathon, *I Am the Dark* was a sprint. I owe my thanks to my partner G, agent Jennifer March Soloway, and alpha reader and friend Victoria Vasquez, as your brainstorms and feedback were invaluable to reaching the finish line.

There are many other authors along the way, like Louangie, Tanvi, Faridah, Tomi, Kalyn, Avrah Baren, Yuva, Trang, Channelle, Clare, Andrea, Miranda, Dera, and Gabi, whose conversations and advice have helped me cling to my sanity.

The team at Macmillan is literally indispensable: Jess Harold, Ann Marie Wong, Mia Moran, Jackie Dever, Katy Miller, Emily Stone, Jacqueline Hornberger, Chantal Gersch, Naheid Shahsamand, Leigh Ann Higgins, Molly Ellis, Gaby Salpeter, Alexandra Quill, Mary Van Akin, Morgan Rath, Sara Elroubi, and Elishia Merricks.

And also my thanks to Ruth Bennett and Amber Ivatt at HotKey.

And lastly, I give my gratitude to you, reader, for following Laure to the ends of the cosmos.

# — ABOUT THE AUTHOR —

Jamison Shea (they/them) is a dark fantasy and horror author, flautist, and linguist hailing from Buffalo, New York, and now dwelling in the dark forests of Finland. When they're not writing, they're drinking milk tea or searching for eldritch horrors in uncanny places. *I Feed Her to the Beast and the Beast Is Me* is their debut novel.